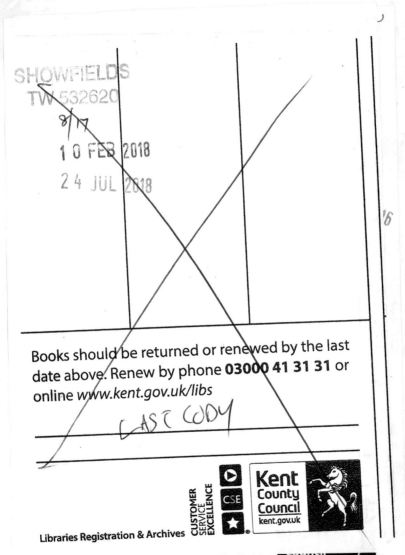

FALLING MORE SLOWLY

Also by Peter Helton

Headcase
Slim Chance
Rainstone Fall

FALLING MORE SLOWLY

Peter Helton

Constable • London

Constable & Robinson Ltd
3 The Lanchesters
162 Fulham Palace Road
London W6 9ER
www.constablerobinson.com

First published in the UK by Constable,
an imprint of Constable & Robinson, 2010

First US edition published by SohoConstable,
an imprint of Soho Press, 2010

Soho Press, Inc.
853 Broadway
New York, NY 10003
www.sohopress.com

A copy of the British Library Cataloguing in Publication
Data is available from the British Library

UK ISBN: 978-1-84901-220-1

US ISBN: 978-1-56947-880-6
US Library of Congress number: 2010019576

Printed and bound in the EU

1 3 5 7 9 10 8 6 4 2

Mixed Sources
Product group from well-managed
forests and other controlled sources
www.fsc.org Cert no. SA-COC-1565
© 1996 Forest Stewardship Council

For Jess

Author's note

Thanks to Krystyna and Juliet. Heartfelt thanks also to Clare and Imogen for making my manuscript readable. Special thanks to Jess for giving me James 'Jane' Austin. No thanks at all to Asbo the cat for jumping on my head just when I thought I had a brilliant idea for my next novel. Gone now.

Chapter One

The ghost of a scream echoed around him. McLusky sputtered into consciousness as he shot upright. He'd screamed himself awake. He hadn't done that for a while, thought he'd stopped doing it. Damn. Blinking rapidly into the twilight while his hammering heartbeat slowed, he took a while to realize where he was. He groped around on the floor until he found his alarm clock, then brought the thing close to his eyes to read the time on the tiny display.

7.29. Nightmare beat alarm by one minute. His meeting with the super at Albany Road station was at nine, quite a civilized time to start a new job. Which he might do if he ever made it off this mattress.

Liam McLusky hadn't slept well. He'd drunk at the Barge Inn, the pub across the road, until closing time then spent half the night lying on his mattress, sipping Murphy's and listening to the strange creaks and groans of his new abode.

Propping himself up on one elbow he fished a cigarette from a pack of Extra Lights on the floor, lit it and inhaled deeply. He had stopped smoking after the attack because he'd been in a hospital bed for a whole month before learning to hobble around again. It had seemed too good a chance to miss when he was already one month ahead in the cravings department. He'd lasted six months without a single puff.

Yesterday he had started again. New city, new job, new pack of ciggies, extra mild. New first-floor flat, rented. He

1

took a quick inventory of the bedroom: one mattress, floor-boards. Zen-like simplicity though perhaps lacking the style. There was a built-in wardrobe with louvred doors the entire length of one side which, after he had flung his clothes into it, remained half empty; a minute fireplace where a gas fire had recently been removed – he could see the old gas pipe protruding from the floor; four empty cans of Murphy's, one of which he was using as an ashtray. A bin-liner full of clothes in need of a wash completed the furnishings. He twirled the cigarette butt into the can where it died with a hiss.

He pushed himself upright. All his adult life he had slept in the nude yet since his release from hospital he had taken to wearing a T-shirt at night. He didn't like looking at the long, curved post-operative scar. It still felt as though that part of his torso where surgeons had delved to repair the internal damage needed symbolic protection.

But really he was fine. He'd been declared fit. He was ready for duty, more than ready. The enforced idleness had been the most difficult part. A fresh start in a new town was what he needed but most of all he needed a start. In the bathroom he turned on the hot tap, opened the gas valve, struck a match and fed it into the mouth of the old-fashioned gas boiler just as the landlady had shown him. Gas hissed and caught with a loud bark that made him flinch. The shower consisted of two plastic hoses attached to the hot and cold taps of the bath and connected to a droopy shower head fixed to the wall. He could only just fit himself under it. It took a while to get the mix right but it hardly mattered, nothing really mattered at this stage. McLusky kept telling himself that. He sniffed the towel and decided it would need washing. Launderette just a couple of doors down, how good was that? He pulled on his socks, then polished his shoes with his right foot. It would do. Chinos, shirt and tie, black leather jacket. He'd considered the suit, first day and all that, and rejected it. Start as you mean to go on. Then he'd remembered he'd been wearing it when they ran him over. At the hospital they had cut the trousers off his blood-soaked legs.

No fridge in the kitchen yet but a gas cooker with three rings, grill and oven, the Newhome 45, its feet standing in small glass saucers to save the ancient lino. This was like stepping back into World War II. Looked a bit like a bomb had landed in here too. Boxes with his stuff stood everywhere. Every surface, and there weren't that many, was cluttered with items that had nowhere to go. No furniture here either apart from a red 1950s kitchen cupboard with glass drawers. He'd seen a junk shop round the corner, it would take no time at all to kit this place out. Some old dear had lived in the flat for forty years and died in here too. He didn't mind. These houses were old, of course people had died there. He liked old houses. He wanted to die in an old house too. What were the chances? He liked places with a history, that's why he had rejected the modern flat in Cotham they had offered him 'until he sorted himself out'; too new, too soulless. And since he would never spend enough time there to give it soul himself, he would have to borrow other people's.

Apart from the kitchen there was only the big, oddly shaped sitting room and a spare room just large enough to accommodate a midget. All that could wait.

In the meantime there was the Italian grocer's next door. He'd soon found out why the flat was cheap: noise from the pub until late and the women at the grocer's setting up the vegetable stalls on the pavement at just after six in the morning, talking loudly in Italian. It always sounded like they were having an argument but they probably weren't. Just loud and happy to be alive. The place also sold pastries and coffee to take away, of which he intended to take full advantage. The grey-haired woman behind the counter showed a strong family resemblance to his Italian landlady but he hadn't yet worked out who was who, so many people seemed to work there. The woman furnished him with both coffee and a Danish and called him Mr

Clusky. McLusky set off towards the centre of town. His new town.

Carl Spranger had spent the night asleep behind the wheel of his BMW and woke with a start and a groan. Shit. He had a raging headache and felt sick to his stomach. It was cold in the car, the windows had misted up with his condensed breath. Fucking bitch. Greedy stupid fucking bitch. He searched for cigarettes amongst the crumpled packets and crisp wrappers but knew there weren't any left. He thumped the dashboard. Shit. Everything was shit now. The devious cow. She'd sent a private bloody detective after him to spy on him and Allie. Paid for with his own bloody money of course.

There was an inch of vodka left in the bottle on the passenger seat. Hair of the dog, always worked. He let the liquid burn down his throat. It was answered by a sharp stab in his stomach. He held his breath until the pain eased. Happened more and more often recently. Ulcer probably. Cancer maybe. And why not? What the fuck did it matter now? Twelve years and now she wanted a divorce. Screamed her demands at him. I want a divorce and I want this fucking house. The house. No one gets the house. One affair and she wanted out. She had it all planned already, his replacement waiting in the wings. A chiropodist, very refined, not coarse, like you. Refined, my foot, ha! He wound down the window, spat, wiped the windscreen. Right front wing had a wrinkle in it. He remembered dimly, he'd hit something in the dark. Large dog, small deer, whatever, he didn't get a look at it. Where was this godforsaken place? Lay-by on the A road leading to the motorway. He'd just driven around, had got too drunk though, cars kept blaring their horns at him, letting him know, probably weaved a bit. Stopped here, slept it off. *The house.* He started the car and pulled out into the road doing a U-turn. Two cars braked hard, parping their horns. He stuck his head out of the window. 'Fuck you too! I'm busy. Fuck you.' *The house*. The house was practically all that was left. She didn't know that, of course. Plant hire business was bad, had been for a long time. He'd had to sell off machinery lately simply to stay afloat. Just him running the place from a Portakabin, with Allie, who had started as a receptionist, manning the phone. Good at telling lies for him, now he was getting more calls from creditors than customers. Lying for him, helping him, consoling him. Allie had more sympathy in her little finger than ... Working late together trying to make sense of the books, trying to salvage something. A friendly word, a hug, a kiss. He'd screwed her in the office. Twice. Twice! And now she wanted the house? She wanted the house for that? No chance. Not-a-fucking-chance. No one was going to get the fucking *house*.

'You can't miss it,' the woman said while eyeing up his almond Danish as though she really fancied a bite. McLusky offered but she just laughed and walked away. Somehow he had managed to get lost, which wasn't good, not for a police officer and not on his first day. Should have called a cab. He checked his watch. Plenty of time.

Of course he'd been to Albany Road station before but not from this direction. He'd looked it up on the A–Z. Easily walkable from his Northmoor Street flat and it would help him get to know the place. Should have brought the map of course. He was in the right district though. The warren of Bristol's town centre had grown over centuries like a rich fungus, the mycelium of its streets stretching senselessly out across the hills behind the harbour area. Dark streets, bright streets, tightly wound streets, steep streets, allowing only brief, surprising glimpses of the harbour basin and the river. The city was built on nothing but hills it seemed. The Romans had vineyards here on the steep, south-facing slopes where the Old

Town had grown up. Or perhaps it was a different hill; he'd read something about it in a guidebook. Some of the houses were tall and narrow timber-frame buildings, a lot of Victorian houses too, but the scars left by WWII bombing had been filled with drab utilitarian concrete buildings, some towering high above their more elegant neighbours.

The most noticeable thing however was always the traffic. These streets had not been built for it and the centre was too busy, too crowded to pedestrianize. Successive traffic schemes had failed. The ever-changing one-way system had become so unworkable half of it had simply been abandoned and the streets handed back to the chaos merchants. The result was a mess of Mediterranean intensity: noisy, polluted, crowded, dangerous and during peak times bordering on anarchy. Delivery vans driving over pavements, taxis going everywhere, car drivers desperate for a place to stop, the usual bikers and suicidal cyclists, the even more suicidal skateboarders, enough scooters for an Italian teen movie and pedestrians dodging the lot. Many cyclists wore dust masks, some wore actual gas masks, probably as a mark of protest against the dense pollution. He had been reading the local paper to get a taste of the place. A campaign was under way to stop motorized traffic coming into the city altogether with protests every Saturday morning, bringing more chaos to the streets. And how were emergency vehicles supposed to get through this, he wondered? How on earth did you move an ambulance through these streets?

McLusky hadn't bought a new car yet, his last having been wrecked in the chase in which he'd been injured. He'd been promised the loan of a plain police unit until he 'sorted himself out' – so much sorting – but taking in this traffic chaos he thought that perhaps roller blades might well have the edge.

He asked directions again, this time of a grey, elderly man rummaging for something in his canvas satchel while pushing an electric bicycle along the gutter. The man looked up with a closed-off face and seemed to consider ignoring him, then pointed. 'Albany Road station? Down those steps, then turn right. You can't miss it, it's the ugliest building in town. Wants dynamiting.'

'Thanks, I'll bear that in mind.' He crossed the street carefully, remembering too well the sound of his own breaking bones as they'd made contact with the car bonnet. He had no desire to repeat the experience. He didn't really believe he could survive a second time. Or even wanted to. Perhaps this would go away or perhaps the feeling might never leave him. Or it might even help him live, the flat feeling that he no longer minded dying. He didn't want to die. But equally he wasn't sure he wanted to survive at all costs. Living and surviving were different things after all.

A shadowy network of alleys and worn, irregular steps connected some of the Old Town streets. Small shops and artisans' workshops clung on here but the business rates and rents had driven many of them out, making way for the national chains that could afford to pay them.

He recognized the place instantly. The man had been right, Albany Road police station was quite the most unlovely building he had come across so far, something he hadn't really taken in when he had come for his interview six weeks earlier.

Comparing the station with the surrounding architecture, a small eighteenth-century church and several well-kept Victorian houses, wasn't really fair. It would be like comparing a plastic stacking chair with Chippendale furniture. This was definitely the stacking kind of architecture. He checked his reflection in the window of an electrical retailer's, too late to worry really. Hair a bit wild though. He smoothed it down.

Reaching for the handle of the tinted glass door of the station he hesitated just a fraction – new job, new era, new life, new crew, new town, new day – then walked inside.

The desk officer buzzed him through the next door. 'Morning, sir, they'll be expecting you.' Just the slightest hint of doubt in his baritone. 'Will you find your own way . . .?'

He nodded and the desk officer gratefully returned to what he'd been doing, far too busy to nursemaid freshly minted detective inspectors.

McLusky remembered his way to CID from his interview though he hadn't met many of his new colleagues at the time since most had been off sick with some sort of virus.

Inside, too, the station was undeniably sixties or seventies. Recently refurbished, the super had said. He'd just have to take his word for it. The place was busy, the stairs echoing like a tunnel with footsteps and voices. Eight forty: he was early, his meeting with Superintendent Denkhaus was not until nine. Straight into the CID room and he instantly felt at home. CID rooms were CID rooms: desks, waste baskets, computer screens, phones – several with detectives attached to them – maps of the force area and city centre on the walls, whiteboard, noticeboard, fax machine, photocopier and kettle. The windows were firmly closed against the noise of the traffic below. The place smelled of printer ink, cheap aftershave and deodorant overwhelmed by sweat.

One man looked up, frowned, then tried for a smile and got up. 'Inspector McLusky, sir? I'm DS Austin.' He stretched out a broad and darkly hairy hand. McLusky shook it. The whole man was darkly hairy and broad, probably worked out. Intelligent, open eyes, blinking fast. The soft Scottish accent sounded like Edinburgh to him, but he was no expert. 'Welcome to Albany. Ehm, your office, sir, is just along here.'

His office. He'd never had his own office. He'd not been a DI long enough for them to even find one for him in Southampton before the bastards rammed him off the road. Then came back and ran him over as he staggered from his car.

Austin led the way back into the corridor and to a door right at the end. 'You're taking over from DI Pearce, it's his old office.'

McLusky had read about Pearce, a bent copper, currently on the run with a goodly amount of drug money, probably in Spain. Enjoy it while you can. Spain was no longer a safe hiding place.

He walked straight in. It was about the size of the box room in his new flat – space for second midget here – and smelled aggressively of cleaning products. It contained a dented filing cabinet, two chairs, an empty bookshelf, a metal dustbin and a small battered desk. The window faced out the back overlooking graffiti-covered walls, chaotic pigeon-shit rooftops and the shadowy backs of houses. In the middle distance, between tall buildings, he glimpsed a sliver of the harbour. Apart from in- and out-trays, monitor, keyboard and phone he'd been furnished with a set of car keys sitting on a form for him to sign and an envelope lying across the keyboard which he knew would contain the gaff he needed to log on to the computer.

'Thanks.' McLusky shivered. He thought he could feel the dampness in the fifty-year-old cement bricks on the other side of the plasterboard, could hear the rustle of their slow crumbling. He pointed to the envelope. 'This is precisely the amount of paperwork I can cope with. Can you see it stays like that, please?'

'We'll do our very best, sir.' Austin's lopsided grin acknowledged the avalanche of paperwork heading for the inspector's in-tray.

The phone on his pristine desk rang. He took a deep breath then picked it up. Anyone could make a mistake. 'DI McLusky.'

It was Area Control. 'Sir, I know this sounds like a job for Uniform, but . . .' The young male voice hesitated.

'Go on then.'

'The original call was made by a Mrs Spranger, sounded like a domestic at an address in Redland. We've sent two units so far and both have gone off the air. We always have reception problems in Redland. We've since had a mobile phone call from one of the officers and he seemed a bit incoherent. There was a lot of background noise . . .'

'Okay, we'll deal. What's the address?' He snatched up the keys, turned the form around and snapped his fingers for a pen. Austin unhooked a biro from his shirt pocket and obliged. McLusky scribbled down the unfamiliar address and hung up then pocketed the pen in his leather jacket. Austin opened his mouth then thought better of it.

'Right.' McLusky held up the paper for Austin to read. 'Where is this place? We'll take my car, just lead me to it.'

The car turned out to be a grey Skoda. 'You sure you want to drive, sir?' Austin doubted the wisdom of it but got in at the passenger side anyway.

'Positive. Just give me clear directions and in good time. The sooner I find my way round town the better.' McLusky avoided being driven if at all possible. He hated being a passenger, always had done. 'Never driven one of these before, though.' He pulled out of the station car park. It felt good to be holding a steering wheel again. Skodas used to be joke cars, now the police couldn't get enough of them.

'Go left here. The new Skoda. 180 bhp, they're okay, actually.'

'We'll find out if you're right in a minute. How long've you been at Albany Road?'

'Two years. Bath before that, then a spell at Trinity Road.'

'Your accent?'

'I grew up in Edinburgh but we left when I was sixteen. We moved around a lot. Straight across here, sir, and keep going downhill till the next set of lights, then left and left again.'

Traffic really was appalling but using the siren sometimes made matters worse, people froze or blundered into each other. 'Keep telling me where I am so I'll learn the streets. I did spend a couple of hours with the A–Z a while back but it's not the same.' After the lights McLusky found a stretch of miraculously drivable road, put his foot down and got blitzed by two speed cameras in short succession before having to slow right down again.

'This is Broadmead, still faster through here this time of day.'

'Trinity Road is district headquarters, right?'

'Right. I hated it. Keep going, but try and get into the left laaaaane.' Austin gripped the dashboard as McLusky braked abruptly so as to narrowly miss colliding with a biker who hadn't expected a Skoda doing fifty across the junction.

McLusky barged on through the traffic. 'It does move, this thing. What's the super like? I mean I have met him, of course, once, but that was formal. To work under?'

'Ehm, Denkhaus?' Austin sounded distracted as his DI drove across three lanes, getting snarled in traffic, weaving, bullying his way through. 'Up Stokes Croft until I tell you. Ehm, he's a no-nonsense copper, can suddenly become a stickler for procedure when the mood takes him. I have book-shaped indentations on my head to prove it. Someone suggested it always happens when he tries to lose weight. Sugar cravings.' He pointed across the street. 'Not a bad takeaway that, by the way.'

McLusky came up behind a bus going at walking pace. He worked the horn, mounted the pavement and managed to overtake in the space between two lamp-posts. Just.

Austin kept his eyes firmly shut until he felt the car regain the road.

'I remember this bit, came down here on my way to the station. But keep up the directions. Albany Road a happy nick?'

'Depends who you're working with, but yeah, it's all right, I suppose.'

McLusky parped his horn at a pedestrian who looked like he might just be thinking of stepping into the road.

Austin hung on tight and gave directions in good time since the inspector was already cornering with squealing tyres. He didn't know a lot about the man and half of that was rumour. He was about five years older than himself, he guessed, thirty-three or -four. He'd transferred up to Bristol from Southampton after nearly getting himself killed in the line of duty there. University man and difficult with it, someone had said. And something about being a bad team player. Unpredictable. Not exactly what they needed at Albany. He sneaked a glance at the new DI. He seemed utterly relaxed despite driving at speed in a new town and an unfamiliar road system. Some system. 'Next left.'

McLusky didn't slow. 'I live down that street over there, next to the Italian grocer's.' He cornered and accelerated up the hill.

'Above Rossi's? What's it like? Left and directly right again.'

'The grocer's?'

'Your place.'

'Well ... Quite cheap. Totally unmodernized, wonky floorboards, no central heating or anything.' No heating at all, now he came to think of it.

Austin shrugged. He could only dream of central heating. He and his fiancée had just scraped together enough for a tiny dilapidated end-of-terrace. Heating would have to wait. 'I quite like Montpelier, couple of good pubs round there. Go left, no idea what that's called, and right up the hill.'

'Keep going, nearly there. Careful, there's often dopey schoolkids wandering across this street.'

McLusky worked the horn again. Austin had never driven through the city at this speed, not even with Blues and Twos. He hated to think what kind of speeds the DI reserved the siren for. McLusky drove up on the wrong side of the road, overtaking everything, barging through, getting a chorus of angry horn play in return.

'Turn right, that should be it.'

'Very leafy round here.' They certainly had the right place. There was no need to look for the paper on which he had scribbled the name of the house. Just beyond the crest of the humpback street was the scene of the disturbance, unlike any domestic McLusky had yet attended in his eight years on the force. Spectators had gathered on the opposite side of the road. He pulled up and jumped out. They were intercepted by a distraught-looking constable. McLusky showed him his ID.

'I'm glad you're here, sir.'

'I bet you are. What the hell's going on?'

The drive of the squat detached house looked like a scrapheap. At various angles stood two squad cars, a BMW and what appeared to have been a green civilian Volvo. All four cars were utterly destroyed, their roofs caved in, windows missing, in fact there wasn't a single surface left undamaged on any of them. Behind all the battered metal, on the once well-kept lawn, stood an enormous wheeled digger, its engine growling, its hydraulic arm pivoting left and right, threatening two uniformed constables with oblivion. At the house the curtains were drawn at all the windows.

'It's a domestic, sir. The individual in the cab of the digger is a Mr Spranger and he is the owner of the house. He intends to destroy it.'

'Did he steal the digger?'

'No, he owns that too.'

'He owns the house and he owns the digger? Well, that's all right then. Why don't we let him?' McLusky shrugged. He hated domestics. Everyone hated domestics. There was nothing more tedious on the planet than people who needed the police to sort out their relationships.

'My sentiment entirely, but we can't. It appears Mrs Spranger is still inside. Though that doesn't seem to bother him. He's going to demolish it around her ears. Told us to clear off his property, sir, and when we didn't he attacked our vehicles. The other cars were already totalled when we got here.'

'Any sign of the woman?'

'No, sir.'

'Has anyone tried to enter the premises to see if there really is a woman in the house?' Because if there wasn't he'd pull those constables out of danger and let the lunatic get on with it.

'Constable Hanham tried and got chased right round the house by the digger. That's how the shed and the greenhouse at the back got it.'

McLusky watched as the burly red-faced man operating the digger took another swipe at an officer. He didn't like the odds. Spranger seemed to be shouting continuously though no one could hear what he was saying over the noise. He looked like a man about to explode. Perhaps he was going to give himself a heart attack and save them all some bother. 'Any ideas, DS Austin?'

Austin scratched the tip of his nose. 'Perhaps if we rushed the cab from both sides one of us could get to him and pull him off or snatch the keys out of the ignition.'

'Fair enough – you up for it then?'

The constable vigorously shook his head. 'With respect, sir, we tried that. He's locked himself in and I caught a nasty whack on my side when he suddenly swung the thing round.'

'Are you okay though? What's your name? Will you need medical attention?'

'I'll be all right. It's Constable Pym, sir.'

'Okay, Pym. Request an ambulance anyway. This looks like it has the potential to get painful for *someone*. And then make sure you keep those civilians out. And move those cars along.' The number of onlookers on the pavement was growing all the time and several cars had stopped in the lane. There were worried faces at an upstairs window in the house to the left, peering across at the noisy yellow digger swinging its bucket arm wildly from side to side. Pym, in his mud-stained uniform, walked off with a slight limp. The digger churned up the damp lawn with its five-foot wheels, lurching forward another yard towards the

14

front of the house, the constables jumping back but not prepared to give way. They'd soon be with their backs to the wall.

McLusky didn't like the look of it. 'Okay, we can't play cat and mouse with him all day. I think the fact that he hasn't actually touched the house yet is a good sign, but all the same. Go round to the right and attract the constables' attention and wave them off. As soon as they're clear I'll try and put the Skoda between him and the house.'

Austin scratched his nose harder. 'Do you think that's wise, sir?'

'No, I don't, but I can't think of anything else short of getting Armed Response out and letting them shoot the place up.' It was his first day back at work on a new force and he wasn't going to mark it by calling firearms officers to attend a domestic. He got into the Skoda and lightly closed the driver door. To make sure of getting out again he also wound down all the windows, then started the engine. Automatically he reached up to pull down the seat-belt, then thought better of it. This was one journey where a seatbelt might just be a hazard. He started the engine and patted the dashboard. 'Been nice knowing you.'

It took a moment for Austin to get the constables' attention since they were concentrating hard on not getting caught by the swinging bucket arm. When at last they both ran off to the right the digger swung in their direction, the moment McLusky had been waiting for. He drove on to the lawn, wheels not gripping well at first, then surged in a tight curve round the back and left of the digger. The Skoda's engine whined in first gear as he drove through what was left of brand new bedding plants in a half-moon bed. He was decimating a row of lavenders just as the digger suddenly swung back. McLusky stopped, threw the car into reverse and flew backwards at the huge yellow thing filling his mirrors. Wheel on full lock now but there was just not enough space left to aim the car properly between the front wheels of the monster. His car made contact with the digger's right front wheel and got bounced back against the other one. The Skoda stalled. Time to get out. He tried the driver door but it wouldn't open far enough for him to squeeze through. The giant wheel blocked his window too. He could see the digger's arm travel up, like a fist drawn back before the deciding punch.

Passenger side. He scrabbled across just as the bucket landed a crumpling blow on the bonnet, bouncing him hard against the roof of the car. A jacket pocket caught on the gear shift. He yanked it free. The door was no use. Head first out of the passenger window, chest and groin scraping painfully over the sill, hands first on the ground, wriggling and kicking himself free just as the bucket smashed through the windscreen and the digger bucked and growled.

'Play with that for a bit, my friend.' He made off towards the left, on all fours at first, then ran around that side of the house. Evidence that the digger had come through here once before was everywhere. Wheelie bin, recycling, firewood shelter all tossed aside or splintered, a giant scrape along the flank of the house. Spranger must have seen him but by the sounds of it was taking it out on the Skoda, as he had hoped. Around the next corner. An aluminium greenhouse stood crumpled and glassless, the potting shed a slant of splinters. At the back of the house he was faced with the choice between a large curtained picture window and a kitchen door. He tried both, finding them locked. The key was in the lock on the inside of the half-glazed kitchen door. Having pounded his fist on both doors and neither seen nor heard a thing from inside, he picked up a heavy glazed pot full of sodden compost and heaved it unceremoniously through the glass of the kitchen door, shattering it completely. He reached through and let himself in. The pot had broken too and vomited its contents on to the kitchen floor.

'Mrs Spranger? I'm a police officer. Are you there?' He rushed through the kitchen, the hall and the enormous sitting room with picture window, large modern fireplace and sofas but saw nobody. In the fish-tank twilight produced by the green curtains McLusky kept calling. As he turned to search upstairs a small sound like a grunt or a suppressed groan stopped him. Back in the sitting room he circled the group of furniture. Cross-legged on the floor behind a two-seater sofa sat a middle-aged woman with wild blonde hair.

'Mrs Spranger?'

She was wearing a quilted sky-blue dressing gown and fluffy white slippers and clutched a brimful tumbler of Southern Comfort. McLusky could smell it. He hated the stuff. The woman looked up, lifted one buttock and farted.

'Mrs Spranger, I'm a police officer, Detective Inspector McLusky. Your husband is threatening to demolish the house. I would like you to come with me to a safe place until . . . the issue is resolved.' He sounded like a twit even to himself.

Her voice was hoarse from crying and shouting and heavy with alcohol. 'He can fuck off, the two-timing creep. I'll keep the house, he can fuck off to his tart. Go and arrest the fucking bastard, he trashed my fucking car!'

'We intend to, Mrs Spranger. Only I don't think it is safe to stay here at present. He seems pretty determined to attack the house with a digger. Come with me, please.' He reached out a hand, offering to help her up.

She slapped it away. 'Huh! I bloody won't. Go and take the bastard away, that's what I called you for. Anyway, you could be anybody, couldn't you? Was that you breaking the windows? Show me some identification.'

'Yes, sorry about the window, I couldn't attract your attention, Mrs Spranger. I do think it's urgent that we get you out of here.' The noise and shouting outside had intensified. He held out his ID but she didn't look at it. 'I really think we should leave now, Mrs Spranger.'

17

She concentrated on her glass of Southern Comfort. 'Bollocks to that. He'll never dare do anything while he knows I'm in here. That's why the house is still standing. The bastard squashed my car. Arrest him. You're useless. You're all useless. Just piss off. He might not love me any more but he loves this house, he'll never do anything to it.'

A crashing and the sound of splintering wood contradicted her. McLusky had had enough. Manoeuvring behind the woman he grabbed her under the armpits and pulled her up. She twisted and screeched her protest, slopping Southern Comfort over both of them. As he bundled her towards the picture window the house shook. He'd intended to get her out by the inset door but she suddenly wriggled free and ran to the hall where clouds of brick and plaster dust billowed. She strutted into it, shouting abuse, throwing the now empty glass at her adversary. McLusky plunged after her, the dust stinging in his eyes and lungs, making him cough. The woman's verbal onslaught had also been cut short by a coughing fit. A large hole gaped where the front door and window had once been and the threatening digger filled the gap, its bucket arm reaching deep into the hall. It jerked up, once, twice, bashing at the ceiling. Mrs Spranger retreated towards him just as the bucket swung sideways and pushed over parts of the first interior wall. He grabbed her arm and hastened her retreat, pushing her in front of him as they were overtaken by another cloud of dust and the crash of falling masonry. In the kitchen Mrs Spranger stalled. 'Look at the fucking mess in here.' The walls shook again. It took considerable strength to push the woman out of her kitchen, even though the ground shook under her feet. Once outside he managed to pull her along by one arm while she clutched at her dressing gown and released a torrent of abuse at him, at her husband and at the constables who took over and ushered her to safety. The street was now full of onlookers, some with cameras and camcorders. The ambulance arrived.

McLusky kept coughing and spitting out plaster dust as he stood on the lawn to watch the end game. One corner of the house had now collapsed, taking large chunks of roof with it. Most of the debris had fallen inwards. It looked like a bomb site. Spranger was still bashing away, but less frantic now, his expression businesslike. He slowly toppled another stack of bricks, then lazily nibbled at the edge of the roof which disintegrated in a shower of tiles.

DS Austin joined McLusky on the lawn. 'Are you all right, sir?'

'Yeah, sure.' He lit a cigarette, offering the pack.

'No thanks, sir, I gave up.'

'Me too.'

'Just the one then.' Austin eagerly lit his and sucked the smoke deep into his lungs. Then he frowned and checked the brand – Extra Lights. It was like smoking stale air. 'That was quite a performance, if I may say so, sir. Wish we had it on video, we could sell tickets down the station, make a fortune.' He jerked his head at the crumpled remains of the Skoda, now lying sideways on the churned-up lawn. 'You didn't get hurt?'

'Nope.' Strange though. He was nervous crossing the street but this hadn't scared him. Proactive. That's what the counsellor had called it anyway. As long as he was acting, taking charge, he was fine. Just standing still waiting for something to happen he couldn't bear. His clothes were a mess.

Austin sniffed. 'Southern Comfort? Did you find time for a quick drink, sir?' For a moment he thought he'd gone too far with this unknown quantity of a DI but McLusky raised a tired smile and brushed half-heartedly at his stained shirt and chinos.

The noise abated as the digger shuddered to a stop, its engine falling silent. Spranger got out and stood for a while staring at it all, trying to take it in. Half of his house had collapsed. Water cascaded where the digger had bitten through the bathroom plumbing and the spare bedroom

19

had now slid into the kitchen. He could see through into the living room where everything was dull and dirty, covered in dust and debris. Only on the coffee table a glass paperweight sparkled in a thin ray of sunlight. He remembered. It had tiny starfish inside it. Probably not real. They had brought it back from a long weekend in Cornwall one autumn. Twelve years. All disappeared. Everything was fucked up. At least his headache was gone now, though his stomach cramps still came in hot waves like his anger. Two constables approached him across the debris-strewn lawn, reaching for handcuffs. God, they looked more like kids.

More Uniform turned up. Two fire engines and the press arrived. Firemen moved cautiously into the rubble to secure water, gas and electricity. The place became very busy all of a sudden. Another ray of sun pierced the fast-moving clouds. 'Oi, no smoking there.' A fireman gestured angrily at McLusky and Austin to put their cigarettes out.

McLusky flicked his cigarette into the lawn where it died with a hiss. 'Let's get out of here, we're no longer needed.' As if in confirmation a uniformed sergeant strutted on to the lawn and started asking questions and dispensing orders in all directions. Mopping up time.

Austin found a likely victim amongst the constables securing the scene. 'Ah, Hanham, glad I found you. You can give us a lift to the station. Our transport is . . . temporarily out of action.'

'Temporarily, sir?' Hanham looked back at the battlefield and the crumpled lump of the Skoda. He'd seen the result of the stunt the new DI had pulled. What a nutter.

Austin shrugged. 'Yeah well, the build quality isn't what it was, they make 'em from tinfoil now.'

McLusky pulled his soiled shirt away from his torso for a better look. 'Drove well though – I'm thinking of buying one myself. I need to change into fresh clothes.' He let himself fall on to the rear seat and spoke to the tidily barbered back of the constable's head. 'Drive us to Northmoor Street first, will you?'

'Sure.' Hanham stole a glance at his senior passenger in his mirror. Typical CID. Not a care in the world. The new DI just destroyed a nearly-new car and now he was worried about a stain on his shirt. If muggins here got as much as a dent in the bodywork of this car he'd never hear the end of it, he'd be spending forever filling in forms. If he wrote it off he'd consider his career more or less finished. CID. They lived on another planet altogether. No one had ever suggested to him that he might make detective one day. He'd stay in uniform forever. And between now and retirement there'd be plenty of chances of dying in it, too.

'Find yourself a parking space, the inspector won't be long, I'm sure.' Austin stood in Northmoor Street holding the door on the little panda car, letting his superior get out.

McLusky hesitated on the pavement. He needed another shower but didn't want to leave Austin waiting in the car. Only his place was a shambles. Hanham would be accustomed to being abused this way and probably thought him a prat anyway. He could send them away and walk back to the station but it looked like rain again. What the hell. He'd never keep up the pretence that he led a normal life. 'Here.' He fished a crumpled banknote from his pocket.

Austin touched one finger to an imaginary cap in salute. 'A tip, sir? That's very kind, am I to share with the driver?'

'Get us all a coffee from Rossi's and bring ours up, I'll leave the doors open, first floor. D'you mind?'

'Not at all.'

'Ask them to put them in real cups, I can't stand polystyrene. Tell them we're honest cops and we'll return them.'

Upstairs he stripped off his clothes and threw them into the corner with the rest of the stuff that was heading for the launderette. He opened his spacious wardrobe and rummaged for a clean pair of trousers. All he turned up was a pair of jeans, slightly frayed at the hem. He found a nearly ironed shirt that would have to do.

The gas from the boiler caught with a bark but he was prepared for it this time. The water didn't seem to mix properly and somehow managed to feel hot and cold at the same time. Plaster dust and grit sluiced from his hair, he could feel it travel down his back. DS Austin seemed all right. Straightforward, didn't ask unnecessary questions and had a sense of humour. Most CID humour consisted of schoolkid pranks and bad jokes which could get tiring after a while but Austin didn't seem the type.

The towel was still damp from his earlier shower and refused to dry him properly. Normal people, *real* grown-ups, probably always had a stack of freshly laundered fluffy bath towels in the airing cupboard. He was still waiting for the day when he'd wake to find he was grown up and mature, the way others seemed to manage so effortlessly, and discover that he had an airing cupboard.

'Room service, hello.'

'Take it into the kitchen, won't be a sec.'

He dressed quickly. A blow-dryer would come in handy, too, now that his hair was getting quite long. It was already beginning to recede a bit and keeping it longer hid that well.

'Real cups, as ordered.' Austin handed back the bank-note. 'And it appears they take a warrant card.'

'You didn't ask for it, though.' McLusky spoke sharply. He disapproved of police officers who solicited free stuff from civilians. Accepting an offer was sometimes the judicious thing to do, asking for it definitely wasn't.

''Course not.' Austin dismissed it. 'Quite . . . minimalist in here. In a cluttered kind of way.'

While they leant against the kitchen counter and drank their cappuccinos McLusky quizzed Austin some more about the area. Downstairs Constable Hanham poured his coffee into the gutter. He hated the stuff but of course no one had thought to ask him what he actually wanted. A simple cup of decent Earl Grey tea is what he would have said, though he doubted you could get such a thing in a foreign shop like that.

Ten minutes later McLusky once more climbed into the

back of the patrol car. He hated being driven so much that he could never stop himself from working imaginary brake pedals, which was why he felt it was safer to keep his feet out of sight in the back. Hanham drove off in the opposite direction to the one he himself would have chosen.

The constable knew that the long way round often saved time. McLusky made careful mental notes, taking everything in like a camera as Austin continued to point out the landmarks, Queen's Road, the Triangle, Browns. Sitting behind Hanham McLusky peered right up a side street and glimpsed a dirty mushroom of smoke growing skywards from among the trees. Half a second later the sound wave of an explosion hit the car like a roll of thunder.

'What the fuck?' Hanham flicked on Blues and Twos and cut across traffic, raced up the narrow street. 'It's in Brandon Hill, this side of the tower.' He drove as far as he could towards the park, then braked sharply. All three officers bailed out of the vehicle and ran along the paths, then uphill across the grass towards the source of the explosion. The plume of smoke now had a ball of fire in its centre, licking twenty foot high towards a stand of trees. People were shouting. Hanham on his radio was breathlessly calling for back-up, ambulance and fire brigade even before they all came to a panting halt at the scene.

A boy and a middle-aged woman were lying on the path that wound around the rise. A wooden structure blazed on the other side of it, halfway up the hill crowned by Cabot's Tower. Debris of the explosion was everywhere. Several people were sitting or standing, nursing cuts and splinters, dazed with shock. Small children were screaming throughout the park, scared by the sudden noise. McLusky noticed different reactions among the people in the park. The cautious were moving away, distressed, or dialling on their mobiles. Others were shouting, rushing towards the scene from all over the park. Some came intending to help, most stopped at a distance they deemed safe, watching. An elderly woman sat hyperventilating on the grass. The

23

teenage boy was wailing, hands clutched to his face, blood dripping from between his fingers. Several civilians were tending to him. The shockwave seemed to have set off every car alarm in the neighbourhood. Hanham ran back to the patrol car for the first aid kit. McLusky knelt by the second prone victim. The woman lay motionless among debris and supermarket shopping on the path. Her face was grey. A little blood trickled from her right ear into the straw of her hair. She looked dead. He pulled off her scarf and felt around for a pulse. It took him a while to detect it. It felt weak to him but despite his job he didn't consider himself to be an expert in vital signs. He thought of putting her in the recovery position but didn't like the look of the bleeding ear. What if her skull was fractured?

'Is she alive?'

He looked up at Austin. 'Barely, I think.' He felt helpless, useless, but pushed the feeling back, swallowing it down. 'What the hell happened here? What was that thing that blew up there?' He gestured with his head at the smoking fire at the centre of the devastation. He was a stranger in town again, he had no idea what this place ought to look like.

'Eh? Ehm, it was just some sort of rustic shelter with benches all round. Kids use it for snogging and cider drinking. Tramps sleep in it sometimes. Uniform move them on.'

'So it was just . . . wooden? I mean, I can see it was, but there was nothing else to it, nothing in it that could blow up like that? It's one hell of a blaze. Can you smell petrol?'

Austin nodded grimly. 'Yeah, that's not a simple wood fire. But it was just a big wooden shelter on a concrete base. Nothing else to it.'

'It was a bomb then. Must have been.' A thin mist of rain began to fall. He looked around him. Constable Hanham was trying to help the howling boy but couldn't persuade him to move his hands off his face. Austin was circling the burning jumble of timber, shooing away some kids. A young woman had appeared next to McLusky, bending down to the victim. 'I'm a nurse.' She spoke in a matter-of-fact way, as though unaffected by what had happened, and proceeded to check that the woman's airways were clear, and covered her body with her coat.

That's what I should have done, McLusky thought, I'm useless. He could hear the first sirens over the screeching and warbling of the car alarms. A small crowd of onlookers had gathered. People were taking photographs; some had camcorders, every other person appeared to be snapping away on mobiles. He pulled out his own and began to do the same, taking a 360 degree shot of the scene of destruction, confusion, anxiety, curiosity. Where was the bloody ambulance? The first to arrive were a couple of patrol cars at the bottom of the hill. They parked some way off on the grass, knowing that fire and ambulance had to come through soon. Thinking ahead, professional. Next to arrive were the fire engines. By now there wasn't much of a fire to put out; the drizzle had increased, keeping the flames down.

A constable pointed a fireman in his direction.

'You in charge here?'

'For the time being. I'm DI McLusky.'

'I'm Barrett, senior fire officer.' He stood next to McLusky and watched his officers deal swiftly and efficiently with the incident, looking after the victims, damping down what was left of the fire. 'CID? You got here quickly. We usually get to incidents long before you lot. You'd send Uniform to scout first, surely?'

'We were passing, heard the explosion. It was quite a bang. I'm no expert but I suspect it doesn't take much to blow up a wooden shelter. Someone made very sure it would go up properly. We could feel the shockwave. Some people got blown over standing twenty yards away.'

'My guess is some kind of accelerant was used, too. There was no warning?' There was suspicion in the man's voice. 'You weren't here because you got a call . . .?'

'Nothing like that. My DS would have mentioned some-thing if things were likely to go bang in this town.' *My DS.* He indicated Austin who was locked in an argument with a tourist about relinquishing the memory card of his camera to him so they could examine the images on it. Camcorder man didn't look happy. 'I think I'd have been made aware of any bomb threats, even though it's my first day here.'

'I know.'

McLusky widened his eyes at him.

'It might be your first day but you do keep busy, DI McLusky. You attended the Nunnery Lane incident earlier but then disappeared before I could talk to you. The house will have to be pulled down, by the way. Let us have your report on that as soon as you can. It's certainly a weird one.'

'Is it?' McLusky didn't think so. People used the weapons that came to hand. If they had sticks they'd use sticks, if you gave them guns they'd use guns. He thought he understood the appeal of a wheeled digger. He squinted with worry into the worsening rain. It would take some creative writing to show that he had made best use of the equipment by stuffing the Skoda under the digger.

'You formed any opinions as to who and why yet, inspector? Terrorism? Here?'

'Strange target for a terrorist. When did they take to blowing up park benches?'

'What then, vandals?'

'Don't know yet. But I intend to find out.'

At last the ambulances arrived, fifteen minutes after Hanham had made the call, and everyone breathed a sigh of relief. Both the boy and the unconscious woman were stretchered off and driven away very soon with Blues and Twos. Those with minor injuries were being assessed by paramedics on the grass opposite the smouldering remains of the shelter. Most injuries came down to splinters and bruises where wooden debris had thumped into bodies. In the end only two more casualties, both suffering from shock, were sent up to the Royal Infirmary. The hyper-ventilating woman recovered enough to be collected by a relative in a taxi.

Austin arrived by McLusky's side, holding several memory cards he had requisitioned from cameras and mobiles, and nodded at the large grey Ford coming to a halt behind the collection of emergency vehicles at the bottom of the hill. 'Super's here.'

The arrival of Superintendent Denkhaus electrified the constable guarding that end of the road. Denkhaus walked straight at him and at the police tape as though neither existed. The constable lifted the tape high over the man's head and the burly policeman walked through without acknowledgement. He was aiming at him, McLusky noticed, but the superintendent's face gave nothing away. After what Austin had said earlier he hoped the man wasn't on a diet.

Denkhaus pointed a fleshy digit as he approached and stopped just short of poking his new DI in the chest with it. 'DI McLusky, you had an appointment with me at nine o'clock this morning.' His voice boomed loud enough for several uniforms to turn their heads.

'I know, I'm sorry, sir, something urgent came up.' He put on what he thought of as his reasonable face.

'I heard all about it. You'd be surprised how quickly news of the complete annihilation of police property travels on this force. You chose to intervene in what was clearly not a CID matter even though you had business elsewhere. With me. Next time I ask you to my office, and I think that might happen very, very soon, you'll make it a priority and will get there on time. Clear?'

'Very clear, sir.'

'I bloody well hope so. So what the fuck happened here?'

Chapter Two

Inside the cramped Mercedes command unit parked in Charlotte Street Superintendent Denkhaus doled out tasks to the team in a practised stream, much of it devoid of punctuation. Then he slowed to add a few more thoughts. 'Colin Keale, most of you will remember, planted three pipe bombs behind the Magistrates' two years ago and got twelve months suspended because of his medical history. I sent Uniform round there to pick him up and see if he's up to his old tricks again. In the absence of DCI Gaunt, DI McLusky, who most of you will have met by now, will be in charge of this investigation. That's all.' He looked around the familiar faces in the room, several of which allowed their surprise to show. Like DS Sorbie: sharp, smart and dark; DI Kat Fairfield: immaculate, eager and self-possessed. DS Sorbie was fiercely chewing his biro while watching DI Fairfield for a reaction to the news that the new man was in charge. Kat Fairfield was looking straight ahead, rigid with anger, avoiding all eye contact. 'Carry on, then. DI McLusky? A word.'

McLusky followed his superior outside. Denkhaus pointed a fat finger straight at his chest, lightly tapping his tie. 'It's your investigation for several reasons. A, because you somehow managed to be first on the scene. B, because I like to shake things up and C, because it'll give you a chance to jump in at the deep end. You won't have to run after anybody, they'll all come to you. You'll not make many friends but then I'm not running a social club. And there'll be a lot of questions, none of which you can answer since you only just got here. My theory is that by the end of it you'll know the answers and feel right at home. Of course there's always the possibility that you'll completely louse it up in which case I'll make your sojourn in the city a short one. You might not be in charge for long, of course. You know how it is, not that this looks much like a terrorist bomb, but anything goes bang and CAT will immediately want to take over. I'm expecting a visit from them soon and I want to be able to show them that we're not a band of yokels waiting to be rescued by the Combined Anti-Terrorism bunch. Colin Keale went before the magistrate for drunk and disorderly, resisting arrest etc. and got a fine. He took exception to this and built some pipe bombs which he set off behind the courts. They weren't really meant to harm anyone, just meant to express his displeasure with one hell of a bang. He's got mental problems, that boy. In a way I hope it's not him, because that would mean his illness just progressed. We'll see. What's your first impression, anyway?'

'Hard to say, sir. It was quite a blast but an unlikely target for even the weirdest terror group. We might be looking for local lads here.'

'Let's hope so. I agree it's a strange place to plant a bomb. But then bombers are weird by definition, which makes them so dangerous.' He checked his improbably thin wristwatch. 'I'll be going to lunch now after which I will be in my office.'

'There's only one thing, sir . . .'

'Yes?'

'I don't have any transport at the moment.'

Denkhaus's nostrils flared. 'Then get a space hopper or something, I fear we're fresh out of Skodas! And you can also stop using my uniformed officers as chauffeurs, they're needed for more important things than driving young DIs around town.' A passing constable smiled grimly. *Too right.*

Despite the extended side pods – the van's 'hamster pouches' – the office of the Mercedes command unit was small for all the bodies crammed inside it. When McLusky went back in a few heads remained studiously down while some of the detectives studied the new man with open curiosity.

He stood in front of the whiteboard. Austin had spent some time bringing him up to speed with the current caseload they were battling. It was quite insane but average for a city this size. He hoped he could strike the right note. 'Okay, I'll make this short. There's always a chance that Mr Keale of past pipe-bomb fame is responsible, but let's not pin our hopes on it. We do however want a quick result on this and we're stretched, with lots of Uniform tied up doing fingertip searches of the park. There's also the matter, I've been told, of hunting a roving gang of mobile phone muggers that appears to be high on the super's list of priorities.'

Some murmurs and groans. The public – and the press – saw the so-called Mobile Muggers as the main menace in the city. Until today perhaps. Chasing them down to get them off the *Evening Post*'s front page had until now been one of the superintendent's pet projects.

'That's why even overqualified detectives like DI Fairfield will be joining in the house-to-house effort to bring in as many witness statements as possible by the end of the day.' A curt nod from Fairfield, a hard stare from her DS. 'Anything to do with explosions will naturally attract the attentions of the Combined Anti-Terrorism people. Several of them may even as I speak be riding west to pay us a visit.' Groans. 'The super feels it would be nice to have something to show our visitors, specifically evidence of our competence, brilliance, efficiency and, I'm sure, cost effectiveness.' Boos and ironic cheers. 'Any questions?'

Only a few hands went up, everyone wanted to get going. He dealt swiftly with the questions then dismissed his troops. 'Right, let's do it.'

Shuffling of papers. The team were getting ready, most to go out, a few to start sifting through the witness statements already taken.

The relief of having started work began to relax his shoulders. He shook a cigarette out of the packet and lit it, mainly to dampen his hunger. That Danish was a distant memory to his stomach.

'Sir?' It was Sorbie, standing by the exit door.

'Yup?'

'It's no smoking in here, sir.'

He grunted an acknowledgement and went to stand outside, watching the detectives troop off, Sorbie and DI Fairfield among them. There'd been no time to talk to the inspector. If she felt resentful about a newcomer of identical rank and seniority being put in charge then she hid it well. Fairfield seemed the efficient type. Very smartly dressed and almost too good-looking for a detective. He wasn't sure himself what he meant by that but wondered how suspects reacted, most of them young and male, in the interview room, for instance.

At least it had stopped raining for a bit. Austin joined him. 'Couldn't scrounge another cigarette, sir, could I?'

McLusky obliged. 'If you're going to keep smoking my cigarettes you might as well call me by my name. I'm Liam.'

'I'm Jane.'

'You are?'

'Well, it's James Austin, so everyone calls me Jane.'

'You don't mind?'

'Not really. Bit late for that anyway. She lived just down the road in Bath, did you know that?'

'Did she?'

Austin nodded. 'She hated it. Too pretentious, too noisy.'

Too noisy. McLusky reckoned here in the park the police made all the noise. Calls, engines, doors slamming, the growls of so-called low-noise generators. 'It's beginning to look like a bloody film set out there.'

It was a gloomy day so arc lights had already been set up to make sure crime scene investigators and Forensics didn't miss anything. This side of the park was out of bounds to the public now, entrances closed off. Lines of uniformed police were doing a fingertip search of the surrounding area. Every bit of debris, down to the smallest wood splinter, was being recovered. A photographer with a large video camera took endless shots of the scene, the surroundings, the entire operation. Press photographers had managed to scramble up through the undergrowth to get as close as possible to the locus of the explosion. They were popping off so much flash photography towards the scene that investigators had to avert their eyes in order to avoid being temporarily blinded. When their protests fell on deaf ears they complained to McLusky.

He sent Austin. 'Go sort them out.' The DS sauntered over, then at the top of his voice threatened to arrest 'the next idiot using a flash for obstructing the investigation'. McLusky approved. He hated the press. Unless he could use them for his own ends, of course.

The chief investigator repaid them five minutes later.

McLusky flicked his cigarette into a puddle. 'What have you got for us?'

The white-suited man twitched his blond moustache. He probably thought he was smiling. 'It was a bomb, home-made. We can't say for sure what type of explosive was used, we'll leave that to Forensics, though I have my own theory. What I can tell you gentlemen is that the explosive material was probably housed in a thin metal canister.' He held up an evidence bag containing a triangular piece of torn metal. 'It's a bit of a miracle that apart from the boy no one else was injured by the shrapnel but then it's quite flimsy stuff. Are you a drinking man, inspector? Does this look at all familiar?'

McLusky took it off him and leant back, angling it into the light coming from inside the command unit. Despite the slight blistering he could still make out the embossed

writing, *Special Reserve* and *Aged 12 years*. The type of metal
canister single malts came in. He half-closed his eyes, visualizing the bottle. 'That'll be Glenfiddich. I prefer the
Ancient Reserve myself.'

'You're a connoisseur, then?' Austin squinted at the bag.

'Not on my salary.' McLusky handed it back. 'Thanks for
the preview.'

'No sweat.' The man left to rejoin the group of CSI technicians working the area.

'The public's new heroes, apparently.' Austin nodded
towards the white-suited army.

'What, crime scene techies?'

'So it would appear. American TV series. All you have to
do, apparently, is run that bit of tin through the lab and
they'll tell you where it was bought, what the perp has for
breakfast and whether he takes water with it. Then you
wash it through the computer and it'll spit out his address.
You haven't seen it either? I can't get Channel Five.'

'I haven't got a telly.'

'Blimey, that's radical.'

'Hardly.' It was probably just another of those things
he'd forgotten to get, like a wife and kids and a group of
close friends he could ask round for supper. He did have
friends of course but they fell into one of two categories:
they were either drinking friends or colleagues and former
colleagues. Both those categories he had now left behind in
Southampton and he didn't expect any of them to come
and find him. *Tabula rasa*. He could start over.

Witness statements had been taken and were now being
collated in the office inside the command vehicle where for
the time being all information came together. House-to-
house inquiries were being made at every property that
overlooked the park on this side.

'All right, Jane, so what are we looking at here?
Terrorists? Kids? A crank?'

Austin rocked lightly from side to side, making himself
comfortable on his feet. 'Not sure what I think. It could

have been a schoolkid prank that went wrong. It was one hell of a bang. Kids do hang out here, though not so much after dark now since the Mobile Muggers have struck here twice.'

'Could well be kids. It's the kind of stupid thing they would blow up.'

'I can't see the terrorist angle at all. It wasn't a big enough explosion for that. And there weren't enough people around. You'd leave it in a crowded place, wouldn't you?'

'And you'd spike it with nails to do as much harm as possible.'

'Then there's always the crank with a grudge against . . . gazebos?'

'Yes, quite. What do we know about the boy who was hurt? Could he have been the one who planted it, only it went off too soon, injuring him in the process? Not forgetting the woman. Stands to reason that the two people who got hurt most were probably closest to the centre of the explosion. We don't know yet how the bomb was triggered but if it was by remote control for instance then they might of course have been the bomber's targets. Do we have any news on their recovery or otherwise?'

'I'll find out.' Austin disappeared inside. McLusky took the opportunity to count his cigarettes. Not enough to get him through the rest of the day. He didn't mind sharing his cigarettes around as long as there were enough of them. Almost without his participation in the process another one appeared between his lips, flaring as he touched the flame from his plastic lighter to it. He walked across the street towards the wet, steaming heap of debris, still being attended by the army of white-suited technicians. The press had given up and returned to their offices, no doubt to fill in the gaps in their knowledge with column inches of speculation. Were he to write the front-page article it would run something like this: *At 11.20 a.m. today an explosive device detonated inside a wooden shelter in Brandon Hill*

Nature Park, destroying it completely. Several passers-by were injured. The identity and motive of the bomber(s) are unknown. End of transmission.

Now it was up to him to provide the rest of the copy. With an incident like this you hoped for a witness and prayed that Forensics came up with something useful, however small. The problem was, forensic laboratories all over the world were stretched beyond endurance. The backlog of items to be examined and analysed was now so great that a simple blood or DNA sample took several weeks to come back. If it was urgent it seemed longer. Even then the most you could usually hope for was another person eliminated from your list of suspects.

Austin reappeared by his side with a scrap of paper filled with his swirly handwriting. 'Good news and not so good news. Uniform went to Colin Keale's place. According to the upstairs neighbour he's on holiday in Marmaris. That's in Turkey.'

'Yeah, I know where it is. We need it confirmed and we need to know when he left.'

'He left yesterday, apparently, so that's him out.'

'Is it hell. The bomb could have been sitting there for days. I want to know exactly when and where he left the country and when he's coming back. Do we know that?'

'Not yet, someone's checking it out for me.'

'What else?'

'The woman who got hurt, an Elizabeth Howe, remains unconscious though they're not sure why. No fractured skull as they first thought but she has damage to both eardrums, hence the bleeding, and probably won't be listening to any questions for a bit even if she does wake up. The boy, a Joel Kerswill, had a metal splinter removed from his right eye. They managed to save his eyesight. They're keeping him in for observation too but we might get a couple of minutes with him.'

McLusky glanced at his watch. The afternoon had drained away. 'All right, we'll have a chat with him then.'

'There's sandwiches now, by the way, if you want. You'll have to hurry, though, they're like animals in there.'

'No, that's fine, I don't eat triangular food.' Everyone seemed to define themselves by what they didn't eat these days, no dairy, no wheat, no carbs, no meat, so why should he feel left out?

'I see. A geometrical diet.'

'Indeed. I prefer a square meal.'

Austin groaned. A constable approached them. 'DI McLusky?'

'That's me.'

'Sign this, please.' He handed over a limp form, A4, folded in half.

'Got a pen? What am I signing?'

'I haven't, sir. It's your transport.' He dangled a set of keys.

'Oh good. Got a pen, Austin?'

'I have. It's in your inside pocket.'

'Genius.' McLusky signed and returned the pen to his jacket and the form to the constable. 'What is it, anyway?'

'VW. There's also a message from the superintendent.'

'Well, what is it?'

The constable looked doubtful. 'He told me to say "space hopper", sir.'

'Right, thank you, constable. Oh, hang on, where's it parked?'

'Right at the end there, behind the Forensics unit. It's a white one.'

'Things are looking up, Austin.' He jangled the keys. 'Sod sandwiches, lead me to the nearest fish and chip shop. No, lead me to the best fish and chip shop in the city. Afterwards we'll visit Joel Kerswill in hospital.'

The street was crowded. Every parked car had to be examined, every owner found and interviewed. Just as the last of the fire engines departed, leaving behind the senior fire officer and one fire investigator, two new cars arrived. The first to park was the superintendent's large grey Ford.

Not bothering to find a parking space at all was the driver of the dark BMW3 series that had followed him here. He stopped in the middle of the road and left it there. Driver and passenger debarked. Sharp suits and cropped hair. Both put on identical grey overcoats. Special Branch or MI5. No matter who they were, McLusky could practically feel himself become invisible. Denkhaus led them straight over. Before the superintendent could make introductions the younger of the two men stretched out his hand. McLusky shook it.

'My name is Kelper, I'll be taking over. You can go now.' He nodded at both of them, then turned his back.

Denkhaus led the new arrivals away, gesturing expansively at the command unit. 'This way. Allow me.'

McLusky offered Austin one of his cigarettes and lit one for himself. 'And there we have it, a bloodless coup. Well, it was lonely at the top anyway. Let's go, Jane.'

'That was damn quick.' Austin consulted his watch. 'Especially if they drove up from London.'

'Oh, I have a feeling Kelper doesn't waste time on motorways. I'm sure he took a plane and had the Beemer waiting for him. Tonight he'll dine with the super and by this time tomorrow he'll be eating rectangular food on the plane home, having effectively put the investigation back a whole . . . Fuck me, our super's got a sense of humour.' They had arrived behind the Forensics van where the constable had hidden McLusky's new transport. It was a little dirty-white car that had been in the police force a lot longer than he had. An appreciative member of the public had scratched PIGS in large angular letters across the bonnet. The scratches were old and had had ample time to rust.

'Looks like you really hit it off with the super then, doesn't it? I like the livery, by the way. But what's it supposed to be?'

McLusky gave the roof a friendly pat and tried to look proud. 'This baby is a 1981 VW Polo. 40 bhp. It does nought to sixty.' The car was unlocked. The doors opened stiffly with ominous metallic yawns.

Austin sniffed doubtfully at the musty interior. It smelled like it had been stored in a cave since the mid-eighties. 'We could drive to the station and pick up my car.'

'Nonsense, man, it's not that bad.' He turned the ignition key and listened to the nasal parp of the exhaust as the engine rattled and shook itself awake.

'On second thoughts, this could be a wind-up . . . did you see them drive it or did it get here on the back of a flat-bed truck?'

Fish and chips from Pellegrino's. They ate sitting in the car. The heater didn't work but right now McLusky was quite happy just to sit out of the rain in the vinegary fug rising from their paper parcels. A traffic warden knocked on the steamed-up window. McLusky cranked it down. It took some effort.

She shook her head at them. 'Sorry to disrupt your meal but you can't stop here, gentlemen.'

McLusky fished with greasy fingers for his ID and held it aloft for the woman to inspect. 'We're under cover, please move along.'

The warden shrugged, then took a last glance at the graffiti'd bonnet before moving on. 'Of course you are.'

McLusky stuck his head out and called after her. 'You blew our cover!'

While following Austin's directions to the Royal Infirmary he wondered how soon he would be able to drive there in his sleep. Every CID officer in every city could sleepwalk to A&E and the mortuary, it was part of the job. He cruised around for a parking space. How could the National Health Service have a funding crisis? The parking fees alone should take care of it. He squeezed the little Polo on to the end of a row reserved for staff and abandoned it, two wheels buried in spiky shrubbery. 'Sorry about that. Get out my side.'

'Are you sure we should be doing this?' Austin levered himself across the gear stick and out the driver's side.

'Yeah, right, if it gets towed away I'll cry.'

'Not that, I mean if whatsisname, Kelper, is in charge shouldn't we await orders from on high?'

'Bollocks to that. You don't think they'll actually do any investigating, do you? They'll throw their weight around for a few hours and get waited on hand and foot. When they're satisfied that Al Qaeda hasn't taken to blowing up park benches in an effort to undermine British morale they'll disappear again. No, we'll carry on as normal. Let's ask at reception here.'

He hated hospitals. Never mind the smell, never mind the lousy food or MRSA superbugs; never mind his unhappy memories of the weeks spent mending after two suspects had reversed over him. It was more than that: McLusky hated hospitals because he felt depression oozing from the very fabric of the buildings. He knew that the cloying, stifling mood would hang around in his clothes and hair like a miasma of hopelessness for hours afterwards. He simply couldn't believe that good things ever happened here. Post mortems he avoided for the same reason. He'd yet to learn anything at a post mortem he couldn't read in a report at his desk or ask over the phone without having to try and shake off the reek of death afterwards. Someone had to attend of course but who said it had to be him? Once a dead body had been removed from the crime scene he was happy to leave it to the scientists and grave diggers.

The boy's bed was by the window in a room with two other male patients who were either asleep, unconscious or dead, it was hard to tell. Joel Kerswill's mother was there, on a hard chair at the bedside. It was clear she had cried recently and since cheered up again at the excellent prognosis. The curtain separating the Kerswills from the bed next to them was drawn but the front curtain was open.

The boy was perhaps fifteen or sixteen. He was sitting propped up against the big hospital cushions with a fierce expression of disapproval on his pale face. His right eye was covered with a white dressing. There were scratches and pock marks on his cheek and forehead where flying splinters had hit, all scabbing over now.

IDs at the ready. 'I'm Inspector McLusky, this is DS Austin.'

Mrs Kerswill was in her mid-thirties. She wore a grey and blue track suit and trainers. Her dark hair had been subjected to a utilitarian cut that she imagined allowed her to forget about it. She clutched car keys and mobile in one hand and a packet of cigarettes and lighter in the other. 'He could have been killed! It's a miracle he hasn't been killed! He could have lost an eye, or both. My son could be blind now, d'you realize that? Just from walking along minding his own business. First London, then Glasgow, now here. I mean, London, fair enough, but you'd never expect them to do it here, would you? Not in a park either. Do you have a lead yet? Do you know who did this to him?'

'The inquiry is well under way.' Platitudes. He turned to the son. What was his name again? 'How are you feeling, son?'

'I'm not your son. It hurts and I want to go home, okay?'

'Joel! No need to be rude to the man.' She turned an apologetic face to McLusky. 'They want to keep him in until tomorrow. As a precaution, they said.'

'Joel, do you feel up to answering a few questions?'

'What kind of questions?'

'Well, for instance, did you notice anyone near the place just before the explosion?'

'How do you mean?'

'Did you notice anyone near the shelter just before the bomb went off?'

'I didn't see anyone. I didn't pay any attention, though. Didn't expect there to be a bomb, did I?'

40

'And you were walking past? In which direction?' Joel's injuries seemed to be on the right side so he presumed the boy had been walking along the path towards town.

Joel Kerswill confirmed it. 'I was walking towards Park Street.'

'Why were you there?'

'To look at it. I'd just got back from the Parks Department. I went for an interview.'

'For . . .'

'Apprenticeship. Gardening. Working in the nurseries and that. At Blaise Castle.'

'Did you get in?' Austin asked.

'Don't know yet. I think I deserve to though.' Joel's antagonism seemed to melt a little.

'Because of what happened?' McLusky asked.

'Yeah, don't you think? I nearly died there. Well, I could have, if I'd sat down for a bit close to where the bomb was. I'd be well dead if I'd sat down. I don't think they should give it to someone else, it wouldn't be fair.'

'I should think so, too. But to come back to the moments before the explosion. You said you didn't see anyone. Was anyone running? Riding a bicycle?'

'Not that I noticed. There was some guy on a motorized skateboard who overtook me? Maybe a minute before? But I didn't see him near that pavilion thing that blew up. Unless he chucked a hand grenade or something.'

'Okay. We'll leave it there then but we might need to talk to you again if anything new turns up. Someone will come and take a written statement for you to sign but perhaps later at home, when you're feeling better.'

'I feel all right, I could go home now.'

'He wants to play on his computer.' Mrs Kerswill smiled and was rewarded with an embarrassed scowl by her son. 'His father walked out on us, perhaps the useless sod will get in touch if he reads about this in the paper. A photographer took Joel's picture for the *Post*.' Her son's scowl deepened. Why did she have to tell everyone? 'He owes us a fortune in maintenance. And Child Support, in case you were about to ask, are bloody useless. If you ever come across him you can give him a message from me. Right where it hurts.'

McLusky promised to keep them informed and left. Just before they gained the corridor Austin nudged his arm and nodded in the direction of the nearest bed. The middle-aged patient in it, propped up in a sitting position, was staring straight ahead, oblivious, under a sign warning *Nil by mouth*. His skin was a cardboard shade of grey.

Once in the corridor McLusky pointed back at the room. 'Wasn't that . . .?'

'Mr Spranger.'

'I didn't recognize him without his bulldozer.'

'Wonder what he's here for.'

'Nothing trivial, one hopes.'

The receptionist made a phone call and sent them down to the Observation Ward. There a doctor was found who could give them news of the second victim.

He was a young man, bright, brisk, alert, not the half-dead, asleep-on-his-feet junior doctor you were meant to expect these days if you believed the papers. 'She still hasn't regained consciousness though all her vital signs are strong. We're a bit baffled by this but for the time being we're just monitoring the situation. She's suffered two perforated eardrums, though miraculously hardly any shrapnel damage. From what I've been told she was on her way home when the blast knocked her off her feet. Have you any idea as to the kind of explosion? A bomb in the park, said the news . . . Who'd put a bomb in a place like that?'

McLusky nodded his agreement. 'That's a damn good question. It's early days yet. What kind of a person is Miss, Mrs . . . Howe?'

'Ms Howe is a retired postmistress.' The Ms, McLusky noticed, fell naturally from the doctor's lips, while he himself could never pronounce Ms without putting undue stress on it.

'Bit young to be retired? How old would you say she was?'

'She's forty-nine. Unemployed postmistress, then. It's the same thing. Post offices are closing and they're not coming back. From what her sister told us she hasn't been unemployed long but didn't expect to find another job. Not at her age.'

'You just mentioned a sister . . .'

'We found identification among Ms Howe's possessions and traced the sister through the hospital records. On a previous visit to the hospital she had named her as next of kin. She's with her now.'

'Do you think we could talk to her?'

'That's up to her. I can ask her. Wait here.'

It turned out that Ms Howe's sister had stepped out for a breath of fresh air, which in her case involved a packet of Superkings and a persistent little cough she didn't know she had. They found her by the nearest entrance. She looked to be the older sister, with hair the colour of concrete and the deep crags of a lifetime's smoking around her mouth. McLusky joined her and gratefully lit a cigarette himself. When he suggested her sister might have been the intended victim Mrs Henley scoffed at the idea. 'That's ridiculous. Who would want to kill my sister? Her? And with a bomb?'

'Your sister isn't married, does she have a partner?'

She shook her head. 'Liz finds it quite a lonely life since the post office closed. Turns out that was where she got most of her social contact. She lives by herself on Jacob's Wells Road. She'd have been coming from the shops, she always comes up through the park. She probably sat down on one of those benches, we did it once when I went with her. Liz'd be dead for sure if she'd still been sitting there but I was told she had moved on already.'

'That's our understanding. We believe nobody was sitting on the benches when the bomb exploded.'

'If only she'd got up a minute earlier. That would have been enough, wouldn't it? A minute? She'd have been far enough away then.'

'That's very possible. When did you last visit your sister at home, Mrs Henley?'

'What's that got to do with anything?' She prised another cigarette from her packet and lit it. 'We don't see each other very often, that's all. It's not that we didn't get on, we just lived our own lives, it's just the way it was.'

'I meant would you notice if there was anything different at your sister's place, an indication that anything had changed in her life, besides her unfortunate unemployment.'

'Oh that. I see what you mean. Well, I was there earlier to pick up some things for her, you know, toiletries and that. It was just like it always was, inspector, there was nothing different, not that I noticed.' She didn't think she ought to mention that the fridge had been empty and the cupboards almost bare. Liz didn't do much shopping these days. The flat had felt cold and lifeless.

Austin noted down addresses for both Mrs Henley and her sister before they left the woman to finish her angry cigarette in the chill evening wind.

McLusky drove the car out of the shrubbery so Austin could enter by the passenger door in a more dignified fashion. 'So, what do you think?'

'Let's see. Do I think anyone wanted to blow up Joel Kerswill as he walked back from his interview? Hardly. Do I think Joel Kerswill set the thing off himself? Perhaps. No, I don't think that either, though I couldn't tell you why.'

'A lot depends on what type of bomb it was. We'll need to know what kind of expertise would have been needed to make it. And the postmistress?'

'An even more unlikely suspect.'

'Also an unlikely target. We don't know how the bomb

was set off yet but it's possible it was just a prank that went too far. It must be hard to judge just how much home-made explosive to stick into a bomb.'

'It'll turn out to be a couple of kids who are at this moment sitting in their bedrooms shitting bricks, waiting for the heavy knock on the door. Another stupid bit of vandalism by kids bored with their computer games.'

'Might well be. Unless . . .'

'You can go left here, less traffic this time of day. Unless what?'

McLusky nosed the car out into the road. This was 'less traffic'? 'Unless it was none of these. Unless it was attempted murder but the intended victim was unharmed. And perhaps even unaware he, she, was meant to be blown sky high.'

'No way. Rubbish way to bump someone off. You'd stick it under their car, surely.' Austin felt he could talk easily to the new DI, who didn't seem precious about his own ideas.

'Quite. Or shove one under his bed. But not his favourite park bench. Always presuming your intended target has a car or a bed, of course. I'm just trying to think of every possibility here since I don't believe at all in the terrorist angle. We get quite a few tourists, of course, so if you wanted to harm British interests then scaring the tourists away would be a good start. But . . .'

Austin took up the baton. '. . . but you would blow up a hotel or Temple Meads station, say, not a pavilion. Turn left here, that's Jamaica Street, that'll take us back to your neck of the woods.'

'Right.' McLusky was committing every turn and street name to his mental map of the city. His new city. It didn't feel real yet. 'And it never works anyway. PKK in Turkey, ETA in Spain, a couple of bombs go off and there's a flurry of holiday cancellations but a few weeks later the bookings go up again.'

'Which makes no sense since all it does is give them time to get the next bomb ready for just when you arrive.'

'Also, you would have to keep up the bombings over a long period to do any lasting harm to the tourist business and not many organizations have those resources. Not the kind that sticks explosives in a whisky tin and blows up park benches, anyway.'

'You've given it some thought then. Are you going back to the station?'

McLusky checked his watch. 'Your car's down there, isn't it? I'll drop you off, but let's call it a day. After all, Kelper, whatever his rank, is in charge tonight and he didn't seem to want us around, did he?'

'It's all right, you can drop me off outside your place. It's stopped raining. I'll walk back.'

He turned into Picton Street. 'If you're sure.'

'Sure I'm sure. Probably quicker, anyway.'

'Are you being offensive about my new motor, Jane?' McLusky turned into his street and stopped outside his house. There were no parking spaces.

'It's a fine example of German engineering. For the transport museum. No, traffic across town is really bad this time of day, is all I meant.' Austin got out. 'See you in the morning.' He pushed the groaning car door shut.

McLusky cruised and eventually found a space to park near Herbert's Bakery. The handbrake squawked and the car rolled back a few inches. He left it in gear.

Standing in Northmoor Street he looked up at the lifeless windows of his flat. He didn't yet recognize it as his own, anybody might live there, it wasn't home. But then where was? With his mother dead and his father God-knows-where he hadn't felt at home anywhere for years.

He had no provisions in the house and the place was still a mess. There was really no point in going back there unless he wanted to go shopping first and then clear up the place so he could prepare some food, by which time he would probably be past caring. He walked into the pub instead. The bar at the Barge Inn seemed to take up most of the space though they had managed to cram a few tables

46

along the windows and the left-hand wall. A pool table had been shoehorned into an adjoining room somehow though you probably had to play with sawn-off cues. There was a door that led to vaulted cellars, available for hire. He ordered a Guinness and asked the barmaid about food. Yes, they did food every night except Thursdays which was quiz night. He perused the blackboard menu. Perhaps the shop across the street was making its influence felt since most of the food was Italian. The most English thing on the menu was probably the chicken tikka. Against his instincts he asked for lasagne to go with his beer and took the only free table, from where he could look up at the blank windows of his own flat. Below it someone was still working at the back of Rossi's though the place was closed with the vegetable displays cleared off the pavement. There was a newsagent's at the corner, a launderette called Dolly's and a strange little shop selling hippy paraphernalia. He knew there was a vet's, a hairdresser's, a greengrocer's and a junk shop just two minutes down the road. A chemist at the other corner completed the impression that McLusky had moved into a small village inside the city.

The food arrived and he ordered a second pint, the first appearing to have evaporated. He certainly felt no different for having drunk it. Halfway through demolishing his lasagne he looked up to catch sight through the window of a man slouching a little unsteadily through the rain towards the pub. He was bleeding from nose, split lip and eyebrows. A moment later he arrived at the bar.

'Oh no, Rick, what happened to you? Here.' The barmaid handed him a clean cloth. 'You been in a fight?'

Rick dabbed gingerly at his nose. 'Mugged. Bastards got everything.'

'Oh no, the Mobile Muggers? What's everything? Were you carrying much?'

'My money, twenty quid. My credit cards and stuff. I was listening to my MP3 player, they got that. My watch.' His voice shook and he winced as he dragged himself on to a bar stool.

'Poor Rick. Here, get that down you.' She put a pint of lager in front of him.

'I can't pay for it, Becky.'

'Don't be daft, it's on the house. And please don't call me Becky, I hate that name. It's Rebecca.'

He took a few deep gulps, pulling a face as the liquid touched his shaky teeth. Blood had dripped on to his jacket which was grimy at the back where he had fallen to the ground.

'Have you called the police yet?' The barmaid's blonde head disappeared below the bar top where she was rummaging about.

'They got my mobile. There's no point, anyway. The police can't catch them. They've had their description countless times now, no point telling them again.'

'You'll have to report it anyway, Rick, just for the cards and your mobile.' She had found a first aid box and produced a bottle of iodine.

'I know but I'll do it tomorrow, I've had enough aggro for one evening.'

'Go and clean yourself up in the toilet and then we'll put some of this on you.'

'No way, that stuff stings.'

'Don't be such a baby. And if you don't cancel your cards now they'll have spent your money by the morning. Here, you can put it on yourself, I've got work to do anyway.' She walked off to serve customers at the other end of the bar. Rick stayed put, dabbed, sniffed and drank. A middle-aged couple who walked in a few minutes later seemed to know him. The story got told again, sympathy was expressed and they bought him a drink before squeezing on to a bench in the corner.

McLusky had finished his meal and brought the empty plate to the bar, next to the mugging victim. Rick was in his late twenties with dark curly hair and a peeved expression on his narrow face, which might have a lot to do with recent events. 'How many attacked you?' McLusky asked.

'Four, there's always four, isn't there? Two scooters, two riders and two big bastards on the back who deal out the shit and do the mugging.' He looked morosely into his pint glass.

McLusky guessed more beer would be required soon. It would numb the pain but the humiliation and anger would take time to dissolve. 'Buy you another?'

He looked up at him. 'If you like. Thanks. The *bastards*.' He drained his glass.

McLusky signalled his order across to the barmaid. She seemed to be running the place single-handedly tonight. 'So what did they look like, your assailants?' There it was, assailants, perpetrators, suspects. Police speak. *Bastards*.

Rick didn't notice. 'Where have you been? Same as what they always look like.'

'I just moved here. First time I've heard about it.'

'Oh, right. Well, they all wear black. Black jeans, jackets, gloves, helmets. They've got balaclavas on under their helmets and they wear sunglasses, one had pink lenses the other yellow. Didn't see the blokes who rode the scooters really, I was busy getting my face kicked in.'

'What were their voices like?'

'Voices? Normal, like from round here.'

'Young, old? What age, do you think?'

'No idea, mate.'

A pint of Guinness and one of lager arrived. The girl put the lager in front of Rick. 'Looks like you're doing all right out of this, anyway.'

'You didn't get a number plate, did you?' McLusky asked.

'I didn't. But they're always either so muddy you can't read them or they're nicked anyway.'

McLusky left it there and returned to his little table by the window. Asking any more questions would have given the game away. He felt he had done enough work on his first day. Starting with that maniac in the digger demolishing his house and the zippy Skoda. He regretted having sacrificed the car now but it seemed the obvious thing to do then. It would read badly in his report, he knew that much. Not at all how he had intended to start his new job but in retrospect not at all untypical. And then the damn bomb in the park.

If it was a prank then whoever planted it had to have been either unaware of the strength of the explosion that was going to occur or completely indifferent to the possibility that people might be killed. What he didn't see was why someone would have planted it in that spot if they had actually *intended* to kill a lot of people. Unless . . .

Unless they had intended to kill a specific person and failed. Or a group of people. Had someone or a whole group of people agreed to be there at a certain time but failed to turn up and thus escaped being blown to kingdom come? Had it been triggered remotely? Was the woman now recovering in hospital the intended victim? At least in his book a bomb to kill a retired postmistress was definite overkill. All these questions had to be worked through and new ones found. Asking the right questions was what CID work was all about. How was the bomb made? Where did the components come from? How was it detonated, etc? McLusky yawned. Tomorrow Albany Road would no doubt be back in charge of the investigation and that's when he would start asking good, intelligent questions of the team. But for now he had had enough. Possibly not enough Guinness but enough of his first day back at work.

Chapter Three

No personal items, no photographs, no Christmas cactus. McLusky was again impressed by the extreme minimalism, even sterility, of the superintendent's office. Apart from the obvious, the computer screen, the blotter, in- and out-tray, phones and fountain pen, there was nothing much to break up the expanse of clean, clear desk. Denkhaus certainly didn't feel the need to create a barrier between himself and whoever had the dubious pleasure of sitting in the ungenerously upholstered chair in front of his desk. The rest of the office was similarly functional. The view across the city his window afforded was unimpeded by pot plants or other decoration.

Denkhaus's impatient, forever slightly irritated energy blasted straight at him. 'Yes, McLusky, interesting man, Kelper. High-flyer, he'll go all the way. You should have heard some of the things he talked about. Well, hinted at, all hush-hush stuff really. The budget they have, especially since the London bombings, it's astronomical. We can only dream ... We dined at the Cavendish in Bath last night and –'

'Then I hope he picked up the bill.' To McLusky's own amazement he had given voice to his thought. He hadn't even heard of the Cavendish before but he was absolutely certain that eating there was beyond a DI's salary. It just sounded like it.

Denkhaus looked puzzled, not used to being interrupted by smartass DIs. 'What?'

'I was just interested, since he wields such a healthy budget. Sir.' He got the 'sir' in far too late to make any difference.

'That's utterly beside the point, DI McLusky, and it was hardly clever to bring up the budget! Ours has a sizeable hole in it since you saw fit to use a practically brand new car as a battering ram. I do wish you could have thought of something less spectacular. We've been plastered across the front pages of the *Evening Post* day after day for entirely the wrong reasons. You haven't been here five minutes and you go and give them more ammunition. Yesterday I felt like sending you straight back to where you came from, I hope you realize that?'

'Yes, sir.' McLusky tried to look contrite. 'And what about today, sir?'

'Today you are back in charge of the bomb investigation. You can count yourself lucky. There's been a spate of burglaries at properties close to the canal; a plague of muggings, as I'm sure you are aware; a runaway ten-year-old boy; a string of random arson attacks on cars as well as all the usual. But unlike your colleagues you have nothing on your desk. You, DI McLusky, will concentrate on finding what the papers are already calling the Bench Bomber.' He tapped an early edition of the *Post*, which looked like it had been ironed. 'I ask you. First the Mobile Muggers, you know, mobile because they steal mobiles and because they run around on scooters. Now the Bench Bomber. They're loving every minute of it. We really don't need this. And of course when we can't give them name and serial number of the perp right away it's "police are clueless". If that woman dies, what's her name . . .?'

'Elizabeth Howe,' McLusky supplied.

'If Elizabeth Howe dies and this turns into a murder investigation then the pressure will really be on. Go after whoever did this with that uppermost in your mind.' Denkhaus punctuated his speech by jabbing an index finger towards him. 'No domestics, no bulldozers. You find damsels in distress, kittens up a tree or toddlers down a drain, you walk straight past. You concentrate on this.'

'Yes, sir. What was Kelper's opinion?'

'Oh, he thought it had nothing to do with extremism. Home-grown stuff, a prank or a crank. And I think we all agree on that. After London they're simply too stretched to investigate stuff like this. They insist we can take care of it ourselves. Let's prove them right, shall we? He also thinks it's a one-off and the target, the shelter, marks the perp out as a crank. A dangerous crank but not a terrorist.'

'Let's hope he's right. Will that be all, sir?'

'Yes, but let me have your report on the unfortunate destruction of the Skoda by tomorrow. And for Pete's sake make it sound good. In fact make its demise sound absolutely inevitable even to the Assistant Chief Constable's ears!' Of course the new DI wasn't the only source of the superintendent's black mood this morning. For the second time in a month the windows of his immaculate 4×4 had been plastered with mud, this time in a restaurant car park in the Old Town. The crudely made leaflet that came with it claimed that *If the 4×4s won't go to the country the country will come to the 4×4s.* Scores of Land Cruisers, Jeeps and Free-landers had recently got the same treatment. Someone, probably one of the Saturday traffic protesters, was waging a low-level campaign against the city's gas guzzlers but since no actual damage was being done no action had been taken. There was even a certain level of public support for the mud throwers, which in turn was branded 'the politics of envy' by the 4×4-driving camp. Denkhaus knew better than most how stretched their resources were, which infuriated him even more. These days you had to fling much harder stuff than mud to attract the attention of the force.

'What have you got for me, Jane?' Without stopping, McLusky called into the CID room by way of sharing around some of the pressure he suddenly felt.

Austin hit the ground running. 'Colin Keale, the pipe-bomb bloke: he boarded a plane to Dalaman airport in south-west Turkey at 22.50 two days ago, the night before the bomb. From here.'

'That leaves him well in the frame. He could easily have planted the thing, with a timer, and then conveniently gone on holiday. As an alibi it won't wash, I want him.'

'We're working on it. It was a flight-only deal, so he could be anywhere, but the neighbours think Marmaris.'

'Okay, we'll start by applying for a warrant to search his hole.'

'Right. Witness statements from the park and the house-to-house are all on your desk.' He no longer addressed McLusky as 'sir' but didn't use his first name, not so soon, even though it had been offered, not within earshot of the others anyway. It was only his second day after all and Jack Sorbie had already ribbed him about 'his new chum'. *Your new chum's getting a right bollocking from the super, mate.*

'And? Close the door, tell me about it.' McLusky sank into the chair behind his desk for the first time. It hissed as air escaped from the faux leather upholstery and creaked metallically as he settled into it. He lit a cigarette and looked around for something to use as an ashtray.

'Ehm, you know this building is no-smoking?'

'Good for the building.' He reached behind him and opened the window.

'Seriously. Even the custody suite went no-smoking yesterday. There's blokes over there screaming that it violates their human rights. They called for their solicitors. They're going to sue us.'

'No win no fag. I wish them luck. Let's get on with it, Jane.' He was suddenly not in the mood for banter.

Jane didn't blink. 'Well, one woman witnessed a man plant the bomb and she recognized him. He's been arrested and admitted everything.'

'Very funny.'

'We got a pile of statements. Looks like we have a lot of

leisured and/or retired people and quite a few home-workers living in the streets bordering the park closest to the locus. Most people who were at home around the time of the bombing did look out of the window earlier because of a bloke on a motorized skateboard. Making a nuisance of himself going up and down the paths. Apparently it made a horrible noise, they use little two-stroke engines –'

'Yeah, I know the things. Bloody menace.'

'Well, quite a few people got annoyed and had a look at what it was and all saw the same bloke.'

'The motorized skateboarder ... the boy, Joel, he mentioned him. Do we have a description?'

'Strictly speaking it's the board that's motorized of course.'

'Jane ...' McLusky managed to ladle quite a bit of menace into the word.

Austin rattled it off from memory. 'Tall, skinny, spiked hair, sunglasses, denims, red scarf and skateboarding gear, knee pads, that sort of thing. Mid-to-late thirties.'

'Late thirties? You'd have thought he'd have better things to do than skating in the park. Right. I want him. He's been up and down the street, he'll have seen something others didn't. Shouldn't be difficult to find. If anyone sees a bloke on a motorized skateboard tell them to kick him off it and bring him in. Illegal except on private land anyway if my memory serves me right.' McLusky stubbed his cigarette out on the aluminium window frame. 'Okay, I'll dive into these.' He pulled the pile of reports towards him. 'Oh, before you go, what does one do for coffee around here?'

Austin stood in the door, suppressing a sigh. 'Milk, sugar?'

'No, no, I'm old enough to get my own. Just point me towards it.'

The DS cheered up immediately. 'Ah, well, in that case it all depends. There's the machine at the end of the corridor if you like your water brown. There's the canteen if you want molasses and there's a kettle in the CID room, bring your own mug and put 10p in the jar.'

'Instant?'

'Instant. DI Fairfield has a cappuccino maker in her office.'

'Has she?'

'Only for the inner circle.'

'And they are?'

'DS Sorbie, DCI Gaunt, the super . . . basically everyone above her own rank and anyone below her own rank who's about to get bullied into doing her a favour.'

'You ever tasted it?'

'Not me. It's not fair trade coffee, if you get my drift. I've managed to avoid it so far.'

'All right. Thanks for explaining the politics of coffee to me, Jane.' He waited until Austin had closed the door before sliding open the desk drawer and taking out a half-eaten Danish pastry from Rossi's. Coffee might have to wait though. He started reading the reports, scattering bits of flaked almond over the pages. Everybody had seen something, everyone remembered someone else, only no one remembered anything significant. Those residents whose houses faced the park had given the most detailed descriptions. It was unsurprising. Those actually in the park were all there for different reasons. 'Taking the air' were the pensioners, using it as a shortcut were the busy people, 'hanging out' were the kids playing truant. Pram pushers, dog walkers and tourists made up the rest; all had their own agendas. But those who lived west of the park had gone to their windows in order to look. Everyone saw the skateboarder. One witness even described Elizabeth Howe, sitting on one of the benches in the shelter, resting with her shopping. This was corroborated by a dog walker in the park. According to him Howe gathered her shopping bags and had just set foot on the path when the bomb went off. Her body was blown forward by the explosion and she twisted while falling, landing back first on the path.

Through some sort of miracle nobody was close enough to the bomb to get killed. Two witnesses saw a couple hugging and kissing earlier on one of the benches. One remembered a young man sitting on the other side, drinking beer from a can. Another saw a three- or four-year-old girl stand on one of the benches before being fetched away by a woman. Lucky family. Nobody saw the container, nobody saw anyone acting suspiciously.

McLusky finished the Danish, licked his fingers and wiped them on his jeans but they remained faintly sticky. He closely read all the reports and notes and got a mental picture of people moving through the park; the skateboarder, woman and child, beer-drinking type, snogging couple, a sprinkling of tourists; Elizabeth Howe and Joel Kerswill walking past each other in different directions. Then the bang. He imagined it from above, watching a silent explosion as from a hovering balloon, saw himself, Austin and Constable Hanham run towards the scene. Too late, it was all too late. McLusky saw it in his mind as though he was there, hovering. He *had* been there and he had been useless. It unfolded in front of his eyes like a movie scene, shot from high above the trees, and he wished he could simply play the film backwards until a figure would walk up, reach for the bomb, put it back into the bag . . . Because there would be a bag, of course, it would also be quite heavy. Perhaps it had been left inside the bag and that had been destroyed by the blast . . .

Impatiently he shuffled the papers into a messy pile and pushed his chair back on its castors. How was he supposed to draw a bead on this idiot from these bits of paper? They were out there, somewhere, either kids reading about their own prank in the *Evening Post* or a malicious crank gloating over the column inches he had been given. Far less likely was an inept assassin analysing what went wrong, planning his next move. Since when did they go around assassinating kids and ex-postmistresses? Post . . . postal workers . . . mail. No, it didn't fire his synapses. All he had was Colin Keale, a known bomb-maker, in Turkey, a retired woman and a kid wanting to be a gardener.

McLusky grabbed his jacket and made for the bathroom down the corridor where he washed the stickiness off his hands, then he clattered down the stairs and out into the thin April light. He never found it easy to grasp a case while locked up inside an office, especially one as dispiriting as the one they had found for him at Albany Road. If you wanted to do policing you had to be out in the street and he didn't even know most of the streets in this city. As a police officer you had to do more than just know them, you had to own the streets and feel in your bones that you did. *My city, my streets, my patch.*

It looked like a good-enough patch, though there was a chill wind blowing through the narrow lanes of the Old Town. The endless procession of traffic snarled like giant knotted ropes up and down the streets as he walked in the vague direction of the river. Cars, vans, lorries, pedestrians, taxies, minibuses, cyclists, motorized rickshaws and of course scooters squeezed through the unquiet heart of the city. Scooters were everywhere now. They seemed to be the new weapon of choice for many commuters and they were being bought, ridden, crashed and stolen everywhere.

Eventually he found himself walking near a ruined church in a convoluted bit of park. He walked purposefully on into a busy area of tall Georgian buildings. He squeezed through a crowded food market in Corn Street, keeping a sharp lookout. He had planned to enter the first café he found but had already dismissed the first two as unlikely candidates for the *best cappuccino in town* which was what he was looking for. In McLusky's opinion there really was no point in drinking imitation coffee. Find the best and stick to it. It should only take me a year, he thought, there were cafés and restaurants and takeaway coffee places every few yards. He abhorred drinks in Styrofoam cups and hence avoided the takeaways. The chances that a barista first brewed the finest coffee in town then poured it into plastic cups were anyway frankly remote. Eventually he simply picked a small café called Cat's Cradle where a table had just become free. He ordered a large cappuccino from the frizzy-haired girl behind the counter and sat on a cold chrome chair at a cold steel table by the window. He watched the people passing in the narrow lane. At this time of day there were mostly women in the streets, he noticed, and the place was busy. The city attracted a fair number of tourists even this early in the season. Museums, art collections, the science park and historic ships, both real and replica, in the old harbour seemed to be the main attraction.

As the girl set the enormous cup of froth in front of him a loud bang outside made her jump and sharply draw in breath. McLusky tried to reassure her. 'Just someone dropping stuff into an empty skip.' He had caught a glimpse of the battered yellow mini-skip at the end of the lane earlier.

The girl relaxed her shoulders. 'Well, after what happened yesterday you can't help thinking. Another one could go off any time, couldn't it?'

'Is that what you think? That there'll be another one?'

'I don't know, do I? But it's scary, isn't it, if someone blows up stupid things like a pavilion. On the tube you'd expect a bomb, but if they blow up stuff like that then anything could explode next. I never thought it would come here.'

'I don't think it has. I don't think it was a terror bomb.'

'Well, if it makes people terrified then I think it is.'

The girl had a point. As she left to serve other customers he tasted his coffee. His scale of coffee-rating only had three levels – 'awful', 'drinkable' and 'the best'. This one was just about drinkable.

It did however have the desired effect of sharpening his senses. As he continued on his erratic march across town he took everything in precisely, filing away into his memory intersections, back streets, alleys and steps, possible shortcuts. He looked keenly, not like a tourist, but like someone taking possession of a new car, a new house, a new lover. Everything interested him from street furniture to the location of the banks and the number of CCTV cameras. His street instincts were good today and eventually he found himself at the western end of Brandon Hill without having consulted the A–Z in his jacket pocket once. The park was still closed to the public and all entrances were guarded by extremely bored uniformed police. McLusky showed his ID and ducked under the tape. He avoided the locus of the explosion and took a circuitous route to the top of the hill dominated by a hundred-foot tower built from pink sandstone. He climbed the narrow winding stone steps that led him breathlessly to the top. From here he had views across the city in all directions but what interested him lay directly below. It wasn't exactly Central Park but for a fingertip search it was big enough. There was a large children's play area, plenty of trees, a pond. The entire area had been combed. There was no separate parks police so Avon and Somerset had provided enough manpower to make sure there were no more devices hidden in the grounds. Suspicious items had of course been found. Two had been blown up in controlled explosions by Royal Engineers; both had been duds. One turned out to be an old dried-up can of yacht varnish. The other had been a rucksack of an Italian tourist, already reported lost. Inside, among other possessions, were his camera and his passport, both now vaporized.

He clattered back down the ancient steps and approached the locus of the explosion. An inner circle had been taped off here, covering the area of scattered debris. A lone CSI technician wearing a coverall was still or again going over the scene, this time with a metal detector. He looked up, annoyed at seeing him approach. 'Can you stay beyond that case, please?' He pointed to an aluminium case standing on the path.

McLusky stopped dutifully by the case and brandished his ID. 'DI McLusky.'

'Makes no difference, I'm afraid.'

'Point taken. Anything in particular you're looking for today?'

'You should get a preliminary report sometime this afternoon.' He hesitated. 'But yeah.' The man came over to him, carrying an evidence bag. He held it up for him to examine. It contained a very small piece of metal that could have belonged to some kind of mechanism. 'The device contained a timer, inspector. They used a wristwatch. A mechanical one works best for this kind of thing. Tick tock, a real ticking time bomb. I've come back to see if I can recover more of the pieces. I'm not saying we'll get it back to work but the more of the pieces we have the greater the chance that Forensics can come up with a make. If it was a new watch then it will probably turn out to have been Russian.'

'Russian? Why's that?'

'Real wind-up watches are relatively expensive but the Russians still make cheap ones you can buy here and there. You would probably not go and buy a precision Swiss watch just to blow it up. So unless you had an old one hanging about you'd probably buy a crap Russian one from a catalogue showroom. It'll last just long enough to do the job.'

'I see.' He looked at his own wristwatch which was a cheap battery job from a catalogue showroom. 'So if it had a timer that means it wasn't radio controlled or anything? Not set off remotely by someone watching for his victim to get near it?'

'That's correct. It was a very simple device, anyone could have built it. It'll say so in the report, I'm sure.'

'So if you're using a wind-up watch how long in advance can you set the bomb to go off?'

'Twelve hours. Enough time to get to the other side of the world, inspector.'

Or Turkey. 'Thanks. Good hunting.' Or whatever one wished people who hoovered grass for a living. Anyone could have built it? McLusky was sure he wouldn't know where to start. His understanding of things explosive began and ended with the kind where you put a match to a fuse and retired to a safe distance. He ducked out of the perimeter on the other side. He called Austin on his mobile. 'I'm in Great George Street. Bring the car. No, your car.' He smoked two cigarettes before Austin crept up on him in a minute Nissan. Not really a convincing car for a big hairy DS, thought McLusky, even in blue.

The car park at Blaise Castle Estate out in Henbury had plenty of space this cold April lunchtime. The man at the estate office glanced at their IDs and gave them directions without asking what they had come about. They had to walk back along the road they had come and long before they got to the nursery McLusky wished they had taken the car. The signs on the gate declared *No Parking* and *No Public Access*. McLusky and Austin weren't public. They pushed through and walked up between long propagating houses and through an open door into a large shed with a concrete floor. There were wooden bays containing various composts and more empty flowerpots than seemed possible. By a still-steaming kettle stood two young men in green dungarees and green T-shirts, chomping sandwiches.

One of them swallowed down a large mouthful, looked like he regretted it for a second, then challenged them. 'Help you gentlemen?'

They showed IDs. McLusky looked around. 'Boss about?'

'On her lunch break. It's about the bomb, is it?'

'Yes, it is.'

'We're putting in for danger money.'

'Good thinking. You wouldn't of course have any idea who would want to blow up a shelter in Brandon Hill?'

'Not the foggiest, and we've been thinking hard.' He reached up a hand as if to scratch his head but changed his mind. His thin hair was ineptly spiked into a ridge that ran down the centre of his head like a flailed hedge.

The other man spoke with a strong Bristol accent,

modified by sandwich. 'We hope it's no one with a grudge against the park, since we're out there all the time, like. We was planting bulbs around there only the other day, all round that shelter.'

'Well, last October actually.' The thin-haired gardener gave his colleague a pitying look.

'A grudge against the park? Or the parks department? Has anyone left under a cloud recently?'

They looked at each other for a split second, seeming to come to an instant agreement on the matter. 'Yeah, Three Veg did.'

'Yup, got fired.'

Austin's brow furrowed. 'Three veg?'

'Nickname. His real name's Tim. He's a veggie, so at school when others were having meat and two veg he used to ask for three veg. It stuck.'

'What did he get fired for?'

The first man had at last dispatched his sandwich. 'What didn't he? Just about everything.'

The two gardeners slipped into their well-rehearsed double act. 'Being late.'

'All the time.'

'Skiving.'

'He'd be out there, like, supposed to plant up a bed and he'd be standing by the fence watching the girls instead, leaving all his stuff lying about.'

'Smoking in the greenhouses.'

'*Borrowing* power tools . . .'

'Driving the minivan through the park like a maniac.'

'Oh yeah, that was on his second day here, nearly got fired for that then, didn't he?'

McLusky had heard enough reminiscences. 'So he got the sack. When exactly was that?'

'Last summer. September? Yeah, it was September.'

'End of September.'

'You seriously think he's behind it? Building a bomb? Three Veg couldn't do it, he hasn't got the brains.'

Rapid shakes of the head from the first man. 'Too thick.'

'Apparently it doesn't take much brains. And we have to explore every avenue. Does he have a surname?'

Hedgerow Hair nodded his chin at a door in the back. 'They'll have that in the office, won't they?'

They did. Timothy Daws, twenty-eight years of age. An address in Bedminster. The admin worker wasn't taking a lunch break. She was eating salad from a plastic container at her desk. 'Yes, we had to let him go in the end. He was charming but a compulsive liar and never did any work. When he did turn up for work at all.'

'Did he have any redeeming features? Was he mechanically gifted, perhaps?'

'We thought so at first. He seemed to be so good at repairing things. Machines appeared to be breaking down as soon as he was supposed to take them out on a job. He would then say, Oh, leave it to me, I'll fix it, and he would, eventually. Only it later turned out there was either never anything wrong with them in the first place or he'd been the one to sabotage them. He'd just sit around smoking, doing nothing. It was another way of delaying the start of any job you gave him.'

McLusky thanked her and walked out the other end between the propagating houses full of row upon row of plants growing in plastic pots. Two more gardeners working at this end looked up from what they were doing and gave him a friendly nod as he passed. One even smiled. People enjoying their work, whatever next? On the way back to the car park he called Albany Road. 'Have we got the search warrant for Colin Keale yet?'

'Still waiting.'

'All right, can you run a name for me? Timothy Daws, as in jackdaw. He got fired by the parks department for being a waste of space.'

'Won't be a tick.' The officer didn't take long to come back over the phone. 'Timothy Daws, yup, petty theft

64

and one caution for cannabis possession, nothing recent. Hardly a career criminal, sir.'

'I don't care, it's all we've got. I have an address out in Bedminster, wherever that is.'

The DC compared it with the one on the computer. 'Yes, same address he gave then.'

'Right. Chase the search warrant.' He slipped his mobile back in his jacket. 'We'll pay Mr Three Veg a little visit.'

Austin drove south and west. 'Does he look like a candidate for our Bench Bomber to you?'

'Not really but who does? If he's a long-term pothead then he could have gone paranoid. Apparently he's a lazy bastard so I wouldn't have thought he'd go to the trouble of learning to make bombs. Also, if you wanted to take it out on the parks department surely you'd bomb the parks department.' McLusky sighed. 'Unfortunately there's no "surely" with these nutters. So we'll go visit.'

The address turned out to be at the end of a dispiriting terrace of small grey post-war houses. Tiny front lawns had mostly been tarmacked to provide parking, since the street itself was too narrow to accommodate the collection of low-budget cars. Only a few front lawns struggled on, some full of the brightly coloured impedimenta of child-rearing, some full of broken white goods. Daws' address fell into the struggling-lawn category. Water from a split downpipe was leaking into the stonework. At the windows the remains of squashed flies dotted grey net curtains. Austin went round the back to stop Daws from disappearing through the garden.

There was a door bell but McLusky ignored it. He squatted down and peered through the letter box. A narrow hall, steep stairs on the right, a tangle of mountain bikes on the left and at the back of the hall what looked like a kitchen. There was movement there. He straightened up, rattled the letter-box lid and pounded on the door.

After a minute the door opened a crack and the pale spotty face of a young man appeared in the gap. 'Yeah?'

McLusky pushed the door wide open and the kid staggered back. 'Hey!'

'Always put the chain on before opening the door to strangers, son.'

The young man looked alarmed. 'There isn't a chain.'

'Then fit one. You Timothy Daws?' He already knew he couldn't be. This specimen was too young and had all the charm of a damp dish cloth.

'No. And it's not my house. Tim isn't here. What do you want?'

McLusky waved his ID. 'Police. Mind if I come in?' He hefted past the skinny youth. 'Thanks. Who are you?'

'Innis Cole.'

'You live here?'

'Yes.'

'You a friend of Timothy's?' Innis Cole, McLusky decided, was barely twenty and nervous. Probably nothing more serious than an eighth of blow in his bedroom, though.

'Not really. He's a housemate. Well, landlord, really.'

'Let's go into the kitchen, Innis. So he does live here?' He allowed the spotty kid to lead the way. Cole stalled however when he noticed Austin trying the half-glazed back door. Austin flattened his ID against the glass. McLusky gave Cole a playful push from behind. 'That's all right, he's with me. Go let him in.'

Austin sniffed as he entered. The place smelled of sour washing and stagnant water. The kitchen was a mess.

Now that he had two officers to put up with the youth appeared even more nervous, looking from one to the other.

McLusky pressed on. 'Where's Three Veg then?'

The use of Daws' nickname seemed to worry Cole. 'Don't know. He doesn't tell me where he goes.'

Austin positioned himself behind him. 'When did you last see him?'

The youth turned around. 'I, er, don't know. Couple of days ago?'

'Three?'

'Maybe.'

McLusky flicked through a small pile of letters addressed to Daws. None of them were personal. 'Does he often disappear for several days?'

Cole turned around again. 'From time to time, yeah.'

'But he doesn't tell you where he goes.' He picked up a chopstick and used it to poke around between the collection of empty takeaway cartons and beer cans on the table.

'What does Mr Daws do for money?' Austin wanted to know.

Innis rolled his eyes and sat down at the encrusted kitchen table. He wasn't going to whirl around any longer. 'I don't know. I think he's signing on at the moment.'

Austin ran a finger through the grime on the half-glazed door, then inspected it and looked for somewhere to wipe it. 'This is a council place, right?'

'Think so, yeah.'

'But you pay rent to Daws.' Austin wiped his finger on the margin of a local free newspaper.

'Yeah.'

McLusky waved a couple of benefit cheques he had found among the letters. 'While Daws claims rent for the entire place from housing. And hasn't bothered cashing these. Curious, wouldn't you say? Can't be short of cash then. When did you last see him, Mr Cole?'

'Is that what this is about? Benefits?'

'Could be. Doesn't have to be. I'm not really interested but I could always take an interest if I got a bit *bored*.' McLusky gave him a warm smile, which seemed to unnerve Innis Cole considerably. 'So?'

'A few days.'

McLusky scissored the cheques between his fingers. Innis tried to count them. 'Two weeks?'

'And where's he gone?'

'He didn't tell me. He's got a job on, is all he said.'

'A job on. What kind of a job?'

'I don't know. Something to do with gardens. He works with someone else sometimes. Or for someone else, I'm not sure which.'

'Does he have a car?'

'A van. And it's no use asking me what kind, it's white and quite clapped out. He was given it, I think.'

'Right. And what do you do, Mr Cole?'

'I work at the video shop.' He jerked his head in the direction of the high street.

'But not today?'

'I'm on a late, we're open till ten thirty.'

McLusky turned on his avuncular voice. 'Okay. Now we would like to talk to Mr Daws about this and that. You might want to give us a call when you see him. But don't worry, we'll pop in from time to time. Whenever we're in the area.' He nodded reassuringly at Cole. As the two detectives left the narrow house Innis Cole did not look reassured.

McLusky sank into the passenger seat. 'Do you realize this is a girl's car, Jane? The baby blue colour won't fool a soul.'

'I know. Eve made me get it. She loves the things.'

'Married? Girlfriend?'

'Ehm, girlfriend, well, fiancée, sort of . . .'

'Sort of? That doesn't sound like you went on your knees and offered up diamonds. It was her idea then.'

'Yes, but not a bad idea for all that. We've been living together for a year now. It really makes sense.'

'Aha?'

'Well, it does when she explains it.'

'Do you love her, Jane?'

'Yeah. Yeah, I do. How about you?'

'Me? I never met the girl. Am I attached? No, not at the moment. I thought I was. Until . . . the accident and me in hospital. It was the last straw for Laura.' He realized that this was the first time he had said her name out loud since the break-up and the shape of it threatened to fill the entire car. He lit a cigarette and found the ashtray crammed with sweet wrappers. 'Any thoughts about Mr Cole?'

'The guy was far too nervous.' Austin navigated the car back on to the main street and pointed it in the direction of Albany Road. 'He was trying to cover up for Daws not being there, so Daws probably told him, "If anyone asks I've only been gone a few days."'

'Get on to the DSS, see when he last signed on and whether he missed an appointment. And also find out when he signs on next, we can easily collect him then.'

'You think he's a possible?'

'He's all we've got, so we'll pull him in.'

'We could always get a search warrant and have a look in his garden shed. It's certainly big enough for a bomb factory.'

'Is it? I didn't see it. Why didn't you say? Turn around, let's have a look at it.' McLusky threw the cigarette out of the window and sat up in his seat, impatiently working an imaginary gas pedal.

Austin slowed, looking for a place to turn round. 'Shouldn't we get a search warrant first, sir?'

'Sir, is it? You can call me Liam, even when you disagree with me. Go on, Jane, make the turn.'

Austin obliged. 'I tried the shed, it was locked and the window was blocked up.'

'Blocked-up windows I like. Mr Innis Whatsisname could be on the phone to Daws this minute, telling him we're looking, or he might already be clearing out the shed. Shit, Daws could be living in it for all we know.'

'But without a warrant –'

'You know, I had a shed once. They are so flimsy. One good gust of wind and they fall over.' He licked his finger and stuck it out of the window. 'Seems quite windy today.'

Back at Daws' house he made Austin leave the car at the street corner. 'I'll go round the back this time, you can take the front. Don't want it to get boring for the boy.'

Along the back of the terrace ran a narrow tarmacked alley full of oozing bin-liners, broken glass and dog shit. He found the back of the house. The flimsy wooden door to the garden was locked. He jumped up and easily pulled himself over it. There was indeed a large shed at the bottom of the desolate little garden. It looked to be at least twelve by eight foot. The double door was secured with a large padlock, the window blocked from inside with fibreboard and chicken wire. McLusky reached the back door just as Innis Cole unlocked it from the inside, dressed to go out. His face fell in resignation and he opened the door.

McLusky stepped into the kitchen. 'Don't mind if I do. Not much of a kitchen gardener is Mr Three Veg. Not even two veg out here. Aren't you going to let DS Austin in? Not very polite that.' Austin was working the bell as well as banging his fist against the front door.

'What is it you want *now*?' Cole looked for a second as though he would stamp his foot in indignation but instead walked off down the hall and opened the front door to the noisy DS who swept him back into the kitchen.

McLusky boomed at the boy. 'We've come to take a look at your shed.' He hooked a thumb over his shoulder.

'It's not my shed, it's Tim's. And I don't have a key. Anyway, you'll need a warrant, won't you? Search warrant?'

'Search warrant? If we came with a search warrant we'd start by searching under your mattress and you wouldn't want that. Nah, son, we don't want to search the shed. You're going to open it and we'll just stand there and look over your shoulder. That's not a search, that's called noticing things. Let's have it then.'

'As I said, I don't have a key.' His eyes strayed involuntarily to a large biscuit tin on the window sill.

McLusky picked up the greasy tin and thumped it down in front of Cole. 'Go on, have a rummage. It's called co-operating with the police and we like it a lot.'

Cole sounded younger by the minute. 'He'll kill me.' He popped the lid and emptied the tin on to the table. Rubber bands, springs, screws, corroded triple-A batteries, leaky biros, fuses. There were several keys, dull from lack of use, and one shiny Yale key on its own split ring. Cole picked it out without enthusiasm. 'This is the spare one, I think.'

'Okay, let's have a look-see.'

Cole led them to the shed with the air of a man being made to walk the plank. 'Whatever is in there has nothing to do with me.' While he sprung the lock and opened the double doors he appeared to be holding his breath. Then he exhaled noisily. The shed was full of tools, mainly for gardening use: apart from three lawn mowers there were forks, spades and rakes, leaf blowers, strimmers and hedge trimmers of various makes and ages.

Cole was visibly relieved. 'Well, what do you know? Gardening stuff. He was a gardener, probably still is.'

'Probably.' Austin leant this way and that so he could get a good look without going anywhere near the door. 'Looks to me though as if he's gone a bit overboard on the tools. You could kit out ten gardeners with that lot. I mean, who needs four hedge trimmers? Three lawn mowers?'

'As I said, nothing to do with me. Can I lock it again?'

McLusky sighed. 'Yes, go on.' The shed was full of stuff obviously stolen but a bomb factory it wasn't – for a start there was no space left inside – and Superintendent Denkhaus's speech from this morning was still fresh in his mind. No distractions, no damsels in distress, no kittens up a tree. This looked like a kitten up a tree.

Austin dug up some professional courtesy as they left by the front door. 'Well, thank you for your cooperation, Mr Cole.'

'That's all right.' Relief at their departure made Cole generous.

McLusky turned round and towered over him. 'Just out of interest, how much rent *are* you paying Daws?'

'What?' Cole's eyes widened helplessly.

The words rabbit and headlight came to the inspector's mind. 'Well? How much? Quickly now.'

71

'Ehm . . . fif . . . fifty pounds?'

'Fif-fifty pounds.' He nodded gravely while the young man tried not to squirm under his gaze. 'Okay, bye for now.'

Cole stood in the door, breathing rapidly, watching them walk to the car. He had to move out, they were bound to come and search the place properly after this. Might as well start packing now. Of course he couldn't leave until Three Veg came back or he'd be in deep shit with him. He had to keep looking after the place though he wasn't sure who was scarier, Three Veg with his explosive temper or the weird inspector and his unblinking eyes.

Chapter Four

'You don't really think he planted the bench bomb, do you? Anyway he couldn't have, he's on holiday.' Colin Keale's upstairs neighbour was a fleshy forty-year-old man with sparse hair and a moist voice. He reluctantly handed over the spare key Keale had left with him so he could water his house plants. 'He would hardly have left me the key to his flat if he had a bomb factory down there.'

'I'm sure you're right.' McLusky took the key off him and thought that he probably meant it.

'Unless you think I'm involved in the bomb plot too, inspector.' He sounded hopeful, relishing the thought. 'I know all about Colin's bit of silliness with the pipe bombs but he wasn't very well at the time. I assure you he's completely normal now. He'd never do anything like it again.'

'We just need to eliminate him from our inquiries, that's all.'

Colin Keale lived in a small basement flat on Jacob's Wells Road, not five minutes' walk from the site of the explosion. If he did plant the bomb then it would seem the height of laziness to do it within hearing distance. Or perhaps it gave the act an added frisson. But surely the ultimate satisfaction must be to watch it happen.

Austin barred the neighbour's way on the steps. 'I'm afraid you'll have to stay up here.'

'What, are you afraid I might interfere with the evidence, or something?'

73

Austin ignored him and followed the inspector down the cast-iron steps into the basement forecourt.

A fig tree in a half-barrel sent fleshy leaves up to the sun and other plants in pots thrived inexplicably in this deeply shadowed sinkhole. McLusky gave the half-barrel an exploratory kick. It felt and sounded solid enough. Next he flicked open the letter box and peered through. The narrow hall looked dark and crowded with jackets hanging from the wall. There was nothing on the floor as far as he could make out. He rang the bell and immediately afterwards inserted the key and opened the front door.

The place smelled faintly of chip shop curry sauce. To the right a door led into a small sitting room; electric heater in a blocked-up fireplace, sofa, stereo, TV and potted plants, lots of them. Everything was tidy. The kitchen was a narrow galley made even darker than necessary by the fact that several house plants crowded around the tiny window. The bathroom was a windowless and plantless hole but the bedroom was a jungle. There was a narrow bed and a couple of chests of drawers. Plants stood on every surface, a big palm grew in a large pot on the carpetless floor. All this vegetation stretched yearning shoots towards the ungenerous basement window. McLusky ran a latex-gloved finger across the front of a bookshelf and harvested a worm of dust. Next he ran a thumb over a polished yucca spike – not a speck of dust. There were books, mainly on the care of house plants. He turned to Austin. 'Go get the neighbour, will you, whatsis-name . . .?'

'Tilley.'

Mr Tilley appeared pleased to be asked at last. 'Satisfied, inspector? No bomb factory here.'

'What does Colin Keale do, fork-lift driver?'

Austin confirmed it. 'That's what it says in his file.'

He turned to Tilley. 'Where?'

'Supermarket depot. He does mainly night shifts. It suits him, he doesn't have to talk to anyone, just gets orders over the radio and picks stuff up and dumps it on the ramp. That's his job, that's all he does. That and growing house plants. Look.' He indicated a low table near the window. It held a plastic propagator full of tiny pots and trays. Above it hung a grow lamp. 'He propagates potted plants. Not pot plants. He's as straight as you and me, inspector.'

Speak for yourself, thought McLusky. 'When's he due back?' He knew already but wanted to hear it from Tilley.

'This weekend.'

'Who'd he go with?' He continued to open drawers without really searching the place.

'By himself. He's not overly sociable but he's no longer the nutter he was a couple of years ago. Colin takes his medication and he stays off the booze, mainly.'

'Mainly?'

'Everyone needs a drink from time to time, you know?'

Too right. He squeezed into the kitchen, opened cupboards, cutlery drawer, oven. This didn't ring any alarm bells at all, he was wasting his time. 'And what does Colin Keale drink when he does need a drink?'

'Scotch, I think. I saw a bottle once, but it's no longer a regular thing, really.'

'Any particular brand?'

'I couldn't say. Glensomething. There's so many of them. What does that have to do with anything?'

'Nothing, just idle speculation. Thank you, Mr Tilley.' He handed him the key. 'Can we leave you to lock up?'

Back on the pavement he shrugged. 'Just because you can't see it doesn't mean it's not there but it doesn't feel right.'

Austin didn't like the implication. He had been taught to mistrust his feelings and go with the facts. He hoped McLusky wasn't talking about instinct. Next thing you knew he'd be saying he'd got a hunch. Hunches didn't go down well in twenty-first-century policing. 'Could be under the floorboards.'

'I know, but it ain't. Maybe it's the potted plants. Anyone who blows up stuff is obsessed with something, a grudge, an ideology, an idea, a fantasy of some kind. But not *Care and Propagation of House Plants, Volume 2*, surely? Send someone round the supermarket depot, see if he has a locker there where stuff could be hidden. Though I doubt it very much.'

'Okay. But we'll still pick him up when he gets back?'

'Oh yes. The moment he steps off the plane, Jane.'

Maxine Bendick dashed through the drizzle to her Mini, fumbled with her seatbelt, started the engine and checked her watch. She had twelve minutes to get across to Park Street for her fitness training. It was an idiotic rush to squeeze the lesson into her lunch break at the best of times but when, as it had today, something came up just before she was due to leave, like a client having a lengthy rant about his council tax bill, not that it had anything to do with her, then she would be late for sure. It was only a half-hour slot anyway but the only one that had been available and nothing was going to stop her. The insane traffic might, of course. She felt vaguely guilty for driving such a short distance – from the 'council services access point' where she worked to the car park behind the Council House – but she would never manage it in time on foot lugging her gear. Getting from her reserved parking space to the Council House car park wasn't the real problem either, she was getting good at that. Only finding a space when she got there could sometimes be tricky, even if there weren't bombs going off. It was a week since the bomb blast. She hoped the police had finished examining the area or it would take her even longer to get to the gym.

Traffic didn't seem as bad today, moving at a steady snail's pace. She was even lucky with a parking space and found one close to the exit. This made all the difference. If her parking space was at the 'good' end she would take the long way to the gym, cutting through Brandon Hill. It was a longer walk but it was worth it, reminding her that there was life beyond houses and housing. Her new Mini bleeped and blinked as its central locking engaged and Maxine walked off at a brisk pace. The drizzle was turning to rain but she didn't mind. A glint caught her eye. Something square and shiny was lying on the tarmac close to the exit of the car park. It looked like a powder compact. A young couple were walking towards it. Surely they would claim it? A little girl's voice inside her shouted *No, I saw it first!* then the couple had walked past it without noticing. Maxine quickly stooped and picked it up. It was indeed a gold compact. It was quite clean and unscratched, so couldn't have been lying there long. Not real gold, probably, the metal was a bit too pale for that, though it was satisfyingly heavy. Maxine slipped it into her jacket pocket. There was no time to look at it now. She shrugged her sports bag higher on to her shoulder and hurried towards the park.

'I was always crap at chemistry.' McLusky had spoken out loud in the privacy of his empty office though he would happily have admitted it in company. He didn't understand half of what the report said. He turned to the end of each section and read through the conclusions. More jargon. The Forensic Science Service at Chepstow had worked fast, had worked miracles, in fact. Getting at least some of the evidence from the locus of the blast analysed within a week was lightning speed compared to normal procedure and had only been accomplished with considerable pressure from the ACC.

Usually there was nothing too complicated about these reports but this time he had no idea what firm conclusions he should draw from the make-up of the device.

Joel Kerswill had given a written statement that offered them nothing more than another description of the skateboarder. Elizabeth Howe, the second victim, had abruptly regained consciousness two days after the explosion. Spookily, it had been at the exact hour of the blast, as though she had heard an echo that had at last awoken her. If so, then it had certainly been a mental echo; she had two perforated eardrums. They'd finally been allowed to talk to her yesterday. The interview had been conducted entirely in writing, to spare Ms Howe's ears. The prognosis for recovery was good.

She remembered sitting on the bench to rest before continuing to carry her meagre shopping home. The next thing she remembered was being lifted up, like in a dream. She couldn't actually remember hearing the explosion.

No new clues about people or events, nothing about the bomb itself. Not one witness had noticed a container under any of the benches.

This much he did understand from the FSS report: the metal container that had held the explosive device – a tin in which Glenfiddich whisky was sold – had also contained an amount of petrol. The device had been triggered with the help of a simple timer constructed from a Russian-made mechanical wristwatch and a run-of-the-mill three-volt battery. The rest of the report was so much gobbledegook. Very precise gobbledegook, naturally. The FSS prided itself on it, which meant their reports were littered with provisos, approximations and qualifications – probably no smaller than but not exceeding.

In other words, what he wanted was an interpreter. He stuck his head round the door of the CID room. 'Jane, the university?'

Austin looked up from a pile of painful paperwork and pointed a plastic biro over his shoulder. 'Yes, Liam. Big thing up the hill, can't miss it.'

'I take it they have a chemistry department?'

'I should think so.'

'Good. I need help with bomb-making.'

'Aha. So what did you make of the forensic report?'

'Oh, I think I've cracked it.' He pulled a face he hoped expressed cheerful disgust and walked off down the corridor.

DS Sorbie was muttering to himself from behind his desk. 'Cracked yourself.' The new boy was swanning around the city running after one single crank who let off a firecracker while the rest of them worked on ten case files at the same time and drowned in paperwork and stupid initiatives. The runaway ten-year-old boy had at least been found, albeit half-dead after what looked like a hit and run on the A road leading to the motorway. There'd been more muggings by the scooter-riding muggers. An attempted abduction of a young woman near the harbour and the never-ending string of drug-fuelled burglaries. Perhaps McLusky would do them all a favour and get himself run over again, then normal service could resume. And maybe then they might promote someone around here rather than import inspectors from outside.

McLusky turned off Park Street into the university hinterland and amused himself by trying to rip the exhaust off the Polo by bouncing it over the ambitious speed humps. After much cruising about he found a parking space at hikable distance from the chemistry teaching laboratories and started marching towards them while dialling the number Tony Hayes at the front desk had found for him. He was put through to the science department and talked to three different people until he found someone who might be able to help him.

'And is there anybody I could talk to today, perhaps?'

'I'll try Dr Rennie for you, see if she's in.' Dr Rennie was and might fit the inspector in sometime late afternoon. 'You're here already? Hang on, inspector, I'll ask her again . . .'

McLusky ghosted through empty, brightly lit corridors until he found the right place.

'Do you always make appointments this way? You must have a lot of wasted journeys.'

'Surprisingly few, actually.'

Dr Rennie didn't offer to shake hands as she held open the glass door of the laboratory to him. Under her open lab coat she was wearing a slate-grey knee-length skirt and an ash-grey roll-neck top. She knew how to throw intimidating glances over fashionably narrow spectacles. 'Sit down, inspector.' She indicated a chair at a desk that faced the glass wall separating lab and corridor. Not a private room of study but one where results were shared, discussed, analysed. The place didn't smell of anything much. McLusky could even make out a faint trace of the doctor's dark perfume. There was only one other person in the airy room, a thin, prematurely balding man endlessly ferrying trays of small containers from long white desks in this room into a windowless store room on the far side of the teaching laboratory. McLusky thought he detected a faint asthmatic wheeze each time he walked past.

'What is it you need help with?'

McLusky handed over the slim file he had brought. 'I got this report from Forensics in Chepstow. What I want to know is –'

She interrupted his flow with a shake of her head. 'Let me read it first, then ask your questions. That way I can read it without bias.'

She really was a scientist then. 'Sure, doc.'

Dr Louise Rennie made herself more comfortable in her chair and started reading. Every time she turned a page she also returned imaginary strands of her fine blonde hair behind her ears with an unconscious gesture of one hand which made him believe that her severely short haircut was a recent development. There was a fan humming somewhere and the wheezy lab rat clinked and padded to and fro, eyeing them with irritation at each passing. Yet it was quiet enough in the room for him to hear the swish of her tights when she crossed, uncrossed and recrossed her legs. He noticed her skirt riding up a few inches above her knee and she noticed him noticing and sighed. She was a very fast reader. 'Yes, that's all quite straightforward.'

'Well, I'm sure it is, really.' Rennie probably thought he was an idiot for not understanding it but he hadn't touched a chemistry book since school, and even then reluctantly. 'I was wondering though if you, as a chemist and being local and . . . being a chemist, if you could tell me . . .' He was making a hash of this for some reason. 'Tell me what you think. What kind of person would use those chemicals to build a bomb like that? How easy would it be? That sort of thing.'

'That sort of thing.' She gave him a quick smile. It vanished as quickly as it had appeared.

'Yes please.' It was the blueness of her eyes, he decided. Same blue as Laura's. Laura, who had had enough. Who had dumped him while he was in hospital recovering from having been run over in the line of duty. Laura, for whom 'getting himself run over' had been the last straw. As soon as he'd been definitely recovering, as soon as she heard him try the first feeble joke about getting a job as a sleeping policeman, she had decided it was safe to go. Police officers needed police officers' wives, she'd told him, and sorry but she knew she would never make one of those.

'Okay, then concentrate, inspector. Potassium nitrate, sulphur, charcoal, surely you must remember that much from school?'

'I was rubbish at science.'

'History, then.'

'What's potassium –' he lent across to read – 'nitrate?'

'Potassium nitrate is saltpetre.' She prompted her slow pupil. 'Saltpetre, sulphur and charcoal . . .'

'Oh, that's gunpowder.'

She nodded slowly. 'Good old black powder, inspector.'

'So we're not talking fertilizer bomb, plastic explosives or dynamite.'

'We're talking cannon, musket, firecracker, rocket. It says here that it was pure, industrial grade, so wasn't home-made from stuff you scrape off a urinal wall and mix with barbecue charcoal, though that can be done if you have enough chaps peeing long enough against a wall. Can't say I'd fancy that route either.'

'So unless it's someone licensed to fire historical weapons that require gunpowder then this is someone who bought a lot of fireworks, took them apart and then filled his container with the gunpowder? So it could be kids, after all.'

'Kids with a bit of pocket money, yes. That amount of gunpowder would require quite a few fireworks.'

'But probably not enough to arouse suspicion if you bought them over a period of time or at different outlets. Enough to kill . . .' McLusky knew this already but was thinking aloud now.

'Oh, certainly. Anyone too close could have been killed by the shrapnel or burnt to a frazzle when the petrol in the container caught. It's just as it said in the paper, it was a miracle no one died.'

'*Burnt to a frazzle*, is that a scientific term?'

'Absolutely. And an apt description of what would have happened had someone been sitting on the bench under which the device exploded.'

'Though if you wanted to make sure to kill and maim lots of people you would stuff the thing with nails etc.'

'Yes. My guess is this was designed to make a big bang and look spectacular.'

'It certainly did that, it sent up a huge black cloud.' A smoke signal. 'Could still just be vandalism then.'

'Yet whoever did it clearly didn't care that people might get killed, maimed and burnt or they wouldn't have left it where they did.'

'Yes. The technical police term for those is *arseholes*.'

'The psychology department is in a different building, inspector.' Dr Rennie pushed the report towards him.

McLusky rolled it up like a newspaper, then patted his pockets for a card. 'I was going to leave you my card but I haven't had time to get any printed yet. I'm new in town.' He spotted a cube of notepaper on the desk and pulled it towards himself, then found a pen in the inside pocket of his jacket. It was a heavy brushed-steel biro he didn't remember buying. Nice, though. 'I'll leave you my numbers.' He scribbled down office and mobile numbers, hoping he'd got them right.

'What are you leaving them for, inspector?'

McLusky had no idea. He shrugged. 'Just in case.'

'I see.' She rose, the interview terminated.

He thanked her, nodded at the lab rat, who ignored him, and left.

Once outside again it took him a moment to remember where he had left the Polo. *Mallzheimer's* they called it now when you couldn't remember where you'd parked your car. Fortunately his stood out by dint of being old, ugly and a shade of white no manufacturer had used for twenty years. He wondered just how this piece of junk had survived to be a police vehicle in the twenty-first century. He turned on his airwave radio and it sprang to life with urgent calls. McLusky answered it and everything changed.

Maxine Bendick dried herself quickly, pulled her shower cap off and shook her hair loose. She had it cut shorter when she joined the gym so as to save even more time. After checking her watch she dressed in front of her locker. It might be a bit of madness but taking the thirty-minute lunchtime slot changed her working day completely. On the days when she trained, lunch breaks were something to look forward to, and not just because it meant a change from the tedium of pacifying irate tax payers on the phone. For years she had spent depressing lunch breaks walking to the Metro Market, cramming a plastic container with as much pasta salad in mayonnaisy gunk as would fit, then eating it with a plastic fork, sitting on the tiny green near her office in good weather but, this being England, for much of the year at her desk. Now she had the frisson of the dash across town, the mad rush to get changed and what usually amounted to no more than twenty minutes of training with Pat. Even though it hardly progressed beyond the warm-up it left her invigorated and helped her survive the afternoon. Pat stood for Patricia but Maxine had been quite happy to let her colleagues believe it stood for Patrick and that he was handsome. She had no idea what had brought on the fitness craze, she had no weight to lose, in fact had put on weight as she built up muscle, and didn't know anyone else at the gym. It had just grabbed her imagination one day and she'd got hooked. Going to the gym meant eating a home-made sandwich in the car while she was driving and less time to chat with colleagues but it was worth it. Even here she didn't have time to make friends at this pace. She'd seen all four other girls that were in this changing room before but never had enough time to do more than smile and nod at them while she rushed. She crammed the gear into her holdall, pulled on her jacket and slammed the locker. As she hoisted the bag over her shoulder she could feel the hard object in her jacket pocket. She pulled it out. Why she had picked it up when she never used face powder or any make-up for that matter was beyond her. Probably because it was shiny and it meant getting something for free. Perhaps she should offer it to one of the girls. She prised the lid open.

The crack of the explosion and the blue, searing flash were simultaneous. Had she not been blinded and distracted by the agonizing pain of her nose being burnt away by a tongue of flame, she'd have noticed the first third of her left thumb fly off and thud into the open locker of one of the girls. All she knew was that her face was on fire. She didn't know that she was screaming, she thought it was the others. Running blindly in the direction of the showers she collided with the door frame and fell to the ground. She clutched at the unbelievable pain in her face. It felt sticky.

'Oh God, oh my God.'

'What the fuck happened?'

'Her face just blew up.'

'Someone call an ambulance.' Someone was screaming it into the darkness. Or perhaps she was just thinking it. 'Someone call a fucking ambulance!'

Then there was nothing, just the hammering rhythm of blood in the dark.

The constable in the viz jacket bravely stepped in front of his car, signalling him to stop. McLusky wound the handle and the window dropped in a series of jerks.

'You can't come through here, you need to –'

'Yeah, yeah.' He cut him off by showing his warrant card.

The PC stepped back a little in order to fully admire the state of the ancient Polo and tilted his head so he could read the inscription on the bonnet. Could the ID be a fake?

'Never mind the car, it's the hard-boiled eggs that are getting me down.' He left him standing there, one constable who was sure to recognize him in future.

The dreaded thing had happened. Not only had the bomber struck again but only a few hundred yards from the first explosion. There was a message in that he didn't want to hear. It was a message about who owned the place. At the moment it sure as hell wasn't him.

The corner of Park Street and Great George Street was busy. The ambulance had already left but the rest of the circus was there. The private little gym had been evacuated and some of its members hung about outside to watch the police machine at work. The entire area was being searched for more devices. He was directed down a corridor past an empty cafeteria. Lanky Constable Pym was standing guard outside the ladies' changing room further along. On one of the benches in the corridor a female officer was comforting a young woman in a dressing gown. Two more young women stood nearby, looking pale.

All McLusky had to do was follow the voices, the police voices, so different from those of civilians – purposeful, using the vocabulary of incident, procedure, of cover-your-back and make-doubly-sure. In the dressing room he found Austin giving instructions to a young police photographer. 'Get shots of every particle of the exploded device *in situ*, get the CSI techies to show you where they all are. Hello, inspector, they managed to find you then?'

'My mobile needs charging.' He didn't mention that he had forgotten to turn on his personal radio until he left the university. He sniffed the air. This place smelled of calamity, of singed hair, roasted flesh, burnt fingernails, gunpowder and sweat, the sweat of fear mingling with that of work and concentration. Blood-spurts covered lockers and benches. There was a pool of vomit on the floor. 'Tell me what happened, Jane.'

Austin talked fluently about the facts so far established. 'The victim is a Maxine Bendick. Late twenties. She comes here for fitness training in her lunch break, works with a personal trainer, Patricia Maine, who's out in the lobby right now giving a statement, but she wasn't in this room when it happened. She was already talking to her next client. There were four women using the changing room when it happened. According to one girl –' he consulted his notebook – 'a Tamara Tasker, Bendick had changed back into street clothes and was about to leave but stopped and took out a gold powder compact which appeared to blow up in her hand.'

'Marvellous.'

'One of her fingers . . .' Austin pointed at an open locker containing blood-spattered clothes.

'Thumb.' A white-suited technician furnished them with the detail without looking up from his task of scraping something unsavoury off the wall next to the locker. 'Left hand.'

Austin continued. 'There you have it. Left thumb. Landed in there.'

McLusky took a good look. It looked like pain, a great deal of pain. 'Other injuries?'

'Her face. Apparently her face is badly burnt. The same witness said her face was actually on fire. Yes. Extensive burns to her face and hands.'

'But she'll live?'

'I think so, the injuries aren't life-threatening per se, unless she dies of shock, of course. Ambulance got here quite quickly for once. Did you know our ambulance service is on the bottom of the league tab –'

'Spare me statistics and league tables, Jane, wherever possible.'

One of the CSI technicians piped up. 'You're not a football supporter then, inspector? Nor a betting man.'

'Got it in one.' It was almost obligatory in the force to like football. He had even tried supporting Southampton for a while just to fit in, but had found it mind-numbing. It seemed a long time ago now when he had still tried to fit in.

The girl would live. But would she want to live once she saw what was left of her face? 'So. Someone fills her powder compact with Semtex? What's going on here, d'you think?'

'Search me.'

'Where's the rest of her stuff?'

'Her bag is over here.'

The pink and white sports bag was sitting on a bench by the door. Austin talked to the nearest technician. 'You finished with it?'

'We haven't touched it. If you must open it wear gloves.'

McLusky wriggled his fingers at him, already clad in latex.

'All right, then. But it could also be booby-trapped of course.'

'Rubbish. The compact blew up after she had changed so she'll have packed this herself. But by all means stand well back, everyone.' A spray pattern of blood adorned the top and left side of the bag. Tight whorls of ashen residue looked like the worm-shaped remains of charred hair. McLusky unzipped the bag in one quick movement and rummaged about. Apart from towel and leotard he found a grey Tupperware box. He noticed his DS instinctively lean back as he prised off the lid. The box contained a home-made sandwich, cut into two chunky rectangles. McLusky approved. 'No revelations here.' He closed the Tupperware box. The aroma of cheese and tomato faded, filling him with regret.

Austin continued his report. 'She was on her lunch break. According to her coach she works for the council at a so-called access point in Hotwells. Inquiries, advice, that sort of thing.'

McLusky recognized the senior CSI man with the blond moustache from the first bomb site and approached him. 'Do you feel like saying something rash, like whether the two explosions are in any way connected?'

The man's moustache twitched. 'Impossible to say, inspector. At this stage. But the sizes of the explosions are very different. This was a very compact design, so to speak.' There were groans from his colleagues. 'This was made to hurt a single person. Almost certainly victim-activated.'

'Victim-activ . . .' The language of these people. 'You mean it was meant to go off when someone handled it?'

'Precisely. The other bomb had a timer. This one could have sat unexploded for years. Until someone opened it, probably, or shook it. Hard to say at the moment. Forensics might be able to tell us more.'

He thanked the man. By now his stomach was rumbling audibly, a result not of revulsion at the awful smell in the room but of hunger, victim-activated by sniffing Maxine Bendick's uneaten sandwich. He gave Austin a push on the shoulder. 'Let's get out of here.' Statements were still being taken in the foyer. They walked straight past and stepped outside. The usual crowd of onlookers had gathered beyond the police tape, including the press who started firing cameras and questions at them as soon as they walked up Great George Street where the police units were parked.

'Inspector, is the victim still alive?'

'Are the two incidents connected?'

'Is it the work of the same bomber?'

'What's the motive behind the bombings?'

'Was there any warning?'

'Is this part of a campaign?'

'Have you made any progress on the first bomb?'

McLusky ignored the press and walked on. 'You've got some of the questions right there.' At least they seemed to have stopped pushing the Al Qaeda angle. Denkhaus had devoted his press conference to stamping out the rumours of terrorism. The city had a sizable Muslim community and everyone was aware of the racial tensions already at work.

McLusky spoke to the nearest uniform. It was Constable Hanham. 'Couldn't you have cordoned off the area *beyond* the vehicles? Press and public are swarming all over the place.'

Hanham was in defiant mood. 'Yes sir, only we ran out of tape and we don't have enough bodies to keep them further back.'

He surveyed the straggly line of police tape strung from a car to a drainpipe to another car. 'Then close off the entire street, that'll only take half the tape, and string what's left across the road up there. Move them right back.'

'Sir, there's people wanting to get to their cars they parked further up.'

'Well, they'll have to walk round then. Do them good.' Naturally McLusky himself avoided any kind of exercise on the grounds that police work was enough foot slog to begin with. He walked on with Austin beside him. 'But there are plenty of other questions. Like how the hell did she end up with an exploding powder compact, for one. And who wants to blow her to kingdom come would be good to know too. If this area is covered by CCTV then we'll examine the footage of course.'

'There's CCTV in the foyer and the gym but obviously none in the dressing rooms.'

'Right. It'll all be a complete waste of time since she could have had the compact for ages, but it's got to be done. I'll even look at it myself, don't worry.' A pale-faced young DC, who he had earlier seen taking statements in the lobby, came out of the front door of the gym. 'Who's that walking question mark?'

'That's DC Dearlove.'

'Good lord.'

Austin wasn't sure if the inspector was referring to Daniel Dearlove's name or looks. Dearlove had bad posture and mousy hair so thin and clogged with hair gel that his pink scalp showed through everywhere. His wispy moustache clung to a narrow pink lip. He looked like a kid dressed up by his mum in a hand-me-down suit.

'Call him over, will you?'

'Hey, Deedee.'

Dearlove looked up from his notebook, changed direction but continued reading as he walked. His lips were moving.

'By the way, Deedee's polyester suits generate enough static electricity to charge your mobile with.'

'Genius.'

Dearlove looked up from his notebook only when he had come to a halt in front of Austin. 'Jane? Inspector?'

McLusky saw Dearlove's fingers were stained with ink from a leaky biro. 'Did you get anything of interest?'

'Ehm, not really. The trainer said she'd never seen the victim use a powder compact, in fact she didn't think she normally used make-up at all.'

'She might have used the compact just for the mirror. Okay. Where was the victim taken? Royal Infirmary?'

90

'No, Southmead Hospital. Burns Unit.'

'Right. Get someone down there straight away, I want a constable outside her room round the clock. Work out a rota and see it's adhered to. Then contact Southmead Burns Unit and tell them I want to interview Maxine Bendick at the first possible. Get both organized and get back to me.'

'Okay, sir.' Dearlove sighed. His shift should have finished hours ago. There was a film on TV he'd wanted to watch starting this minute and he hadn't thought of setting the recorder. Once you joined the police force you had to record the rest of your life, just in case you weren't there to see it. And as usual there wasn't enough left in the budget to pay overtime, even before flashy bastards like McLusky wrote off brand new cars.

'Right.' McLusky had already forgotten Dearlove. 'Let's get everything collated and see if any of it makes sense when looked at together.'

'Okay. We have lift-off . . .' Jane walked briskly away towards his little car.

McLusky cast a weary eye over the scene. The press hung about patiently or perhaps were just resigned to boredom, hoping for developments, statements, things to photograph. Someone had found more tape by the looks of it, constables were busy fluttering the stuff in more sensible places, ordering people beyond the line. Tourists were getting extra entertainment and were making the most of the pause in the rain. Shoppers with carrier bags walked slowly by. Strangers talked to strangers.

He spotted the superintendent heaving himself out of his spotless car at the street corner and his stomach responded with a protesting growl. Danish pastry for breakfast was okay but you got hungry again after five minutes. He walked off in the opposite direction and ducked under the tape. It was the wrong colour. It also read *Caution, Electric Cables Below*. Someone had shown initiative.

Doubling back towards Park Street, putting distance between himself and his superior, he felt like he had when

91

skiving from school, something he had done a lot of. But he felt no guilt. He couldn't think too long on an empty stomach without becoming short-tempered, even absent-minded. He hoped this wouldn't mean he'd end up in the same shape as the super, who clearly liked his food and, according to Jane, his beer.

He stopped briefly to look back towards Brandon Hill and the bomb site, now completely cleared. All that remained was the blackened concrete base on which the shelter had stood. The council had already announced that it would be rebuilt. He wondered morosely if any such announcements would be made about Maxine Bendick's face.

Near the museum he had adopted a bistro that served tapas, a drinkable cappuccino and wine by the glass. A few tables stood empty on the uneven pavement, waiting for the arrival of spring. The waitress smiled in recognition as she handed him the menu. Would she still smile at him if she knew that he was a police officer? He ordered bread, olives, a dish with spicy sausages and something that looked like overcooked ratatouille but tasted fine. The food here, although Spanish, reminded him of Greece but was conveyed to his table with un-Mediterranean haste.

If murder and mayhem spoilt your appetite then the police force was clearly not for you. McLusky enjoyed every morsel of his food and his glass of red precisely because he had a bad feeling about these explosions. Over the past few days he had completely convinced himself that he was dealing with a one-off, whatever the target had been, whatever the motive. The second explosion changed everything. And the super had put him in charge. He raised his eyes from his empty plates and found the wait-ress looking at him from behind the high bar. He nodded at her, intending to ask for his bill, but when she arrived at the table found himself ordering more wine instead.

The second bomb had nothing prankish about it. It was a deeply malicious thing. This could not be misconstrued as someone wanting to create a bang. Someone had wanted to hurt Maxine Bendick. Someone had gone to considerable lengths to hurt Maxine Bendick, constructed the device, concealed it inside her compact. It took a particular kind of person to imagine the injuries the device would cause and still persist in building it, planting it. It took an extraordinary depth of feeling, like hate or the desire for revenge, on the one hand, and a complete lack of empathy on the other. The person behind this was not lashing out, here was forethought and planning. Malice aforethought. McLusky drained his glass. Two could play that game.

Chapter Five

'What I was afraid of most has happened, then, a second device has been detonated. I had hoped we were looking at a one-off, a badly judged prank, but I was wrong.' McLusky was glad about the two glasses of wine he had had. The incident room that had been set up at Albany Road in record time was tiny and crowded with tables, computers and personnel. He had perched himself on a folding table to appear casual as he talked to the assembled crew, only to find that the table was so rickety he felt it might collapse under him. Yet he stayed where he was. To compensate he lit a cigarette. Sod the no-smoking rules. He would stop smoking at work when people stopped killing, robbing and mutilating each other. This time nobody objected. Just a short while later one or two other cigarettes were furtively lit elsewhere in the room.

Addressing the troops was nothing new, but getting new troops on your side was important for anyone hoping to lead an investigation. Any roomful of detectives contained a selection of bright, intelligent sparklers, competitive climbers, dullards treading water, skivers, sharp operators and sometimes downright villainous specimens of police-hood. You couldn't afford to take your time over finding out who was who, that would come later. You had to size them up as you would a roomful of drunks where you were expected to restore order. Who were the trouble-makers, who could be an ally, who would slink away, and who might stab you in the back?

'But we were told the two devices were quite different.' DI Kat Fairfield was holding her biro like a dagger, jabbing it against her notebook for emphasis. 'The first could still have been by a different perpetrator. Could still have been an act of vandalism, in fact. While this one was personal. Aimed at one specific person, Maxine Bendix.'

'Bendick. It could be. It could be a copycat thing, someone suddenly getting a taste for blowing up people. It could be coincidence even, but I don't believe that. No. Making these devices takes time, getting the ingredients for the bombs together, that alone takes a lot of time.' Every shop in the area that had sold fireworks over the past twelve months was being contacted, staff and owners quizzed about large amounts of fireworks being purchased. That too took a lot of time, a lot of man-hours. 'Of course we can never rule out anything until we have bagged our man.'

'Do we know it's a man, sir?'

French? DC Claire French, was it? He was good with names but the DC had a face so plain it bordered on the expressionless and he only vaguely remembered seeing her before. She took plain clothes to an extreme, too, and would disappear into any shopping centre crowd without leaving a trace on the retina. A good trait in a detective. 'No, you're right, we don't know that at all, nor do we know that we are dealing with a single perpetrator. We can make the thing as complicated as we like, really. We could have two separate perpetrators or one, a single bomb maker or a group, an original bomber and a copycat bomber.' Some nodded in assent, let's keep it simple by all means.

A sudden thought struck him and a dark vista of horrors opened up before him. He was about to throw this into the ring, then decided to keep his suspicions to himself. Concentrate their minds on what we've got. 'There has been no communication from the bomber, no declaration, no demands. In the absence of that we'll need to look at the victims for a motive.'

A hand was raised with pointed index finger in schoolboy irony. DS Sorbie. 'What if the attacks are motiveless?'

'Have you ever come across a motiveless crime?'

'Loads.'

'I doubt that. Unprovoked, yes, senseless, certainly, motiveless, never. Since we know little or nothing about the suspect we might find a lead in who the victims are. At the moment it's all we've got, though I admit I'm a bit baffled. We have three victims so far. One, a boy returning home from an interview at the parks department. He makes an unlikely target. Perhaps for a bomb built by his old school mates but that's a little outlandish for me. Elizabeth Howe, recently-made-redundant postmistress. It is hard to imagine a less likely target for a bomb attack. Surely something involving brown paper and string would be more appropriate. Which leaves Maxine Bendick. What do we know about her? Who wants to harm her?'

DS Sorbie looked contemptuous. 'She works for the council – spoiled for choice, I should think.'

'What department, was it housing?'

'Yes, mainly, but she also did stints in other departments, processing forms, sorting out queries. Half the people who come in there must feel pretty murderous about backlogs, delays and such, waiting lists, council tax, fines etc.'

'Good point, Sorbie. Find out if anyone has made any threats, are there any particular disputes between the council and a member of the public where Bendick was the one dealing with them, either directly or by letter where she could be identified.'

'Sir, we . . . DI Fairfield and I, are supposed to get urgent results on the Mobile Muggers as well.' It simply wasn't fair on them and if Kat wasn't going to speak up then he would. 'The super is leaning on us to get a result re the muggings and make arrests, yet now we're supposed to work on the bombings as well. There's also been a spate of burglaries all along the . . .'

DI Fairfield shot Sorbie a look and his complaint fizzled out. The last thing she needed was for McLusky to get the impression she couldn't cope with her workload.

'I'm aware of the pressures on you. I'm leaning on you, the super leans on all of us, so go lean on some other poor sod.'

DI Fairfield's biro was poised over the paper. 'This second device. Was it designed to kill?'

'No, too small, by all accounts and a different kind of explosion apparently.' He watched Fairfield scribble it all down without even looking at her notebook. McLusky was impressed. He had tried writing without looking once and produced an undecipherable mess.

He doled out more tasks to the troops then let them loose. It felt like firing shots into the dark with a weapon he hadn't loaded himself. He might be firing blanks. Which reminded him. He turned to Austin. 'Where's Dearlove?'

DC Dearlove had managed to hide throughout the briefing, even in this cramped room, behind the broad back of DS Sorbie. Austin spotted him and called across the noise of the meeting breaking up. 'Hey, Deedee, can we borrow your brain for a minute?'

Dearlove stood up. 'Yeah, okay, what for?'

'We're trying to build an idiot.'

'Funny, Jane.' Then he felt himself skewered by McLusky's unnerving green eyes and was compelled to walk over after all.

McLusky wondered how the gawky youth with a suit full of static had made it into the police force. Would there really be a Detective Inspector Dearlove one day? 'Bendick has round-the-clock protection? When can I see her?'

'I left a note on your desk, sir.'

'I'm not a great note reader, Deedee. Find me, talk to me, call my mobile, send a pigeon. Don't leave bits of paper lying around expecting people to have read them, you get into trouble that way. Always make sure information is passed on properly and you know it's been received.'

'Okay, sir. Is that all, sir?'

'No, Deedee, it isn't all. What did you write in your damn note?'

'Oh, sure, it's all done, there'll be a bod outside her room, 24/7. There was no word from Southmead on when she can be interviewed. They were operating when I asked. They'll let us know.'

'They never do. Keep asking, okay?' He turned to Austin. 'If this was a murder inquiry what would you be doing right now, Jane?' Austin opened his mouth but McLusky was already walking away. 'I'm going to watch a video.'

In his office he found notes, performance targets, preliminary reports, memos and other things he hated with a passion. But no CCTV footage. Of course he hated CCTV footage too. What you saw there was already over, could no longer be prevented. CCTV showed you crimes that should never have happened, accidents that could have been avoided, people who by now had disappeared and victims already dead. He hated everything about it. Yet it was sometimes useful and it often secured convictions.

He phoned the desk. The footage from the gym and surrounding area should have arrived by now. There was no answer. He let it ring for a while then left his office and clattered downstairs.

It was the public who really liked CCTV. They couldn't get enough of it. They liked being watched, it made them feel safe. To like being under surveillance you had to have a childish faith in the benevolence of those who were watching you, a faith McLusky didn't share. All this stuff looked good practice now but nothing lasted forever, not even democracy.

The noise level coming from the lobby was alarming for this time of day. When he let himself in through the security door he could see why no one had answered the phone. Down here at least two phones were ringing incessantly. Everyone was arguing loudly with someone. The place looked more like a bad Saturday night than mid-afternoon on a weekday. Two half-naked drunks were being noisily processed. One of them was being restrained by two PCs while he screamed abuse at Tony Hayes, the desk officer. The other drunk who, judging by the state of his rancid trainers, was the author of a pool of vomit on the floor, gave slurred support to his friend. 'Too fuckin' right, Bobby . . . they've no right . . . you fuckin' said it.' Two officers were waiting to check in their customers, two girls arrested for shoplifting. Repeat offenders, scrawny smack heads who whined with hard flat voices that grated in McLusky's ears. Their hair was thin, their skin pale and slack. A middle-aged black woman wearing an ensemble of Day-Glo clothes stood under the noticeboard, talking loudly to herself in impenetrable angry patois while treading from one foot to another like a child needing the toilet. An elderly Asian couple walked into the lobby. Both said something that to McLusky's lip-reading skills looked like 'Oh dear' and walked straight out again. The drunk and disorderly would sober up in the cells, the shoplifters would be processed and eventually released back on to the streets. Having been relieved of the stolen goods the girls would of course have to commit some crime as soon as possible. If the shops were shut by then they would have to mug someone to get the money for gear or else they'd smash their way into a car to find stuff to sell. Meanwhile politicians congratulated themselves if the price of heroin went up because of Customs and Excise seizures. They imagined it a success while all it meant was volume crime had to rise with it to match the escalating price. But the price of heroin was still shockingly low compared to a night out at a club.

Addiction . . . He craved another cigarette. For McLusky an air of futility seemed to rise from the vomit- and dirt-covered floor. Here were six police officers who would spend hours dealing with four teenagers who had made drugs and alcohol the centre of their universe; a universe so tiny there was no room left inside for anyone but themselves. The screaming bloke was handcuffed now and got tired of struggling but kept up the verbal with moronic repetitiveness. Tony Hayes, who had been abused by experts during his many years in the job, showed no sign of strain, though he briefly raised one eyebrow when one of the girls shut up long enough to spit in his direction. Tony Hayes liked a clean lobby. Tony Hayes was also wearing his stabbie as a matter of course, ever since an irate customer had vaulted the desk and attacked him with a sharpened screwdriver last summer. McLusky let himself into the relative security of the area behind the desk. Hayes acknowledged him but kept his concentration on logging the details of the drunk. McLusky looked around, spotted a likely-looking carrier bag with a yellow post-it sticker on one of the desks and grabbed it.

'I meant to send them up as soon as I had a minute.' Hayes spoke without turning around, having excellent hearing as well as eyes at the back of his head.

The bag was suspiciously light. 'There's not a lot here.'

'That's all that came, sir.'

Back upstairs McLusky found a DVR and monitor in the CID room. It was quiet, most officers being out for a change, chasing something. Austin was there chewing a cheap biro into oblivion in front of his computer. McLusky loaded the footage. There was none from the gym. He complained about it to Austin.

'There wouldn't be, the system's not switched on during the day.'

All that had come was CCTV from the Council House car park. Footage of the whole day was there but for the moment he was only interested in that covering the time and area of Maxine Bendick's approximate arrival. The image was in black and white and a time counter ran at the bottom right, accurate to one tenth of a second. Once he knew what he was looking at he could safely fast-forward until the car whizzed into view, then he rewound and pressed play. The Mini came into the picture on the bottom left, speeded up and slotted neatly into the space in one movement. At this moment there were no people and no other moving cars visible. All the spaces at this end were taken now. After only the shortest interval Maxine Bendick got out of the car. He paused the tape. So that's what she looked like. He mentally corrected himself: this is what she had looked like, before half her face was burnt off. He released the flow of the image. The woman sprang to life again, retrieved her bag from the passenger seat then pointed her key, which was answered by a silent flash of the car lights. She walked off briskly through the rain. An undamaged, unburnt Maxine, untouched by the madness, walked into the wilderness without noticing it. The car park was on a slight slope. The picture angle was a little awkward but adequate, looking across from the top of one of the high lamp-posts. Maxine was making her way towards the edge of the picture which only showed a narrow strip of pavement. A couple, man and woman, appeared from that direction. He would later follow their movements and, if they walked to a car, try and identify it and trace them. Maxine speeded up now and then disappeared out of the frame. End of story. Nothing had happened.

Or perhaps ... He rewound a little, replayed the sequence. Maxine disappeared off the screen but a sliver of her bag, which stuck out behind her, didn't. It bobbed down, then up again before finally going out of shot. McLusky's opinion was succinctly summed up. 'Shit.'

'Found something?'

'I think so. Come here, Jane, look at this.'

Austin arrived at his shoulder. He replayed the whole sequence for him. 'Gets out, grabs bag, walks towards the exit, right? Here comes a couple towards the entrance ...'

'She puts on a bit of a spurt.'

101

'Yes. Keep your eye on the bag.'

'Oh, she stops and bends down, that's what that looks like.'

'I think when she's fit to be interviewed she'll tell us she found the damned thing right there.' McLusky tapped the edge of the screen with a fingernail. 'Only she didn't open it until later because she was in a hurry.'

Austin nodded. 'Possible.'

'Possible. Though I hope not. I sincerely hope not. How long do you think the thing could have been lying there? Minutes? Hours? Days?'

'That's hard to say. It's a busy car park and a lot of people go in and out, not to mention those walking along there. Not long. It was bright gold.'

'That's what I'm thinking.' He scribbled a note for Deedee Dearlove to try and trace the couple in the video. Naturally he expected others to read his notes.

Austin scratched the tip of his nose. 'Why were you hoping she hadn't found it there?'

A couple of civilian operators walked in. McLusky jerked his head towards the exit. 'My place.' Austin followed him into his office. McLusky wedged open a window and pulled open a drawer. He produced a small ashtray with a lid and his cigarettes. Austin accepted one. Still this ridiculously light brand. What was the point? You had to smoke twice as many. He accepted a light from the inspector's tiny plastic lighter, filled his lungs with smoke and repeated his question. 'Why are you hoping she didn't find the thing there?'

'Because.' He swivelled his chair and shot upright. 'Because I very much want someone to have it in for Maxine Bendick. I want to please find that someone has been trying to blow her up.' He stood by the large-scale map of the city centre which nearly covered one entire wall of the tiny room and tapped his fingers on the green shape that represented Brandon Hill. 'Here's the shelter, was the shelter, I should say. Here's the car park, here's the way she habitually takes through the park. Maxine Bendick goes to her gym three lunchtimes a week. She went on the Monday of the bench bomb. The pavilion went up an hour before she was due to walk within ten feet of the thing.'

'So you do think Maxine Bendick was the intended victim?'

'I was hoping. Until I saw the footage we just looked at.'

'I see what you mean.'

'Good. I don't think anyone else does yet. If someone really was after Maxine Bendick then we shouldn't have much trouble finding him. They must connect somewhere. If you have made an enemy who goes to this kind of trouble to get at you then he'll stick out a mile. Ex-boyfriends, husbands if any, cranky relatives, anyone who asked her out and was turned down since the beginning of time needs to be checked out. Anyone she could have made an enemy of at work or members of the public, all still have to be followed up, of course.'

'It's what we're doing. But if she found the powder compact by the steps . . .' Austin puffed up his cheeks as he shared the inspector's vision.

'Jane, if she found the thing then we're in deep, deep trouble. The words shit and creek spring to mind. If she found it then it wasn't aimed at her at all. It was aimed at To Whom It May Concern. *Anyone* could have picked it up, the couple who walked past, for instance.'

'But a powder compact, surely it was aimed at a woman.'

'It was golden, shiny. Any normal child would pick up something like that, anyone, probably. All that glitters. It means that whoever planted it has no connection to the victims at all. The motive lies elsewhere. God help us, Jane, we might as well run up the white flag now and call in a psychiatrist. Because we haven't got the first idea of where to look.'

'One place I did look was the DVLA.'

'Oh yeah, Three Veg. Got anywhere?'

'There's no record. Timothy Daws, van or no van, never had a driver's licence or anything registered to him, now or ever.'

'That makes a change. I had him down for dizzy driver, uninsured and untaxed. Still, two out of three isn't bad. Any joy at the DSS?'

'He's on Incapacity for a bad back, so he doesn't have to come in and sign on.'

'Right, we'll pull him in when we can but he's way down the list now. Another bomb in the park and I'd have been out there like a shot in a helicopter looking for white vans, but this powder compact doesn't fit. It's near the park but not in it. It's in the wrong place and the wrong kind of object if you want to revenge yourself on the parks department for being dismissed. If you wanted to get back at them you would, I don't know, booby-trap a flower pot or something.'

'Forensics might come up with something.'

'Oh yeah? If the pickings are as rich as last time we'll be no further. There was no DNA found at all on the debris of the last one, which is hardly surprising after the explosion, the fire and the hosing down it got. And even if there had been it would do us no good unless his DNA was already on file. This is a new customer. This will turn out to be everyone's favourite nightmare. Like the guy in the States who shot people at petrol stations from the comfort of his car, I forget his name. This is a bastard who doesn't mind who he hurts. And this won't be the last explosion we'll hear in the city either. This, as they say, is just the beginning. He gets a kick out of this and he'll need a new fix soon. And what are we going to do about it?'

'Let's say you're right. Let's say we have a nutter out there who just likes to blow up people and he isn't fussed who it is he hurts.'

'Yes?'

'Then why give Maxine Bendick police protection?'

'Because, Jane, I've been known to be wrong.'

Chapter Six

Dave Hands slammed the front door to his tiny, first-floor council flat with some force and clattered down the stairs. He hadn't planned on going out but the bastard leccy had just run out and he could hardly be expected to sit in the dark without the telly all night. So it was off to the convenience store to charge the meter key. He was forever on 'emergency' which constantly ran out, usually just before the kettle boiled. Unlike this bloody rain. There seemed to be an endless supply of that.

He crossed the glistening road and walked the few yards past the darkened shops to the battered door of the convenience store. The shop was empty of customers. The hard, suspicious eyes of the shopkeeper followed his every move. He hated this place. Everything in here was crap, crap food, shit fags, tins of crap. Everything in here was a rip-off. Rip-off electricity, rip-off booze. The price of bog-roll was fantastic. You had to be rich to buy this shit. Rich and stupid.

He was supposed to stay at home and save his money, pay off his ridiculous overdraft. Sod it, he had been good all week, now that he was out anyway he would go for a beer and make it worth his while. No point getting rained on just for the bloody leccy, that would just depress the shit out of him.

Even the cash machine in this place was a rip-off. It charged you for each withdrawal. Better to take out next week's money all in one go, it was cheaper in the long term.

Extra tenner for the pub. Fuck it, make it twenty, it needn't mean he would spend it all. He folded the notes into his card wallet, all apart from the twenty for the pub which he shoved into his jeans pocket. He felt better already.

Once outside he breathed in deeply. You needed to take a break from being good sometimes or life became unbearably dull. He crossed the empty road. The rain came down heavily now. A couple of pints up the road then.

That's when he saw it. Just there on the pavement, at the edge of a slimy concrete bus shelter, lay a fat wallet. A man's leather wallet, in the rain. Now that would be fantastic if there was actually money in it. There was certainly something in it, it was positively bulging. His steps quickened. Money, he hadn't found any money in the street since he was a kid. It looked new. And expensive. He bent down and picked it up.

'Oi! Fuckwit!' A large black shadow jumped from behind the shelter, another appeared from behind a parked van. 'Leave it! Your phone, your money! *Now!*'

They wore helmets, visors halfway down. Shouting. One pushed him towards the other. Two scooters appeared from the nearest corner.

It was them. No way were they going to get his money. 'Fuck off!' He kicked back at the one who grabbed him from behind. The big guy in front punched him straight in the face with a gloved fist before he could even get his own up. He heard the crunch as his nose broke. Blood spurted. Two, three hard jabs to his right kidney from the bastard behind nearly made his knees give way. He heard himself scream in pain and lashed out at the guy in front who grabbed him by the throat with a vicious grip. He couldn't breathe. The helmet smashed into his face. Once, twice, three times. After the third impact he fell backwards, spurting an arc of blood. When he hit the edge of the bus shelter the back of his head exploded in pain as the impact cracked his skull. And everything went dark.

* * *

DI Kat Fairfield hated being driven nearly as much as McLusky did but she would reluctantly concede that Jack Sorbie's skills behind the wheel matched her own. She actually felt quite safe when the DS drove, even at speed. At the moment she had him just cruise about the edges of the city. A leaden sky made it darker than it should have been at this time of the evening. Headlights reflected in wet streets, kerbside puddles sent up neon-coloured spray. What, she might ask, was sweet about April showers? This was the dampest, coldest spring she could remember, hardly better than the winter that had preceded it. This was what a volcanic winter would be like, endless dreary rain from an obsidian sky. She could really do without it, thanks very much. Denkhaus's new protégé McLusky she could also do without. She had no intention of staying a lowly DI forever, so the last thing she needed was the superintendent's new Golden Wonder. It was a shame DCI Gaunt was away. She felt that she'd been getting somewhere with him. She didn't care that no one seemed to like Gaunt. You didn't have to like people to work well with them, sometimes it was easier when you didn't, it made the relationship simpler. But Denkhaus was a difficult man, with mood swings of menopausal monumentality. Somehow she found it difficult to get on the right side of him.

There was only one thing at work that had improved recently. The single thing that had eased off was the frequency with which male colleagues, civilians and officers alike, were trying to drag her under their duvets. She had turned every one of them down, politely and firmly. Well, firmly, anyway. Then recently Claire French had warned her that a rumour had sprung up that she was gay. Offers of drinks, meals and the cinema had drastically fallen off since then. Not that she'd ever consider starting a relationship with someone from the force anyway. She'd never been attracted to another officer. First she had wondered why, since she liked her job well enough and couldn't now imagine doing anything else. But lately she had come to think that two police officers, even if they didn't have to work closely together, could only succeed in getting in each other's way – or worse, dragging each other down. And surely the job was tough enough as it was. Anyway, didn't sleeping with someone from work display a certain lack of imagination? It wasn't as if she didn't have the opportunity to meet other people. She encountered new people every day. Problem was they were either victims or perpetrators, and she didn't fancy either much. There was the life-drawing class, when she managed to attend, but the current intake didn't do much to inspire her.

It wasn't true, was it, DC French had asked eventually. Of course it wasn't. Though she had felt a bit of a fraud for asserting it so bluntly. She was by no means sure. Fairfield thought she was probably bisexual, or would be, given half a chance, only so far it simply hadn't presented itself. Well, not since school anyway and she doubted if that really counted. Ultimately it had remained an unconsummated affair anyway. And even if. She'd hardly tell DC French about it, the nosy cow.

'Another circuit, Kat?'

It was Katarina but she didn't mind the 'Kat', not from Sorbie, anyway. It had been Katarina Vasiliou until what her mother called, had always called, 'Rina's disastrous marriage'. Of course any marriage not involving a *nice Greek boy* would have been disastrous in her mother's eyes. It had lasted all of one year. Well, technically she was still married and the name was useful, at least. Fairfield was an easier name to get on with in the force than Vasiliou, she was certain of it. No, she didn't mind Sorbie calling her Kat when no one else was around. Jack was all right. Loyal, anyway. 'Yes, just keep cruising.' She went back to concentrating on the photocopy of the map she'd stuck to the dashboard. On it she had marked all the muggings attributed to the same gang with yellow marker pen. She was willing the resultant mess to turn into a revealing pattern that would instantly tell where they would strike next, preferably with a loud *ta-dah* sound, but however long she stared it still looked random. Just like herself and Sorbie, the scooter muggers cruised around town, looking for a likely victim. They struck three, four or five times in quick succession, then disappeared from the radar. All she had gleaned so far was that the gang operated strictly outside the zone covered by CCTV. As expected, the cameras installed around the centre had never brought down the overall incidents of street crime, they had simply succeeded in moving certain types into adjacent areas.

Into the yellow dots, in her clear, upright handwriting, she had logged the time of each incident. Now, with a notepad on one raised knee, she sorted the times into a list. Forty-two incidents so far. Not to have caught them by now, after all the effort expended, was becoming embarrassing. They didn't need the *Evening Post* to point it out. Denkhaus was screaming blue murder that their clear-up rates were beginning to look ridiculous. As she listed the times in barely legible handwriting due to Sorbie's driving, a pattern did begin to emerge. So far all they had realized was that the gang struck from dusk onward. They obviously liked the relative darkness but for some reason had never attacked after eleven in the evening. Now she noticed something else. So far they had never struck at weekends.

Sorbie was stunned by the news. More, it seemed to upset his sense of how decent criminals ought to operate. 'I can't get over it, you're telling me they work Monday to Friday and about seven to eleven? They treat it like a job?'

'I know. They've certainly got better hours than we have. I wonder what their pension plans are like.'

'And their job's getting easier. Since Denkhaus told the paper it was safer for victims not to resist, people have just handed over their stuff. The last victim was completely unharmed.' Sorbie snorted contemptuously as though that was a failing on the part of the victim. 'The bastards just had to ask nicely and were given the stuff.'

'Denkhaus was absolutely right to make that statement. It's much safer to just give them what they ask for. They have clearly demonstrated that they are willing to use a lot of force. But it's the kind of advice that sticks in your throat. You see what I see, Jack?'

'Yup.' Two identical blue scooters had joined the stream of traffic from a side street and were now weaving across the lanes ahead of them, going south along the Bath Road. The scooters the gang used had been reported as being all kinds of colours. But Fairfield had noticed that they seemed to get progressively darker and had come to the conclusion that the gang used spray paint to change the appearance of their transport. It was easier to do dark over light with a spray can.

'No passengers though. Shall I hassle after them?'

'Just try and keep them in sight, might as well have something hilarious to look at.'

Sorbie obliged and noted the index numbers as he got close enough. Both scooters were sporting L-plates and were being ridden accordingly.

Sorbie snorted with contempt. 'All over the place. Makes you wonder how they survive long enough to take the test. Someone ought to drag them off the things and read them the bloody highway code. *In Braille.*'

The traffic was still heavy, the wet roads glistened. As the rain thinned to a fine drizzle the windscreen wipers slowed to an occasional squeak. He kept the scooters in view, as instructed, but knew they weren't the ones, not just because of the L-plates which could come off quickly. No, when he saw the muggers he would know them. And these guys ahead of him were criminally stupid rather than criminal. They appeared to be keeping up a shouted conversation between themselves as they drove through and around traffic and scooted side by side in the middle lane.

'Still going south.' Sorbie kept up a murmured commentary to himself.

Fairfield looked up. 'Let's carry on up here, then turn round at the old brewery, then back towards the centre. This place is due a mugging or two, I feel.'

Female intuition, Sorbie thought, but kept it to himself. 'That route takes us past Mitchell's place of course.' He looked at his superior.

Fairfield stiffened. 'So?'

Ady Mitchell was a fence. Fairfield knew he was a fence, but proving it was something else. Normally she'd hardly be interested but since he set up in the city theft and robbery, mostly of mobile phones and PDAs, had shot up. Certain types of burglary too. He had plenty of previous. Fairfield refused to believe this was a coincidence and she didn't believe he'd gone straight. It had become a pet project of hers but so far proving a connection had eluded her. Mitchell had finally made a complaint against her when out of frustration she had taken to sitting in her car near his lock-up, one in a row of brick-built Victorian warehouses at the edge of Brislington, without official sanction. She knew at the time it was obsessive behaviour and that she ought to get a life but it had gnawed at her pride and still did. It had earned her an official reprimand for unauthorized surveillance.

They had visited the lock-up twice before that and not seen anything suspicious. It was an Aladdin's cave of junk of every description, from china to electrical goods. Second-hand goods, buying and selling, eBay trader, fence – it was all the same to her. And it would be low on her list of priorities if only it hadn't meant children being targeted for their mobiles and business types for their BlackBerries. If she could link him to any street robberies that would be sweet indeed, only now she couldn't even go near him without landing herself in serious trouble. 'That's okay, we're following these two, nothing to do with Mitchell.'

Sorbie kept his eyes on the road. 'If we got stuck in traffic near his lock-up would that be interpreted as

111

unauthorized surveillance too? If we happened to look and see something?'

'Like stolen goods being unloaded by known criminals? Only if they can prove you deliberately brought along your own traffic jam. Hey, you're giving me ideas now . . .'

The scooter riders turned off to the right. 'There they go. Mitchell's place coming up in a sec.'

'I know, Jack, I've been here before, you know?'

'Just saying.'

'Well, don't. Just drive.' Fairfield engineered a yawn as they drove past the lock-up. All of the warehouses looked dark and deserted at this time of the evening and the clapboard café that served them had long closed for the night.

Drizzle gave way to heavy rain again. Sorbie turned right at the traffic lights by the brewery and drove back east. They saw several scooters on their way in. 'If you're looking for scooters there's always scooters. It's like being told to look for a kid wearing trainers.' A few minutes later he turned back towards the centre. They passed the large drive-through burger place. At this time of the evening it usually played host to hordes of teenagers, many on scooters. Tonight it looked deserted.

It was while he swept through a few side streets to relieve the monotony that the radio came to life. They no longer crackled (though from time to time they stopped working for no reason) but the controller still sounded reassuringly like she had a bad case of hay fever. Street robbery reported in Kensington Hill. Four suspects on two blue scooters leaving the scene along Hollywood Road going south.

Sorbie slowed down. 'Hey, that's us, Hollywood's just behind us. They'll come this way any second.'

'I'm not so sure. Quick, do a U-ee! They might feel like a burger after a good mugging. We can always turn again.' She steadied herself against the dashboard and gave their position to the controller. 'Was the victim hurt?'

'Yes, victim is male, in his thirties, collapsed with head wound, ambulance en route, ETA four minutes. The victim is receiving first aid from a taxi driver who is a trained first-aider. A passing couple who made the call saw the scooters leave in your direction.'

'Get shifting, Jack. Looks like this one put up a fight for you.'

'Bastards.' He performed a ragged U-turn using the entire width of the road, the pavement and a bit of road-side shrubbery. It took him no more than thirty seconds to get to the bottom of the hill. There was no sign of any scooters. Sorbie bullied his way up the hill, scanning the road, his mirrors.

'Damn, they could be miles away, those damn things can squeeze through any traffic too. Keep going.'

'If we do meet them, do we try and stop them?'

'We'll follow.'

Seconds later they approached a narrow side street. It spat out two blue scooters. Sorbie knew this was the genuine article, he had always known he would know. Two scooters, four muggers; black clothes, black trainers, black full-face helmets. Only they were going the wrong way.

'Rats. I was half-right, anyway. Turn round. Let's get 'em. Make a noise.'

'It'll only make them split up.'

'I know, Jack, but it's in the rule book.' She gave their call sign to the controller. 'In pursuit of four suspects, possibly male, on two blue scooters travelling west on Bristol Hill, index number . . .' She gave the number of the closest scooter. Sorbie brought their plain unit closer to the rear of the nearest scooter before turning on Blues and Twos. Blue light strobed under the grille of the bonnet and the siren howled.

Riders and passengers turned around and the scooters swayed, then picked up a bit of speed. It was a moment they had discussed many times. A single police unit would never persuade them to stop. It would take at least two units to have any chance of cutting off even one, after which they would probably abandon the scooters and run. If by then they had a helicopter up they should be able to apprehend them. Only it hadn't worked the last time a patrol had caught a glimpse of them. They'd lost them on the ground and the helicopter had circled the area and found nothing.

Sorbie knew this pursuit could only go two ways and he was certain he already knew how it would end. If it went on long enough they might crash or they would disappear down an alley where he couldn't follow. He had also discussed the possibility of 'nudging' them off, as he had delicately put it to Fairfield, but the inspector wouldn't hear of it. Sorbie had met Australian police on a visit to Sydney and had admired their attitude. Over there suspects were 'crims' and crims got what they deserved. There was no time to pursue this favourite gripe of his, however. The front scooter was signalling left to alert his partner behind him and both scooters turned side by side, slicing across the inside lane and turning down a side street. A startled car driver slammed on his brakes, blocking Sorbie's path.

'Whose side are you on, blockhead?' Sorbie cranked the wheel and took a lot of pavement in cornering around the vehicle. It only cost him a few seconds but it had put the entire length of a street between him and the scooters. They were cornering again. Sorbie shot after them.

Fairfield pointed ahead. 'They're going down there, that's a dead end.'

'It is for us but not for them. There's a pedestrian entrance into the supermarket car park, they'll go through there. We'll have to go round. We've lost them.' Sorbie drove on without slowing but turned the siren off until he needed it to cut across the next two junctions, then turned it off again. It might relax the riders if they thought they had lost them. He doubted it would. They were too well organized not to have an escape route planned in advance.

Having circled the supermarket he slowed in the middle of the junction long enough to avoid colliding with a green-grocer's van, then sped north.

Fairfield, who had kept up a commentary on the pursuit to the controller, asked if any units were in the area and was told there were none on that side of town. Several had been drawn off to help with a multiple RTA on the motor-way, which kept the helicopter busy as well.

'Are we packing it in?' Sorbie asked, still overtaking vehicles at speed. They had come full circle, once more on the Bath Road.

Fairfield's voice was gritty with frustration. 'Carry on past Mitchell's place. You never know, we might get lucky.' Minutes later the lock-ups flew past her window, dark and deserted. 'All right, cut the lights and drive me towards my coffee machine, Jack. I'm seriously pissed off now.'

Chris Reed loved computers. He loved everything about them. And especially the net. It was the most liberating weapon unwittingly given into the hands of the ordinary man, and now it was unstoppable. It brought together like-minded people into supportive communities that could be fostered and nurtured into global movements. The estab-lishment could never monitor them all, there were too many of them, too many sites, too many users. Computers helped keep in touch, organize action. Computers gave you ideas. And they cost next to nothing. This one had come from a skip, like most of the things in his room in fact, and it was okay. It was ancient and had less memory than a middle-aged pothead but it did most things, albeit very slowly.

The printer on the other hand was a pain in the arse. Reed cleared another paper jam. The print on his home-made leaflets was too pale and a bit stripy, not at all the stark-looking warning he had been aiming for. But they'd get the message.

He could only do a few cars at a time. Of the five students in this house all but Vicky were totally apathetic. A couple of them had come on the Saturday Traffic Protest once and that was it. Direct action wasn't their style. Any action really. They didn't even bother to vote. As far as he could see they were all at uni so they could one day become part of the establishment and add their own 4×4s to the madness and consume until the planet was dead.

He left the printer chewing on the leaflets and went and knocked on Vicky's door. Loud, synthetic dance music thumped on the other side. He knocked harder.

The music blasted him as Vicky at last opened the door. 'Oh, hi.' She went back to piling her hair into a mess on top of her head in front of a narrow length of mirror glass, giving a grunt of frustration when the arrangement snaked apart. She started all over again. As she lifted her arms her short dress rode up high enough to gave him a glimpse of black knickers.

'You're wearing a dress?'

'Yeah. Look all right?'

She'd forgotten. Obvious. 'Not very practical.'

'That always depends.' She could see Chris in the mirror. He was so scruffy. Someone should take the man in hand. For a mature student he was all right really. He had some valid ideas, stuff to say. But it got boring very quickly. Chris the one-trick pony. 'I'm going out tonight. We're meeting at the Watershed.'

He crossed the room to the mini system and turned down the moronic music. 'We were going to do some cars tonight. You said you'd come.'

'No, don't do that, it gets me in the mood.' She turned it up again and returned to her mirror. 'I must have forgotten. Next time. I'll come with you next time. Who else is going anyway?' She asked purely for something to say, she really wasn't in the mood for Chris tonight and she knew there'd be no one else. In theory Chris's raids were quite a laugh, in practice they were cold and yucky.

'It's just us.' He knew she wouldn't change her mind now, she had her make-up done and everything, but he wouldn't let her off so easily.

'Sorry, we could do it tomorrow night, what's wrong with tomorrow?'

'I'll do it by myself then. Won't be able to do many cars but at least it's a start. Then we can do some more tomorrow.'

'Oh no, just remembered, I can't tomorrow, I'm going up to see my parents for a couple of days, aren't I? Dad's birthday, they sent me a train ticket.'

He left her room without a word and slammed the door behind him, regretting it instantly. He couldn't afford to alienate the girl. But how were they ever going to make a difference if dancing and birthdays took precedence over saving the planet? He found lots of support for what he had to say on the net, in the forums and chat rooms, but actually getting stuff off the ground yourself was a lot harder. He hadn't managed to find many recruits and of the few he did find, only Vicky was left to help him. When she felt like it. Ah well, he'd do it tonight and he'd do it by himself.

Chapter Seven

Tiny, tiny hairs. Backlit by the weak morning light that modelled the contours of the girl's stomach. There had to be thousands of little downy hairs and he liked them. From this vantage point – his head resting on her thigh – he could see some of them moving in his breath. The pierced belly button was, on close inspection, not an improvement on the original design. During their lovemaking he'd been scared of catching his hair on it, ripping it out by accident. It was quite safe, Rebecca had told him. Didn't he like it? No, no, it looked fine. A tiny enamelled daisy. He touched it now with his middle finger, waggled it about a bit. It made him shiver. Rebecca remained fast asleep. Or pretended to be fast asleep, sometimes just as good.

Why couldn't they stick to earrings? Earrings were all right, much nicer in fact. Was it a sign he was slipping into 'young middle age'? Was that why he'd chatted up the barmaid in the first place, to reassure himself that everything was still there, everything was just as it was before Laura?

The two-bar heater from the junk shop had been on all night while they slept and the room was unnaturally warm. The girl had kicked away the duvet after their last, lazy lovemaking. McLusky propped himself up on one elbow and studied her body: the hollow of her stomach, her taut flanks, her breasts unbothered by gravity, her long neck curved away from him, her exactly shoulder-length blonde hair, the perfect ovals of her nostrils.

He had enjoyed her body but images of Laura had constantly intruded, offering themselves for comparison. Sight, touch, smell, energy and size, everything was different. No better or worse, just different and somehow vaguely irritating, not exciting and energizing as it should have been. But these tiny hairs he liked.

Somewhere under the jumble of clothes and duvet by the side of the mattress his mobile chimed faintly and patiently. He scrabbled around for it, leaning across the girl's body as he did so, making her stir. At last he found it and answered it. 'McLusky.'

Rebecca opened her eyes. She gave him a look from sleep-narrowed eyes to go with her brief ironic smile.

The voice at the other end sounded bright and showered and wide-awake. 'Morning, inspector, it's Louise Rennie . . . Chemistry department? Bristol Uni?'

'Ehm, yes. Morning. Morning, doctor.' The girl wriggled from under him into an upright position and started clinking through the Pilsener bottles by the side of the bed, lifting each in turn without luck. 'Have you had a new thought, Dr Rennie?' He was wide awake now.

'Yes, you could call it that. I have two tickets for *The Duchess of Malfi* at the Tobacco Factory for tonight and I wondered if you'd like to come.'

'Ah. I see. Ehm . . .' The girl lit one of his cigarettes and got up. McLusky's eyes followed her breasts out of the room. 'Yes, that would be . . . great. Shakespeare?' So that's what he had left her his number for. He lit a cigarette himself and inhaled deeply.

'No, the other guy. The performance starts at eight. Can you meet me in the café at seven?'

'I'll do my best. Which café?'

'The one at the Factory, inspector.'

'Makes sense.' The flush from the toilet seemed excessively loud. The girl padded back into the room and broke into a cough. McLusky coughed unconvincingly, trying to claim it as his own.

'You should try and give up smoking. Both of you. See you at seven, inspector.'

He put the phone down and checked the time. Rebecca was dressing. He watched her legs disappear into pre-ruined jeans and her breasts under T-shirt and sweater. The little pang of regret he felt made him wonder if he was likely to see them again.

By the afternoon five hours of meetings, report-sifting and fruitless phone calls had nearly succeeded in driving Rebecca's breasts from his mind. Now, in stark contrast, he was staring at his least favourite thing, CCTV footage. The CCTV operation for the city centre was being coordinated from a single suite of hi-tech offices. McLusky had spent half an hour there, in an office where recorded incidents could be analysed and copies made, before he decided that he couldn't concentrate in the place. The subliminal electronic buzz of hundreds of monitors thickened the air around him into an electronic fog and produced a dull headache behind his eyes.

The few staff were helpful but they were also very busy. When he'd arrived and been shown around they'd been in the process of directing police by radio to a fist fight outside a launderette, a car break-in, shoplifters tracked through the centre, a speeding pair of scooters and a group of kids lobbing bottles from recycling bins at each other across a pedestrianized street. On yet another monitor McLusky saw a middle-aged woman, perhaps drunk, perhaps taken ill, lying on the pavement near a newsagent's. Pedestrians were neatly stepping around her, pretending not to notice.

All the staff here were civilians of course, which was another source of worry. He didn't want anyone drawing the same conclusions he had until it became inevitable. As soon as he had the copies he had asked for he took the footage back to Albany Road.

At the station he had requested and received three battered TVs and three DVD players and had managed to cram them all into a corner of his tiny office, one balanced on top of the other, and plugged them into the only available socket via an adventurous knot of extensions. Ensconced in his chair and with a notebook beside him he wrote endless, detailed and systematic notes. Having long recognized his woeful inadequacy when it came to paperwork he tended to overcompensate by sifting everything into separate sheets, columns and folders, with large simplistic headings. This would generate piles of papers all with directions at the bottom like 'cf. DOGWALKER 1' or 'see also SECOND NOISE REPORTED'.

The angles on the cameras covering the entrances were shallower and allowed number plates to be read. The time counter helped him to synchronize the footage. Any person walking in or out who could have simply dropped the booby-trapped compact he tracked from camera to camera. Those that walked out he tracked backwards, those that came in he tracked forward. Some people of course merely used the car park as a shortcut but most were coming from or walking to their cars. He then noted down the appearance of the people and the make and age of car and laboriously tracked the vehicle back to when it arrived or left, noting the index number if possible. Nobody however could be observed placing the bomb by the entrance or dropping it, though the camera might not pick up such sleight of hand. The area was just outside the picture, perhaps by less than a yard, he estimated. After two hours of this he reminded himself that he was acting on the assumption that what he had seen in the original footage was indeed Maxine Bendick bending down to pick up the glittering find that later claimed her face. His headache had got steadily worse. Time for a break. He stopped the playback and called the hospital.

Sitting on the sill of the open window he was glad of its unprestigious view over the backs of houses, away from the eyes of punters, colleagues and superiors, because it allowed him to defy the smoking ban. While he was waiting for a doctor at Southmead Hospital to come back on the line there was a knock at the door. It sounded like Austin's knock but you could never be sure. Just in case it wasn't he hid his cigarette by balancing it on the window frame behind him. A slight breeze made it roll off and fall into the void.

'Shit. Come in.'

It was Austin. 'Shit come in? Charming. Or did you think it was DCI Gaunt? I forget, you haven't met him yet.' Seeing that his superior was on the phone the DS sat down. He produced his own cigarettes and lit one with a silver lighter. Not before time, McLusky thought – the man's addiction had been costing him a fortune.

Austin frowned at the tower of TV sets. 'Why didn't you use the computer, you could have had all three on a split screen?'

'Really? Now he tells me.' The doctor came back on the line, armed with files and superior advice, no doubt, to refuse his request.

McLusky had expected no less. 'Dr Thompson, I said interview. I have no intention of *interrogating* Miss Bendick. She's a witness and a victim of crime. I only need to ask her a few questions.'

'Not for a few days, I'm afraid.'

'One question? I tell you what, doctor. *You* ask her one question for me and I might not have to interview her at all, how's that? Would you do that? It might just help stop more cases like Miss Bendick coming through your door.'

A short pause during which McLusky rolled his eyes for Austin's benefit.

'I can't promise you anything. It might depend on the question. She needs rest.'

'It's a simple question. Just ask her where she got the powder compact.'

'That's all?'

'Nothing else.'

'I'll call you back.'

'Oh no, I'll hold.'

'You're a suspicious man, inspector.'

Too right. Waiting for people to call back, being abandoned by operators in little-explored corners of the switchboard, phantom messages left with imaginary people and all things 'in the post' were part of an officer's daily round and high on McLusky's list of spirit-draining nuisances.

He wedged the receiver between ear and shoulder, stretched his legs out along the window sill, folded his arms and turned to Austin. 'You found nothing, I take it?'

The DS had just returned from supervising a search of Colin Keale's locker at the distribution depot where the man drove a fork-lift at night. 'Nothing relating to bomb making. An overall, a newspaper and a vacuum flask that had whisky in it.'

'Whisky? Mmm. Glenfiddich, by any chance?'

'I don't have your nose, Liam. I could tell it was whisky but not which one. We'll send it off for analysis of course.'

'And wait four weeks? Bollocks to that. Give me one sniff, Jane, and I'll tell you if it is. What time does his plane land?'

'16.55.'

'We'd better get a move on soon. Is the flask still here? Then go and get it.' While he waited for Austin to return he fluted bored invective down the line where Dr Thompson and Southmead Hospital were offering him nothing but static.

Keale's Turkish holiday was over and he was flying back into Bristol Airport this afternoon. It would be good to have at least something to scare him with when they questioned him. Of course an awful lot of people drank Glenfiddich. Few stuffed the tin it came in full of gunpowder and shoved it under a park bench.

123

'There you are, impress me.' Austin handed over the red plastic flask. It was scratched and grimy.

McLusky unscrewed the plastic cup and popped the old-fashioned cork stopper. He inhaled the fragrance deeply and was instantly troubled by a strong desire to put the half-litre flask to his lips and empty it. 'It's Glenfiddich all right.'

'Sure?'

'Can't be a *hundred* per cent sure without tasting it, but we can't go around drinking the evidence.'

'Am I bothering to send it off?'

'Pointless at this stage, it wouldn't prove a thing. We'll wave it under his nose first during the interview and ask him. Then we'll send it off.'

'Because you've been known to be wrong?'

'Indeed.'

The receiver against his ear crackled to life. 'Inspector?'

'I'm here.'

'Miss Bendick told me she found the compact at a car park that day. Is that any help?'

On the contrary. 'It is. Thanks for doing that, Dr Thompson. I must ask you to keep that detail to yourself for the time being. It's important it doesn't become public knowledge at this point in the investigation.' He returned the receiver to its cradle with exaggerated gentleness.

'Is it what I think it is?'

McLusky slid his jacket on. 'Yup. Let's go.'

By the time they had arrived at Austin's car the implications were sinking in. 'Bastard. Now what do we do?'

McLusky strapped himself into the back seat as conscientiously as someone about to loop-the-loop in an open-cockpit plane. 'You have my permission to panic. Meanwhile we continue to have every available bod explore every possible avenue. How are we doing with the fireworks sales?'

'We're nearly through them all. Nothing. No one reports any suspiciously large sales or people coming back for several purchases, though that's very hard to keep track of if you have several staff. If our bomber has any savvy he'll have gone round lots of shops anyway.'

'Quite. I expect he did. What about people licensed to handle gunpowder?'

'We're still checking those too. There's not many in our area. The licence conditions were tightened up several times recently, Prevention of Terrorism Act etc. Did you know you only need a lightning conductor if you are storing more than 500 kilograms of the stuff?'

McLusky frowned at the traffic. 'Fascinating, Jane. And what a shame, otherwise all we'd do is look for a suspicious lightning conductor and make a quick arrest. Are we going to make the airport on time?'

'Yeah, no sweat. I'm using a shortcut.' Austin swung the car through a couple of roundabouts and dived into the suburbs where he could avoid much of the traffic that was building up again on the more obvious routes. One day soon they would experience gridlock in the centre again. Last summer it had only taken a few simultaneous incidents and the city had ground to a complete halt.

He was keen to discuss whatever little progress they had made, the angles they had already covered, while he skilfully negotiated the network of streets and lanes that would spit them out near the airport. The DI on the back seat however did little more than grunt and for the most part stared past him out at the narrow lanes as though their final doom lurked just around the next corner.

New security arrangements at the airport meant they could park nowhere near the entrances but it didn't matter, they had arrived in time, thanks to Austin's shortcuts. McLusky never had much faith in shortcuts and was impressed. They hadn't got stuck in traffic once and that was a rare experience. Still, being driven was a nightmare. 'You've got to show me your shortcut on the map.'

'I'll photocopy you a map.' Austin checked his watch. 'He'll land in five minutes.'

Colin Keale was going to do no such thing. At this very moment he was looking out from his window seat at the duvet of cloud obscuring his view of the Mediterranean. His departure from Dalaman had been delayed by two hours. But that didn't worry Keale. What worried him was whether or not he was going to get the contents of his holdall through British customs and what would happen to him if he didn't.

'Didn't you think to check before we set off?'

Austin rolled his eyes. 'I was going to but I got distracted by the whisky thing. Airport police should have let us know really, they're the ones tracking him. Are we going back to Albany or are we waiting?'

'God no, we'll wait.' Shortcut or not, under no circumstances did he want to do the journey three more times. 'And since it was you who got distracted by the whisky thing you can distract me with a cappuccino thing.'

They installed themselves in one of the cafés in the arrivals lounge, but not before McLusky had colourfully expressed his displeasure at not having been informed of the delay to the airport police sergeant supposedly in charge of picking up Keale.

When Colin Keale at last arrived he simply couldn't believe it. How had they known? They hadn't even looked inside his bag, just scooped him up in customs and frog-marched him out through a side door where these two CID clowns were waiting, and he knew CID clowns when he saw them.

McLusky put his ID away. 'You know why we are here?'

'Yeah, I guess so.' Keale looked tired and deflated. Apart from his nose, which had caught too much sun, he looked pale. He hadn't gone to Turkey to sunbathe, that seemed obvious.

McLusky was surprised but never looked a gift horse in the mouth until he had got it home. 'In that case, Colin Keale, I'm arresting you for causing explosions, attempted murder, causing actual bodily harm . . .'

'Wa-wa-wait!'

He didn't let himself be interrupted and finished the caution: '. . . something which you later rely upon in court. Anything you do say may be given in evidence. Do you understand?'

The man looked incredulous. 'No, I fucking don't.'

'Well, we can talk about it down the station, Mr Keale.'

Which is what they had done now for the last hour in this depressingly neutral interview room at Albany Road. Spread out on the table stood part of the contents of Colin Keale's holdall, the reason, he had assumed, for his arrest. There were several plastic nets and paper bags full of what had at first looked to McLusky like onions and shrivelled potatoes, and a carrier bag stuffed with packets of plant seeds, some of them in little brown envelopes with Turkish handwriting on them. And a litre bottle of whisky. It wasn't Glenfiddich. None of this looked like a major breakthrough to the inspector.

'I suppose this contains Glenmorangie too?' He produced the thermos flask from a carrier but thought he already knew the answer.

'Where the hell did you get . . . did you break into my locker at work?' Keale was brimming with righteous anger but struggled to keep it in check, in view of the contraband on show on the table in front of him. So he had been stupid once and built some pipe bombs. They'd been glorified fire crackers really, just something to piss people off with. Now they were talking about blowing people up. And he hadn't even been in the country. He had made one mistake, one error of judgement, and from here to eternity they were going to arrest him every time a car misfired in the city. He hadn't been well, had gone through a period of mental instability, you might say. He was better now but of course to the police it had to be him if some bastard started blowing up people. He hadn't really wanted to hurt anyone, he just wanted to make them look stupid. What a fucking mistake that had been. 'Yes, yes, it's Glenmorangie. I suppose you told my employers and lost me my job as well now? That's great. That's dandy. It wasn't easy getting any sort of job with my history. And you've no idea how cold it is in those bloody warehouses in winter. A couple of tots get me through the night shift.'

Austin had brought in a photocopy of a leaflet produced by the Plant Health and Seed Inspectorate. McLusky read it. He was getting bored with all this. They'd been over Keale's movements on the day before the explosion countless times. He cited his neighbour as an alibi and McLusky had little doubt that it would check out. The man was just a plant nut. The things on the table between them were bulbs and corms, he wasn't sure where the difference lay, and there were enough seeds in this one carrier bag alone to keep a garden centre going. He hadn't brought in anything illegal, he swore it, just far too much, he admitted it. Everything was so cheap there. He wasn't doing any harm, was he?

McLusky checked his watch. He was already over an hour late, the play had started a while ago and he had no idea if Dr Rennie had got the messages he had left for her.

And now, since he had whisked Keale away before his bags had been checked at customs, he had more or less helped the nutter smuggle these things into the country. He didn't feel much sympathy for Keale. The man was a creased, slightly greasy-looking type. Perhaps it was the plane journey that had shrivelled him or maybe it was finding himself back inside an interview room at Albany. He was just another slightly strange, unhappy man who liked growing stuff in a basement. What did it matter? This was all a waste of time.

'Right, you can go. But don't leave town, as they say, we might want to talk to you again.'

Keale crossed his arms in front of his chest. 'What about my bulbs and seeds though?'

'None of these are . . .' McLusky picked up some of the shrivelled-looking things. 'None of these are dangerous? Or endangered and what have you?'

'No, as I told you, I just went a bit overboard.'

'Well, then pack them up and get out of here.'

Keale sprang into action. In less than a minute he had cleared the treasure into his holdall and rushed away. In his eagerness to be out of there he left his duty-free whisky behind.

Back in his office McLusky found a place for the litre bottle of Glenmorangie in the bottom of his desk, making a mental note to get a couple of glasses from the canteen.

A fine drizzle began to darken the pavement as he waited for his taxi.

On the other side of the river in the Knowle West district of the city Frank Dudden was pissing in the street between two parked cars while shouting at the *bastards* in the George and Dragon behind him. 'Fascist wankers! If you won't even let me piss in your fucking stinking toilet then I'm pissing right here!' He half turned to look at the pub from which he had just been evicted and splashed urine against the back of a car, over his shoes and one knee as he swayed backwards. 'Fuck.' He buttoned himself up, wiped his hands on his trousers and steadied himself. *Wankers*, all of them. As he passed the pub he aimed a kick at the door through which he had been propelled by the landlord. His kick glanced off the slick woodwork and hurt the side of his foot. 'Fascists!' Dudden steadied himself against the wall before steering an approximate course down the pavement. First they sold you the drink then they told you you'd had too much. What was the world coming to when a man couldn't even get pissed in peace to drown his sorrows? What was so bad about that? It was any decent and honest Englishman's right to get rat-arsed if his girlfriend of seven – seven! – years ran off with his month's takings. Which, okay, he should have banked earlier. Still. Running off with it. Without him. Because of one bloody scuffle. And to Spain! Toremo-fucking-linos! Just how tacky was that?

Dudden reached his car at the street corner and stopped to focus on the object standing on its roof. 'What the fuck?' A can of Special Brew. An unopened can of Special Brew. You're hallucinating now, Frank, because you're thirsty. He looked around him. There were people walking on the other side of the street, cars driving by, but nobody in the immediate vicinity. Well, if it was standing on his car he'd fucking have it anyway. He reached across and picked it up. Heavy. It really was full, unopened. 'Well, thank you, very thoughtful of you, whoever you are, Mr Special Brew delivery person.' He sniffed, hawked and spat viscous, slow-travelling mucus between his feet. Having fumbled the car door open he let himself fall behind the wheel and pulled the door shut. 'Manna from fucking heaven. No offence.' He tilted the ring-pull up with the long nail of his index finger and pulled.

The confined explosion knocked Frank Dudden against the roof while separating him from his left hand and most of his genitals. Sprays of blood from his multiple injuries blinded the ruined remains of the windows. His lungs had been crushed empty by the force of the blast. By the time Dudden managed to suck up enough breath to scream he was already too weak to do so. Instead, a pink bubble escaped from his mouth and popped while his heart pumped his blood into the upholstery.

The play wouldn't finish for ages yet. He wasn't really dressed to mix with a theatre crowd either, though the

Tobacco Factory didn't look all that posh. Like many cultural venues in the city a theatre had found a home in one of the many rundown commercial Victorian buildings that had once served the busy port on the river Avon. Cigarettes were now made in China, no doubt. He wondered if one day Chinese tobacco factories would turn into fashionable theatre venues.

Webster, so that's who the play was by. He studied the poster behind the glass door. One of those ancient plays performed in modern dress, presumably to show how relevant it was to the present. Or perhaps because it saved money on the costumes? He probably would have hated it anyway. Two people stood outside, smoking, twelve feet apart, having nothing in common but their craving. He entered the lobby. The place was quiet. It had been immaculately restored and looked modern and cheerful. McLusky hated the nursery school of architecture. The man behind the reception desk barely registered him.

'Where's the café?'

'Upstairs next to the auditorium.'

Bare brick walls, blond wood tables, medieval music. Three bar staff oversaw a practically empty room, probably waiting for the interval crush. He registered with a sigh that the only thing on draught was lager and ordered a bottle of Guinness, then corrected himself. 'Make it two.' He'd just remembered how small those bottles were, they got smaller too as he got older. 'What time's the interval?'

The barman checked his watch, pulled a face. 'Ten minutes.'

'Will there be a crush?'

'Oh yes, stand well back.'

Only two of the tables were occupied, by couples talking in low voices, not noticing him. McLusky took a table as far away from the bar as possible from where he could still keep an eye on the door, and emptied the first bottle without bothering to pour it, then took more time over the second one. He was relieved to see that one of the men at the tables was also wearing jeans and he relaxed a little. Laura had been keen on the theatre, though he could only remember having gone with her twice. He had enjoyed it, but it all seemed a bit of an effort, mainly the dressing-up part. This was okay.

There was no mistaking the moment the interval started. A wave of voices and footsteps approached and poured through the door, breaking against the bar. Dr Louise Rennie was among the first. She received instant attention from the barman and signalled to McLusky that she'd get him another drink, seemingly taking his presence here for granted.

'I didn't get any messages.' She added another bottle of Guinness to his collection and took a sip of her orange juice.

'I'm sorry. I called the uni. They said they'd pass it on.'

'I'm sure I'll find a note in my pigeonhole tomorrow. Today's my day off. It really doesn't matter. It's not a good production and I would have been embarrassed having dragged you out to see it. Were you busy catching the bench bomber?'

'Is that really what people are calling him?'

'It's what they call him in the papers. Why, what do you call him?'

'You don't want to know.'

'Though I can imagine. Can you talk about it? I mean the case.'

'Some of it.'

'Is the new explosion, the poor woman with the powder compact, is that related? Is it the same guy who did that?'

'I think so, though so far there's no evidence to support that theory. It just seems unlikely that two people in the same city are planting bombs at the same time. Forensics may be able to confirm that it's the same perpetrator but I'm pretty certain anyway.'

'But the bombs were very different. That's what the papers said, anyway.'

132

'They were. It was a different type of explosion. The bomb was much smaller, obviously. And it didn't have a timer, it was set off when the compact was opened.'

'So the first one was a time bomb? That wasn't in the papers.'

'Keep it to yourself. I shouldn't have told you that. We need to keep back details so we can weed out the cranks and attention seekers claiming responsibility. We've already had several cheerful souls on the phone.'

'But how did the woman get hold of it? Was it her own compact that someone filled with explosives?'

McLusky hesitated. 'That's . . . one of the things I can't tell you.'

Louise Rennie looked away over his shoulder at nothing, pondering the answer. 'I see the implications, I think. If it wasn't hers then . . . Things could get interesting.'

McLusky went through a series of helpless facial expressions that signalled, 'Yes, you're right, but I'm not saying anything.'

'And the bomb was much, much smaller. Was it the same type of explosive?'

'There's no word yet. But what did the most damage to the victim was the tongue of flame that shot from the device. It set her face on fire.'

'That might not have been the intention. It might just not have worked properly.'

'That's always possible.' This was like still being at work, only with the addition of beer and beauty.

They both reached for their glasses and drank. 'What are you suddenly smiling about, inspector?'

'Well, doctor, I was thinking that this is a most peculiar topic of conversation for a date.'

Rennie sat back in her chair. 'A date? Is that what this is?'

'Well, no, I didn't mean . . .'

'It was meant to be a visit to the theatre, which has now turned into a drink, or in your case, three drinks.'

133

Why had he said that? He didn't even like the word 'date'. Nobody 'dated' in Britain. McLusky searched her face for signs of annoyance but found instead what he hoped was an ironic sternness. She wasn't wearing her glasses but peered at him over their rims anyway.

'Sorry, it's not really what I meant. I was just wondering if any of the other couples at their tables are talking about bombs and mutilation.'

'The other couples? You can obviously see us as a couple, then?'

'Jesus, one has to choose one's words carefully around you.'

'I'm a pedant, inspector. Take no notice.'

McLusky knew that 'take no notice' without exception meant 'please note'. A change of subject might help. 'So, how's the play? Rubbish, you said? Thanks for the invitation, by the way. That was quite unexpected.'

She waved it away. 'I had a spare ticket.'

'And you asked everyone else but no one could make it?'

'Well, no, it wasn't quite like that. I just thought you're new in town, probably don't know many people yet . . .'

'That was kind of you. I'm afraid I came straight from work, I'm not dressed for the occasion.'

'Neither am I, really. The Tobacco Factory isn't that kind of theatre, you wear whatever you feel like.'

Rennie wore a simple grey knee-length dress, matching shoes and handbag. It reminded him of the sixties. No jewellery apart from pearl ear studs, yet she looked fit for the catwalk. Her eyes weren't like Laura's at all, he decided. 'So, are you going to bring me up to speed about the play?'

'Oh, stuff the play, you'll never get into it now and I'm not fussed about it. I thought we could go and eat something.'

'There's a bistro here, I saw.'

'It's a bit too studenty here for me. I didn't book anywhere but I know one or two places where we might get a table.'

He tried not to let his relief show. 'Okay, if you're sure about the play. I'm quite hungry, now you mention it.'

'So am I. We'll finish our drinks and go.'

'Good. So the interrogation starts here. Have you always lived here?'

'Me? God no . . .'

The conversation flowed easily, mainly because Rennie talked freely and happily about herself. She gave him her potted autobiography from her peripatetic childhood when the family followed her father from failed venture to failed venture, her travels, her eventual studies at Liverpool and her subsequent teaching posts. They both had a stint in Southampton in common, she teaching chemistry, he on the force.

As they left the Factory they found the rain had stopped. McLusky offered Rennie a cigarette.

'No thanks, I'm a chemist, I know what's in it. But you go ahead.'

He lit one for himself with a shiny silver lighter he found in a pocket of his leather jacket and didn't remember owning. It was satisfyingly heavy. They were walking towards Rennie's blue Toyota when his mobile rang. In a city full of strangers this could only mean bad news.

It was DS Austin. 'At last. Your airwave isn't turned on or something and your mobile was saying you were unavailable.'

McLusky's mental image of his airwave radio lying at home next to the cooker made him swallow hard. 'No signal, I guess.'

'Your predictions are coming true. Another bomb, by the looks of it. The victim is male. Blew up inside his car.'

'Is the victim alive?' McLusky made an apologetic gesture to Rennie who shrugged her shoulders.

'He was still alive when the paramedics got there but

135

he died at the scene. It's in Knowle West.' Austin gave the address.

'Hang on a second.' He fumbled about in his pockets.

Rennie had anticipated it and handed him a folded envelope from her handbag. She watched him note down the address with a heavy, brushed-steel pen. The man had a certain style, she had noticed it before, no plastic biros or disposable lighters for him. He looked good in a leather jacket, too. The inspector probably drove a good car and owned solid, quality furniture, he seemed that kind of a man.

McLusky folded his mobile. 'Something's come up. I'm afraid I have to go and find a cab somewhere. I came without my car.'

'I'll drive you there, much quicker.' She released the central locking then went to the back of the car and squatted down low, inspecting the tail pipe.

'What on earth are you doing? You're not looking for bombs, are you?'

Rennie straightened up. 'No. Just making sure it's clear. It's the latest craze, it seems, blocking the exhaust pipes of cars. It was my turn a couple of days ago. Car wouldn't start and I ended up having it towed to a garage. It took them half a day to find a rotten apple in the exhaust pipe.'

As Rennie drove off McLusky spotted a man standing alone beside the entrance of the building, watching. 'Isn't that ...?' Rennie drove off fast and he lost sight of the figure.

'Isn't that what?'

'The ... the bloke. The chap who was at the laboratory when I came up to ask your advice. I thought I just saw him by the theatre.'

'What, Harmer? Most unlikely. I don't think Steven even knows what goes on inside a theatre.'

'What is he, your assistant?'

'Yes, well, not just mine. He's a lab technician. Am I driving you to the scene of a murder?'

136

'I'm afraid so.'

'Another bomb? You might as well tell me, it'll be in the paper tomorrow, save me the expense.'

'I was going to. Yes, another explosion. That's all I know, really. A man died.'

'That then rather looks like a bombing campaign, doesn't it?'

'If it turns out to be our man again, yes.'

'But what's he campaigning for?'

'That's a good question.'

'You haven't received any demands, then, something else you can't tell me?'

'No, nothing at all.'

Rennie was driving them south, confident of where she was going, hardly referring to her sat nav. To him all this looked new, alien, yet somehow universal. A cityscape of suburbs, becoming poorer and more depressing the further they went. Even in sunshine, without sodium-lit rain, this place would look drab and dispiriting. Here and there a building site hinted at recovery, yet mainly what they drove past were drab streets full of cars that looked dumped rather than parked; a boarded-up house, a playground full of rubbish, a van without wheels.

Knowle West. McLusky recognized it instantly, though he had never been here. It was Costcutter Country, and markedly different from the other Bristol west of the river. Here problem neighbourhoods, high unemployment, failing estates and failing schools had created a ripe market for hard drugs and the crime they spawned. Gangs of children, often led by young adults, defended their imagined turf and were responsible for an impressive percentage of the crime, knifings and shootings in the city.

Rents here were lower, yet even hard-up students shunned the area, not being keen on too much reality all at once. Besides, it was too far from the university, from the clubs and the gigs. Even pubs were failing here as more and more people stayed in to drink supermarket booze and watch TV in the imaginary safety of their homes.

Judging by the number of drinkers standing outside its doors the George and Dragon was bucking the trend. The area around Frank Dudden's car had been completely sealed off and the road junction was closed. Despite the persistent drizzle many of the neighbourhood's residents had deserted the fantasy world of television and computer games for the arc-lit reality of death on their own streets and formed a noisy cordon beyond the police tape. Many had brought drinks, bicycles, babies and camcorders. Pictures and videos were being taken on mobile phones.

On the other side of the tape police cars, Forensics vehicles, ambulance, undertaker's van, technicians' cars and Denkhaus's Land Rover were already there. Everyone had crammed their vehicles across the junction and on to a triangle of grass which they soon realized was the neighbourhood's dog toilet, the pub's vomit bucket and a used-needle repository.

'Looks like you're the last to arrive, inspector.' There hadn't even been time to move to first names.

'Looks like it, doctor.'

'So this is what policemen's wives can expect, is it?' She checked her watch. 'Forty-seven minutes, not much of a night out.'

'Yes, I'm sorry. It's not always like this, honestly. Thanks for the lift. Perhaps we could . . .'

'Yes, inspector. Next time I have fifty minutes to fill I might call on you again.'

'I look forward to it.'

But don't hold your breath. 'Good luck, inspector.'

Watching her drive off McLusky was assailed by a sudden feeling of loss that cut him raw across his chest. He ducked under the police tape and stood in the shadows between the police vans and lit another cigarette. *This is what policemen's wives can expect.* He took a deep drag on his cigarette then walked coughing towards the arc lights at the street corner. It was all policemen's wives' husbands could expect.

DS Austin had spotted him and lifted a finger in greeting but McLusky steered a course towards Superintendent Denkhaus who was talking with a sharp-suited man standing close to a metal briefcase and holding aloft a black umbrella. The two were shaking hands as he got there. 'Ah, glad you could join us at last. You might try keeping your airwave turned on if you want to head this investigation.' He turned to the umbrella'd man. 'This is DI McLusky, new to our troubled parish. Dr Coulthart, Home Office Pathologist.'

Coulthart was in his late fifties, wore rimless spectacles and had a suspiciously full head of dark hair. He seemed to look through McLusky. No offer to shake hands was forthcoming. Instead the pathologist gave a curt nod. 'Inspector.' He picked up his briefcase and turned away. 'Good luck, Rob. I think you'll need it.'

Denkhaus grunted at his retreating shape. Coulthart had taken his umbrella with him, leaving the superintendent standing in the incessant drizzle. He had come without his hat and was bristling with discomfort and irritation. If DCI Gaunt hadn't been in Spain trying to assist in the arrest of that bastard DI Pearce, he wouldn't now be standing in the sodding rain. Again. He gripped McLusky's shoulder hard. 'It was only a matter of time before someone got killed. This shit always escalates, by accident or design. This one may have got killed by accident but we can't count on it.' He released him and jerked his head towards the wreck of the car at the street corner. A large enough tent had at last been found and crime scene technicians were erecting it around the vehicle. 'You go get a good eyeful, I've seen enough. It's all yours, detective inspector.'

McLusky stood in the rain and gave the scene time to sink in. Glass and bits of fittings from the car were lying in a wide orbit. Technicians and Forensics were busy all around the area, closely watched by the press and

139

neighbourhood. TV had arrived and bribed their way into the upstairs bedrooms of nearby houses to get a better view. Austin was talking to one of the white-suited technicians, himself still wearing overshoes and latex gloves. Uniform were everywhere.

The four doors of the victim's car were wide open now. Having donned protective gear himself McLusky approached it from the driver's side. Everything he saw was dark red, thoroughly sprayed with blood from the explosive dismemberment of the victim. The car's interior felt like the inside of a giant mouth with broken teeth and a half-chewed man on its tongue. Paramedics had got some dressings on to the victim in a vain effort to stop the bleeding and had managed to get a drip into his arm before he died. The dressings were so soaked in blood it was difficult to tell them apart from the charred clothes and the stained upholstery. The smells were of blood, faeces, urine and burnt flesh mingled with the aroma of spent gunpowder. The rain drummed harder on the polypropylene sky above. He looked closely at the dead man's grey face, smeared with his blood. The eyes were closed, the mouth wide open, showing much dental work. He knew little could be gained by this. There wasn't much he could glean from this carnage that the finely detailed reports he would soon receive couldn't tell him. Yet something compelled him to absorb fully the aftermath of what had occurred here. Somehow he felt more of an obligation to engage with this filthy corpse of an out-of-shape middle-aged man than he had felt towards the survivors of the first two blasts. He owed this man more than the others.

Austin had appeared behind him. He had taken one look at the carnage and since then studiously avoided the corpse. He felt guilty now, seeing what time the inspector took. But as far as he could tell, what had happened here was quite obvious.

Paramedics had crawled all over the front and back of the car, their uniforms more red than green when they finally gave up, no doubt giving Forensics a headache. They had found the shredded remains of a can of lager that had contained the device. The smell was gross. What was Liam studying so closely? 'Booby-trapped beer can. Found anything else?'

McLusky broke off his vigil. Failure is what he had seen. The picture of the dead man had imprinted itself on his retina. Perhaps they should allow the press in, allow the TV cameras close and make them transmit this on the news in fine detail. Could the bomber really have wanted this? Would the bomber look at this and think he had *done well*? Would he be shocked? Or was he too weird, too far gone to care? Perhaps it was a stupid question. People had been blowing each other up quite happily ever since explosives were invented. 'Has Denkhaus named a crime scene coordinator?'

'Yeah, me.'

'Right. No, I didn't see anything special. Just brewing up a good head of resentment. So, tell me about it.'

'Victim is a Frank Dudden, a small trader at St Nick's Market, sells T-shirts with your own designs printed on them, that kind of thing. Got thrown out of the pub because he could hardly stand up straight. We have an eyewitness for what happened next. The old boy who lives in . . . number fourteen, across there.' He indicated the little grey house across the street where every window was lit up. 'A Mr Belling. He keeps a diary of all the nuisance in his street so he can complain to the council about it. He heard shouting and came to the window. Saw the whole thing. '

'Right, let's talk to him.'

'He's already given us a statement. He saw the can of –'

'I want to hear it myself.' He marched off and Austin followed in his wake.

They found the front door ajar. McLusky announced himself. 'Hello, police. Can we come in?'

A man appeared at the end of the corridor. 'Oh yes, in here, if you will.'

They stepped into the brightly lit hall and squeezed past an electric bicycle to get to the back. The witness was at home to visitors in his kitchen. Mr Belling was a small wiry man in his late sixties. He wore a thin steel-grey sweater over a pink shirt and thin grey tie. His wrists were encircled by two wristwatches, one on each side.

PC Purkis was enjoying a mug of tea at the kitchen table and Mr Belling was glad of the policewoman's company. The thing had been quite a surprise. He also hadn't enjoyed this much attention since he broke his collarbone five years ago. And here were more people coming.

McLusky showed his ID and introduced Austin. They gratefully accepted the offer of refreshments.

Belling fussed over the tea for the newcomers and when everyone was settled around the table McLusky invited him to repeat what he had seen. Belling made himself comfortable on his chair. His was the one with the cushion. McLusky suspected that Mr Belling spent many hours sitting on that cushion, writing letters to the council in blue biro.

Belling took a sip of tea first. 'I had of course spotted the tin of lager on top of the car earlier but I had assumed it to be empty. These days people chuck their rubbish wherever they like. For instance, you are only supposed to put your bin bags out on a Tuesday but sure enough every week the people in number twenty . . .'

McLusky drank his tea and let the man get there in his own time. It was dry and warm in here.

'It was the shouting that made me look out this time. I was upstairs so I could clearly see him standing outside the pub, shouting. Well, I say standing but he was swaying. You could tell he was drunk, he had that leery kind of voice they get. Then he urinated right there outside the pub, between the cars, that's usually a good indication of drunkenness, I find. Then off he went, nearly fell over

142

twice before he made it to the car. I couldn't read the number plate, even with my binoculars, because of the angle. But I was going to call the police right away if he drove off, because he was obviously dangerously over the limit. He picked up the tin from the roof and I thought he was going to throw it away, which would have been typical of his kind, but he took it with him when he got in. I was waiting for him to start the engine but instead the car just exploded. Just like that. Bang. Except it didn't sound at all like it does on the radio, it sounded much nastier. All the windows blew out, stuff all over the place. It rattled my window and set off every damn car alarm in the neighbourhood. I called for an ambulance straight away, of course.'

McLusky thought he knew the answer but asked the question anyway. 'What did you do after that?'

'Well, I went back to the window, of course, to see what would happen next.'

'You didn't go outside to see if you could offer any assistance?'

'Go outside? A bomb had just gone off! I was hardly going to go where I could be blown up. Everyone in the street had to have heard it, some of them would go, no need for me to go outside.'

'Quite. Let's go back a little. You said you had noticed the can of beer on the car roof earlier. How much earlier?'

'Oh, now let me have a look in my journal. I keep a journal, you know, of all the happenings around here. You'd be surprised what goes on. It's upstairs, I'll fetch it down.' Belling disappeared.

The three police officers exchanged glances. Austin nodded ironically. 'Very organized.'

PC Purkis agreed in a low voice. 'Everything in this house is very proper and in its rightful place.'

McLusky looked around the kitchen. Everything was. Immaculately straight, spotlessly clean, nightmarishly tidy and neon-lit. He already knew the old man would tell him to within two decimal points what happened when. CCTV had nothing on Mr Belling.

He returned with a brightly coloured child's exercise book. 'Here, you see, I did note it down. I came to the window because number seventeen were having a fresh row, shouting at the top of their lungs as usual, but the tin wasn't there then. Then I came back to the window because the motorized skateboard was coming through again with that awful two-stroke noise.'

McLusky perked up. 'Motorized skateboard?'

'Yes, trailing blue smoke too, as if there wasn't enough pollution in this city, now they have to fit engines to their skateboards.'

'Do you think you could describe the skateboarder for us, Mr Belling?'

Mr Belling could. 'One of those chaps who dress like a child even though they are clearly over thirty. Spiky hair, you'd think they'd wear a helmet, wouldn't you, but I suspect that would spoil the image. He does have gloves and knee protectors. A red scarf and sunglasses, even when there is no sun, of course. Yes. Now ... 19.04 p.m., that's when I noticed the tin. And the explosion occurred at 20.15 exactly.'

It was exactly midnight when McLusky left Albany Road by taxi. The rain had stopped but the snakes of traffic hadn't. Hordes of young people, wearing surprisingly little considering the weather, were pressing through the narrow streets and alleys of the Old Town, shouting, some staggering, some drinking from cans and bottles. He spotted two teenage boys pissing side by side against a shop window, talking happily while the urine sloshed around their trainers. Flying insults, laughter, angry argument, excited howls. Twice the cab stopped for drunks swaying across the street, the driver muttering under his breath but

144

keeping his opinions to himself, for which McLusky was grateful.

Reams of statements had been taken during house-to-house inquiries and from the landlord and patrons of the George and Dragon. McLusky had spoken to the landlord himself. The man was visibly shaken by the death of Frank Dudden, who had been a regular. He had thrown him out that night 'for his own good' as he had believed. Now he felt that somehow he had sent him to his death and felt responsible. He had neither heard nor seen a motorized skateboarder, 'not today, not ever'. Not that kind of pub, he had assured him.

Belling's description matched exactly those of the residents of Berkeley Square and Charlotte Street who had been annoyed by a skateboarder prior to the first bomb in Brandon Hill. Could it be a coincidence? McLusky didn't like coincidences.

Only two other residents in the immediate area remembered the skateboarder but neither had seen or heard him recently. The proliferation of underpowered scooters howling up and down the streets probably meant that the sound was too unexceptional to be noticed around there.

A description had now been circulated force-wide and he was sure they would pick him up eventually. Was he the bomber? He'd certainly like a chance to ask him.

If the skateboarder was connected to the bombs then he wanted to be caught – why else make yourself conspicuous? – and McLusky would oblige. And when he caught up with the bastard he'd better be wearing his knee-pads.

Chapter Eight

McLusky had overruled Austin's decision to set up an incident room near the scene of the murder. Austin had tried to argue but McLusky was adamant. 'This won't be the last. The devices are going off at such close intervals we'll still be stuck out here in Knowle West when the next one blows.'

Secretly Austin had been relieved. There would have been very few facilities out there and setting up at Albany Road was always far easier and quicker. And closer to the canteen.

McLusky had been impressed by the speed with which things had materialized – tables, chairs, phones, terminals, printers, monitors, civilian IT staff, fax and kettle. It couldn't really be called 'well rehearsed'. The murder rate in the city was so high rehearsal was unnecessary. It was now simply routine.

This morning, as McLusky looked at the civilians and officers talking on phones or clacking away on grey, battered keyboards, he felt panic beginning to bubble on the floor of his stomach. But why? What was different this time? Precisely nothing apart from the fact that the victim had died. It would be no easier or harder getting a lead. Strikingly different was the effect the bomb had had on the media. The press was making much of beer, booze and bomb alliteration. The unusual packaging of the bombs had attracted the national press too. Everyday items like powder compacts and cans of lager were not supposed to explode. There was much speculation about the choice of item. The beer can was surely aimed at drunks and the powder compact at the vain. Yet the more intelligent writers did spot what McLusky had said from the start, that anyone might have picked the items up and become a victim. That didn't mean of course that there was no connection in the mind of the maniac behind the bombings.

He noticed several of the computer operators sit up straighter which meant Superintendent Denkhaus had once more appeared in the open door behind him. A desk facing away from the door had been a bad choice. The super appeared at his elbow and without comment added another national paper to the pile already there. He managed to see *Deadly Drink* in the headline before Denkhaus leant a fleshy hand on it and bent close to him. 'I'm giving a press conference at half eleven. Have you got any pearls for me that I can throw before the lions or are you sending me out there naked?'

A moment of metaphorical bafflement made McLusky hesitant. 'Ehm, no. I mean, nothing new since we last spoke, super. We have the skateboarder near two of the incidents but I'd rather you didn't use him to protect your modesty. So to speak. Just . . . following your metaphor, sir. I don't want him to know we are looking for him. He can easily unspike his hair and float the skateboard down the river.'

Denkhaus shrugged heavily. 'On the other hand someone must know who he is. If your friend or neighbour rode a skateboard with an engine on it you would know about it. We could be looking at an early arrest . . .'

'I doubt it, sir. The man's a loner. He makes bombs, so he's unlikely to sit on the pub quiz team. He's too busy hating someone, something. His neighbours might have no idea he's got a motorized skateboard. I imagine he takes it in the back of his car. He drives to a car park, puts on the gear and gets on the skateboard. Then off he goes. The

147

same in reverse. If he has a garage his neighbours might never know.'

'Someone will have seen him take the thing out and start it up.'

'Sure. It's what I'm hoping but I don't want to spook him. As long as he's using the skateboard he's conspicuous. I'll find him.'

Denkhaus didn't like the way McLusky said, 'I'll find him.' Police work was team work. He knew the McLusky type. They thought they'd invented detective work, thought that it was all down to them and that they could bend the rules. Cocky guys full of 'I' when the going was good. When it all came to nothing it was back to the collective 'we'. I succeed, we fail. 'Do you really think he could be our man?'

'He's all we've got at the moment.'

'You were quite sure about letting Colin Keale go. You don't want to pull him in again, apply a bit more pressure?'

'Not until we've exhausted everything else. Not until I'm getting desperate.'

'Don't worry, McLusky, I'll tell you when you're getting desperate.' Denkhaus straightened up and squinted at the window. Rain clouds hung low over the city. 'I hate going out there fielding questions without having anything positive to feed them. There's no progress on the muggings and no progress on the bomber. All the press are ever looking for is incompetence or negligence. They're forever trying to blame us for what's happening out there. In fact what gives the media the biggest hard-on is resignations, hounding someone until they are forced to resign. Makes them feel their crummy little lives are worth living. I'm already getting my ears chewed from upstairs about this. They're afraid the bomber might cause a panic. If people start panicking then we really aren't doing our job properly. What's happened to the spirit of the blitz? All it takes is one little . . .'

The phone on the desk rang. 'Excuse me, sir.' He answered it. It was Lynn Tiery, the superintendent's secretary. She had the Assistant Chief Constable's office on the line for Superintendent Denkhaus. 'It's the ACC for you.'

Denkhaus suppressed a groan. 'I'll take it in my office. Keep me informed. About every detail. Whether there's progress or not.'

When Denkhaus was out of earshot the civilian computer operator at the next desk looked up from the lists on his screen. 'No pressure then.'

'Not yet. Is it me or is it bloody freezing in here?'

A cheerful chorus answered his question. 'It's bloody freezing in here.'

'Can we do anything about that?'

'Nope. The heating shuts down automatically on this day every year irrespective of the actual temperature. Centrally managed. It would probably take an Act of Parliament to get it changed.'

'Marvellous.' If he had to be cold he'd rather be cold out there where he could do something useful. Footage from the car park where the compact was left was still being sifted. A check on all identified vehicles was being done. It would take time to cross-check if any of the registered owners had previous and those would end up on the top of the list to be interviewed about their movements. Endless man-hours. Of course it had to be done but McLusky was almost certain it was a waste of time. Unfortunately he had nothing rational to base this conviction on so could do little about it. What he could do was get out of here.

Damp humanity crowded the lobby. An entire minibusload of day-trippers were reporting all their possessions stolen, including their bus. A couple of pale, thin-haired teenage boys were being processed, the evidence of their thieving in a clear plastic bag on the desk: CDs and DVDs. They wore nothing more than jeans, T-shirts and trainers and looked like they'd swum there. The rain appeared to

149

do little to dampen the public's enthusiasm for mayhem. Theft, shoplifting, burglary and naturally all crime connected to drugs continued unabated. Domestic violence rose slightly. Only the figures for indecent exposure were significantly depressed by cold, wet weather.

McLusky turned on the windscreen wipers of the Polo. They were useless. It was even colder in the car. The lack of heating meant he had to drive with the window half open to stop the windscreen fogging up completely. He kept wiping a patch so he could peer through. The route to Forthbank Industrial Park in the east forced him to battle through some of the worst traffic snarls in the city. Wedged between two articulated lorries in his underpowered car and barely able to see through the spray kicked up by other vehicles he darkly pondered his transport problems. When the sign to the industrial park appeared out of the gloom he gratefully pulled off the busy A road and through the open gates. Among a monkey puzzle of signposts McLusky found what he was looking for.

The place looked like an enormous upturned mushroom punnet, appearing to have practically no windows, and advertised itself with three-foot comic-strip lettering above the entrance: Blackrock Sports Park. He was about to lock his car when he changed his mind, checked that the glove box was empty and left the Polo unlocked.

In the lobby he showed his ID to the man behind the counter. The receptionist looked about fourteen. 'Are you looking for someone?'

'Could be. This is a skateboard arena, right?'

'Skateboarding and rock climbing.'

'Do you ever get people with motorized skateboards here?'

The kid laughed. 'No fear. Total no-no. Anyway, they're crap.'

Perhaps he had better talk to a grown-up. 'I see. Who runs this place?'

'Spike.'

'Spike who?'

'*I* don't know, just Spike.' His tone suggested this was an unreasonable question.

'Is he in? Can I talk to him?'

'Sure, he's on the course. Through those doors and then the next. You can't miss him, no one else wears yellow after all.'

'Why's that?' McLusky suspected some arcane rule of skateboarding.

'Do you wear yellow much, inspector?'

He thought the kid might have a point. By the next set of double doors a sign instructed him to take off his street shoes before entering the echoing hall and he complied, carrying his shoes and feeling slightly ridiculous. The arena was an artificial landscape of ramps and pipes and rails, flights of steps and curves. It was a big place. He wouldn't have called it busy but it still surprised him how many people had time and money to skate around here on a weekday.

A spiky-haired man in what looked like a yellow romper suit made from shiny synthetics was chatting to a diminutive girl. When he spotted the unlikely-looking intruder he came rolling over, flipping up his board as he stopped in an automatic gesture. 'Help you?'

'McLusky, CID. I've already been told by your receptionist, no motorized skateboards here.'

'Certainly not. Why d'you ask? Someone making a nuisance of themselves?'

The place echoed to the sound of rubber wheels and grinding boards and the rain drumming on the giant roof. 'I'm looking for someone who rides one, he could be a witness. Spiked hair, skinny, same age as you perhaps, mid-to-late thirties. Wears denims, scarf, shades. He rides a skateboard with a little two-stroke engine and wire control.'

'Yup. It's for idiots. A gimmick. You won't find anyone using them here, that's for sure.'

'What, because of the noise or the pollution?'

'Nah, that's not the point. It's like bicycles and motor-bikes, right? It just don't mix. And you can't really do a thing with 'em.'

'So what do people do in here?'

'Well, as you can see, we've got the lot. You don't skate, I take it?'

'You're very astute.'

'You'd be surprised. We get all sorts here. Well, there's basically two types of skating, there's street skating and ramp skating. In street skating you could for instance jump up on a bus-stop seat or suchlike and do grinds and board slides, tail grinds and stuff. In half-pipe skating you go up and down the ramp and do tricks on the ledge. Over here we've got a couple of half-pipes, a jump ramp . . .'

The man got into the swing of it and McLusky let him carry on without really taking in much. Spike seemed to talk in a different language and each sentence contained at least three words that appeared to be English but which McLusky had never heard before.

At the opposite end of the hall a skater coasted quietly towards the exit. He didn't like the look of that man who had just come in. He had seen the suit show some kind of ID and somehow he didn't look like a health-and-safety guy. It might have nothing to do with him but he'd make himself scarce anyway. As he slipped through the doors while the copper's back was turned he thought that per-haps it was just as well they made you wear helmets in here. Spiky hair was too conspicuous. He'd change it, slick it back from now on. Not bothering to shower and change, he just cleared the things from the locker and went straight to his van. He stowed his gear in the back, next to his brand new motorized board, still in its box. Electric, rechargeable, much quieter and even faster than the two-stroke one. And environmentally much more sound, mustn't forget that, of course. Apparently it had a range big enough to get you right across the city. He saw himself skating silently, magically, across town. *Stealthboard*. But first it needed to be charged. Then he could use it tomorrow night.

The Polo was still there. Ah well, give it time. Somehow the musty interior managed to feel colder than the outside. What McLusky had learned from Spike seemed to fit with what he himself thought of the bomber. A motorized skateboard was regarded as uncool and according to Spike you 'couldn't do a thing with it'. No tricks. Whoever the skater was he wouldn't be hanging out with kids at the half-pipes in the park. Motorized skateboards were for nerds and dweebs. For loners. Spike had in fact suggested that anyone using one might be more interested in fiddling with small engines than skating. Someone with engineering skills.

While he fought his way back towards the centre through lunchtime traffic the rain began to fall more slowly — and then abruptly stopped as the sun broke through the clouds. After weeks of relentless rain and monochrome dreariness the brightness of the light seemed Mediterranean in its intensity. Colour returned to the city and patches of blue sky were reflected in the long kerbside puddles. All this light made McLusky hungry.

The Albany Road canteen served a type of food specially designed to minimize the chances of police officers enjoying their pensions for too long. The chip-fat and wrinkly-sausage smells that pervaded the neon-lit basement cavern reminded him of school dinners, as did the hubbub of voices albeit an octave or two lower now. Standing in the queue behind a young constable with unusual BO he surreptitiously surveyed the room, conscious that as the new kid on the block some diners would be checking him over. He spotted DI Fairfield sitting by herself and decided to join her. Things had been so hectic there had never been time to get really acquainted.

153

When it was his turn there was little left to choose from in the beige-and-brown section under the heat lamps. Something called 'cauliflower bake' looked the least lethal. As he carried his food on a tray in the direction of Kat Fairfield the DI looked up. Spotting him she drained her glass of water and, leaving her tray on the table, made for the exit on a tortuous route specially chosen to avoid him.

Someone waving attracted his attention. It was Austin, also sitting by himself in front of a mug of stewed canteen coffee. The DS shrugged his shoulders. 'I wouldn't take it to heart. I'm certain DI Fairfield is a great admirer of yours, she's just shy and retiring.'

'I'm sure.' He drove his fork through the dried crust of industrial cheddar into the anaemic concoction beneath and faltered. 'Is today a special occasion or is the food always crap?'

Austin waggled his head. 'It's a bit late, the best stuff disappears quickly. The food's not so bad as long as you strictly avoid anything with "bake" in its name.'

'Ah.' McLusky put his fork down and pushed his plate aside. 'Thanks for the warning. I take it nothing's come up to get us any further in the Frank Dudden murder?'

'Not really. Did you go out to the skating park?'

'Yup, nothing. I was given the impression that no one would admit to owning a motorized board anyway, if they ever came there at all, and the description didn't seem to ring a bell.'

'Well, after what the old guy said about the skateboarder I had a look at the map. Around the harbour basin, the Floating Harbour and out Ashton way are tarmac paths he could use. There's also the cycle paths. One cycle track runs from here all the way to Bath along the river. He could be running around on that.'

'Do a lot of people use that path?'

'No one with any sense. We had loads of problems along that path. People got kicked off their bikes left right and centre. They'd rob them, take their bikes and then ride off on them.'

'Why don't they close the paths then?'

'I wish they would. Unfortunately you can get a lottery grant for making cycle paths but not for getting rid of them. It's anarchy down there. It's where St Paul's kids take their stolen mopeds to ride and the glue-sniffers hang out there. Closer to the access points you get the prozzies using it if it isn't raining. We had people grow cannabis on the verges. Last year one guy tested his home-made jet-engine down there. Strapped it to an old children's go-cart. Hadn't thought of fitting brakes. He fell off and the jet went on and set fire to everything it passed. It's pretty much nutter country so our skateboarder should fit right in. We have stepped up patrols.'

'I'll check the place out.'

'*Don't go alone after dark* is my firm advice. Oh yes, I was told to remind you about Frank Dudden's autopsy.'

'What time is that?'

Austin checked his watch. 'In about fifteen minutes, actually.'

'Then what are you sitting around here for? Get going, DS Austin.'

Austin's face fell. 'Me? I thought you ... Oh, right. Okay.' He took a gulp of his coffee and rushed off, clearly indignant.

McLusky reached for Austin's abandoned mug. If police work were a popularity contest he'd never get anything done. He sipped the coffee. It tasted appalling and he knew it would give him heartburn. As a kind of penance he drained the mug anyway.

Five hours later the heartburn was still with him as he wrestled with paperwork at his desk. Whatever had happened to 'freeing front-line officers from unnecessary red tape'?

Not even a nano-second passed from the perfunctory knock to his office door opening. Denkhaus, back from the press conference, filled the frame.

'Where the hell is that report on the written-off Skoda? The ACC is asking. And as if I didn't have enough to contend with, Phil Warren needled me about that very escapade at the press conference.'

'Who?'

'Reporter on the *Post*. Never mind that, where's the damn report? I thought I'd asked for that days ago!'

'And I went straight to work on it but I kept getting distracted by the noise of explosions.'

'Don't get distracted, McLusky. If I ask for something I expect DIs to deliver.'

McLusky nodded his head at the computer screen in front of him. 'I'm actually working on it right now. Nearly done.'

For a moment it seemed as though the superintendent was going to walk around the desk to take a look at it. Had he done so he'd have found that McLusky was frowning at a fish-tank screensaver with the bubbling sound turned off.

But Denkhaus just grunted. So far he was singularly unimpressed by the new DI. He sniffed the air. 'Has someone been smoking in here? You realize the entire station is a no-smoking zone?'

McLusky made a show of sniffing and nodded. 'This office always smells of smoke. My predecessor must have smoked heavily.'

'That he did.'

'The smell got into the furnishings.'

Denkhaus seemed satisfied with the explanation. He gave a curt nod with his chin towards the computer. 'Get on with it. I'll be in my office. *Waiting*.' He closed the door heavily behind him.

McLusky breathed a sigh of relief when he heard Denkhaus in the corridor bark at his next victim.

Around four o'clock Austin returned from witnessing the autopsy. As it turned out it had been his first and he hadn't enjoyed it much. He had been berated by Dr Coulthard for being late. The pathologist had been expecting a DI and showed his displeasure by treating Austin as though he suspected the DS had suffered brain damage on the way to the morgue. Even though the viewing area was separated from the theatre by a glass wall and he had been spared the smell of the mutilated corpse, Austin had felt his stomach churn. The pathologist dug up no surprises. He pronounced that in life Dudden had been a slightly overweight middle-aged man with a troubled liver and straining kidneys who, had he not picked up a booby-'trapped beer can, might have had another ten years' drinking in him before his own internal time bomb put an end to it. Austin reported to McLusky in short sentences then quickly disappeared to the incident room.

To McLusky it only confirmed his belief that going to autopsies was a waste of time and put one in a bad mood for the rest of the day. 'I wonder who else I can piss off on this shift.' He pushed the other bumf aside and pulled his keyboard towards him. *How I destroyed a good-as-new Skoda fifteen minutes after it was issued to me and how it was unavoidable by Detective Inspector Liam McLusky. . .*

When after one hour and three drafts he eventually brought the sober report to Denkhaus's office Lynn Tiery, his steel-eyed secretary, knew all about it.

'Ah yes, the super's been waiting for this.' She put it on a pile of papers on her desk and went back to clacking on her keyboard.

'You'd better take it in to him then.'

She smiled up at him without slowing her typing. 'No rush, the super went home an hour ago.'

While McLusky had been buried under his fast-accumulating paperwork the return of the sun had worked a transformation on the city. The late sunshine softened the architecture. People looked brighter, happier, moving more slowly. As he walked along Albany Road he caught a glimpse of the old harbour between two buildings. A tall ship was moored down there and the old harbour ferry chugged across the brightly mirrored water. The footbridge looked like a spindly limb in black silhouette against the sun. In this light the sprawl of the city felt mysterious to him, so large, full of the unknown, full of new people, the promise of a new life. For a brief moment he was visited by a feeling he had last experienced as he first arrived by train in Southampton. Then he had looked across the busy harbour and thought the place must contain everything a man could possibly want from life. Now he snatched at the feeling, wanting to own it again, but it escaped him like the tail end of a dream. He blinked it away and walked on. It was of course all an illusion, there was nothing mysterious about cities. With all those people climbing over each other like so many ants the only mystery was why the pavements were not stained with blood more often.

A few turns left and right brought him to Candlewick Lane. He stopped opposite the Green Man. It was a CID pub and he should go and make himself known, drink, socialize, talk shop. Not tonight. There was plenty of time for that, preferably with Austin in tow and when he was in an indestructibly good mood. Tonight all he wanted was a quiet pint. Or perhaps more than one. He turned down several steep flights of uneven medieval steps between narrow timber-frame houses, getting into a rhythm and letting his feet make all the choices. It brought him close to the harbour on Ropemakers, a surprisingly quiet one-way street with cars parked on either side. Just as he scanned its low brick buildings the sun dipped behind clouds and the lights of a pub sprang to life. The illuminated pub sign proclaimed this to be the Quiet Lady, above the picture of a woman in a yellow dress carrying her own head under her arm. Inside, it was an unreconstructed drinking hole, just the way McLusky liked it.

'Have you got a garden or somewhere I can smoke?'

The landlord set a carefully poured pint of Murphy's before him. 'Upstairs. The room marked Private. You can kill yourself there.'

'Ta.'

Everything about the room was small. A couple of logs smouldered in a tiny grate, rickety tables for two stood in front of three slits of windows and a skinny bench opposite the fire completed the furnishings. The room was empty. Just what the inspector had ordered. Sitting by the window closest to the fire he drank and smoked. Below him lay the warren of the Old Town and beyond that the harbour basin. The sun soon set over the wasteland on the opposite shore, briefly throwing disused loading cranes and a few surviving structures into silhouette against the sky.

Somewhere out there the next episode was being planned. Somewhere out there a man, surely a man, was dribbling gunpowder into a harmless object, turning it lethal. Out there his next victim walked unawares. Unless . . .

Footsteps outside, then the door opened. The invasion force consisted of just one woman in her forties. She was carrying a drink in a tall glass and lit a long cigarette already dangling from her lips. Her hair looked an unlikely shade of brown and was held in a tight twist at the back of her head. She acknowledged him with a nod and sat facing the window at the next but one table, sucking greedily at her cigarette. 'Can't smoke at work, can't smoke on the bus, can't smoke in the bloody bar. This country is beginning to piss me off.' She spoke not to him but at the window in a hoarse, aggrieved voice.

McLusky nodded and lit another cigarette himself.

After a minute's silence she turned to him. 'What about the bloody bombs then? Did you hear the copper on the telly? We're all supposed to go about our business and stay calm but vigilant. They'll ask us to dig for victory next.' She snorted smoke through her nostrils.

That sounded like Superintendent Denkhaus had been rolling out the spirit-of-the-blitz platitudes. But what else could he have said to them? He nodded in agreement. 'Yes, I wouldn't go around picking up things off the street. Gold compact, can of beer or whatever. God knows what'll blow up next.'

'It's human nature though, isn't it, you find something interesting, you wouldn't just leave it. You don't look at a can of beer and think, That could blow my hand off, do you?'

'Perhaps people should from now on.' Of course a lot depended on where you found the thing. Unless . . .

She took a long gulp from her glass. 'Now tell me this, though. What's the motive? Who's behind it? What kind of person does such a thing?'

He shrugged. 'A coward. Also someone quite mad. It doesn't look political so I guess it's personal. Psychotic bastard would be my guess.'

'D'you think they'll get him? Any time soon?'

'I doubt it.' He realized that he very much meant it. 'He'll be difficult to find. He might be living quite a normal life otherwise. People compartmentalize their minds. When he's not making bombs he's probably Mr Boring of Sleepy Street and kind to birds.'

McLusky didn't really feel like talking. When the table between them was taken he took the opportunity to leave the room. He drank another pint downstairs where the place had filled up, mainly with men drinking in groups or by themselves. He wondered whether the name of the pub kept most women away.

By the time he made it back to the Albany Road car park he reckoned he had worked off a sufficient amount of alcohol to drive home. Via another drink at the Barge Inn.

* * *

Chris Reed pushed his bicycle along the sparsely lit street in Redland. It was an excellent district for his purpose. It was middle class but not too posh. In some middle-class areas all the 4×4s were in the garages and only the second cars left on the streets. But the tarted-up terraces in this street had no garages and the agricultural machinery was parked where he could get at it.

Earlier he had visited the covered market at closing time and had stocked up on all the fruit they were going to throw away at the end of the day. What a waste. Just because they were bruised or a bit past it they were going to chuck it, as if there weren't enough poor people in this town who would appreciate it. He had come away with a good haul, apples and oranges mainly but also an overripe pineapple. He kept that and a couple of apples for eating, the rest he was using for his new double-whammy. Every 4×4 got the exhaust blocked with fruit and the windscreen splattered with mud. The leaflet – *If the off-roader won't go to the country then the country will come to the off-roader* – went under the windscreen. First they would have to read his leaflet, clean the mud off, then they'd find that their engine wouldn't start. They'd get the message. And the windscreens weren't easy to clean either. This wasn't just any old mud. He got it from a special place near the Floating Harbour. It was dark, sticky and slimy from decades of spilled oil from a refuelling point for boats and barges. The reservoir on his bicycle was nearly empty but there really wasn't any point in using the mud sparingly. The mud had to represent a real inconvenience for the drivers, not a symbolic one. He'd get some more of the stuff some night soon. He didn't need any help. Sod Vicky. You couldn't rely on others. He'd work by himself from now on.

A black Mercedes four-wheel-drive gleamed. It was parked in the pool of light from a streetlamp, which wasn't good but the car was so shiny it was practically screaming out for the treatment. Putting the bike on its side-stand he took a half-rotten orange from the left pannier and rammed it expertly up the car's exhaust. The second pannier held two containers made from sawn-off petrol cans. The mud really was nearly finished yet he managed to scrape together one more ladleful. The splat across the windscreen was also expertly executed, without getting a single drop on his clothes. As he reached for the leaflet in his jacket the door of the nearest house opened. From it a man came charging towards him, swinging a walking stick like a weapon. 'What the fuck are you doing to my car?'

Chris jumped on his bike and pedalled off furiously while the man gave chase. Christ, he looked quite fit, if he caught up he'd be in trouble. The road climbed uphill here and it was difficult to get any speed up on this boneshaker, another skip-find. At last he was pulling away from his panting pursuer. 'Just delivering an important message!' He shouted it across his shoulder when he was sure he was getting away. The man issued a stream of insults that echoed along the street, then he hurled the walking stick after him. It fell short.

When he reached the safety of the next street corner and realized he had lost his pursuer Chris laughed. It was the laughter of relief. He'd have to be more careful from now on, or his one-man campaign could easily come to a premature end.

McLusky left the Polo unlocked at the first parking space he found and walked briskly down to the Barge Inn. Another couple of drinks would see the day out in agreeable enough fashion. It was Rebecca's night off. The pub was busy but he found a stool at the corner of the bar and was soon sipping a pint of Guinness served by the bald landlord. He found it difficult not to think about his work. It was his case and he was responsible. There would be another bomb, therefore he was already responsible for the next victim because it was up to him to stop the bombs. But you couldn't work twenty-four hours a day, even though it felt like you were. Especially at the very beginning of a murder investigation there was pressure to work non-stop for the first forty-eight hours which is when a result was most likely. Of course most murders were committed by the victim's nearest and dearest or by rival criminals, so you had a pretty good idea of who to look for to begin with. Not here, not this time.

He suddenly felt ravenous and ordered a double portion of chips from the landlord. It arrived together with another pint and a hefty bottle of ketchup. He was warming to this pub. As he glugged ketchup over his chips a group of men detached themselves from the bar and headed for the exit. Through the gap they had left he spotted Rebecca. He could tell it was her day off since she was wearing her paint-spattered multi-coloured art student gear. She sat very close to a boy of about nineteen or twenty, their legs entwined, hands on each other's thighs while they talked. When the girl looked up her eyes met McLusky's. She acknowledged him with a brief smile and a nod. Then she bent to the boy's ear and spoke a few words. The boy laughed.

'That's a lot of ketchup, my friend.' The landlord blocked his view. 'Might have to start charging extra.'

McLusky looked down. His chips had drowned in a red sea of sauce. He suddenly felt tired and no longer hungry. While the landlord collected glasses behind him he picked up his pint, hid it under his jacket and stole out of the front door. He would drink it at his place and bring the glass back some time. As he crossed Northmoor Street furtling for his keys a sudden movement in his peripheral vision made him look right. Nothing. Yet his mind filled in the blanks and furnished him with an after-image of a figure standing by the corner, now vanished. He wanted to run to the corner but was hampered by the pint he was carrying. By the time he had speed-walked there and looked down the road there was nothing suspicious to see, a few cars, a few people walking. Nobody he recognized.

163

Chapter Nine

'With respect, sir, since I can't go anywhere near Ady Mitchell I might not be the best officer to work on the muggings.' DI Fairfield sat very upright in front of Denkhaus's desk. From somewhere she found the strength to control her expression and keep her voice calm. Any betrayal of emotion, any sign of anger, and the superintendent would put it down as hormonal. In this environment a woman had to be careful not to react in any way that could be construed as 'typically female'. If you could make people forget you were a woman, if you made them believe you were one of the lads, then you would be taken seriously and get ahead.

'Nonsense, Fairfield, you have it back-to-front. We found no evidence that Mitchell is dealing in stolen goods. These days you can make a fortune selling crap to morons on eBay without having to break the law. You had a shot at him and nothing turned up. Now concentrate on the guys who are doing the actual mugging. Because in the absence of any evidence –'

'Mitchell does have –'

'Please don't interrupt me, DI Fairfield. If you know what's good for your career then you'll leave Mitchell out of it and catch the scooter gang, preferably red-handed. Because that's the kind of headline the force needs right now. That's what you'll concentrate on, Fairfield.'

'We've simply been unlucky, sir.'

'Since when does intelligence-based policing rely on

luck? Our statistics prove that whenever resources are targeted in the correct . . .'

Fairfield just nodded and nodded. She would never convince the super. He had already told her she had to make do with the resources she had, which was basically DS Sorbie, since everyone was working on the beer-can murder or buried deep under their own caseload. The quicker she agreed to everything the sooner she'd be out of his office. To make matters worse she had heard this morning that DCI Gaunt wasn't coming back for at least another fortnight. The chief inspector would surely have backed her up and shielded her from this continuous pressure from the super.

'. . . and we simply have to learn to live with it.'

It sounded as though Denkhaus had talked himself to the end of a treatise. Quick, before he jumped on the next passing hobby horse. 'Yes, sir, of course. Will that be all, sir?'

Denkhaus supposed it was. Fairfield had to learn to be flexible and get results with the resources available. She was too ambitious and so took things personally. 'Yes, that's all.'

Fairfield left the super's office with as much grace as she could muster and closed the door with exaggerated care. Ten minutes later she was in her office, sipping the blackest espresso from the tiniest cup. As the bitter fragrant liquid revived her spirits she managed to raise the ghost of a smile. One day she would sit where Denkhaus was now and all this would be nothing but a footnote in the ancient history of drudge.

McLusky hammered away at his keyboard while issuing sporadic bulletins of bitching that others had already learned didn't want answering. 'Of course one good reason for having an incident room in the first place is that without it the amount of *useless misleading dead-end crap information* murder generates would bury a detective and his desk so deep in dross you'd have to get a dog team in to dig him out . . .'

At a desk opposite him Austin had another crank caller on the phone, the third one so far to claim responsibility for the beer-can device. 'And you packed it with TNT you bought over the interweb?' There was stifled laughter among the computer operators.

McLusky wasn't in the mood. Austin had been talking to the moron for ages. 'Get rid of the wanker.'

Austin covered his mouthpiece. 'No, this one's a special wanker, he's calling from a landline. It's an address in town so I've sent a note down to Uniform, they're on their way there to read him the riot act.' He uncovered the mouthpiece. 'Is that your door bell I can hear, sir? I think you'd better answer it. There'll be a couple of officers there to explain the meaning of *wasting police time*, okay? And the same to you, sir.' He returned the receiver to its cradle with a flourish. 'This call has been recorded for training purposes. Right, what's next?' He pulled a file off the pile beside him and started flicking through witness statements, or *witless statements* as he liked to think of them. And if he ever found the microsoftie behind the phrase 'paperless office' he'd add 'justifiable homicide' to the man's vocabulary.

McLusky had had enough and logged off. There was a whole world of madness waiting for him outside, with spring sunshine to go with it. He would walk. It was Saturday and nearly lunchtime. The Saturday Traffic Protest should still be going and he wanted to see for himself what it looked like.

Every Saturday, to maximize attendance and optimize disruption, protesters met on the Cathedral Green before spreading out into the traffic arteries near the council offices and around the harbour. Every Saturday the place came to a virtual standstill. From where he was walking now he could see that traffic across the Old Town was hardly moving at all. Most drivers sat talking on the phone or fiddling with their sat navs and radios: there was little else they could do. In this otherwise picturesque one-way street, he came across a new development. Traffic here hadn't moved for a while. The narrow street was solid with stationary vehicles. One driver of an ancient Fiat had got out of his car in front of a café with small tables on the pavement. He was now sipping coffee in comfort and nibbling on a biscuit. Since then traffic in front of his car had moved by a couple of car-lengths before grinding to a complete halt again. It was enough to get the drivers who were waiting behind his car agitated. A uniformed police officer was engaged in an argument with the man at the café table. As McLusky passed the scene the officer stopped him. It was lanky Constable Pym. 'Ah, Inspector McLusky, I'm glad it's you, sir.'

To McLusky this was such an unusual sentiment that his face expressed severe doubt. 'What is it, Pym?'

'We got a call from one of the drivers behind here, the second one along, I think. You see, sir, this gentleman here is the driver of that Fiat, which he simply abandoned in the street.'

The driver, a hungover-looking man in his thirties, shook his head. 'I have not abandoned it. The keys are in the ignition and it's unlocked and I'm having a coffee. Look, it's gridlock, or as near as. I forgot it was Saturday or I wouldn't have come into town at all, it's always like this.'

'I've been trying to tell the gentleman that it is a violation of the highway code to leave a vehicle unattended in a place where it is likely. . .'

The man raised a hand in protest. 'It's not unattended, I'm right here, I'm attending it, but I'm *attending it while drinking coffee.*' He demonstrated this by taking a sip of frothy coffee and fixing his eyes on his car.

Pym scratched his neck with the pen from his notebook and turned to McLusky. 'You see, sir, the problem is, if he refuses to go back to his vehicle I'll have to arrest him but if I arrest him who's going to move his car?'

'Arrest him? I'm not sure you can force people to sit in their vehicles, unless they're actually in motion. At least I think so, though don't quote me on that. Well, I mean look at it . . .' He swept an arm in the direction of the cars stacked up the hill. 'Nothing's moving, and somehow you'd think they'd turn their engines off . . .'

Somewhere in the queue someone gave an impatient blast of the horn. Several others joined in for a short concert. A shout of 'Get a fucking move on' came from somewhere. McLusky turned to the owner of the Fiat. 'Is that cappuccino you're drinking, sir?'

'So?'

'Is it any good?'

'It's not brilliant but okay, I guess. You do get a biscuit with it.'

'Amaretti?'

'I think that's what they're called. Has a sort of almond taste. You could always ask the waitress.'

Constable Pym couldn't believe his ears. Out there a riot was brewing and the inspector was discussing the quality of coffee.

McLusky noted the name of the café, Carlotta's. 'Well, finish your cappuccino by all means, sir, but after that pull your car forward. With any luck there might be another café further along.'

The man grinned. 'Yeah, there is actually. Okay then.'

McLusky widened his eyes at Constable Pym: and where was the problem?

'But, sir, we might get a public order situation in a minute.' He nodded the back of his head at the snarled-up traffic.

'No we won't, 'cos you're here. Talk to them. Have a chat. But don't let them pee in your helmet, however desperate. You'll be fine.' He moved on.

168

Pym watched him saunter down the road. *McLusky*. Where on earth did they find *him*?

Wherever McLusky went it was all the same: traffic crawling or stationary, and short-tempered drivers using their horns with un-British frequency and ferocity. Cyclists still squeezed through some streets, many no doubt feeling that their day had come, and pedestrians walked freely between the cars and into the path of the unexpected cyclists. He followed the fingerposts towards the cathedral, through narrow alleys and down uneven flights of steps, and soon got to the heart of the chaos. He stopped next to a grey-haired sergeant from Traffic who was standing in his viz jacket by his car parked on the broad pavement. Showing his ID, McLusky explained that he was new in town and they both watched the spectacle for a while.

It had the air of a carnival. Many of the protesters had dressed up in bright costume; a great number of them wore dust masks or gas masks. Whistle-blowing and drumming syncopated the slow march. There was a surprising number of elderly people too. A few children, some wearing Hallowe'en death masks, were being pulled along in soap-box-and-pram-wheel carts shaped and painted to look like coffins.

The earlier protest marches along the main arteries had been judged illegal because of their disruptive quality and the damage done to city centre businesses. These new tactics by the protesters were simple but just as effective. Strings of protesters simply crossed and recrossed strategically chosen streets at the centre of the traffic system in a continuous loop. The zebra crossings they had chosen were all within sight of each other. Many protesters worked the pavements too, giving out leaflets to pedestrians. The braver ones stuck them on windscreens.

'Looks like we have all types of people here.'

'Yes, it's quite a disparate group, concerned citizens as well as the usual lot. There's a few students, cycling clubs, Green Party activists, Friends of the Earth, old hippies, skip

169

divers, concerned citizens. Not so many parents of school-age kids of course.'

'Why's that?'

'They're mainly the ones in the cars, sir. Everyone thinks it's the other people who should drive less.'

According to the sergeant there was nothing they could do about the zebra crossings. In fact police were now employed in stopping irate car drivers from trying to simply barge their way through the crossing protesters. 'Clever and simple. But we're not so worried about the fact that the traffic comes to a standstill, that's a matter for the council to address. Because frankly, a few more cars and you won't need a protest march to have gridlock on a regular basis. We had real gridlock once already, one Saturday, last year. We analysed it. All it took was the crowds from the kite festival trying to get home, a drunken fight in the middle of Park Street, a broken-down tourist bus just over there,' he pointed to the junction, 'and an abnormally wide load arriving from the motorway, delivering a boat. Oh yes, and some big football game on telly so the pubs were filling up. For several hours nothing much moved. You couldn't get emergency vehicles anywhere. Even the motorcycle ambulance came a cropper. One arsonist could have levelled the town centre, we'd have needed bucket chains to put it out.'

McLusky stepped into the road and picked up a couple of discarded flyers. One had the picture of a dog wearing a gas mask on it – an image he seemed to remember from a book about the blitz – and carried stark warnings about the health impact of car fumes, especially on children. The second flyer concentrated on the contribution of car traffic to global warming.

'These aren't the ones we're worried about, sir. I have two children myself and my youngest has asthma. They have a point about the pollution.' He reached into the car and took out a blue folder, flicking it open. 'But these have started appearing now.' The leaflet in the clear plastic sleeve was simply produced on a computer's printer and exhorted in large letters: HELP SAVE THE CITY, DISABLE A CAR TODAY. 'That's clearly going beyond legitimate protest. We're trying to catch who's been distributing them but we're too late for today, I think. We do video the protests of course but we're not exactly MI5, our cameras can't tell one flyer from another.'

'Is there any indication that people might follow this advice?'

'There is indeed. Nothing too drastic as yet, just a spate of motorists finding all their tyres let down. Sometimes it's a whole street and of course nobody's got four spares so it is quite effective that, if you want to stop people from driving. Then there's that nutter sticking fruit up people's exhausts and splattering mud all over 4×4s.'

'Yeah, I heard about that. Our super's had his 4×4 treated thus twice.'

The officer's face briefly brightened. 'Denkhaus? I'm not saying a word. But the mud they use is very dark and sticky. We were wondering if perhaps we could get the mud analysed. Maybe if we knew where it came from we might be able to catch the little toerag.'

McLusky sadly shook his head. 'Not a snowball's. Oh, you can try sending in a sample, only by the time it comes back from Chepstow the internal combustion engine will be a distant memory. You'd have a better chance with a poster saying *Have You Seen This Mud?*'

'That bad, is it?'

'Even if you're investigating murder.' Unless . . . Perhaps mud was the answer. Perhaps mud was just what he needed. 'Tell you what, though. I do know a chemist at the uni who might take a look at it. I can't promise anything, of course.' He gave a prolonged shrug. 'But it might be worth a try.' It might be a good excuse to see Dr Louise Rennie again.

Now the officer had visibly brightened up. It wasn't every day a CID officer took an interest when he didn't have to. 'Really? That's very . . . that would be good, yes. Where . . .?'

'I'm working out of Albany Road. Send the sample direct to me, McLusky.'

As he walked on he spotted one of the offensive leaflets on the pavement and picked it up. *Disable a car today*. It had a clean logic to it. Stop the car and you stop the pollution. As he climbed back up the streets towards Albany Road he got a good view of part of the city centre around the cathedral, the council offices and the enormous Marriott Royal Hotel, the streets all around solid with cars. It looked like madness. All these people surrounded by painted metal, going nowhere.

One man's misfortune, of course, was another man's opportunity. Shoplifting and other petty crime had risen dramatically on Saturdays because the thieves knew police cars were practically grounded during the protests. Foot patrols had been stepped up. Bicycles had been issued to several fit constables to respond in a traditional, low-tech way. They were a hit with the public and had produced some arrests as well as sprained wrists and ankles and in one case concussion.

If only he could take a good look at his own case from a great height too, perhaps he'd be able to see what kind of madness lurked in there. He turned into the still-stagnant one-way street with the intention of trying the cappuccino at Carlotta's, perhaps get a bite to eat too. For some reason he had felt perpetually hungry ever since coming to this town. When he got there he was drawn further along by the french-fry-and-ale aroma emanating from the Neptune Inn a few doors along.

The interior design leant heavily on the pub's name, with tridents, bladder wrack seaweed and fishing nets on the ceiling. The blackboard menu included several fish dishes to keep up the theme and he ordered the simplest-sounding one, with an extra portion of chips and a pint of Guinness. The food arrived by the time he had half-drained his pint. When his mobile chimed with the sober factory-setting ring tone he recognized the caller as DS Austin. A premonition made him stuff his mouth with chips before he answered it. 'Mn-nn?'

'Liam, it's Jane. Where are you?'

McLusky swallowed. 'Lunch.' He broke up some of the fish with his fork. 'Where's the fire?' He quickly shovelled as much fish, chips and peas into his mouth as was feasible. From across the pub the barmaid eyed him with disgust: that man in the leather jacket ate like a pig while talking on the phone.

'You'll be lunch if the super is to be believed. And the fire will be under your posterior if you don't get it over here quickly.'

'What's it about?'

'Can't talk, just get here.'

'On my way.' He pocketed the mobile and looked at his barely touched food. Five minutes wouldn't make any difference, would it? Perhaps it would, Austin had sounded worried. One more mouthful and he was on his way. He couldn't even use the traffic as an excuse, the Polo had been sitting in plain view in the station car park all the while.

At Albany Road he caught the atmosphere at once. Everyone in the incident room tried to look heads-down busy. He was hoping Jane would fill him in but all DS Austin managed was to wave a newspaper from across the incident room before Denkhaus darkened the door and growled, 'McLusky, my office, now.' As the super turned away Austin held up the early edition of the *Post* so he could read the headline: PSYCHOTIC BASTARD.

He shrugged his shoulders. Who, me? As he walked past the CID room Sorbie's smile followed him down the corridor. Another nail in the man's coffin.

Denkhaus had left his door ajar. Lynn Tiery, his secretary, arched her eyebrows and puckered her lips but didn't look up.

McLusky slid into the superintendent's office and closed the door behind him. He remained standing and wasn't invited to sit. Denkhaus slapped a copy of the *Post* across the desk, then slammed his open hand on the front page and began bellowing. 'Have you lost your mind, McLusky? How dare you talk to the press without authorization? Since when do junior officers give interviews? What do you think the bloody press office is for?'

'I'm really not sure what this is about. I didn't talk to the press and I gave no interviews. Can I have a look?'

Denkhaus put an unpleasant smile on his fleshy face. 'You haven't seen the *Post*? Then by all means borrow my copy, DI McLusky.'

He picked it up and read while Denkhaus impatiently quoted bits at him from memory. 'Police have branded bomber a psychotic bastard! We are looking for a coward! Investigating officer *doubts bomber will be caught any time soon*! God knows what will blow up next!'

An evil feeling stole into his stomach which had nothing to do with lack of food. He recognized his own thoughts but how ...? Then it came to him. The chain-smoking woman upstairs at the Quiet Lady. 'I didn't know she was a journalist, sir. Just a chat with someone over a pint.'

Denkhaus thumped the top of the paper. 'Phil Warren, that's who she was.' That's what came from letting brand-new DIs loose when they didn't know their way around town yet. He blamed himself. But McLusky should have had more sense than to express his opinions to a civilian like that. 'It was underhand bloody tactics from Phil, which you should always expect from her. Of course we'll make an official complaint but the damage is done now. The phones have been running hot. McLusky, you just can't go and tell a civilian you think it'll take a long time to catch this bastard. What's the point of me giving press conferences, reassuring the public and managing the press if you shoot your mouth off in the pub? Were you drunk?'

'No, sir, I don't have that excuse.'

'You think I'd accept drunkenness as an excuse? Don't make things worse. You're not endearing yourself to me, *detective inspector*. What's more, did you mean it? Are you going to tell *me* you don't think we'll apprehend him any time soon?'

'I'm not sure, sir. If the bomber turns out to be our skateboarder then we might wrap it up soon. But I have my doubts. In the absence of useful DNA or witnesses we'll be hard pushed to make an early arrest. If the devices aren't targeted, if they're just left lying about, then the usual connection between victim and perpetrator isn't there to tell us anything. Needless to say I have every confidence in the team. Jane, James Austin, I mean, is a first-rate detective.'

'I know. But are you, McLusky?' Denkhaus swivelled his chair and looked out over the city, hazy with pollution. There was no point giving the case to someone else, it would simply set the investigation back and if the papers got wind of it they would try and make something of it. McLusky would have to do for now. But he would have to do better. 'I expect results. I want to see you making progress on tracking this guy. What do Forensics have to say?'

'Very little, sir. Home-made devices, commercial gunpowder extracted from fireworks. There's no report on the beer can yet but the preliminary report on the powder compact said it also contained a proportion of magnesium, which burns with a bright, intensely hot flame. That's what did the damage there. All the ingredients, everything about the devices is freely available to anyone, though we are checking with suppliers of course.'

'And no useful DNA?'

'None at all, sir. If there ever was any, then it was destroyed when the devices went up.'

The faint cries of gulls penetrated through the glass along with the sound of car horns. Denkhaus nodded sagely. *Destroyed*. That reminded him. One thing he had to give McLusky: he wrote a good report. His account of how

175

he had used the plain unit against the digger so he could get the woman out of the house read very well. It was bound to be pure fabrication but the ACC would be satisfied with it and that's what really mattered. 'Right.' He swivelled round to face the DI, who was still standing. The man had one hand in his pocket and looked far too relaxed. 'In future you will play your cards close to your chest and be a lot more careful who you talk to. I'll see what I can do to calm the waters but it will be difficult. Stirring up panic sells papers which means they'll milk this for all it's worth. The next time you have something you wish the public to know you can talk to the press office. *After* talking to your superiors. I am very disappointed, McLusky. You have seriously undermined my public relations efforts. Now get out there and catch the psychotic bastard before the coward kills again.'

McLusky bit back the remark that actually he had been out there when he was called in here. He just nodded and left the office. Lynn Tiery's eyebrows had returned to their normal position but she still didn't bother looking up.

DI Fairfield was glad when she could reasonably call her shift finished and leave. Since it was Saturday she had left her Renault at home and taken the bus in. At least if that got stuck in the Saturday protests you could get off and walk. Miraculously she had managed to get to work this morning before the traffic seized up. Now she was walking home. Cars were still crawling through the centre and going on foot would probably be quicker. What she really needed was a drink. She had briefly considered the Green Man but the prospect of a pub full of colleagues, mainly those with no real homes to go to, failed to rouse her enthusiasm. Not that she felt great fervour for anything much at the moment. There seemed to be no movement anywhere, not in her work and not in her private life. The recent upsurge in burglaries had them all playing catch-up;

176

sometimes householders didn't see police until days after the event and complained bitterly to the poor officer who eventually did turn up. At least the Mobile Muggers gave it a rest at the weekend, though other street robberies increased. As a result her last two, or was it three, drawing classes had slipped away because she had simply been too tired to contemplate them. On the plus side McLusky had been reprimanded today for shooting his mouth off to the press, which meant her day had not been a complete write-off.

Fairfield was nearing her Cotham maisonette. The place seemed full of students, all walking in the opposite direction to her, knowing something she didn't. It had taken her over half an hour to walk. The wind was now in the south; unseasonal cold had given way to curiously mild air. Abruptly she stopped walking as though her energy supply had been cut off. What was she going home for? There really was no point. She was tired but it wasn't the kind of tiredness that could be cured by sleep. It was a tiredness of the mind that hung in strength-sapping billows around every thought. Her place would be empty. There was nothing she'd fancy eating in the house because the last time she'd been shopping she had foolishly decided to be virtuous and leave all her cravings unanswered. Damn. She didn't want to spend another night drinking supermarket plonk in front of the telly. It was Saturday, when had she started staying in on Saturday nights? Probably years ago, she could hardly remember when she'd last been out having a good time. Or even trying to have a good time. Or just been out, even. She used to have a couple of girl-friends who could be relied upon for going into town with, but one had moved to London and the other was busy night-feeding twins.

If she was going to go out for a drink she should really go home and change first. And eat something. Only by the time she'd showered, changed, eaten something sensible in her sensible kitchen and come out again she'd be too fed up to enjoy a drink. She'd end up in front of the telly drinking supermarket plonk, she just knew it.

The kebab place was open and willing. When she emerged with her hot and soft parcel of junk food she looked guiltily up and down the street. She should arrest herself for crimes against nutrition. What would her mother say to this bad imitation of Greek food? Her mind went back to the light and heat of Kerkyra, where one of her numerous distant cousins had sweated cheerfully in a real *psistariá*, handing her fragrant kebabs in soft pitta bread at the price of a smile. On Sundays he would take her to the beach on the back of his tiny scooter . . . Kat blinked the images away. She hadn't been back there for years. It seemed so long ago, so far away, it might as well have happened on a different planet or in a different life. Perhaps it had happened to someone else.

A distant rumble of thunder made her look up. Black clouds were drifting across on the warm southerly breeze. It didn't matter, she knew where she was headed now. With practised timing she made the last morsel of junk food disappear just as she arrived at the Black Swan. It would be full of men, drinking with one or both eyes on the giant TV screen, but at least there would be no loud music. Any port in a storm.

The place was busy, all the tables taken. She found a free bar stool. The men occupying the others checked her over, some staring unapologetically. She was resigned to the fact that she would have to fend off some kind of unwanted attention sooner or later. It was the price you paid for being a woman and daring to drink alone.

She decided that after what she had just eaten only lager would do. The barman obliged. After draining half of her pint she was beginning to feel that perhaps the evening might be rescued after all. Fairfield relaxed her shoulders.

Then she heard the voice. There was no mistaking Ady Mitchell's flat vowels and sloppy consonants. At first she couldn't make out what he was saying above the general noise. He was talking excitedly, then there followed the laughter of several men. She turned slowly around to look, hoping that she hadn't been discovered. He was sitting at a table with three other men she didn't recognize. Mitchell himself was about forty, large, with a spreading tonsure of baldness. He was holding forth to his younger audience with his flat hard face grinning straight at her. Fairfield thought she heard him say, 'Watch this, guys,' as he made a big show of getting up, taking a drink, then working his way across the pub towards her.

Why did the bastard have to be drinking in this of all places? After her official reprimand for 'harassing' Mitchell outside his lock-up this was a bad situation. And Mitchell knew it. Fairfield reached for her glass, intending to empty it before leaving, but it was too late. Mitchell appeared beside her, elbowing her neighbour in the ribs to make space for himself. The man looked up ready to take umbrage. Recognizing the hunger for a fight in Mitchell's face he changed his mind and retired to a safe distance, taking his drink with him.

Mitchell talked loudly, to give the pub the benefit of his wit. 'Well, if it isn't the delectable *detective inspectorette*. You just can't resist my charms, can you?' He smelled of aftershave and Southern Comfort. His thin wet lips stretched into a broad unpleasant smile. Fairfield realized she had reacted too late. If she slipped off the bar stool now he'd be towering over her by at least a foot and there was hardly space to turn around, the place was so crowded. He slapped a hand on the bar, attracting the attention of those who weren't already watching. 'The girl can't help herself. The little inspector has the hots for me and just can't stay away. I even had to take out a restraining order against her but here she is again like the proverbial bad penny.' He was almost shouting now, no doubt for the benefit of the grinning audience at his table. One of his mates was filming the entire scene on his mobile. This wasn't good. 'What is this, police harassment or sexual harassment? Haven't you got any mates that you have to follow me about? I told you before you're not my type, sweetheart.' Waggling his mobile in front of her he lowered his voice and spoke straight into her face from a distance of less than three inches. 'You must think I'm real stupid if you think you can get to me like this. I could easily make life real difficult for you, love. One phone call from me to your boss Denkhaus and you're up to your neck in shit. So fuck off, you stupid little bitch.'

Fairfield found that her hand was still holding on to her pint, gripping it hard. The urge to smash it into Mitchell's face was strong but there was a stronger voice telling her to let go. Let this one go. There are too many witnesses. Say absolutely nothing. Back off. You'll get him later. Be professional.

It was a career decision. She let go of the glass, took her leather handbag off the bar and used it to create enough space between herself and Mitchell to slide off the stool without colliding with his steamed-up face. The exit seemed a long distance away. She walked across the floor, people making way for her, many eyes following her. The boy with the phone was recording her retreat.

'Piss off, copper!' Not Mitchell's, a young voice brave with anonymity. Someone near the door attempted a la-la-la version of a cop show's title music. Applause broke out at Mitchell's table, then she was outside, the door falling shut behind her, muting the noise.

Rain was bouncing off the pavement. Shit. She rummaged in her handbag for her tiny umbrella but it wasn't there. There was no point in calling a cab, she couldn't hang around here. It was only water. She struck out towards home through the hard city rain. And if she should cry, in this rain who would notice?

Chapter Ten

Libby Hart checked her watch. Six minutes to nine, very nearly done. She hated the new late opening hours. But libraries were struggling and it had been decided that more people would use the place if they stayed open late once a week. First Sunday opening, now late opening, soon all-night opening? She didn't know if this really was improving library use since the numbers had not been worked out yet. She did know they had more problems with drunks when opening late, especially when it rained hard, like it had earlier on. Attracting new clients. Or was it 'end-users'? What was wrong with calling them 'people'? The library had changed over the last few years and she didn't think it was for the better. People now came to watch videos and to use the internet. It certainly meant that more people came to the library without ever taking a book off the shelves. The noise level had risen with it, especially around the computers. You often heard mobiles ringing and being answered too despite the notice at the door asking for them to be turned off.

'Goodnight, my colleague will let you out.' She gave the young woman a relieved smile. That was the last one, she was sure. While Doug let the woman out she went on one last tour of the entire library just to make certain there was no one left ignoring the announcements or sitting asleep or hiding between the canyons of shelves, hoping to be locked in.

The woman had left a heavy red book lying on the table where she'd been sitting. Libby picked it up and took it on her tour of the library. *A Chronicle of Crime. Infamous murderers and their heinous crimes,* promised the subtitle. Why would anyone want to know about this stuff? She had reached the last corner of the library, the quietest one furthest away from the entrance. No one here either, the library was clear. She walked with the book towards the issue desk and wondered what had brought the woman to the library on a rainy evening to study this grisly tome. Grainy images of convicted murderers looked up at her from the cover. She opened it at random. *Woman Kills Rival: Dumps Body on Wasteland.* Libby hoped the woman who had studied it tonight hadn't been looking for inspiration. She closed the book with a determined slap and set it heavily on to a trolley. One for the morning shift to sort out.

At the desk Doug had cashed up, locked the sliding cupboards and was now tidying away the last things on the desk. She liked working with Doug. He was near retirement age and only worked two days a week which meant he was a lot more cheerful than some she could mention.

'I think we've done it, Libby.'

'Yup, I think we have. And it's even stopped raining.'

'Good.' He waved a fat silver biro. 'Someone left this behind. If no one claims it by the end of the month I'll have it. It's nice.'

'Put your name on it then.'

'Certainly will.' Doug ripped a square of yellow notepaper from a block and clicked the biro. It exploded in a gas-blue flash that left a red after-image on Libby's retina. Doug's hand was a pulpy red mass and there was blood streaming from his neck. His head trembled and his dimming eyes were fixed at a bloodied horizon thrumming with fear. His body crumpled and slumped behind the smouldering desk. For several heartbeats Libby stared at the space where he had stood. Then she filled her lungs and ran screaming for the door.

'Will he live?' McLusky was standing on top of a desk from where he could appraise the bloodstain on the carpet, the bloody foot- and handprints, arcs of spatters and the bloodied work station where the victim had stood. Scene of Crime were still hunting for bits of tissue as far as twenty feet away from the point of the explosion. The victim had been removed to the Royal Infirmary.

Austin, knee-high to his superior, shrugged. 'Touch and go. If he does then it's entirely thanks to his colleague who called the security guard who's a first-aider. The ambulance would never have got here in time. He was losing a lot of blood from the wound in his neck.'

McLusky took another look at the bent and blackened stub of metal in the evidence bag he was holding. It was all that was left of a polished steel biro, thick as a finger, solid and seductive. Anyone using the library could have picked it up, staff or punter, man, woman or child. It was rigged to blow up as soon as someone tried to use it. A whisky tin, a beer can, a powder compact, a biro. It made no sense. McLusky jumped off the desk. 'It makes no bloody sense. There's no rhyme or reason I can see. Who's he after? Just anyone? Does he have a grudge so vague that it doesn't matter to him who he blows up?'

'Perhaps he just likes building bombs and all else is incidental. Or perhaps Sorbie was right, there's no motive.'

'Then God help us.' The large device in the park had merely been the overture, the rapping of a conductor's baton in order to get everyone's attention. Now the bomber was playing his tune and leading them a dance.

'There's no CCTV in here, I'm surprised. They're relying on their alarm system.' Austin nodded his head at the big security gates that would sound an alarm if anyone tried to smuggle out any items.

McLusky looked morose. 'You'd need a camera between every two shelves. And you could still drop a biro without it being picked up. And that's basically our problem. The devices are small and can be delivered any time. We have no idea where this guy picked the biro up but it could have been sitting between a couple of books for ages. His bad luck. Someone else could easily have picked it up, put it in his pocket, carried it around then used it miles from here. And then if he'd died we'd never know. We wouldn't have a bloody clue where it came from.' He lowered his voice. 'Forensics have been less than useless so far.' He gave the item in the evidence bag one more exasperated look then handed it back to the chief technician, who dropped it into his case.

There was nothing more to do here. He had spoken to Libby Hart, the librarian who had witnessed the incident. She'd barely been coherent enough to make sense and had repeated the same things over and over: how he had just crumpled, how his thumb just disappeared, how it all happened so suddenly.

That was the nature of the thing, you couldn't very well have a slow explosion. It was clear that the woman was deeply shocked and when it transpired that she lived by herself he had made sure she was accompanied home. If she didn't settle the officer would know to call a doctor who could administer a sedative. All she probably needed was to talk it out of her system and get some sleep. Sleep . . . McLusky checked his watch: two in the morning. The discovery instantly provoked a yawn. He turned to Austin. 'We're done. There's nothing here. The woman didn't know where or when her colleague picked the thing up but if he pulls through and tells us then we'll try and match the area where it was found with today's book issues. Yesterday's, I should say.'

Austin scratched the tip of his nose with the nail of his index finger. 'Ehm . . . I'm not sure I follow.'

Austin read the note twice. 'He sounds quite a loon. Look at the capitalization. Odd language, too. You can't smoke in here, public building.'

'Closed to the public due to pyrotechnical writing accident.' McLusky inhaled deeply from a freshly lit cigarette.

'Good thinking.' Austin lit one for himself. 'Those capitalized words, could they add up to a message or something? Have you tried stringing them together?'

'You've watched too much Inspector Morse.'

'It was worth a thought. He's just mad then?'

'Mad as a box of frogs. You didn't really expect anything else, did you? But he's made contact. It's a classic "Don't call me stupid" thing.'

'He thinks *you're* a "very Very Stupid Man".'

'Good. Underestimating the opposition can be fatal. The important thing is that we got him riled enough to take risks. Contacting me was a big risk. His first mistake.'

'Shame he didn't sign it while he was busy making mistakes.' He fanned the thick smoke between them with the letter. 'Do you think Forensics will find anything on this?'

'Apart from my fingerprints? I shouldn't think so. But you never know. The postmark is central.'

'That covers several districts, including yours. What he doesn't tell us is why he's doing all this.'

'Oh, but he does. Here.' McLusky tapped the letter. 'The madness is out there and I'm going to stop it, or something. He thinks the world has gone mad and only he has remained sane. He's going to shut us all up.'

'Yes. He's threatening you personally though.'

'That's the beauty of it.'

'How?'

'Because it wasn't part of his plan. I've irritated him. If he comes after me it'll interfere with the rest of his crazy scheme. Which is obviously planned in advance. What I have to do is wind him up some more.'

'Careful, Liam. It could backfire, then what?'

'Admirable choice of words, Jane.'

'Let's say it was found in the music section then we'll check on the library computer to see who took out CDs and interview them, see if they remember anything.'

'Oh, right. And if the guy doesn't live?'

'Then we'll interview everyone.'

'Oh joy.' Austin gave the library, still full of crime scene officers, one last disapproving look and wondered just how many people wandered in and out during a day. He hoped fervently he'd never have to find out.

Later the next day at his desk and dealing with the paperwork that had begun to litter it, McLusky felt he was in hiding from the case. Unlike some CID officers he had known who seemed happy to spend most of their working life behind their desks, it made him feel resentful and guilty. This paper and computer stuff had to be dealt with but sometimes it seemed like it was deliberately designed to keep him away from his work. There was enough red tape in this building to tie the entire station in knots. While being new on this patch had kept the mail and paperwork down – compared to what some of his colleagues were suffering – he knew it wouldn't take long to catch up with him. He threw his biro down in disgust, looked at it for a moment, then picked it up again, weighing it in his hands. It was the brushed steel biro. He was sure he hadn't bought it and almost certain it hadn't been a present. Which meant he had picked it up somewhere. Just like the librarian. It was so easily done. Something as simple as picking up a pen could mean you ended up fighting for your life in intensive care, like Douglas Boon who had a hole in his throat the size of a pound coin where part of the pen's metal casing had hit. He'd been doubly unlucky. The device had been designed to take the victim's fingers off. Which it had also done. He had lost part of a thumb and the tips of two fingers.

McLusky reached for the only letter that was not internal mail and slid it open using the biro. It contained a narrow slip of paper, densely crowded with lines, typed single spaced. Randomly capitalized words danced through the text. Before he had taken in a single sentence he knew what he was looking at. It was from him.

He withdrew his hands from the paper as though it was on fire and let it glide on to the computer keyboard. One hand crept across his desk in an unconscious search for cigarettes, the other towards the phone, while his eyes remained nailed to the page.

I am Disappointed to read such Nonsense reported about me in the Paper. I expected Better from an Officer of the Law. If you really think I am mad then you are a very Very Stupid Man. The Madness walks Out there and it is I who Will Stop it. And to this Fight which is a Good Fight I bring a Courage You Cannot Appreciate. I Am Not A Coward. You Are Part of the Problem if you Lie To People About Me. I will not waste Any More Time with you But if you give me More Trouble and Lie to people Again then I will come and Shut you up. I will Shut You all up, and then there will be Quiet Again!

Using the biro and an unopened letter as levers he flipped the page over. Nothing on the other side. It was less than a third of an A4 sheet, typed in a common font.

Bloody hell, did he need a cigarette now. A short and hectic hunt produced only empty packets. The part of his brain not engaged in keying Austin's mobile number into the desk phone painted scenario after scenario of the future and for once not all of it seemed gloomy. At last Austin answered.

'Jane, get in here and bring your ciggies.'

'In where, boss? I'm at the library.'

'Oh. Thought you were down the corridor. Okay, stay where you are, I'll find you.'

McLusky only consciously registered that he was driving once he got stuck in traffic for the second green-light sequence at a junction near the harbour. According to an article in the *Post* it was theoretically still faster to drive in the city if your journey was longer than two miles. Anything shorter and a pedestrian would beat the car. Now he wished he had tried it. For one thing it would have allowed him to buy cigarettes. When at last he had fought his way to the back of the library he parked the car on a single yellow line with two wheels on the pavement. He pushed the groaning door shut, leaving it unlocked. For several seconds he stood, unmoving. Then he opened it again, put the keys back into the ignition for good measure and pushed the door shut once more.

A PC guarded the library entrance. Both lending and reference libraries were still closed to the public while a meticulous search for more hidden devices was under way. McLusky's footsteps echoed in the stone corridor inside the solid Edwardian building. He found Austin in the lending library checking his notes. The DS had spent his time interviewing all the staff that had turned up for work and drawn a blank.

Austin shook his head in answer to his superior's raised eyebrows. 'Nothing out of the ordinary, nobody saw anything or anybody suspicious. No one saw the biro. So what was so urgent? A nicotine crisis?' He held out his packet cigarettes and box of matches.

'Swap.' McLusky handed him the letter inside a seal evidence bag. 'Let's step into the foyer.'

'Shit, it's from him. You got him narked with that art and it flushed him out.' The DS looked at McLusk admiration. 'Did you plan it like that?'

'What? No. No, nothing as clever as that, I honestly no idea, I'd never heard of Phil . . .'

'Warren.'

'. . . Phil Warren, I thought she was just another p

'You know what I mean.'

'I'll be careful. I'll try not to pick up any strange objects.'

'I'm not sure the super will go for it. Provoking the bomber doesn't sound like a Denkhaus strategy. He'll scupper it.'

'I mean it as a last resort. But you're right, Jane. Best not burden Denkhaus with the knowledge of this.' He took the evidence bag from Austin and made it disappear in his leather jacket.

'You mean not tell him you got a communication from the guy? Are you serious?'

'Why bother the man with operational detail? He's far too busy with public relations and performance targets.'

'This could mean real trouble, especially if –'

'Okay, look, it's my problem. I never showed you the letter, you need not be involved. And if it has to be mentioned later, well, it's not dated and I might lose the envelope, I can be so sloppy, and I'll pretend it only just got there.'

Austin thoughtfully scratched the tip of his nose. This kind of thing could easily go wrong, especially if the case came to court. 'Just so long as you know what you're doing . . .?'

'That's very unlikely. But it makes me feel less naked having this up my sleeve.' Perhaps this metaphor-mixing was catching. 'So far he has all the weapons and we're just mopping up behind him, waiting for him to make a mistake. It's a costly strategy.'

'Depends on how quickly he can make the bombs.'

'Yes. Unless . . .'

'What?'

McLusky prised a cigarette out of the packet Austin was holding and walked off, talking to the echoing foyer. 'Unless he's made them all in advance. For all we know there could be fifty of them already out there.' He turned at the end of the corridor. 'And then what? We're up the creek then. Catching him wouldn't make a blind bit of difference then.'

McLusky stocked up on Extra Light cigarettes at a nearby newsagent's. Lunchtime had crept up on the city and everywhere people were rushing to join queues in cafés, post offices, supermarkets and sandwich bars. His own internal clock appeared stuck at breakfast time. He bought a sticky Danish pastry at a nearby bakery and ate it while he walked.

When he returned to his car he found it unmolested by car thieves and traffic wardens. It was another warm spring day. The fungal damp-canvas smell of the Polo's interior had intensified with the rising temperatures. McLusky suspected a dead mouse or rat under the broken upholstery but had so far failed to locate it.

Back at Albany Road he found the station car park was crowded with a large army truck awkwardly parked. Not having been allocated a permanent parking space yet meant he only just managed to squeeze into a corner at the back. Here he made sure to lock the car, in case someone was watching. He looked up. There was. There were faces at every window. He saw DC Dearlove wave at him which had to be a bad omen.

Outside the main entrance stood a group of Uniforms plus Tony Hayes, the desk officer. 'You can't go in, sir. Suspect package. The ground floor has been evacuated and no one from upstairs is allowed to come down.' He pointed at the army truck. The cab door was marked *33 Engineer Regiment*. 'Explosive ordnance disposal. The package was addressed to you, sir.'

'What? Get out of my way.'

'But, sir . . .'

Impatiently McLusky shouldered his way through the group and opened the door to the lobby.

Inside three engineers in full body armour looked up and shouted at him almost in concert. One rushed towards him, arms outstretched. 'Please move outside, sir.'

190

McLusky held up his ID. 'I'm McLusky.'

'That's who it was addressed to. But it makes no difference.'

'It does. I don't want the thing to blow up. No controlled explosions if you can help it.'

'Please, sir, let's talk outside.'

Away from the door and the uniformed officers McLusky and the engineer, a man with freckles and a moustache, talked quickly.

'Try not to blow it up. If at all possible we need it intact. Why hasn't the rest of the station been evacuated?'

'Because all personnel would have to practically file past the thing, this station is badly designed.'

'How big is the device?'

'Big enough to demolish the lobby but perhaps not enough to do structural damage. It's heavy, according to the desk officer, and looks to be about four by three inches and three inches deep. Rectangular. We have a portable X-ray already in the lobby and are about to have a shufti, that should give us a better idea.'

'It relates to a case I'm working on . . .'

'Yes, we have followed that with interest. We expected to be called sooner or later. Fortunately we're never far away.'

McLusky tapped the man's bulky armour. 'Got another one of these?'

'We have but I'll have to ask my superior about that. Please wait here this time.'

It seemed an age until the engineer returned. 'Follow me.'

Inside the truck he found that putting on the bulky body armour took him longer than expected. 'I thought a stabbie was heavy but this weighs an absolute ton.' The weight of the helmet with its blast-proof visor gave him a headache in less than the time it took him to walk across the car park. Tony Hayes' ever-mobile eyebrows had risen to maximum elevation. He had asked if he could be there when they dealt with the package – after all, it was his lobby, or at

191

least he thought of it like that. They had flatly refused to entertain the thought. How come the new DI always got what he wanted?

Inside the lobby McLusky found the other two engineers busy around a grey contraption balanced on the counter. Two station phones were ringing unanswered in the background.

One soldier waved him over. 'Come and have a look, inspector.'

On the small monitor beside the X-ray machine was a faint grey image that to him looked like nothing identifiable.

'There are no metal parts in this package and it looks like no device I have ever encountered. There is a dense mass at the centre, hard to draw any conclusions. On that basis I'm willing to proceed and open the package. Please stand off.'

The package, he could now see, was wrapped in brown paper and sealed with clear tape. 'How did it get here, does anyone know?'

'It was hand-delivered but no one saw it arrive. They sensibly evacuated the ground floor. It has your name on it, as you can see, nothing else.' The man slid a scalpel around the sides of the package. 'Nothing in the wrapping, no resistance.' He gently folded up a flap of paper. 'Red plastic container.' He removed the top of the paper, revealing a red plastic tub with a white lid. The engineer laid his heavily gloved hands on it. 'Here we go then, I'm opening it now.'

On cue the phones stopped ringing and the lobby fell silent. The plastic creaked as the engineer prised the lid off the container. McLusky strained to see clearly. The engineer produced a plastic screwdriver and gingerly prodded the content with it.

'Well, inspector, it appears to be full of mud.'

* * *

192

Twenty-four hours later, while trying to beat the traffic by finding his own intuitive route to the university, McLusky wondered just how long the mud jokes would keep running at the station. Not that Superintendent Denkhaus had found anything even remotely amusing in the incident which had paralysed his station for hours. And he had left him in no doubt about that either. Denkhaus had once more sharply reminded him that his brief was to avoid anything that might sidetrack him and here he went offering his services to Traffic Division. Naturally he wanted the mud-flinging little scrote caught but if McLusky had a mind to have a go then it was definitely to be in his spare time.

Which is why he now found himself driving to the university during his lunch break, in order to spring some muddy suggestions on Dr Louise Rennie. This time he knew where he was going and parked close to the building next to a red Fiesta with its driver window knocked out. He left the keys in the ignition and went in search of Rennie.

For a while he was walking against an outgoing tide of students in the science block but by the time he found the laboratory again the place had fallen silent. From the corridor it looked empty. He knocked on the glass door and entered.

'Anybody home?'

The door to the store room at the other end was open, its strip lighting on. A small tinkling noise came from there, then stopped. He walked over and stuck his head round the jamb and found himself looking at the balding head of the laboratory technician, who was standing motionless in front of a steel locker, one hand on its chromed door handle.

He found he couldn't recall the man's name. 'Hi, Dr Rennie about?'

The technician turned around slowly and laboriously cleared his throat. 'She's gone to lunch.'

It was the man he had seen by the Tobacco Factory, he was sure of it, no matter what Dr Rennie thought. 'Where?'

'Common room.' There was a definite wheeze to the lab rat's chest and the pallor of his neon-grilled skin made McLusky want to shudder. He decided to ask elsewhere for directions.

Once he had been shown to the senior common room it took him only seconds to spot Louise Rennie. A man sitting opposite her talked animatedly while Rennie nodded at her lunch. She looked up long before he had got near her table. A few words spoken to the man opposite her made him get up and leave.

'Don't tell me, inspector, another forensic report? I may have to start charging.' Rennie's food looked as yet untouched.

'Would you mind if I joined you for lunch, doctor? If I can get some food here, that is.'

'Yes, go ahead. Just go and choose something. Don't look so worried, you could pass for a lecturer, no problem. And you still have to pay for it.'

McLusky didn't know why the thought of being mistaken for a lecturer should give him such pleasure since he didn't mind being a detective. Until it came to canteen food. He asked for the trout and while piling salad into a bowl noted the complete absence of unidentifiable brown stuff shrivelling under hot lamps.

When he sat down at her table Rennie's food still looked untouched. 'You shouldn't have waited, it must be getting cold.'

'I found I'm not really hungry. *Bon appétit*, inspector.' Rennie smiled, leaning back. Her grey silk top shimmered like water across her chest as she did so, tugging at McLusky's eyes. 'Is this a social call then?'

He waggled one hand. 'Expect further attempts to impose on your time and good nature.'

'You think me good-natured? Interesting. Does it have anything to do with what's in your carrier?'

'It has.' He put his fork down.

'No, no, you eat. You look like they've been starving you.' She pushed her tray aside and pulled the bag towards her. 'A tub. It's heavy. What's in it?'

'Mud.'

'You know how to treat a girl. How does this fit in with the bombings, inspector?'

'You can call me Liam, doctor.'

'You can call me Louise, Inspector Liam.'

'It's a different . . . case. I was wondering if it was possible to tell where it came from.'

'Liam. Mm.' She moved her lips as if savouring the taste of the name. 'I do already have a job, did I not mention that?'

'I know, that's quite okay, you don't have to do it, I just thought it was worth asking. I was hoping there might be a really easy test for that kind of thing.'

'Did you now. Only if you're looking for something specific or if you know what's what. It's a job for the forensic lab, surely.'

He reached over and put the tub back in the bag, shoving it aside. 'Too busy. It's low priority stuff. Not really important.'

'Important enough for you to come up here, though. Oh, I get it.'

'Good.'

'You didn't really need to bring an excuse along, you know.'

'Good. So how are you?'

'Fine, I'm *good*, I'm having a good day.' She checked her watch. 'I'm teaching a bunch of first years next, keen but dim. I enjoy it. And you?'

'I'm enjoying this.'

'Yeah, the food's all right here.'

'No, I mean this.' He waved his hand between Rennie and himself.

'You're easily pleased.'

'I don't think so. I've been thinking about you. It was a shame our evening the other day got interrupted.'

'Truncated would be a better word. Severely pruned. You arrived late and left early.' Rennie reached an arm across and retrieved the mud-filled tub. She peeked under the lid and poked a well-manicured finger in. 'Sticky stuff. I'll spend five minutes on it and it'll cost you dinner whether I find anything or not. Deal?'

McLusky smiled at his food. 'Deal.'

Chapter Eleven

'Result, Moneypenny.' Sorbie flung his imaginary hat towards the invisible hatstand in the CID room, then tried to plant a kiss on DC French's cheek.

French pushed him away good-naturedly. She didn't really mind Jack's attentions, not that he actually meant them. No one else seemed to even notice that she was a woman, certainly not while the glamorous Fairfield was about. 'You've been celebrating, I can smell it. You made another arrest then?'

'Traffic scooped him up for us, but he's ours. We can link the little scrote to at least eleven burglaries through his lavish and evil-smelling DNA donations in his victims' underwear drawers, the stupid wanker. That's the second outstanding warrant sorted and all from the council car park. We must do this more often. McLusky might be less than useless at catching the bench bomber but he does wonders for *my* clear-up rate.'

'I'm glad to have been of some small service to you, DS Sorbie.' McLusky walked past him on his way to the tea kettle.

'Ah, ehm, sorry, sir, didn't see you there.' Sorbie sat down heavily at his desk and busied himself with logging on.

McLusky took his time making himself a mug of instant coffee, leaving Sorbie to squirm in the ensuing silence. Secretly he had to agree with the sergeant's assessment. In terms of his own investigation the car park CCTV had been of no help at all. Yet the prodigious number of man-hours spent marrying faces to number plates from the endless footage had resulted in no fewer than three arrests of known criminals. The hapless suspects hadn't counted on police officers looking at the footage, which only ever attracted police attention if an incident occurred. Once they had been recognized and their number plates read it had only been a matter of time until they were picked up. Two had been outstanding warrants in Fairfield and Sorbie's open files. A third was a missed court appearance who had been scooped up because an officer spotted a 2002 number plate on a 2003 car. That man too was now in custody.

McLusky thought he could hear the CID room breathe out collectively behind him as he left carrying his mug of coffee. He hadn't really meant to pour cold water on Sorbie's celebration; there was never quite enough to celebrate for police officers as it was, and the sergeant had made good use of the footage and followed up well. Only there was something about DS Sorbie that made McLusky suspect that he probably deserved the odd bucket of cold water occasionally. He would mention Sorbie's good work in his report while not forgetting to point out that only the footage watched by police officers had yielded fortuitous results. Those worked on by civilian operators had drawn a blank since they were unfamiliar with the faces of the suspects.

Perhaps he should have mentioned to Sorbie though that he thought smelling of quite so much booze after lunch was never a good idea in a nick where the superintendent had a habit of prowling about.

Two hours later Sorbie viewed his dispiriting surroundings through the metallic pulse of a dehydration headache; Nelson Close was an unheroic huddle of three dozen pre-fabs, a third of them with their flimsy backs to a ghostly road that once serviced a now derelict industrial estate. The council ought to have bulldozed them years ago only some of these poor deluded people refused to be rehoused into nice new high-rise flats with a view. They liked their 'bit of garden' and didn't want to move. The council had lost their court case against them and now they had to wait for the tenants to die off before they could develop the site along with the rest of the area.

He burped acidly. His stomach had turned sour after all that cider he had gulped earlier. Kicking about impatiently at a mouldering cardboard box in one of the empty plots he looked about for a place to relieve himself. He just couldn't bring himself to ask one of these weirdos for permission to use their toilet. Only a dozen of the creepy little bungalows were still being lived in, if you could call this living. The rest did service for target practice by passing kids. The ones that were inhabited were being broken into one by one, three so far. The empty ones had now been boarded up to try and keep the junkies out.

Behind him he could hear Kat doing her 'reassuring the public' bit with two wrinklies, probably a lot better than he could himself, he had to admit. But then women were always going to be better at that kind of thing. What a dump this was. It had probably been all right fifty years ago but even then these flimsy things must have been freezing in winter and roasting in summer. And anyone in possession of a tin opener could break in. Pathetic.

DI Fairfield said her goodbyes to the old couple and soon joined him with her clipboard. 'You didn't spend a lot of time with your lot, did you?'

'Well, there isn't really all that much to say, is there? If you live in a stupid place like this it's no wonder you get broken into.'

'You didn't tell them that, did you?'

'Not in so many words, though I did point out that if they don't have locks on their windows then they might as well leave them open. Same thing to a burglar.' Sorbie rubbed his unruly stomach, which was churning. 'I've never been any good at this stuff, not when I was in uniform and not now. And this is definitely a uniform job.'

'I know. They've been round too.' Fairfield sniffed the air and didn't look at all put out. The sun was going in and out of the clouds, beginning to burn away the greyness that had hung around her mind all winter. When she first joined the force she'd never imagined it would mean spending so much time sitting indoors hammering on keyboards, filling in forms, chasing targets, following initiatives. She much preferred being outside, talking to people away from neon lights and computer screens. She should move away from the city, get a job in a little seaside town ... it would take forever to make DCI. 'You know exactly why we're here.'

'Yes, so Denkhaus doesn't get his gold stars tarnished.'

'It's politics, Jack. People need to see that we take this seriously, that's why the ACC wants us to show our faces. To reassure people. We'll have one more chat before we go. That chap standing in the door, last-but-one house.' Fairfield cheerfully waved at a man in his sixties standing in his front door. He didn't wave back. 'That's the last of the inhabited ones. It's vulnerable that one, it's the last-but-one, has empty houses on either side and it backs on to the old service road. He hasn't been burgled yet, perhaps we can convince him to get some security. This is all about perception of crime anyway, not actual crime. Denkhaus doesn't want another newspaper crusade over this one. Or more suggestions that we're not protecting these people because the city wants them to pack up and go. Of course the fact that these prefabs are isolated and full of old folks was publicized by the stupid papers in the first place.'

The morose expression of the man didn't change when Fairfield showed her ID and introduced DS Sorbie. 'Caught them yet?' He snorted dismissively before Fairfield could draw breath to answer. 'Thought not. According to your own statistics it isn't likely you ever will. And if you do, the courts will let them off with a slap on the wrist so they can go and do it again.'

'Not quite, Mr . . .' She looked down her list.

'Cooke.'

'Mr Cooke. We have been quite successful in driving down the rate of burglaries in the city. One of the ways in which householders themselves can help of course is by fitting locks and shutters to windows. Has anyone spoken to you about that yet?'

'They have. I told them what I'm telling you now: fitting window locks won't make a blind bit of difference to the criminals. They just go somewhere else. Do you think they'll go, "Oh dear, window locks, well, I'd better go straight then and get a respectable job"? Rubbish! It won't stop a professional housebreaker and it'll just make the drug addict try next door. You don't stop criminals with locks on your windows, you stop them with locks on their cells. And by keeping them locked up.'

'There might be something in that, Mr Cooke. In the meantime I hope you're not making it easy for them.' She looked down the sad cul-de-sac. One more boarded-up house separated Mr Cooke from a derelict and overgrown site where a brickworks had been demolished. She certainly wouldn't feel safe living here.

'Making it easy? It's the council who are making it easy for them. The burglars and the kids who throw empty beer bottles at our houses and the drug addicts who leave their needles lying about, they all come down the service road. Then they come through the fence. We've asked the council to put in a decent fence several times but they'd rather wait until we've all been robbed blind or brained by a flying bottle.'

'I'll look into that for you and tell the council what I think about it.' What was left of the flimsy wooden fence that separated the cluster of prefabs from the derelict road was richly overgrown, the gaps full of builder's waste, fly-tipped rubbish and rubble. It wouldn't keep out anyone.

201

Even to her it looked like the council had deliberately let the area become run down to make staying there less attractive. Fairfield had the heavy feeling CID would sooner or later be down here again, perhaps sorting out worse than plain house-breaking. Sorbie was right, she thought, these people should have moved away. Only now did she notice that Sorbie was no longer standing behind her. 'Mr Cooke, you wouldn't by any chance have noticed where DS Sorbie has got to?'

'I would. He's down there, throwing up against the back of number twenty-two.'

Witek Setkievich could already see the end of his shift. Getting there was another matter. He only had three punters left on top, the others had got off at the science museum, but passenger numbers hardly mattered. Getting back to the starting point at Broad Quay and handing over at the end of his shift was all that mattered. The ancient red Routemaster open-top bus may have been fitted with a low-emission engine but it was still as big as a house and nearly as hard to drive. In this traffic it could take ten minutes to cover the last five hundred yards to the harbourside stop. This was where the company's touts hunted for tourists, trying to entice them to take the 'hop-on hop-off' tour of the city. A few hundred yards away near the Hippodrome the company kept a draughty little ground-floor office.

As was usual at lunchtime the roundabout was clogged with idiots not knowing where they were going and all getting in each other's way. But Witek didn't really mind. He liked driving the bus. Getting a licence was the best thing he had ever done. It had fed him since coming to this country. And driving the city tour bus was much, much better than driving a regular bus around the city which he had done for a year before landing this job. Tourists were much more polite than the passengers on ordinary buses.

Especially foreign tourists. They hardly ever wanted to beat him up, did not call him stupid Polack, didn't tell him to 'go back home to Moscow' and didn't spit at the security screen. Tourists never pissed between the seats and didn't throw up so much.

Traffic moved on for a few car lengths and he could at last cross the junction. The road system in this city was madness, of course. Three times they had changed the layout, reversed the one-way systems, and nothing they tried worked properly. Some people wanted tourist buses banned to lighten the traffic but looking at this chaos that would be a drop in the ocean. It did worry him though. Driving was all he had ever been good at and he liked this job. He liked the bus.

Witek strained to see who was doing the afternoon shift handing leaflets to the tourists. He recognized Ben and yes, there she was, her blonde hair shining in the sunlight: Emma.

Witek liked Emma. He liked her so much he could not bring himself to shorten her name to Emm like everyone else did. Of course he had no chance. Emma was nice and polite with him but that's all it was. She was on her gap year and would go travelling to Asia and Australia soon, something he could never do. Afterwards she would go to university. And he would still be driving a bus.

When at last Witek swung the Routemaster into the reserved bay by the harbour Emma was talking to Ben and neither of them even turned their heads to see which driver was pulling in. Dave, who would relieve him and drive the next shift, was slouching by the railings. He gave a slow wave and carried on smoking.

Witek announced the end of the tour over the microphone and added a reminder. 'Everyone please be sure to take belongings with you.' He opened the doors and waited for the three single passengers to alight. Each one said thank you as they left, so polite. The last thing he had to do was check that the vehicle was reasonably clean and pick up any rubbish and anything accidentally left behind. He checked first downstairs then the upper deck, collecting a few chocolate wrappers and a plastic sandwich carton. Right on the last seat lay a small pink lady's umbrella. He picked it up. It looked cheap. Nobody would call for it at the office, they'd simply go out and buy a new one. But it was company policy to keep all found items for a couple of weeks before letting the staff take them home if they wanted to.

Dave was downstairs leaning in the open door, lighting a last cigarette before the start of his shift. Witek checked his watch. Dave's shift started in one minute but he would hang around for another five in plain view of the office, something he himself wouldn't dare to do.

'What you got, pink brollie? They never leave anything useful like a carton of fags or a hundred quid. What's traffic like?'

'Is crap. Always is by now.' Witek smiled over Dave's shoulder at Emma who was looking in his direction without registering him.

'Yeah, I don't know why I keep signing up for the afternoon shifts, they're so much worse than the morning ones. I just can't hack the early start, know what I mean? Not that I couldn't drive this heap in my sleep. Watch this.' After one last drag from his cigarette he flicked the butt at a council rubbish bin and missed.

Witek's voice was heavy with the tragedy of it. 'Every day you miss, Dave. Never get better. Always miss rubbish bin.'

'Tomorrow, Witek, my son. Now excuse me while I drive this rubbish bin.'

Emma had moved and was busy working on a tourist couple who were already holding a leaflet each. She was standing on the wrong side of the parking bay for him to walk past casually, perhaps exchange a few words, ask how she was. The office, where he had to sign out, lay in the opposite direction. Now she moved even further away.

Witek sighed. He'd sign out and somehow contrive to walk past her afterwards. It would mean taking quite a detour around the roundabout since home was in the opposite direction but it would be worth it. Witek smiled to himself as he walked quickly towards the office. Emma was very pretty even though she was English. Polish girls were famously pretty, much prettier than the English. But Emma was very beautiful in a very English way. Hard to explain. Different pretty.

Sally, the office girl who almost single-handedly did all the admin jobs for the company, comically waggled her head while chewing down the cheese sandwich she had just dispatched. This one was not pretty. Sal was nice, though definitely not pretty. But she was always so cheerful, so perhaps she didn't mind.

'Hello, Witty, another day done? S'all right for some. Driving round in circles, calling it work, then knocking off early. I've got another four hours to go.' She handed him the relevant clipboard holding the form for the drivers to tick and sign. Witek gave her the umbrella in exchange. 'Oh, cute, can I have it if no one comes for it?'

'Is not my colour, Sal. I don't think is your colour too. You can have it, of course.'

Sally made a note of the date then bent down to the cupboard where left items lingered among till rolls and boxes of rubber bands. As she found room for the umbrella her eyes fell on a plain white carrier. 'Oh yeah, the egg, Witty, the egg! That's one of yours and it's been here more than two weeks now.' She slipped it from the carrier and placed it on the counter between them. The heavy papier mâché Easter egg rocked gently between them. Its varnished shell was brightly decorated with Easter bunny motifs and a paper banderole around its waist promised *fine dark, milk and white chocolate* treats inside.

'Nobody came for it? Someone somewhere is sad now.' He gripped the shiny ovoid with one long-fingered hand. 'Can I take the carrier too?'

205

Disappointment spread over Sally's face. 'Oh, Witty . . . You're not taking it home to snaffle by yourself, are you? I thought we could share . . .' She tilted her head and fluttered her eyelids in a parody of silent-movie seduction.

Witek hesitated with one hand resting on the egg, the other stretched out towards the carrier bag. He had thought of presenting the egg to Emma. His eyes wandered towards the window. He could see the quayside but no sign of her. Happy Easter, Emma . . . But then she might know that he had found the chocolates on the bus and not bought them for her. She might think it was a cheap gesture. And if he took it away Sally would think he was mean and greedy. Everything to do with girls was complicated. You always found you wanted to please them and it broke your heart to disappoint them. 'I remember now, I don't really like chocolate. You will eat them, Sal.'

'Are you sure? You don't want any of it? They're expensive chocolates . . .'

'Total sure. You will enjoy them more. I go home now.' On a sudden impulse he gave the egg a vicious twist, leaving it spinning on the counter in front of a mesmerized Sally as he walked out of the office.

He stood on the pavement, squinted towards the bus stop and tried to make out Emma among the people on the quay. The force of the explosion made him stagger against an old lady. With a cry of dismay she fell to the ground beside him. Witek thought he heard the crack as her hip bone shattered.

They walked to the locus, McLusky had insisted on it. Austin was glad he had as the traffic turned out to be particularly bad. They were easily keeping pace with the cars and by the time they got within sight of St Augustine's Parade traffic was stationary everywhere. As they approached the Citytours office it didn't take them long to discover why. The building that housed Citytours had been evacuated, along with the buildings to either side. The stretch of road in front of them was closed to passing traffic. The tarmac beyond the police tape was crowded with police cars and Forensics vehicles.

Something about the way the police tape hung limply across the road threatened to drain McLusky of his goodwill to mankind. He grabbed the first uniformed officer he saw. 'What's with the bloody roadblock?'

'Standard procedure, inspector, with a bomb threat.'

'I thought the bomb had gone off.'

'It has. There could be secondary devices, though. Couldn't there?' The constable looked unsure now.

'What kind of bomb was it?'

'A small device. Hidden in an Easter egg, is what I heard.'

'Any Easter eggs in the road?' He didn't wait for an answer. 'What about the victim?'

'Two victims, sir. An old lady got knocked off her feet, suspected pelvic fracture, the ambulance has just left. The other was an office worker, she was closest to the blast. Slight bruise and a nasty shock, otherwise she's fine, apparently.'

'That's the first good news I've had since this thing started.' He saw that Forensics were already at work. 'Where is the office worker now? Not still inside, I take it?'

'No, she and a co-worker are in that café further along, with PC Purkis.'

'That's the second good piece of news. How did the egg get here, any idea?'

'Left on one of their buses, I believe. Driver found it.'

'Right. Do you see any Easter bunnies in the road? No? Then get the damn traffic going, constable. Pronto.'

The constable set about getting all the police vehicles moved while muttering about sarky CID gits and making up one's bloody mind. McLusky ignored the Citytours office and swept on to the café. Here he found PC Purkis sharing a large pot of tea with a pale woman sporting a burgeoning bruise on her forehead and a broad-shouldered blond man with mournful eyes.

'Every time I see you, constable, you seem to have a cup of tea in front of you.'

Purkis didn't know how to answer that, since it was true, but then she had only met the inspector once before, at the old man's house in Knowle West. He seemed to be in a foul mood so perhaps he was in need of a cuppa himself. 'That's true, inspector. Best thing in a crisis, I always think.'

McLusky sat down on the last free chair, next to the broad-shouldered man. 'Jane, you heard what the officer always thinks, so get us a large pot of tea. And a chair for yourself. Hang on, I'll give you the money.'

'I think I can manage.'

The café was crowded with refugees from the evacuated buildings and the voices sounded excited, even happy, perhaps at the interruption of an otherwise dreary day at the office.

Purkis made the introductions. McLusky noticed that Sally's hands displayed a small tremor as she lifted her teacup. 'Has that bruise been seen to?'

PC Purkis resented the implication that she might have neglected the basic care for the victim. 'The paramedics took a look and ruled out concussion.'

Sally spoke up. 'They offered to take me to the Royal Infirmary just in case but I'm fine, really. Considering. Even my ears have stopped making that horrible high-pitched sound. I mean, compared to what could have happened I'm all right. It could have blown my fingers off.'

'That's probably what it was meant to do. Do you feel like telling us exactly what did happen? I know you already told the story but I'd like to hear it myself.'

'Sure.' Sally told the tale right from the beginning, from how and when the egg arrived to how Witek had left it spinning on the counter. Halfway through her account Austin arrived with the tea then disappeared again in search of a chair. By the time he reappeared Sally's tale was coming to its conclusion. 'The phone rang. I went to my desk to answer it. I had my hand on the receiver when it happened. It blew me over. It was like a big wave on the beach that knocks you off your feet. And I nearly brained myself on the edge of an open drawer. Stuff from the counter was flying everywhere. It looked like a storm had blown things about. Nothing broke or anything apart from the egg, that was just gone completely. It took me a while to realize what'd happened. Do you think it was a time bomb?'

'I doubt it, though it's possible. It's more likely that it was meant to go off when someone opened it and that the spinning motion set it off prematurely. Forensics will tell us, no doubt.' He turned to Witek, who was pale and looked preoccupied. 'You found it, Mr Setkievich.'

'Yes. Ehm, two weeks ago.'

Sally waved her hand in disagreement. 'Three weeks this Friday, actually.'

'Is there CCTV on the buses?'

'No. We do not need TV. Is peaceful, nice people normally, nobody makes us trouble.'

'Can you remember where you found it?'

'Lower deck, I think. On the floor, in a white plastic bag.'

'You don't remember who sat there?'

'No, no. Could be anybody. I don't look at passengers, I look at the road. And people move about. We go slow, is quite safe.' Witek nodded reassuringly.

For once McLusky wished for more CCTV. 'People don't book these tours in advance, do they?'

'Mostly they pay me. They come and go as they want. No booking.'

No bookings, no names, no CCTV, no witnesses, no memories. 'I suppose I'll have to talk to your boss too, just to cover all the angles. Where would I find him?'

'Her.' Sally sniffed at the built-in sexism of the inspector's question.

'Her, sorry.'

'Madeira. For another week.' She sighed. 'On the plus side it's been raining there ever since she arrived, I checked on the net.'

McLusky decided that Sally would recover from her experience soon. 'Mr Setkievich, what time of the day would it have been when you found the egg?'

'I found it after the first tour. So about twenty past ten is when I pull in again, depends on traffic. Sometime is later.'

'And you'd have set off when?'

'Nine thirty.'

He turned to Austin. 'Right, we'll work backwards, get the route, get all available CCTV for that morning and find footage of the bus going round the city. Mr Setkievich, how many Citytour buses are there?'

'Two. But the other was not running that day. I remember because someone made sabotage on bus. Mechanic took all day to find rotten fruit in bus exhaust. I think apple.'

'Well, that makes it easier. If we spot the bus then we might catch a glimpse of the passengers.' He nodded at the civilians. 'Thanks, you've been very helpful. We will need written statements from both of you in due course.'

Sally looked put out. 'Will we have to come to the station to do that?'

'Oh, no. PC Purkis here will visit you at home. You can do it over a mug of tea.'

Purkis perked up. 'Yes, sir. Thank you, sir.'

Outside the scene had changed. Traffic was once more flowing in normal treacle fashion. Behind the now much smaller police cordon stood a bevy of reporters and photographers. He spotted Phil Warren just as she looked his way. Her gaze was interested and unrepentant. McLusky signalled to her with one hand at waist-height, you/me, flashed an open palm for five, mouthed Marriott Hotel. Warren widened her eyes in surprise, gave a slight nod, then walked away casually. The whole transaction was so quick no one else appeared to notice, including Austin who walked beside him.

'There's that Phil Warren slinking off. Probably scared you'll have a go at her.'

'Oh yeah, so it is. I'll get a chance to mess with her mind some other time. Right, Jane. Get on to CCTV, grab as much help as you can find, see if we can spot anything at all.'

'What will you be doing?'

'Me? Just . . . stuff. I'll catch you up.' He ducked under the tape and stuck his head into the door of the Citytours office but didn't cross the threshold. Forensics were everywhere, picking the place over. The team leader with the blond moustache looked up from bagging fragments of bomb mechanism. 'Someone was damn lucky, inspector. This could have removed more than her sweet tooth.' The team groaned. 'Blinded her, more likely. Common fireworks injury. There must have been a pound of gunpowder in this one.'

'Any chance it was a time bomb?'

'No, we can safely rule that out. Same type as the others, perhaps not as lethal.'

'How so?'

'It's all about containment, the tighter the charge is confined the more powerful the explosion. You see, the can killed the bloke because it was soldered shut. The pen too was bad news because of the metal casing, that's what nearly did the librarian in.'

'It didn't look good at first but he's recovering well.' He would send Jane to speak to him. They were constantly playing catch-up, going with the slow grind of the police machine, giving the bastard time to get the next bomb off. This egg proved just how easy it was for the devices to travel in time and space before they went off. Planted nearly three weeks ago, a safe distance. 'How are they set off, just out of interest? Do they have detonators that might be traceable?'

211

'Detonators? Good lord no, nothing as snazzy as that, inspector, you don't need any of that. It's simplicity itself. The action of opening the device completes an electric circuit. At the centre of the gunpowder sits a filament from an ordinary torch bulb with the glass removed. Connected to a battery. The moment the circuit is closed and the filament is connected to the battery it glows white hot. Works just like a fuse. Simple but deadly effective. Low-tech is always best. Take a revolver, for instance, as opposed to a semi- . . .'

'Fascinating, thanks for that.' McLusky withdrew his head and walked off briskly.

The interior of the hotel surprised him. He had expected something more traditional, a little worn perhaps. What he found was a champagne bar and a well-appointed lounge and Philippa Warren on a sofa by the fireplace.

'Another one of those?' McLusky nodded at her drink, clear liquid, ice and lemon.

'No thanks, I have the distinct feeling I ought to be sober for whatever is coming. Or will I need the alcohol to numb the pain?' Her voice was as hoarse as it had been at the Quiet Lady, so presumably this was a permanent feature.

'You'll be fine.' He ordered a cappuccino and sat down next to Warren, their elbows almost touching.

'You mean you're not going to be tedious and berate me about dubious journalistic practices? Because I have an answer for all that.'

'You have? Let's have it.'

'Tough.'

'That's it? That's your answer?'

'You talk, you'll get quoted. Whatever you say in a public house is by definition in the public domain.'

'You may have a point there.'

'"May" doesn't come into it. Okay, I knew who you were and had the advantage. A girl's gotta live.'

'And you were only doing your job.'

'Quite.'

His coffee arrived. Someone had sprinkled grated chocolate over the froth. McLusky hated chocolate and laboriously scraped it off before trying the liquid underneath. It was barely drinkable by his standards. 'How did you find me? Were you following me?'

'Yup. Though not very far. Only from the station to the pub. I expected you to nip into the Green Man in Candlewick Lane but you had other ideas. You're a loner.'

'I'm not a loner. You didn't follow me home a few days ago?'

'Nope, don't know where you live. So someone's been following you?' She drained her glass, rattling the remaining ice in it which attracted the attention of the waiter. 'I think I will have another drink after all.'

'And I'll have a different drink. What was that?'

'G&T.'

'Two gin and tonics.'

'Thanks. Are you going to answer my question?'

'What was the question?'

'Has someone been following you?'

He picked up the spoon and prodded the collapsing froth of his vile cappuccino, remembering the figure by the street corner. Perhaps, perhaps not. A bit of paranoia, most likely. 'Only you, it seems.'

'Mm.' Warren filed the answer under 'evasive'. 'The new bomb was hidden inside an Easter egg? Were there chocolates inside apart from the bomb?'

'D'you know, I never asked?'

A superior smile. 'Only a man could forget to ask that.'

She was right. But what would it signify? An added bit of perversity? Or the fact the bomber didn't care for chocolates either? 'Unimportant.'

'Shame on you, inspector. It's the kind of detail my readers want to know. Are you guys still maintaining the choice of container for the bombs has no significance? Chocolate, beer, make-up, there's got to be a theme here.

To a puritan soul they might all be indulgences he'd disapprove of.'

'Biros?'

'Nobody is perfect.'

McLusky used his mobile rather than his radio, to get the information, calling Austin at the station. 'Jane, find out if the egg contained anything other than the device. Like the chocolates that were supposed to be in there?'

The mention of Austin's nickname attracted Warren's attention. 'Who's Jane then?'

'My DS.'

'Pretty?'

'Very. I'll point Jane out to you sometime.'

Austin came back to him quickly. 'Yes, they are finding traces of chocolate but very small amounts. You think it could be significant?'

'No. Just wondered.' He terminated the call. 'A small amount of chocolate. A token chocolate. Symbolic chocolate. Which leaves us with a man who eats chocolates but has a perverted sense of humour. He gives you one chocolate but blows your fingers off. And that is what I want you to concentrate on in the next piece you write. He is a *bastard*. He's a *coward*, he has a twisted sense of humour. He thinks he has a good reason for doing what he does but he hasn't. It's his *delusions of self-importance* that make him think he's justified, not any cause he might have. And by using an Easter egg he's clearly targeted children, which makes him the biggest coward imaginable.'

'Says Detective Inspector Liam McLusky?'

'Says *a source close to the investigation*.'

Warren's face lit up. 'You are trying to provoke him.'

'Two can play.'

'So you had contact before? He contacted you after my last piece, am I right?'

McLusky drank silently.

'I knew it. What did he say? Did he call, write, email?'

214

'Can't tell you. You can't mention it, it would put the entire investigation at risk. And that's official. If I hear about it I'll issue a warrant for your arrest.'

Warren snorted dismissively. 'You won't make it stick, no witnesses. So what's in it for me?'

'Exclusive when I get him.'

'Can I have that in writing?'

McLusky drained his glass and stood up. 'Don't be daft. I gave you the piece of chocolate, that proves you have inside information. Go make the bastard feel small.' He turned away towards the exit.

'Do you drink at the Quiet Lady often, inspector?'

McLusky didn't turn around. 'No, never.' In an inside pocket his mobile vibrated. A text message from Louise Rennie. *Mud analysed. Collect results 8 pm at the Myristica, King Street. Smart casual.* He texted his acceptance. Then he remembered the bin-liner waiting to be taken to the launderette and went in search of the nearest clothes shop to stock up on smart casual.

Sorbie fiddled with the strap on his helmet, having trouble remembering how it went through the double metal loop. It was such a long time since he'd ridden a motorbike. His hands fluttered a little with the adrenalin of it and he turned away from the patiently waiting vendor. No point giving the teenage mutant opportunity to sneer.

But it seemed the kid was more interested in the state of his helmet. 'That's old-fashioned lids for you. The new ones are all seatbelt style. I'm not being funny but you really should get a new one anyway, looks like yours has been dropped, you've got a scuff on the side. '

The scuff on the side of Sorbie's helmet was the result of the spill that had interrupted his biking career ten years ago. His bike had not been worth repairing and a car had suddenly seemed a sensible alternative. Yet he had held on to the gear, along with vague dreams of one day making a

215

comeback. And here it was. The teenage mutant with the nose-ring and eyebrow studs who now had a significant wodge of his hard-earned in his pocket was right, of course, the helmet was junk. It would probably come apart like a raw egg if his head hit the tarmac, but it satisfied the demands of the law. He had intended to buy a new one with the money he got off the asking price for the bike but had surprised himself again by how completely inept at haggling he was. 'It'll do for now.'

'On your head be it.'

'Ha, very good.' At last the strap fastened. He shook hands with the kid, pulled on his gloves and straddled the tall trail bike. The engine growled into life and Sorbie's excitement mounted. Ten years. He gingerly pulled away. In his mirrors he thought he saw the teenager shake his head. In response Sorbie accelerated away hard along the dimly lit street, trying to remember the way out of the estate back to the main road. When he reached it he opened the throttle wide and took off towards the dual carriage-way at twice the speed limit. 'Yyyyyes!' He shouted his delight inside his helmet, born again. The engine on this thing had enough grunt to catch any scooter and the bike was skinny enough to go wherever they went. Solo units with their half-ton of equipment and modifications could get stuck in traffic nearly as easy as a police car. But not this. This could go anywhere, on the road or off the road. And if he caught up with the bastard Mobile Muggers he'd blow them into the weeds for good. Unofficially of course. In his spare time.

Well, someone had to show some initiative round here.

Chapter Twelve

Carol Farr could hardly believe how late it was. She should have been back by seven but her coach from London had been stuck on the motorway for two whole hours and even after that the traffic had crawled along. Two massive accidents, apparently. Once the traffic started moving again they had made the driver stop at a service station, the whole coach was dying for a wee and the onboard toilet was out of order. They had run out of refreshments for the passengers so half of them also queued to buy stuff like drinks and sandwiches. In the end it had taken another half-hour to get everyone back on board. What a nightmare journey.

She hated walking home in the dark but she had spent her last penny in that service station on a Coke, some chewing gum and a magazine just to alleviate the boredom. Should have bought a sandwich, starving now.

The bridge seemed to go on forever tonight. There was still quite a bit of traffic, which made her feel safer. She had turned her iPod off now she was in the suburbs. With the music and the wind and the traffic noise you wouldn't hear if someone came up behind you. She checked over her shoulder – there was nobody walking on the bridge at all. Just her. The wind blustered in her ears and snatched at her clothes. It had been a good gig, worth going, just a shame Jo had managed to get ill at the last minute leaving her to go by herself. She'd bought her tickets ages ago, there was no way she was going to miss it. And it had been worth it.

Then today, after leaving Jo's friends who had put her up on the sofa, she'd done Oxford Street, mainly clothes and record shops. She didn't have much money left to spend so in the end she'd bought three CDs and that was that. Sensible. She could have got more money out but the whole trip had already cost too much.

Well, that was the bridge done. Not that this was civilization yet, Bedminster Bridge led you into some scenery that was bloody depressing. Coronation Road seemed to go on forever, nothing but the muddy river and shrubbery to the right, supermarket car park and shrubbery to the left. And she had to walk right to the end of it to get home, what a boring end to a brilliant couple of days. Carol turned her iPod back on.

They were just sitting there, on their scooters, two on each on both sides of the road. Suddenly there was no more traffic. Why was there no traffic? She just knew it was them. They closed in quickly on their scooters, surrounding her. Two of them got off.

They all shouted at her. 'Your bag, your money!'

'Hand it over!'

'Now!'

The biggest one ripped her bag open, took her mobile and the CDs. 'Your money, where's your fucking money?'

The pillion from the other scooter grabbed her hair and twisted, yanked back her head and grabbed at her throat. 'The money, now!'

Carol tried to prise away his gloved hand but he tightened his grip and kneed her in the back. 'I – I haven't got any.' She only just managed to squeeze the words out.

'Don't lie!' The big man in front of her went through her outer pockets, then ripped her jacket open, pawing at the inside pocket.

She glimpsed one, two cars going by. Couldn't they see what was happening?

The punch in the stomach came as a surprise. The man behind her let go of her throat, spun her head around by her hair and kicked hard into the back of her knees. Then she was on the ground and they were kicking her. She shut her eyes and covered her head, curled up, as the kicks rained. Then it suddenly stopped. A car horn blared, the engines of the scooters whined. They were gone. Only when all was quiet did she dare to open her eyes again. Two more cars drove by slowly, the drivers curious, but then accelerated away. Carol hated them more than the muggers.

McLusky was glad it was a mild night because it meant they could walk. If he had thought about it he'd have found he was simply glad all round. The evening was going unexpectedly well, he hadn't put his foot in it once, the food at the Myristica had been excellent and the night was curiously mild, giving it an almost Mediterranean feel. Even the Georgian houses around here didn't look a million miles away from Italian architecture, though you couldn't quite imagine people stringing washing across the streets. He hadn't really known where else to walk so he had steered Louise towards his flat in Northmoor Street and she seemed happy to walk without asking the destination. He had been gently teased about his obviously brand new clothes that clashed with his comfortably worn shoes. What Dr Louise Rennie would make of his flat, even after the hour-and-a-half he had spent clearing up the worst mess, remained to be seen. At least the sofa and coffee table he'd bought from the junk shop down the road had been delivered and she wouldn't have to stand. He had bought a bottle of red too, just in case.

As they turned into Northmoor Street he couldn't help feeling that it had been presumptuous to lead her here. 'Well, this is where I live, doctor, thanks for walking me home.'

'Is that what I've been doing?'

'Looks like it.'

'And are you going to ask me in?'

'I was going to try that next. Would you like to come up for a drink?'

'Thank you, I would.'

'I must warn you, I haven't had time to decorate yet. Or buy a lot of things, there hasn't really been the time to do anything much yet, careful, the tread is broken on that step.' He noticed he was talking too fast as they climbed the narrow stairs and with some effort stopped apologizing until they got to his floor. His mail had been left by the door. He scooped it up without checking it and inserted the key in the lock. 'Well, here goes, don't say I didn't warn you.'

'Yeah, yeah.' She dismissed his warnings as self-deprecation but only until she had negotiated the empty hall and stood in what was meant to be the living room. There were no curtains and no lampshade on the bare bulb dangling from the ceiling. In fact it would have been much quicker to list what actually was there: an unfashionable blue sofa and a pine coffee table standing on a thin ethnic rug. The walls were white. 'Interesting, who's your decorator?'

'Warned you. The rest is worse. The spare room is still full of boxes, I'm not really unpacked yet.' In the kitchen he popped the cork on a bottle of Australian red while Louise took in the spartan fittings with a deepening frown. McLusky noticed it. 'I ordered a fridge, should come any day now.'

She ran a finger over the cream enamel of the WWII gas cooker. 'A nice steam-driven one, I hope. Do all policemen live like this?'

'No, I doubt it. Though I'm sure a lot of them survive on canteen food and pizza.' He looked for wineglasses, couldn't find any and had to settle for a couple of tumblers. 'It's only temporary, I'll get it all sorted once I've got my bearings.'

The sofa was hard and smelled of dust and long storage. It reminded Louise of her student days in shabbily furnished accommodation, all that was missing were the posters of rock groups on the walls. She watched McLusky light a cigarette, manipulating the expensive-looking lighter with slender fingers. He used a saucer as an ashtray. This was like dating a teenager in his first digs away from home. She fortified herself with half a tumblerful of wine, reached out and gently grabbed and twisted his new blue shirt, pulling herself closer. 'Okay, time you came clean. Unless this fabled spare room with all your boxes is one hell of a cavern you don't seem to have ... well, let's just call it *stuff*. What happened? Did your last place burn down? Burglary? Repossession? Left somewhere in a hurry? Or did you just upgrade from a caravan?'

McLusky smiled down at Louise's fist holding on to the shirt material. The grab had turned into a small, two-fingered caress. 'I'm trained to deal with shirt-grabbers, you know?'

'Well, you can show me that later. This is *my* interview technique. So. What happened? You've been very cagey all evening about your life in Southampton while I've told you practically every story of my life.'

'I just don't do stuff very well, that's all. In Southampton I moved in with someone who seemed to have all that kind of thing already, fridges and cookers and heated towel rails. So I never accumulated any. When we split I simply threw some things into a few boxes and bin-liners ...' It had been Laura in fact who had packed all his possessions into boxes, carefully wrapped naturally, while he was still recovering in hospital. It was all there waiting for him at the section house when he got out. Half of it had never been unpacked since. 'I'm not hung up on material things.'

'Neither am I. Just a place to lay my head, really.' She let herself sink back along the length of the sofa, bringing him with her by the shirt. Slipping her fingers into his hair she pulled him close until their lips met in a series of slow, tentative kisses. His aftershave seemed to have mellowed and blended with his own particular fragrance into faint hints of cinnamon and musk. She enjoyed the weight of his body on hers and wriggled lower, sliding her hands down his back as their kisses grew longer. His hands insinuated themselves smoothly into the small of her back, the arch of her neck. A hum of pleasure vibrated his chest and he pulled her body harder towards his own. Louise walked her fingers over the unfamiliar topography of his muscles under the shirt material, a whole landscape in urgent need of exploring. The unfamiliar buzz of the door bell froze both of them in a silent, trembling pause. The door bell sounded again, longer, more insistently.

'Bugger.' His first instinct was to ignore it. It was what the cast of Louise's eyes and the pressure of her palms against his back seemed to suggest too. Only his mobile had been turned off, his airwave was in the kitchen and he could still hear the super's warning that he might keep himself more available in future. The buzzer sounded for long seconds, someone was leaning on the button downstairs. 'I'll have to check.' With an involuntary groan of frustration he disentangled himself, moving swiftly to the intercom by the door. 'Yes?'

'Liam?' A woman's voice.

'Who is this?'

'It's me, open the door.'

'Laura . . .?'

'Give that man a coconut. Are you going to let me in or not?'

McLusky pressed the button while his mind raced. What was she doing here? And at this time of night? How had she found him? What could it mean? When she appeared in his doorway the sight of her drove all speculation into the background.

'Well, can I come in?' She peered past him. 'Or is it inconvenient?'

'No, not at all.' He stepped aside to let her pass and

caught sight of Louise whose expression suggested he might have worded that differently. 'Come in, now you're here.' In the sitting room he made the introductions, feeling a little dazed. Unexpected didn't begin to describe this. She looked well, her hair was shorter, she looked younger too, somehow, or just different? 'What are you doing here? And how did you find me, I mean, why?'

'I did call your mobile but it was always unavailable. They gave me your number and address in Albany Road, after they checked with Southampton that I was who I said I was.'

'Laura, what are you doing here?'

Louise got up, smoothed her dress and picked up her handbag. 'I'd better go, I can see you have things to discuss.'

'No, wait, I mean, I'll call you a cab.'

'I'll be fine, I'll call myself one.'

'If you're sure.'

'Sure I'm sure. Bye-bye, Liam.' She twisted lightly away from the hand he had laid on her arm and didn't look back as she descended the stairs. McLusky closed the door gingerly behind her.

'I did call, honestly, Liam. I thought I'd see how you are, I couldn't have known you'd be having company. So soon.' Casually opening the doors to both spare room and bathroom she nodded knowingly, went on into the kitchen where she stalled in mock astonishment for a moment, then tested the weight of the kettle before flicking the on-switch.

He leant against the door frame, hands buried in his pockets. 'Make yourself at home, Laura.'

'Well, it does all look so familiar. It's an exact copy of the place you had when I first met you. I don't even have to see your bedroom, it's a mattress on the floor and a bin-liner with dirty laundry in the corner, am I right?' Her smile finally reached her eyes. 'But even then you at least

223

had a fridge. You need a bit of help with this nest-making thing.'

'Is that what you came here for, to help me build a nest?'

'Oh no, not at all. I had an interview today at the university here.'

'To do what? And why here?'

She turned her back on him while she pretended to look for tea and mugs in the dresser. 'It's for a degree course. I'm going to be a student.'

'A student. Studying what?' Laura had never before given the slightest hint that she wanted to resume her education.

'You could sound a bit more pleased for me. Archaeology. Field archaeology.'

'You're going to . . . dig up stuff.' It figured.

She turned, folded her arms and leant back against the dresser, the search abandoned. 'That's the plan. I had an interview today, it went well. At least I think it did.'

'And what brought this on? I mean, you never talked about archaeology before.'

'Yes I did. Well, I always watched stuff on telly.'

'What about your job?'

'The surgery is merging with a larger one and they don't need two administrators so I took the redundancy they offered. It'll pay towards my degree.'

'But why here? Don't they do archaeology at Southampton?'

'They do but here I get to study with the good-looking bloke from the telly.'

'You're kidding.'

'I am. The fees are lower and I prefer the course programme.'

'I see. Well, I . . .' He let out a deep breath through puffed-up cheeks. 'That's . . . brilliant. But why are you still here? In town, I mean?'

'There's a field trip for interested applicants tomorrow, we'll spend the weekend on a dig near here. They didn't tell us what, I think it's to test our dedication.'

'Could be a Roman villa.'

'Medieval midden heap.'

'Ancient burial.'

'Who was that woman?'

'Someone who helped me with a case.'

'But she's not an officer.'

'No, she works at the uni.'

'Might get to see more of her then. Me, not you, I mean. Ehm . . .' Laura frowned at the kitchen again. 'I'm not sure I really want a hot drink.'

'There's some red wine . . .'

'You know I'm allergic to red.'

'There's a late-night place down the road, I'll get you a bottle of white.' He picked up his jacket, shook it but didn't hear his keys. 'I'll ring the door bell, I won't be a sec.' While he walked quickly along the road McLusky marvelled at how Laura had managed within two minutes to drive away the woman he had hoped to take to bed yet had him trotting along to the late-night pub to fetch a bottle of overpriced white for her. Three years, that's how. Three years of living and fighting and scratching their names into each other.

Laura walked through to the one door she hadn't opened yet. She pushed it wide without entering. A mattress on the floor, as she had expected. Yet there wasn't the accumulation of beer cans and empty cigarette packets that used to complete the picture and there were no black bin-liners either. Another sure sign that she had interrupted something was the fact that the bed was made. Liam never made a bed unless he expected to share it. And only then for the first half a dozen times. Unless the accident, as everyone had insisted on calling his attempted murder, had miraculously changed him into a tidy person. It had left him looking leaner and paler than she had ever seen him but underneath she suspected the same old Liam. So why was she here?

The door bell rang, two short pings, the way he always rang it. She pressed the button on the intercom until she heard the door open downstairs then on a sudden impulse went into the bathroom. Here she was back on very familiar ground. Several damp towels draped wherever, the wash basin encircled with used razors and a tube of toothpaste spilling its guts. In the corner behind the door, a stray black sock. This chaos had always infuriated her, so why did a fierce nostalgia bite at her now? She heard the clinking of bottles and quickly checked herself in the mirror, make-up, hair, teeth, then pulled a face at herself.

From the sitting room came a girl's voice. 'Liam? I pilfered six bottles of Pilsener from the pub and I want you to arrest me. I suggest a strip search and a night in custody. Where are you?'

Laura found the voice belonged to a blonde girl showing surprise, a pierced belly button and a lot of leg below the hem of a frayed denim miniskirt.

'Oh sorry, hi, didn't know he had company. I'm Rebecca.' She was cradling half a dozen bottles of beer in front of her no doubt perfect chest. 'Where is he then?'

'He just popped out, he'll be back in a minute. I was just leaving.'

'You sure?'

'I am.' She picked up her handbag. 'Absolutely certain. Abso-bloody-lutely.' She slammed the front door and clattered noisily down the stairs. As she left the building she nearly collided with McLusky carrying a bottle of wine by the neck like a weapon.

'Where're you going? I just got your wine, I thought we were having a drink?'

She didn't stop but walked a few steps backwards. 'Some other time, Liam, you're far too busy right now.' She smiled and waved then walked quickly away. Just around the corner she passed a man in a blue rainproof examining his shoes. She couldn't be absolutely certain but hadn't he been there examining his shoes when she arrived? Not that it bloody mattered.

Chapter Thirteen

Charlene Kernley hated this bit. She didn't like walking home in the dark and she hated walking right by the river but it was such a shortcut. At first she used to take the bus but the return ticket had gone up so much she would have to work forty minutes each day – she had worked it out on a calculator – just to pay the fare, so now she walked and this shortcut made it just about bearable.

There were the lights around the swing bridge but the further she walked the darker it got. The council should really put some lamps here. She never used it in winter, far too dark before and after work, she always went the long way round. But at this time of the year there was still some light left in the sky and it was only in the middle between the bridges that it got really scary. She shouldn't walk home alone, there were so many places where someone could lie in wait and jump out at you. She knew in theory that things like that happened but they didn't happen all that often, surely, and never to anyone she knew.

At intervals Charlene checked over her shoulder to see if anyone was there. If she saw someone she would run. Not that she could run very far, not with her asthma, but there were cars driving up there, she would make it that far.

There was no one. No one but her. No one else was stupid enough to use this shortcut, she thought icily.

Charlene could feel herself go wheezy – hell, she could *hear* herself go wheezy, it was so quiet on this stretch. She stopped, got out her inhaler, always in her left jacket pocket, shook it and took a deep suck into her lungs. That was better. Her biggest fear was that one day it would simply stop working. One day she would use her puffer and nothing would happen. She was only seventeen now, could you really live all your life relying on your inhaler being there when you felt that someone had stolen all the oxygen from the air? But then you never knew, they might find a cure for asthma though she wasn't sure they were actually looking for one.

As she set off again, aiming for the weak puddle of light that a sodium lamp from the bridge threw on to the path, a shiny object near the edge of it drew her eye. It gave her something else to aim for, would take her mind off things for the next few yards. Probably broken glass, there seemed to be a lot of it lying about, mostly beer bottles. But this was no beer bottle, the thing looked square. As she got closer she thought she knew what it was and quickened her step, despite still feeling a little wheezy. No longer checking behind her now.

It was a mobile phone. Not the latest model but not a crap one either. Black and silver and so heavy in the hand. Not a scratch on it, it looked polished in the gloom. Charlene didn't own a mobile, simply couldn't afford it at the moment. Every kid in the street had a mobile, the parents probably picked up the bill. Even though she was working five days at the canteen she couldn't afford it. She wondered whether this one worked, it would be just her luck to find a broken one. Where did you switch this on? This button at the top, she supposed.

The tongue of magnesium-powered flame that shot straight into her mouth seemed to consume all the oxygen in the world. She had swallowed live coals and now her head was on fire. While the melting plastic of the phone's casing fused with the burning flesh of her hand she staggered back, trying to escape from the blinding swirls of coloured pain in front of her eyes. With her airways soldered shut with fear, panic and fire she whirled around, unseeing, hoping to extinguish the fire in her face and hand. She didn't realize that she was already falling, pitching sideways into the oily water with a silent scream. The other reason she hated walking by the river: she had never learned to swim. The ice-cold grip of the black water mixed with the fire in her mouth, indistinguishable. Charlene kicked her legs and thrashed her arms, straining towards what she thought was the surface, what she hoped was up, but it was dark now, cold and black. The pain in her chest was raging, it became huge, it became unbearable, her heart punched like a fist into her throat. Nowhere was up, it was all down, it was all black. Charlene stopped struggling and the pain popped like a child's balloon.

'Mum being in and out of hospital all the time is how I learnt to cook. No, it's a lie, my dad trying to cook for us, that's what did it. He was awful. In the kitchen, I mean. Can you cook?'

'Don't know, never tried it.' His stomach rumbled but McLusky didn't mind waiting. He lit another cigarette and poured more wine. What for him made this unexpected domesticity quite acceptable was that the cook was messy and dressed in nothing but a T-shirt.

At first Rebecca had just been there, then been there again, then been there still. Soon a portfolio, a messy bundle of drawings and a toolbox had appeared, along with a holdall full of clothes. On cue the fridge-freezer was delivered. The empty fridge had given rise to shopping. This in turn had spawned cooking.

'Seriously?'

'I've been known to boil potatoes and shove lamb chops under the grill.'

'That's cooking. One step up from heating up ready-meals, anyway.'

The sound of his airwave springing to life next door made McLusky even hungrier. He groaned theatrically.

Rebecca turned round to face him. Blood red sauce spattered from the spoon she held aloft on to the floor. 'What?'

'Work.'

'Tell them you're a hundred miles away, visiting sick relatives. That's what I always do.'

'Ah, that doesn't work any more. Airwave radio has GPS. They know exactly where I am.'

'Then don't answer it.'

'There's always that, I suppose.'

He answered it, scribbled down the unfamiliar street references and promised he was on his way.

'But what about your supper?'

The sentence had a painful familiarity about it, despite coming from the lips of a half-naked girl he barely knew. Her voice still had the fresh tone of surprise, regret and genuine commiseration it would soon lose. Given time the tone of that same sentence would change first to resignation, then resentment and accusation.

'Leave me some.' He stooped to kiss her goodbye. 'What is it, anyway?'

'Not telling you now.' She kissed him, wrapping arms and one leg around him, a hero's goodbye. 'Is it at least something important?'

'It is to someone.' He took a deep breath, his nostrils filling with the fragrance of her hair, the aroma of her food. He pulled away with twin regrets.

A short necklace of arc lights had already been strung along the riverside. He abandoned his car at the end of a line of police vehicles on the road and stood next to a muddy bicycle by some railings near a large landlocked ship's anchor. This stretch of water was called the Cumberland Basin, he had learned over the radio, and somewhere close by was something called the Floating Harbour. Here a paved path ran along the basin between the bridges. Now it was busy with officers and crime scene technicians but before their arrival it had to have been deserted at this time of the day and year. Another blank patch on McLusky's mind-map of the city had been filled in. But ultimately it made no difference where this was. Death loved dark water but had never been choosy. If what had occurred down there turned out to be murder then this dismal stretch of water would forever appear as a stain on the emotional map he carried to navigate the city by. When the stains on the map began to run into each other then it might be time to move on. Or take early retirement.

Flashing his ID to the constable standing guard at the anchor was unnecessary: the PC recognized him from the Easter egg bomb as a sarcastic CID bastard. When he saw McLusky bend over the edge to get a look at a frog-man in the water he fervently wished someone would nudge him in.

Most of the activity was concentrated in an area where the body had been pulled from the river. The pathologist was there already, kneeling white-suited by a rectangle of tarpaulin on which rested the body of a woman. It was fully clothed, which was always good news.

McLusky suited up; it gave him time to remember the pathologist's name before approaching him. 'Evening, Dr Coulthard.'

'Inspector . . .'

The pathologist concentrated his examination on the face and neck of the victim. Here scorch marks were the prominent feature, clearly discernible even under the covering of oily slime. The victim's right hand was encased in a clear evidence bag, secured at the wrist with a soft tie.

'Any clues as to the cause of death yet?'

'Mm? Not really, but my guess is that she drowned.'

'Then what's with her face, are those burn marks around her mouth?'

'They appear to be.'

'Did that happen before death?'

'Rest assured, I think we'll find it did.'

'Thank the gods for that. I can deal with *strange* but I hate *weird*.' So far McLusky saw no reason why he

231

shouldn't hand this over to someone else. He was, after all, supposed to concentrate on finding the bomber. Drowned girls didn't fit the remit. 'Still, very strange, how do you burn yourself on an empty path next to the water? It wasn't one of those fire-spitting accidents?' It was not unheard of that unwise street performers who spat and swallowed fire reached for the petrol when paraffin was unobtainable. The results were invariably disastrous, occasionally fatal.

Coulthard straightened up, shaking his head slowly. 'No, nothing like that.'

'So, what, a freak accident?'

'Almost right, inspector. My guess is accident arranged by a freak.'

McLusky's mood took a nosedive. He pointed to the victim's wrapped hand. 'She picked something up?'

'Yes. It looks to me like the melted remnants of a mobile phone, fused into her charred skin. The phone must have contained some kind of accelerant, possibly similar to the one used in the powder compact. Once it went off she couldn't have dropped it if she'd tried. The thing must have burnt instantly with such a fierce heat that it stuck to her hand. My guess is she tried to douse the pain, fell in and drowned. This is definitely another one of yours. Sorry. I could see you were hoping otherwise.'

McLusky straightened up and looked about. 'What a shit place to die too. I wonder where she found the thing.' Would the bomber leave it here, where few people came? Why not? But more than likely she had picked up the phone, if that's what it turned out to be, somewhere else. And they might never know. Unless.

A preliminary search of the area was already under way, the fingertip search would have to wait until daylight. Austin appeared by his side. 'We got a tentative ID, she was carrying a library card. No photo ID though. Charlene Kernley. We came up with an address near Ashton Gate. I think she was taking a shortcut.'

232

'Walking alone after dark ... Not that it would have made any difference. How old do we think she was?'

'No more than sixteen, seventeen.'

'Who found her?'

Austin pointed to a man in his early thirties, sitting morosely with his back to a bollard under the watchful eye of Constable Pym. 'This character over there. He flagged down a Traffic unit that happened to be passing. I don't think he's happy about having to hang around, though.'

'Well, that's just tough. Let's have a quick chat with him.'

Even when he stood in front of him the man didn't get up until he addressed him. 'Do you think we could have a word? I'm Detective Inspector McLusky. And you are?'

'Reed.'

'You found the body.'

'Yes.'

'Where exactly was the body when you first saw it?'

'Just there, where they pulled her out. She was sort of floating, face down. Just by the edge.'

'Did you pull her out?'

'No, didn't touch her, I know not to touch dead bodies. I went and found a police car and stopped them. They pulled her out.'

'Good thinking.' McLusky turned around, contemplated the group of crime scene technicians near the water's edge for a few seconds, then turned to Reed again. The man's boots were muddy, and his hands were a little grimy. His fingernails were positively black. 'What's your first name, Mr Reed?'

'It's Chris, Christopher. I gave all my details to that policewoman . . .' His gaze moved about, trying to spot the officer who had taken his details.

'Never mind. And what do you do, Chris? You don't mind if I call you Chris?'

'Ehm, no, I'm a student.'

'At the uni? What are you studying?'

'What's that got to do with it? I didn't have anything to do with the girl dying, I just found her. I was just passing. Why are you asking me questions? Is that what you get for helping the police, endless questions?'

This kind of reaction always rang little alarm bells with McLusky. 'Bear with us, Chris, we'll have you on your way in no time. So, what were you doing down here?'

Reed shrugged. 'Just passing, riding my bike.'

'Right. Is that your bike back there? By the railings?' It was difficult to make out from here. 'Do you have lights on your bike?'

'There's a dead girl and you ask me about the lights on my bike?' He made a silent appeal to Austin but got nothing in return but a lizard stare. 'Okay, no, I don't have lights, are you going to arrest me for that?'

'And where were you going?'

'Home.'

'Which is?'

'In Cotham.'

'And you were coming from where?'

'Nowhere. Just riding my bike.'

McLusky shot Austin a questioning look. Austin's eyebrows rose and he took over. 'Just for fun?'

'Yes. That's allowed, isn't it?'

'Sure. Only Cotham is quite a ways from here . . . *Chris*. And your bike, if I remember rightly, is just an old boneshaker with no gears. It's pretty dark down here too with no lights and there's broken glass about.'

McLusky took up the baton again. 'Okay, Chris, let's try again. What were you doing here?'

'Nothing illegal, I've done nothing wrong.'

'I would like to believe that, really I would. What did you say you were studying?'

'Political science.'

'Not horticulture then.'

'What?'

'Your hands, your fingernails, you look like you've been gardening or something. You said you didn't go near the body, how did your hands get that dirty?'

'I . . . the chain came off my bike. Now look . . .'

The body had been pulled out at a spot more or less equidistant from the two bridges, where it would be darkest. 'So how did you spot the body in the water if you were cycling and had no lights?'

'I was pushing it at the time. As you said, there's lots of glass around here.'

'Okay, you were pushing your bike along this dismal bit of path in the dark for no reason whatsoever, on the wrong side of town, near a row of houses, several of which have recently been burgled.' He had invented the burglaries but it seemed to pay dividends, Reed became visibly scared.

'Burglary? What else are you going to accuse me of? First that I have something to do with the dead girl, then burglary. You're completely mad.'

Behind Reed an elderly man at the cordon started heckling the police and technicians, his hard-edged face a mask of anger in the ghoulish light. 'I could have told you that would happen. It was only a matter of time. Decent street lighting and constables on the beat is what we need. You lot only turn up when it's all too late. You're useless.'

A PC ambled over to have a soothing word with him. McLusky opted for a change of venue. 'Do you have anything on you that you shouldn't?'

Reed shook his head. 'No.'

'Sure? Okay. Show me your bike.'

Reed didn't budge. 'It's just back there.'

'Come on then, let's have a quick look at it.'

'It's just an ordinary bicycle.' Despite his resistance he became the reluctant filling in a CID sandwich as Austin led the way, McLusky following close behind.

'You see, it's just an old bike.' Somehow Reed stood back from it, as if trying to dissociate himself from it.

'It's a wreck. Can you open the panniers for us, please.'

Reed's hands fumbled with the fastener of the first pannier. He opened it and stood back.

'Fruit. That's a lot of fruit, Chris. And in bad condition, most of it.' He picked up an orange, flicking a thumbnail over its mildewed rind.

'Yeah, I forgot it was in there actually. I got it cheap from the market. I'll probably need to chuck that away now.'

'Okay. What's in the other one, more fruit?'

'The other one?'

'Yes. The *other* one.'

Reed opened it with an impatient flick. Snugly fitted inside was a plastic container brimful with dark, oily mud. The hooked handle of a ladle was just visible.

McLusky impatiently wriggled his fingers. 'The leaflets, hand them over.'

Reed shoved a hand deep into his jacket and produced a wad of his home-made pamphlets. DISABLE A CAR TODAY ... McLusky handed them on to the PC. 'Here, get Fruit 'n' Mud and his bicycle down the station for a chat. If he gives you any grief at all, caution him. We want to chat some more and when we're finished I know a few people from Traffic who are keen to have a word.'

Sorbie shifted on his bar stool, checked the time on his mobile and swore silently. He was on his fourth mug of stewed tea at the clapboard café that served the lock-up owners, delivery drivers and the workers from the nearby trading estate. From where he was sitting he had a good view of Mitchell's lock-up, just two doors up. Entrance to the warehouses was on alternate sides to give more forecourt space, which meant that old cars, broken-down vans, stacks of wooden pallets and nests of bins proliferated on both sides.

There was no guarantee that Mitchell would turn up before the tea and sausage rolls Sorbie kept ordering at intervals gave him the heartburn from hell but it would be worth it. A bit of banter, some sleight of hand – he'd always been good at that, card tricks, shoplifting as a school kid – and soon Mr Mitchell's emporium would lie wide open to explore. After that a bit of luck and good timing was what was needed. Quite a bit of luck, come to think of it. And here was the bastard at last, getting out of an unfashionable old Jaguar. And he was by himself which was perfect. Sorbie moved fast; he had to time this just right. His bike was parked close to the huge double doors, giving him the excuse to walk over. As far as he knew Mitchell had never set eyes on him yet it was important he would not recognize him later, so Sorbie put his helmet on and pretended to fumble with his straps just as Mitchell snapped open the enormous brass padlock that secured the doors.

Heavy in Sorbie's jacket pocket weighed another padlock of identical make, already flipped open. 'S'cuse me, mate. I was wonderin' . . .'

Mitchell turned around suspiciously. 'What?'

'I was wonderin' . . . me and a couple of mates was thinking of maybe renting one of these lock-ups for using as a workshop. For fixing up bikes for the bike club.'

'And?' Mitchell turned his back on him and opened the door just wide enough to let himself in.

'I was wonderin' how big they was and how much the council charged and that.'

Mitchell flicked a wall switch and high up in the ceiling two banks of neon lights blinked on. By the time he turned round to face Sorbie again the padlocks had changed places.

'Mind if I have a quick shufti?'

'Sorry, can't allow you in there, security, see? But, I mean, you can get an idea of the size from here. And what you pay depends entirely on what state the place is in, whether it has leccy and water and all that. All right? Ask the council.' Mitchell was closing the door on him.

Sorbie turned away, nodding, as though totally satisfied. 'Yeah, cheers, mate.' He started his bike and rode off straight away, without looking back. At the next junction he turned off, parked the bike next to a waiting Renault and got into the car on the passenger side.

DI Fairfield started the engine. 'Okay?'

'Piece of piss, guv. I still think you should let me go in instead.'

'We've already had this talk, twice, DI Sorbie. I'll not discuss it again. You've done your bit and I'm grateful, now shove off, you're off duty. If it goes tits up then at least it'll be my tits. Hand over the lock.'

Sorbie dropped the weighty padlock into her out-stretched palm and got out, closing the door with disapproving but not insubordinate force. Fairfield waited until he had ridden off then drove fast in the opposite direction to the warehouses, turned into the potholed customer car park of the Railway Tavern and parked in a spot from where it was just possible, albeit at an extreme angle, to observe the doors of Mitchell's lock-up. They'd been very lucky, the timing couldn't have been better. It was cashing-up time now at the café. Through her lightweight binoculars she observed the girls as they took in the menu boards and closed the shutters of the squat wooden hut. At all times she kept the doors of the lock-up in view. She didn't expect to see anything surprising. When they had first targeted Mitchell they had watched ad nauseam as nothing much happened. No one except the owner was ever seen visiting and the eventual search of the lock-up had produced nothing but more or less legitimate junk. A search of Mitchell's garden flat had equally drawn a blank. Yet she remained convinced that Mitchell was behind the scooter muggings. Not that there wasn't enough other street crime to keep them going, but the persistence of this gang and the arrogance of the man she suspected to run it rankled. She knew she was damaging her career in pursuit of a small-time criminal but she didn't care. Other officers had a more sanguine attitude to criminals who got away. They consoled themselves with the thought that you could never catch them all and that if you couldn't get them for a particular offence you were bound to get them for another one later. It was an attitude she found hard to cultivate. For her, letting a criminal carry on meant she was failing to protect the victims of his crimes. This, too, was probably not a practical stance. She knew that some of her colleagues loathed the victims of crime almost as much as those perpetrating it. It was true some people seemed to invite crime.

The only thing she felt slightly guilty about was leaving Sorbie under the impression that she had thought up the padlock trick herself when in reality she'd remembered it from a crime story she had read years ago.

It wasn't long until Mitchell emerged, carrying a box. Through her binoculars she could make out the picture of a DVD player on its side. Transferring the box to his left hip he hefted the heavy door shut with his shoulder, then hooked the padlock in place and snapped it shut one-handed. A conscientious tug to test it had fastened, then he walked left out of sight to where she knew his car stood. Moments later the Jaguar passed her field of vision going west in the direction of Mitchell's home.

Once she was sure the café staff had all gone Fairfield didn't waste any time. She had come prepared with gloves, pencil torch and a small digital camera that had excellent night vision. As she started across the car park, eyes fixed on the lock-up on the other side of the road, four young men heading towards the pub in high spirits called out to her. 'You're going the wrong way, sweetheart, the pub's over there.'

'Yeah, come and join us, come for a drink.'

Fairfield gave them a non-committal smile. And just in case they took further interest she kept walking until the pub was out of sight, allowing time for the lads to disappear inside, then walked back, crossed the road and sauntered up to the lock-up, making it look as though she belonged. The cold brass lock released after one turn of the key.

'Open sesame.'

A huge, sprawling hive. A big, convoluted, up-and-down-switchback town full of noise, full of life, full of everything a man could want. Here were all the pubs and clubs, all the theatres and museums, restaurants and takeaways you could stomach. Its streets made you feel that anything might happen, to someone, somewhere, for some reason. He loved this city. He'd grown up here, knew every corner and alley as well as his adversaries did. Sometimes he knew them better, since he had made it his business to better them. He owned this place in a way an incomer like McLusky would never do, however long he hung about. Which is why he, Sorbie, would make a fist of it. An angry fist but one that served well. Career mattered, clear-up rates mattered, yet just fighting the war also mattered to him. They could never *win* the war, not even a police state could win this war, but you had to keep winning battles, at least some of them, keep putting the fear into them, or the streets would become unmanageable. Once that happened, ghettos and no-go areas would follow, parts of the city abandoned, handed over to the dregs of society to be administered by the criminally insane. It could happen. But it must not happen. Not here.

Which is why Sorbie was riding noughts and crosses around the areas not covered by CCTV in his spare time, listening to Control on his radio, waiting for business.

While waiting he worried about Kat. He should be there covering her back, but she had told him in such vehement terms to keep away that he had obeyed orders, reluctantly and under protest. By the same token he had kept his own crusade secret, knowing that she would disapprove, even disallow it. Now both of them were engaged in irregular warfare, by themselves, without back-up, each putting their own career in jeopardy. It didn't make sense.

But how else . . .? He would never have got permission to go after the Mobile Muggers on a private bike, not without lengthy special training and as part of a wider operation. Not that he imagined himself to be as competent as a trained police rider, yet his confidence was growing. He'd ridden the bike every day for a week now and it all came back to him. Though this was only the second time he had seriously looked for business in the hours he knew the muggers operated in.

Sorbie completed another sweep that had taken him all the way from St Anne's to Ashton Court. He was on his way back towards the centre, bemoaning the waste of petrol under his breath, when his radio spewed out the message he'd been waiting for.

The muggers had struck in an alley near a fish and chip shop, then ridden off on two scooters heading in his general direction. The victim had been badly beaten. An ambulance was on the way, a car was being routed to the area. Only the helicopter was not available again and without it they had little chance of picking them up.

Keeping his freelance status intact by leaving the radio unanswered Sorbie sped towards the area, riding just close enough to the speed limit not to attract too much attention. The last thing he needed was to get stopped by Traffic Division. If his mental calculations were right and luck was with him he might just run into them somewhere around Ashton Gate. He could already see from the absence of floodlights at the stadium that the area would be quiet apart from the main thoroughfares.

The raw noise of the engine gave him confidence. No scooter however fancy would be able to outrun him on this bike. From what he had seen of the scooter riders and their pathetic style they had never taken a bike test. Sooner or later one of them would crash and, if not, they should certainly be encouraged to.

Where the hell were they? Drab streets stretched in all directions. He hesitated at an ill-lit junction. Across the road from the midst of a rubbish landslide piled against the blind wall of a house a smouldering sofa sent up dismal smoke signals. A fine rain had begun to drift on the breeze and would soon extinguish it.

The radio under his jacket burbled. A Traffic unit had sighted them, not far from his own position. He turned right, hassling the bike towards the river. Soon he heard the disappointed voice of the pursuing officer on the air-wave. 'We've lost them now. Suspects drove between a couple of bollards down a footpath. We won't catch them now on our own. Usual story. Do you want us to continue?'

'Negative, Delta One, can you attend a disturbance in Stackpool Road instead . . .?'

Sorbie approved. They'd be less than useless and might get in his way. Better for the scooter guys to think they had shaken off any pursuit. Footpaths, alleys and cycle paths were a safe bet for them as long as there wasn't a helicopter up. Even then they could split up, doubling their chances. The fact that they hadn't been picked up so far showed that someone had given it some thought.

Tonight, without a helicopter, it would take busloads of officers to flush them out. Or one detective sergeant with a second-hand bike and a tankful of luck. Several intuitive corners and fast squirts of the throttle later, Sorbie's luck appeared to hold.

Perhaps they didn't know the area as well as they thought they did because there, a few hundred yards in front of him on the main road, ran two dark scooters side by side. 'Past your bedtime, boys.' He opened the throttle wide to catch them up.

He had underestimated the noise his engine would throw along the quiet evening streets. The already alert pillions both turned suspiciously and soon the scooters sped off around the next corner. Twenty seconds later he was there, in time to see them leave the road, cross the pavement and disappear across the grass behind a graffiti-covered sub-station. He gave chase. The grass was slippery and Sorbie was no off-road expert but the trail bike behaved impeccably and had the advantage over scooters made for city streets. Here was no man's land, the dispiriting non-space between the tangles of uncrossable streets into which pedestrians had been forced. Nobody in their right mind walked here at night. Several streetlamps stood lightless, victims of a spate of air rifle shootings. Sorbie's single headlight illuminated the litter-strewn paths and verges and allowed him to dodge the abandoned shopping trolleys and sagging cardboard boxes that had found their way here.

There was now no sign of them. He stopped, turned off the engine and lights. For a moment all he heard was distant street noise. The helmet didn't help. A flicker of light and the sudden echoing amplification of a scooter engine's whine from below and to the left. Of course, the underpass. Sorbie restarted the engine and rode fast along the snaking, dipping path, avoiding drifts of broken glass and sodden, slippery takeaway cartons.

Before the entrance of the tunnel he braked hard. Its square mouth gaped darkly. Around it huge spray-paint tags like heathen warnings, red, blue, black. Sorbie directed the headlight into the opening and flicked to full beam. The uneven concrete floor was puddled and strewn with litter, the grey tiled walls glistened with damp and the spray of mud. Halfway along the tunnel's length sat a nest of sagging bin-liners spilling rubbish, beyond it lay the frame of a child's bicycle.

Sorbie suddenly felt cold. Shouldn't be going in there without back-up, not even on a bike. It's what he would be telling any constable. But they had come through here and were getting away. Inhaling deeply Sorbie thought he could smell the sweet rotting fumes escaping from the rubbish bags. He shrugged off a shiver: what the hell. As he twisted the throttle the bike leapt forward eagerly. Just a few seconds and he'd be through it. Eyes fixed on the exit. The cavernous space boomed to the sound of his engine, amplifying it. Halfway through now. A headlight appeared just beyond the exit and halted. Black scooter, black-clad rider and pillion. He checked his mirror knowing what he would see: another headlight in the darkness behind. He braked too suddenly, the back wheel stepped out, but he caught it and came to a skewed halt in the centre of the tunnel.

Behind him the other scooter crept nearer. Gunning engines echoed as they sized each other up. Now much depended on how tooled up they were. There was no point in waiting until they both managed to get close to him. He had to joust with the one facing him. Sorbie moved the handlebars to direct his headlight and to line up the bike. The scooter's lights were on full beam, making it hard for him to see. Engine fumes fogged the beams of light.

Then it began. Both scooters started their race towards him but he concentrated on the one ahead. The pillion was swinging something, a stick, no, too straight, a length of piping. 'Ah, fuck. Fun and games.' Sorbie closed his visor and revved up his engine. 'Let's do it then, you wankers.'

With the door pulled shut behind her the darkness was complete. While most of the lock-ups had a narrow slit of window on the wall opposite their entrance, usually covered with galvanized wire on the inside, not even a glimmer of the streetlight reached inside this place. Fairfield turned on her pen light. Its beam was woefully inadequate in this darkness. A big darkness. It was too feeble to reach the end of the lock-up but she knew that the window had been painted blind and partially blocked. There was a light switch on the wall yet she preferred to rely on the torch. One chink of light escaping outside might be enough to advertise her presence.

She knew she didn't have much time. One or two of the lock-ups were in use at night. Someone might pass and notice the absence of the padlock on the hasp outside and decide to investigate. Or worse, call the police. As she let the beam of her torch travel over the high double row of shelving that ran along the centre of the cavern some of her determination evaporated. The place hadn't changed much since the official search; if anything it was piled even higher with junk. A lot of this stuff had to have fallen off the back of various lorries but Mitchell's paperwork had been quite convincing. And of course according to him whatever he couldn't account for came from car boot sales.

Yet that was over sixty muggings and countless burglaries ago. Mitchell had had plenty of time to get careless and the bastard had complacency written all over him. She remembered it well. Fairfield opened a box at random. It contained a lava lamp with a Continental two-pin plug. The next was tightly packed with vinyl records, *Abide With Me – Fifty Favourite Hymns, Christmas with Des O'Connor* . . . The next box contained a jumble of cables and several clock radios. This could go on all night. There was no system here, it would take Mitchell hours to find a specific item unless he had a photographic memory. Most of it was junk too, he'd never afford the flat in Clifton and a Jaguar, however naff, on selling old tea kettles.

A rustling sound near her feet made her flash her light that way. A cockroach scuttled under the shelf. She moved on, glad she was wearing trainers. Towards the end of the space against the right-hand wall stood a large metal locker with double doors. She turned the black iron door knob and pulled. It opened quietly on well-oiled hinges yet the two shelves inside displayed nothing but oily rags, a few computer magazines and a chain of outdoor Christmas lights. A sudden eddy of cold air around her calves made her shiver and she closed the door.

Against the damp back wall stood a warped table supporting a grimy electric kettle, plastic bottles of water, a carton of tea bags and a tower of polystyrene cups. The plastic bin next to it was heaped high with used tea bags and cups. Fairfield examined a pint of semi-skimmed for freshness. It was well within its use-by date. A lot of tea was being drunk in these less than salubrious surroundings, half a stone's throw from the café. It didn't constitute a punishable crime but seemed a strange economy measure. Unless a lot of tea was being drunk outside café opening hours.

Fairfield prodded a few more boxes in the centre aisle. Strictly speaking it was she who was committing a crime here. This is where her stupid obsession with one unimportant lowlife had got her: standing in a mouldering lock-up with nothing but cockroaches for company. It was time to get out of here. It was definitely time to get a life. Perhaps she would go and take those lads up on their offer and have a quick drink in the pub. Or have a lot of quick drinks in the pub and leave the car. And should anyone ask, she could be an aromatherapist or a postie or something else people didn't have issues with.

The sound of the neighbouring lock-up being opened up seemed unnaturally loud. Time to go. Fortunately, because the entrances alternated end to end, the neighbour would be unaware of the missing padlock on Ady Mitchell's door.

Despite the thick walls Fairfield felt compelled to tiptoe along the shelves. Yet she was wholly unprepared for the sudden movement right by her side when the entire locker she had examined earlier swung inwards with a metallic groan. Light from the lock-up next door flooded in. Fairfield dropped on to the dusty cement and lay still. No wonder they'd never found anything in here. The two lock-ups connected.

Fairfield lay on the floor listening to the footsteps moving to the end of the lock-up. Water was being poured and the kettle began to hum. So far Mitchell had not turned on the strip lights, making do with what illumination fell through the hole in the wall from the lock-up next door.

The increasing noise of the kettle gave Fairfield the confidence to retreat backwards, in a crouch, to the furthest aisle where it was practically dark. Reminding herself that she was on the right side of the law made no difference: she knew that if she was discovered it would jeopardize any chances of convicting Mitchell and put the brakes on her career forever. But she had to get a better view. Slowly she advanced up the aisle until she found herself opposite the open metal locker on the other side. Through a chink between boxes she could just make out a van parked in the lock-up next door. A greengrocer's van. So that's how it was done, it had to be. The scooters were launched from the van and, after the muggings, disappeared into the back of it. Greengrocer's van . . . you wouldn't even register it if what you were looking for was a couple of scooters.

Fairfield moved back to the darkest corner while Mitchell's distorted shadow jumped jerkily across the back wall as he made his tea. Mitchell's mobile chimed. 'Yeah, what the fuck happened to you, where were you? I waited for you . . . Oh, for fuck's sake. On a motorbike? What did you have to mess with him for? I can't believe I'm hearing this. Stay where you are and I'll pick you up. What a complete fucking mess.' A change of tone suggested the phone call had been terminated and Mitchell was on the move and talking to himself now. 'Fucking morons. Brainless stupid thugs. Psycho fucking junkies. You just can't get the fucking staff.'

A scrape followed by a metallic groan and clang left Fairfield in darkness once more, yet breathing more easily. Almost immediately the van's engine started next door. As soon as she was sure Mitchell had driven off she switched on her pen light and let herself out at the front. The original padlock clicked into place. She gave it a quick wipe, snapped off her gloves and walked towards the Railway Tavern. Even as she dialled the CID room's number she was beginning to feel as though she had unexpectedly recovered from a long illness. There seemed to

247

be more oxygen in the air, too. 'Dearlove, just the man I was looking for. DI Fairfield. Listen, Deedee – yes, I know it's the end of your shift but speed is of the essence here. Listen, I had an anonymous tip-off about the Mobile Muggers . . .' She rattled off a list of what she wanted, from the officers required to form a welcome committee at the warehouses to an arrest warrant for Ady Mitchell. Then she tried DS Sorbie's mobile and got a service message – his number was unavailable.

There was not much time for strategy. Sorbie's bike leapt forwards, the front wheel briefly lifting as the acceleration pushed it towards his adversaries with a satisfying growl. The higher the speed the more stable the machine. He raced up through the gears. The overloaded scooter screamed towards him on the clear strip of concrete in the centre of the tunnel, the pillion brandishing a piece of lead piping in his right hand like a mace. Nothing in his left though, he was holding on with that. As the gap rapidly closed between the two machines each occupied the left margin of the centre as though traffic rules still mattered. 'Tales of the unexpected, morons!' At the last possible moment Sorbie cut across the oncoming scooter's path, causing the rider to swerve to his right. His pillion swivelled to get a right-handed swing at him on the wrong side. It was enough. The scooter bounced into a pile of rubbish at 30 mph, spat off its passengers and crumpled as it slid along the wall.

For a few breathless seconds Sorbie's own bike snaked and bucked in the rubbish until the wheels regained the tarmac of the path at the exit of the underpass where he braked hard. His hot breath had steamed up the visor. He flipped it up and looked back into the dusk of the tunnel. The other scooter rider was performing a wobbly turn, abandoning his crashed team mates. 'No honour among thieves.' His own turn was hardly less ragged but once back on tarmac there would be no contest. He'd kick the bastards off their scooter and run over their sorry arses if they still had a mind to get up afterwards. He stopped beside the crashed riders, noting with satisfaction that both of them remained on the ground. It looked like broken ankles to him. For a moment he hesitated. He had two in the bag, not a bad night's work. But his adrenalin demanded the chase go on. These two wouldn't scoot much for a while anyway. He left them lying in a cloud of his exhaust.

By now there was no sign of the other scooter. Back in the sodium light of the road he stopped again, visualizing the streets, putting himself in the other rider's shoes. He rode off, sprinted along for a bit, then circled a roundabout, still thinking. He'd only get one shot at it ... Then he knew: they'd be running north on Clanage Road then sneak back on the cycle path along the river. It was what he would do. He opened the throttle and dialled through the gears in pursuit. Traffic was light. Easily overtaking several cars he quickly reached the access point for the cycle path, a narrow stone bridge across the railway cutting.

Like magic their solitary rear light came into view after only a few moments on the cycle path. 'Shouldn't have stopped to chat, boys.' They were running fast from the sound of the pursuing bike. Despite his efforts he lost direct sight of his quarry several times, such was the speed at which the fleeing rider negotiated the turns of the narrow path. Surely the guy had to crash out any second now even without his help? Should he let him go, return to the crashed riders and make sure of those two? He slowed down. Call an ambulance? They might need one. At least he hoped they needed one.

What was he thinking? They could use a bloody mobile and call their own. He speeded up again. Here the cycle path skirted the river which was at high tide and swollen from weeks of relentless rain. There was no exit until the harbour basin, they didn't stand a chance, he would soon catch up, just had to concentrate now. Vegetation to the right, the river close to the left, Sorbie knew at these speeds there was little margin for error. He put a spurt on, getting flayed by the vegetation crowding the path. He nearly had them now, bouncing along at panic speeds. Sorbie opened the throttle further. Each time the fleeing rider looked over his shoulder to measure the ever-closing distance to his pursuer the scooter weaved dangerously on the narrow path. Nearby streetlights now illuminated parts of it and the dark, muddy waters of the turgid river. He closed the gap. Twenty . . . ten . . . five yards, this was it, he had them now. Sorbie got ready, his foot itching to deliver the kick that would destabilize the scooter. The pillion turned round, his face invisible behind the visor, but his panic obvious as he slapped the rider's shoulder. The rider looked back and in doing so swerved right. Trying to straighten up he overcompensated and ran out of road. As the scooter carried rider and pillion over the water's edge at over 40 mph each assumed a separate trajectory. The scooter buried itself in the black waters with a crash and hiss, followed by the rider's somersault. The pillion hit the surface in a helpless tangle.

Sorbie braked hard then looked back. In the gloom he could see very little on the water. He turned and directed his beam at the crash site. The scooter had disappeared. One helmeted shape frantically splashed and thrashed about, shouting something. Sorbie turned off his engine but kept the lights on.

'I can't swim! Help! I can't . . . fucking . . . swim!'

There was no sign of the second mugger. The helmet dipped under water, arms thrashed, a wordless scream. Even a proficient swimmer might have trouble swimming after a crash, clothes and boots heavy with water and wearing a helmet, probably injured. The figure bobbed up again, coughing, screeching. 'Help me!'

Still no sign of the other one. And all that was holding this one up was probably the expanded foam in his helmet.

Sorbie swung the handlebar to direct the light here and there but nothing was visible on the surface apart from bits of plastic debris from the scooter and the thrashing figure of the drowning man. He had sounded like a teenager. Now he was just gurgling and retching. Sorbie looked about him. Just when you needed some rubbish to throw in the water for the bastard to hold on to there was none around. He took off his helmet. 'Ah shit.' The black, oily water didn't look inviting. 'Tell me it's nice and warm in there, you bastard.' Quickly he shrugged off his jacket and grappled with the zips of his boots. He dropped them disconsolately just as the mugger's helmet disappeared under the surface. 'Oh shit. I can't believe I'm doing this. I can't believe I'm fucking doing this.' DS Sorbie jumped feet first towards the empty spot where the man had slid under.

Chapter Fourteen

Eleni. Gary loved the name. It suited her. A simple name, old-fashioned, unpretentious, yet classy. He was glad the new owners hadn't insisted on renaming her. Not only would he have considered it bad luck for a boat to be renamed but a modern name would not have fitted a classic motor yacht like the *Eleni.* Laid down in 1915, completed in 1920, she was a gentleman's yacht and every one of her seventy-three feet and seven inches a lady. Loved, abused and neglected in turn, she had been at home in the Adriatic, had languished in a lonely berth in the thirties, had seen action in WWII on harbour defence patrol and had survived a near miss off Dunkirk. Gary tapped the soft soles of his shoes on the wooden deck. Beautiful women had sunbathed here under tropical skies, soldiers had huddled here after having been picked off the beaches. Both tanning lotion and history had soaked into these planks and would stay sealed inside them now for as long as she stayed afloat, no matter who walked on them. He would miss her, missed her already. The refurbishment had taken six months and he had worked on her almost from the beginning.

In the light of the setting sun the *Eleni* inspired nostalgic dreams. Here, moored at the very end of the harbour basin, surrounded by nothing but boat sheds and the gutted hulls of barges and houseboats waiting for a second chance for a useful life, it was easy to forget which century you lived in. You could lean back against the woodwork and dream.

Almost as soon as the press had finished scribbling notes and taking pictures of smiling people holding aloft glasses of champagne everyone had packed up and left. Gary was not important enough to have been invited along to the celebration dinner, only the project leader, engineer, vendor and new owners went. He himself, along with Dave the mechanic and Sharon the general dogsbody, had been given money to celebrate in the pub. But he'd declined and Dave and Sharon had left without him. All day sadness had crept up on him, and more than sadness. Not far below it nagged an irrational anger as though the yacht had been stolen from him. Sold into slavery. Like a beautiful woman the *Eleni* could inspire jealousy as well as love.

The fact they had chosen to celebrate in a restaurant rather than here, probably for fear someone might spill champagne on the polished fittings, simply added to his resentment. If they felt any real connection to her they'd have celebrated on board, started up her two Gardner engines and taken her out to sea, where she belonged. But the new owners were not really interested in her, she was a business tool now, to be used for corporate hospitality around Majorca. He wasn't likely to see her again let alone be allowed on board. In the end he had chosen to remain behind and say a quiet, undisturbed farewell.

What he really wanted to do was to cast off and take her back in time all the way to the Indian Ocean of the nineteen-twenties and -thirties, to Ceylon and on to the islands off Siam. He ran his fingers over the cool, polished teak of the wheelhouse. He'd had a hand in restoring it, as in most other things wooden on the yacht: her steamed oak beams, rock elm timbers and teak deck. He wouldn't really call himself a shipwright yet, though he had when he applied for the job. He'd lied a fair bit but got away with it and learnt on the job. Now that the project was finished there was no more work here for a while. Perhaps he would move to Cornwall or up north, he hadn't decided yet. There was still boat building going on in Scotland, he knew.

Dusk had crept through the harbour and the sodium glow of the city lights threw workshop and sheds into sharp relief. Without illumination from the boat or the office there was just enough residual light in the west for him to take one more turn around her deck. Trailing the fingers of his left hand lightly over the familiar surfaces of the wheelhouse, the edge of the coach roof, the radar mast and finally the wheelhouse again he completed his last inspection. As he got ready to go ashore via the short gangway connecting the yacht to the deserted quay his foot nudged a heavy object that did not belong there. Gary stepped back and picked it up. It was a bottle.

A full bottle of champagne. An *unlikely* bottle of champagne. He could just make out the label, a supermarket own-brand! How did it get there? All the champagne drunk earlier had been vintage stuff. He knew, he had been given a glass, well, half a glass, most of it had been froth, and he had seen the bottles, it was Something & Something French champagne. Had this one been bought for the lower deck to drink and then forgotten about? Yet he was pretty sure that a bottle of champagne, supermarket or not, would have been spotted if it stood on deck right by the gangway. In fact he was pretty sure it hadn't been there a few minutes ago when there had still been more than enough light to spot it.

Stranger things happened at sea. The bottle felt well chilled and it was perfect for the occasion. Even the fact that it was cheap champagne fitted well with his tiny contribution to the story of the *Eleni*. He would drink a private, quiet toast to their parting. The foil top slid off easily. Unused to opening champagne bottles, a little fearful of the bottled power behind the cork, he pointed the neck of the bottle well away from himself as he untwisted the wire clip and set his thumb under the rim of the cork. His nervousness and the sturdiness of the champagne bottle probably saved his life. The neck of the bottle disintegrated as the small explosive charge ignited the petrol in the bottle. The content self-propelled in an imperfect arc towards the door of the wheelhouse and splattered flames across the varnished teak. Gary fell backwards on to the deck with his hair and clothes enveloped in petrol flames. He wasted no time rolling towards the guard rail and heaving himself overboard into the harbour. When he resurfaced the shock and pain made him gasp and thrash as he struggled in the freezing water towards the quay.

Above him the *Eleni* burnt. Oiled planks and varnished timbers caught easily even as the petrol burnt itself out. *A petrol bomb.* One minute he was going to toast her, the next she was ablaze. He had set her on fire. He had to make it to the quay, he had to put it out somehow, call for the fire brigade. She mustn't burn, not after all the work they had put into her, not after all she had survived. It was his fault. It was insane, completely insane, but it was. When he reached the quay a few yards away from the burning yacht and the raw flesh of his palms closed around a rusty ring set in the harbour wall, Gary screamed.

'It doesn't smell as bad as I expected.'

'Yeah, quite pleasant really.'

'The owners might not agree of course.'

'Perhaps not.' McLusky sniffed audibly. 'Or is that your sandwich I can smell?'

Austin folded up a corner of sliced white from his home-made sandwich. 'Bavarian smoked cheese. You've got a good nose.'

'It's house fires I can't stand, they smell truly awful. It's all those burnt plastics and melted TVs.'

'No plastics here, she was a posh boat, all natural ingredients.' Austin rocked lightly on his heels beside McLusky as they continued to look down on to the charred hull from atop a tarpaulined nest of oil drums on the quay.

The *Eleni* had remained afloat but her wheelhouse had disappeared and the galley had burnt fiercely after a small propane bottle had exploded there with the fire spreading to the saloon. There were two holes in the deck, which was blackened from bow to stern. Now that there was daylight fire investigators were going through the treacherous remains.

Further up the quay, at the perimeter of the taped-off area, a silver Porsche was being carefully parked. As the driver approached the police tape he was challenged by a constable and after a short conversation allowed to proceed. McLusky watched him take his time as he picked a route through the harbourside snake pit of hoses, cables and ropes. His hand-made shoes crunched reluctantly over crushed glass and eroded concrete. He was talking on a mobile. 'Place is a mess. I can see the boat, she's a goner. It's a disaster from start to finish. I'm flying into Palma this afternoon, you can kill me then.'

'Jane, go and ask him what . . .' McLusky rolled his eyes at Austin who appeared to have stuffed the entire sandwich into his mouth at once. 'Forget it.' He called to the new arrival. 'Hello. Are you the owner?'

The man walked over before answering. 'Was. One of them. Nothing much left to own.'

'She might be worth restoring . . . not that I know much about boats.'

'Then what, may I ask, are you doing here?'

McLusky held out his ID for the man to peruse.

The man shrugged: so what? 'It was arson, I'm told. Have you got someone in custody?'

'Not yet.'

'What about the shipwright chap? Wasn't it him?'

'We don't think so. He just happened to be the one who picked up the incendiary device. He's recovering nicely in hospital, by the way.'

'Good for him. Meanwhile we are short one motor yacht. I'm going to get the blame for this. There are plenty of yachts for sale in Majorca but, like an idiot . . . I saw her advertised, liked the style and persuaded my partners. She was hardly seaworthy then. We had her brought up over-land from Cardiff last year. They worked like demons, only finished her yesterday.'

'Why here?'

'I'm from here. My children live here with their mother. And I wanted to give work to the last surviving boat builders here. Bloody disaster.'

'She was insured?'

'Generously. That's not the point. Might not look it here but in Majorca the summer is well under way. There's people waiting.'

'What do you do there?'

'Financing development. Balearics and southern Spain. I hope you find who did this. Not that it'll make much dif-ference. I'm flying back to face the music now. Goodbye.'

'Goodbye Mr . . .'

The man was already walking back to his car and didn't bother to turn around. 'Chapman.'

They both watched him blast off, blaring his horn impatiently at an elderly man wheeling a bicycle along the harbour front. Austin rolled the tinfoil wrapping of his sandwich into a ball and flicked it in the direction of the departing Porsche. 'Cheery chappy, Chapman.'

McLusky didn't comment. Something had disturbed him this morning and it wasn't the extremely early appear-ance at his door of DS Austin with news of a suspicious incendiary. No, the early hours of the morning he had always considered to be the best of the day, still fresh, untainted, at least if you avoided police radio. It was some-thing else that niggled at him now, back of the mind, tip of the tongue. Something he heard, saw or smelled but he couldn't grasp it. Hopeless. It slipped away like the tail end of a dream, back into his unconscious. He was out of cigarettes, too. He thought better with a cigarette, a walk and a cigarette. 'Got a ciggie, Jane?'

'Didn't I say? I've packed it in. As of today. Eve is making me, she was livid when I started again.'

McLusky looked hopeful. 'So ... no doubt you have stocked up on mints, chewing gum and chocolate-covered peanuts then?'

'No, I'm going cold turkey.'

'Well, that's no use to anyone. You're really not getting the best out of your addiction, DS Austin.' He hopped off the oil drums. With his mobile phone held at arm's length he turned through 360 degrees, recording the entire scene, ending with Austin's glum face. 'Smile, Jane, think of the money you'll save. See you back at the station, I'm taking a walk.'

At a newsagent's McLusky handed over his bank card to pay for two packets of cigarettes. Austin's fiancée was right. Quite apart from the health risk the damage to your finances was insane. There were people out there earning less per hour than the price of a packet of twenty. But this was not the right time to stress over it. Or the fact that even Extra Lights made him cough like a coal miner in the morning. He would compensate with fresh air, go for a walk, set his brain working, try and retrieve the disappearing strands of thought in his unmethodical mind.

He had simply turned his back on the harbour, intent on exploring a few more streets of his new home, and was pleasantly surprised when he came across a small park. Queen Square with its tree-lined perimeter and its lawn dissected by a star of paths was just what he needed. He would walk its perimeter under the trees and think.

Only when he had walked one length of the square did he allow himself to light the cigarette he'd been craving. Games, they were just games, he had to pack it in for good. When he caught the bastard. The day he caught the bastard he would give up smoking. Just please don't let it be today.

It promised to be a warm, sunny day yet here in the shade under the trees it was cool and the smells of the nearby river and of early morning lingered. At this time of day there were few people in the park, mainly mothers with children and the elderly. A community support officer on a mountain bike was making the rounds, cycling past him at a leisurely pace. There had to be worse beats than one that included Queen Square in the morning.

Two devices in two days. Phil Warren's latest article on the bomber had graced the front page of the *Post* only yesterday. True to what McLusky now recognized as her form she had called the bomber not only a coward but also a twisted loner and a perverted madman who had clearly targeted children when he hid explosives in Easter eggs. Neither the bottle nor the phone would have been planted in response to the article, it would have taken too much time to build them. If the bomber was to react his response was still to come.

The mobile might have been there for days, there was not enough left of it for Forensics to give a verdict on that. The champagne device had clearly been tailored to the occasion. But why the boat? Why include the yacht in his list of targets when all the others had been left where they could be triggered by anybody who found them? The apparently random nature of the attacks suggested a man – surely a man – who hated everybody. Random attacks always meant that the perpetrator was dissociated from real people. The man he was looking for was isolated, a loner, a man for whom other people had no real substance.

Only the yacht was different. How could the yacht offend a man like the bomber? Did it stand for something, symbolize something – luxury, conspicuous consumption? Did all the places and devices have a symbolic value? Or did that only happen on TV, where eventually you found that it all corresponded to some damn poem or Shakespeare play or verses of the Bible? Unfortunately it was difficult to tell what was significant to an unhinged personality until after you had caught him and taken a good look at the hinges. Few murderers had a poetic streak and

259

in his experience the poetry-writing, opera-going, hard-drinking but lovable CID officers who solved such crimes were thin on the ground in the force. Hard-drinking, maybe . . .

Unhinged, another word Warren had used. As instructed she had also used 'according to a source close to the invest-igation' more than once. So far there had been merciful silence about that from the super's office since Denkhaus probably assumed Warren had simply made it up. But the bomber would assume no such thing.

He dropped the butt of his cigarette on the ground, refusing to feel guilty. Well, why didn't they supply ash-trays? The great outdoors was one of the last places you were allowed to smoke after all. For now. His mood hadn't lifted, far from it. He clawed another cigarette out of the packet. Extra Lights just didn't work as well as real cigarettes. As he focused his eyes on where he touched the flame from his lighter to the end of the cigarette a blurred movement entered his line of sight. He looked up, refocused. Away to his right beyond the equestrian statue in the centre moved a skateboarder. McLusky stared hard at the small receding figure. Move your legs, let me see you move your legs. The figure didn't, just glided on in effort-less, lazy zigzags. It might be his imagination, might be wishful thinking, but the skateboard looked larger than normal, chunkier. He couldn't hear an engine but what of it, perhaps the guy had silencers fitted, whatever. He screwed up his eyes as the quickly disappearing figure moved into the shadows under the trees. There it was, the hand holding the control wire – a motorized bloody skate-board. Which way was he going? Left.

McLusky fell into a trot on the path across the green. After a few yards he dropped his cigarette and speeded up. The skateboarder looped sharply and moved in the oppo-site direction. McLusky turned too and jogged back under the trees. Fingering his radio he thought of calling for back-up, then thought better of it. Just a hunch, could be anybody, and by the time they got here ... Denims, red scarf. Looked like a red scarf. He was wearing blue, anyway. If he left the park he'd never catch him. McLusky speeded up. Definitely give up smoking. If he caught him and it turned out to be him, he'd quit. His legs ached already. Definitely quit. He had to cut him off without alerting him. When he saw the community police officer cycle back towards him he stopped running, rested his hands on his knees for a second to catch his breath, then he flagged him down, waving his ID.

'I'm DI McLusky.'

'CID? I wasn't aware –'

'What's your name?'

'Botts, sir.'

'I need to borrow your bicycle, Botts.'

Community Support Officer Eric Botts hesitated, standing astride his bicycle. 'I'm not sure, I mean, when will I –'

'Get off the damn thing, he's getting away.'

'Who, sir? Do you want me to pursue him?' To Botts, who went swimming on Tuesdays and cycled everywhere, the inspector didn't look too fit. But he sure looked furious. 'Okay, here. Third gear's a bit sticky, mind.' As soon as he had got off it the inspector dragged the bike around, swung into the saddle and started pedalling away furiously. Botts felt uneasy. He'd never heard of a Detective Inspector McLusky. What if it was a fake ID? You could run up anything on a computer now and laminate it. If so, then he'd just been mugged of his police issue mountain bike. He'd never live that down. He called after the man who was riding his bike straight across the grass now. 'I'll just wait here then, shall I?' No answer. Sod this. He started jogging after him under the trees.

McLusky bumped on to the grass into the dazzling light. Where was the bastard? A glimpse of red on the far side, moving too fast for a walker, was all he could see. McLusky pedalled. As the bike's tyres left the grass and reached the hard, flat surface of the path he gained more speed. He could see him clearly now, the age was right, the clothing, he was wearing sunglasses, all fitted the description apart from the hair, which wasn't spiked. So what? It was him and he would cut him off in a minute. How did you make this damn thing go faster? Impatiently he pushed at the gear lever: the gears crunched, the chain raced and became slack. The bicycle rolled to a stop – the chain had come off. McLusky told the square what he thought about it: 'Crap!' Then he got off and started wheeling the bike back. The skater was still gliding along the perimeter. He lost sight of him on the other side. The man's description had been circulated internally, though no one had been told what he was wanted for. 'In connection with a serious incident' was the euphemism. Why hadn't that dopey hobby bobby spotted him then? He wheeled the bike across the grass and back under the trees. No sign of the support officer. This hadn't turned out to be the stroll he had had in mind.

'Sir!' He turned around to the voice behind him. It was Botts. And behind Botts, blissfully unaware, approached the skateboarder, doing a showy slalom around the promenading people.

McLusky pointed. 'Botts, stop that skateboarder!'

The officer turned around, walked into the man's path and opened his arms wide. 'Stop, police!' The skateboarder careered past him with an easy manoeuvre and turned the speed up, looking panicked across his shoulder at the officer.

'Not like that, Botts.' McLusky picked up the bicycle and threw it at the skateboarder just as he whizzed past him. It hit him at waist height and sent him sprawling on to the tarmac. 'Like that!'

Botts trotted up. 'Sir, my bicycle.'

The skateboarder groaned as he disentangled himself. He remained sitting on the ground, massaged a wrist and bellowed at his assailant: 'You fucking maniac!'

McLusky held out his ID for him. 'The nice officer asked you nicely. I'm not so nice, of course.' He wagged a finger. 'Motorized skateboards – not allowed in the park.'

'You can't be serious. I could have cracked my skull open.'

'Yeah, that's another thing. No helmet, so I thought I'd have a word.'

'You're nuts. I'm going to sue you for assault. I'll have you investigated and thrown off the force.'

Botts went to help him up. 'Calm down. What's your name, sir?'

'I'm going to sue him for endangering my life –'

'Up you get.'

'I don't need any fucking help. I can't believe this.'

McLusky briefly wondered how his method of stopping skateboarders might go down with the super. Not so well if he had got the wrong man, perhaps. 'Actually, you might be an important witness. Tell us your name.'

'It's John. Witness to what?'

'Any other names?'

'John Kerswill.'

The name rang a distant bell. Ah, yes. 'You wouldn't be in any way related to Joel Kerswill?'

'What if I am?'

'Well?'

'He happens to be my son.'

'Visited him lately?'

An hour later McLusky still kept up the pressure on John Kerswill in interview room 2. 'You were seen near the Knowle West bomb, shortly before a man died in his car there.'

'I told you I live near there now. I must have been just testing it out, I don't often ride in the street, only when I've been working on the engine. The new electric board needs no work at all, of course.'

Austin couldn't contain himself. 'We're very happy for you.'

McLusky impatiently flicked at a file of photographs containing pictures of the bomb victims. 'Come on, Kerswill, the jury is never going to believe that, it's too much of a coincidence. You just happened to be right there on Brandon Hill moments before the bomb went off, too? And you skated right past your own son.'

'I didn't know that, did I? I didn't see him. It really was coincidence. Stuff like that happens all the time.'

'Are you telling me you didn't recognize your own son?'

'I didn't really look, did I? I was skating. People just sort of become obstacles, you don't look at what they look like, really, you're busy skating.'

Austin nodded knowingly. 'People become obstacles. Of course with bombs going off in parks you might have fewer obstacles to avoid.'

'When the bomb went off, where were you? How far away?'

'Already at the bottom of the hill. Nearly. Close to the exit.'

'Did you go back?'

'Yeah. A bit. But not close.'

'Why not?'

Kerswill took a sip of polystyrene tea. He stared at the grey liquid left in the cup and shrugged. 'I've been sort of avoiding things. I thought people might be after me.'

'For . . .?'

'Child Support. They do go after people.'

'The story of your son's injuries was plastered all over the front page. Did you visit him in hospital?'

'I couldn't, could I? And it said he'd only been lightly injured.'

'Well, I myself did visit your son in hospital. And I met your wife. She wanted me to pass on a message in case I ever ran into you.'

Kerswill looked up. 'Yeah?'

'You don't want it, son.' The 'son' had just slipped out. The man was older than McLusky yet he dressed like a teenager and ran around on a skateboard. In broad daylight.

Kerswill looked contrite. After a long silence he spoke slowly, eyes unfocused. 'I suppose you would call it a mid-life crisis.' A slow shrug. 'We were married for what seemed like forever. I just thought I saw my life slipping away, work, home, work, home, the wife at me all the time about money, nothing but work ... I mean, they get taken care of when there's no one there earning, it's not like they're starving and I never meant it to be forever. I hadn't planned it, either. I just flipped one day, took the van and left. I didn't even take much of my stuff, I was going to go back, only I really needed to get away for a while.'

'But going back got harder.'

Kerswill brightened up. 'Yeah, that's right. The longer I'd been away the more I couldn't imagine going back. I knew it was selfish but with every day it got even more selfish. I mean, I felt much freer again doing just enough decorating work to keep me going. I could do what I wanted.'

'Riding a skateboard.'

'Not just that, but yeah. A powered skateboard is ... it's like magic, it transforms things.'

'Your own son didn't recognize you, so I expect you have been transformed, Mr Kerswill.'

'Well, I had the hair spiked and all that ... It said in the papers he'd been to an interview for an apprenticeship when the bomb went off. I wonder if he got it.'

'I strongly suggest, Mr Kerswill, that you call him and ask.'

Where was the camera? She couldn't go to Barcelona without a camera. Rebecca toured the flat again, finding yet more of her things to throw into the holdall or stuff into a bin-liner. Five days in Barcelona, what would she need?

It was a college trip and they'd be traipsing through museums, Picasso, Miro, Gaudi. Didn't he fall out of a tram and die? She subjected the clothes she picked up from the floor to a sniff test and dispatched them into holdall or bin-liner respectively. She'd find somewhere else to live when she got back. Liam was all right but he was a bit old, over thirty. There was no way she could introduce him to any of her art school friends, that would really freak them out. A policeman, he would never fit in there. Especially since he was so down on drugs too, any kind of drugs. She couldn't make him see that there was a difference between hard drugs and, let's say, a bit of E. He wouldn't even let her smoke one piddly joint in the house. It got really boring and there was no telly. Why would anyone want to live like that?

Sketchbook, drawing stuff, she'd need that, had packed it, but she wouldn't go without the camera, the one on her mobile was rubbish. Well, she'd looked everywhere twice, there was only one place where it could be now, and that was Liam's manky old Polo. She vaguely remembered having it last time he'd given her a lift, perhaps it fell out of her bag. He'd gone to work this morning with DS Austin in his nifty Nissan, why didn't he get a car like that? They were cute. So she'd go and check, the old wreck was always parked round the corner. The car keys were nowhere to be seen but he never locked the thing, probably hoping it might get nicked but she doubted even a joyrider would go near it.

It was a shame it couldn't work out because she really liked Liam, he was quite funny and really kind but he totally cramped her style. It made her feel like she was living in two different worlds, living a double life almost, with college friends in one and Liam in the other. She couldn't really tell him what she got up to with her mates, he wouldn't approve, and she couldn't take him with her. He was always busy and on call anyway and liable to be dragged out of bed at unholy hours like this morning. Bed, now that was the one thing she would really miss him for. He was so different from the other guys she had slept with so far, a lot gentler. And a lot rougher, too. Liam always had that puzzled look when he woke up next to her and then he'd break into a smile as though he'd just been given a present. Every time. She'd miss that. She'd probably miss that most.

Halfway up the next street there was the car, with a brick behind the offside rear wheel since the handbrake was as dodgy as the rest of the thing. Some old cars were quite cool but this one was just embarrassing. Rebecca opened the hatchback door. Impatiently she rifled through the empty plastic bags and rubbish – nothing. She opened the passenger door and looked in the footwell then searched the glove box – nothing. There was a letter on the passenger seat. She picked it up. It just said Inspector McLusky on the envelope and no stamp or anything, someone must have dropped it in the car, someone who knew it would be unlocked or they'd have stuck it under the windscreen wipers. Probably someone wanting him to park his eyesore somewhere else. Well, damn, no camera. Where the hell was it, then? She pocketed the letter and slammed the passenger door shut with all the force of her frustration.

Like a biblical column of fire a gas-blue flame rose from the centre of the driver's seat, reaching up to the roof with a fierce hiss. Seconds later flames and smoke spread out and began to engulf the entire interior. Now all she could see was a dull red glow at the centre of the blackness, filling the car like an evil eye. Incredulous and transfixed by the spectacle, she forced herself to move backwards away from the car, just as the first window blew out.

The further the interview had progressed the clearer it had become that John Kerswill simply didn't fit the bill. He was far too busy reclaiming his lost boyhood to litter the city with explosives. McLusky hadn't had much time or inclination to think about the effect the bombs were having on the rest of the city. In sharp contrast Superintendent Denkhaus, in whose office he found himself after releasing Kerswill, had been only too aware, having had to field urgent questions from the press, business leaders and the Assistant Chief Constable.

'It's the randomness of the attacks, McLusky, that scares people. I'm told hotel and B&B bookings are down by forty per cent. Businesses are hurting. Even if we apprehended the culprit today the damage is already done, people are going elsewhere. And it's not just the tourist industry that's suffering, I mean some people have taken their kids out of school.' Denkhaus stood and turned his back on McLusky while he took in the panoramic view his large window afforded him. Policing had ramifications well beyond crime prevention and detection: it influenced economics and politics and was in turn influenced by politics and dictated to by economics. It was as well if young DIs understood that. He was under constant pressure, not just from the ACC but from the mayor's office and representatives of the business community. 'Our citizens don't feel safe any more, small retailers report a drop in sales. Pubs and clubs get fewer people through their doors. People shop at the supermarkets and spend more time indoors. More worrying still, two major conferences have been moved to other cities and the organizers of the half-marathon are thinking of postponing until the autumn, and the kite festival was nearly cancelled.'

'Kite festival nearly cancelled?'

Denkhaus turned to face the young DI. He couldn't remember, did he have children? Not that it mattered. 'Yes, so you see how far-reaching and unexpected the consequences of these attacks are. It simply can't be allowed to continue. A valuable yacht was destroyed in this latest outrage. People will seek mooring for their expensive boats elsewhere. If that happens then the plans for the harbourside development could be jeopardized. The development depends entirely on investors having complete confidence that our city is the right place to be.' Denkhaus quoted almost verbatim from the tirade he had endured from the ACC earlier that day.

McLusky nodded distractedly. 'Indeed, sir.' Kite festival, now why did that ring a bell? The bell it rang had an uncomfortable sound. It conjured up a nagging, like a thing he'd forgotten to do, like an unposted letter. He would look in his notes . . .

'I presume DI Fairfield's success didn't escape your notice? We finally got the Mobile Muggers off the streets . . .'

'Quite literally, too.'

'Yes, quite.' Denkhaus allowed himself a smile. 'It was pure good fortune that DS Sorbie happened to be there on his day off. And he reacted professionally and bravely. Even saved the life of one of them. Jumped after him into the river and dragged him to safety. The other one either drowned or got away. And practically at the same time Fairfield got an anonymous tip-off and was able to catch Mitchell, a notorious fence, red-handed as he was bringing the rest of the gang to his lock-up. We were there ready and waiting. Intelligence-led policing, McLusky. The man was actually running the gang, even supplying them with the scooters. So you can see, persistence and hard work pay off. It certainly didn't do Fairfield and Sorbie's clear-up rates any harm. You on the other hand appear to be –' There was a loud knock. 'Yes, what is it?'

Lynn Tiery appeared in the door, frowning at a piece of paper in her hand. 'Sorry to interrupt. There's an urgent message for DI McLusky, concerning his car.'

Denkhaus insisted on driving them there, despite McLusky's protests. The superintendent's lecture continued on the tortuous drive across town but drifted at last into reminiscences, how he himself had risen through the ranks, starting as a beat officer in a small West Country town, grasping every opportunity, applying himself, not bucking the system. And here he was, ambitions fulfilled. He had no desire to rise any higher, not wanting to lose touch with real, frontline policing.

The street was blocked with police, fire engines and a fire investigator's car. They abandoned the Land Rover in the middle of the road and walked up without speaking. Accident, vandalism or the bomber, all depended on the verdict of the fire investigators.

They showed their IDs and approached what was left of the Polo, a blackened evil-smelling shell. A sulking Rebecca was there, being shadowed by a PC. She pounced on McLusky. 'You took your time getting here, they're treating me as though *I* set fire to the damn thing. It just caught fire, I swear, I just slammed the door and whoosh, up it went. I was just looking for my camera.'

McLusky calmed her down and sent the PC on her way. Almost immediately a fire investigator confirmed their suspicions. 'A small device wired into the springs of the driver's seat. Nasty. Had you sat in it you'd have been in trouble. There was no explosion, it was an incendiary device, probably a mixture of accelerant like petrol, some flammable adhesive perhaps, magnesium, some kind of trigger.'

'Shit, I nearly sat in it! Ouch!' Rebecca's hand made an involuntary move to her behind.

Ignoring her, Denkhaus raised an impatient eyebrow at McLusky. 'Who's the young lady? How did she come to search your car?'

'Ehm, she's staying at my –'

'I'm his girlfriend.' Was his girlfriend. Definitely was. He had the same problem she did, obviously, he had practically disowned her there and then. 'And the coach to the airport goes in less than an hour from college. Can I go now?'

Denkhaus turned away to talk to the leading fire officer about the safe removal of the car.

'I gotta go, Liam. Oh, here, nearly forgot.' She pulled the letter from her pocket. 'Sorry, bit crumpled. Found it on the driver's seat.'

Same typeface, same envelope. McLusky folded it non-chalantly into a jacket pocket. 'When are you back?'

'Seven days.' It was only five but she gave herself a couple of days in hand, time to think, make a final deci-sion. 'Can't remember what time the plane lands, I'll call your mobile.' She kissed him hard on the mouth but dis-engaged herself almost immediately. 'Don't want to embar-rass you any further. Really gotta go now. *Buenos dias.*'

'*Ciao bella.*' Or was that Italian? He'd never been much good at languages. He watched Rebecca walk away. She was a kid, really, and she could have been seriously hurt. He would never have forgiven himself. As she reached the street corner he got ready to wave if she looked back but Rebecca walked on without turning.

He slid the letter open and read. *Perhaps This will Shut you Up. I have Warned You. Now I will employ My Armies everywhere. Homes and Churches will be safe but Silence will settle on the Parks and Streets of this City.* This one he couldn't possibly keep to himself. 'Superintendent? Rebecca found this in the car before it went up.'

Denkhaus read. 'I wonder if he intended you to read this before or after you were incinerated. I'm sorry this invest-igation has got a bit close to home for you. The man knows where you live, what car you drive. All, no doubt, a result of you talking to Phil Warren. You weren't all that hard to find once the bomber knew your name. Is there somewhere else you can stay until he is apprehended?'

'I'll have a think.'

'Think fast, McLusky, this guy wants to hurt you.' He returned his attention to the letter. 'Mm . . . *I have warned you,* what does that mean, I wonder. We hardly need any more warning.'

'I think what's significant about the letter is the mention of parks.'

271

'He exploded his first device in Brandon Hill . . .'

'I think he's going to target parks again. This kite festival, where is that held?'

'That's at Ashton Court.'

'Well, I think it should be cancelled.'

'Bit late for that, McLusky, it's today.' He checked his watch. 'Started an hour ago. Do you have any particular reason for thinking the festival could be a target?'

McLusky hesitated. If only he knew why the words 'kite festival' reverberated in his mind. 'No, just . . . a feeling. The place will be full of children, sir, they'll pick up anything, no matter what they've been told. It's a golden opportunity for the bomber to spread panic.'

'And you think on the strength of your . . . *feeling* I should order the festival interrupted? Send everyone home and have the whole bloody park searched?'

McLusky held the superintendent's critical stare for a few seconds before answering. 'Yes. Yes, I do, sir.'

'I thought you might say that.' Denkhaus was already walking away shouting instructions at uniformed police. 'Constable! Get yourself across to Ashton Court at the double, it needs to be evacuated. You may be the first there but back-up won't be long.' The constable made a tentative move towards his car, then stopped and opened his mouth to ask how on earth he was going to evacuate a huge place like Ashton Court but Denkhaus cut across him. 'Use your initiative, go.' In his car he gave orders over his airwave radio for several units to converge on the park and to use loudhailers to clear the area. 'Don't create a panic, I want an orderly evacuation.' He turned to McLusky. 'Let's go and watch your drama unfold, shall we?'

By the time Denkhaus had threaded the Land Rover through the traffic, across the river and into Ashton Court a thin stream of people were moving towards car parks and the nearest exit. Many were adults with children. Practically all carried one or more kites, large box kites, Chinese dragons, kimono girls, birds, stunt kites. The bright colours of kites and children's clothing were enhanced by rays of sunshine piercing the grey, threatening cloud that had rolled in again from the west. Many more people were still on the slope where the main event took place, packing up. There were refreshment marquees and trading stands selling everything from kites to crystals. A patrol car drove slowly up the gently curving lane beside the hill using a public address system, telling people to leave the park by the nearest entrance, not to run, not to pick up anything that did not belong to them.

They stood by the Land Rover and watched. McLusky was shocked at the extent of it. 'I had no idea it was that big.'

'Spring kite festival. People come from all over the country to show off with stunt kites and what have you. It's a big deal.'

'I thought it was just a couple of hundred kids flying their kites. There must be a thousand people here.' He took out his mobile and started recording the panoramic scene of exodus from the festival site.

'We usually get two-and-a-half thousand visitors, perhaps fewer this year thanks to our little problem.'

McLusky saw the plume of smoke and the man falling a second before the crack of the explosion reached his ears, like the blast from a large-bore shotgun. People started to converge on the spot halfway up the slope, others hurried their children away. Some waved kites and clothing in the air to attract the attention of the paramedics parked on the road. They didn't need telling. Having heard the noise they had started their engine and were now already driving on to the grass.

Denkhaus fixed him with an evil stare. 'McLusky, I hate intuition and hunches and especially hunches that come too late to be of any bloody use. I want to know how you knew!'

McLusky's mobile told him he had reached the limit of his recording facility. He pocketed it. 'I didn't know anything, sir. I don't even know where I heard about the kite festival before, on the radio perhaps.' They made their way up the slope, walking fast, following the tracks the ambulance made on the grass. 'I think we can expect many more devices to go off. He says in his letter something like . . . can I have it again, sir?'

Denkhaus stopped, glad to catch his breath for a moment, and handed him the note, now protected by a clear evidence bag.

'Here. *Now I will employ my armies*. The devices are his soldiers. I think he has a suitcase full of the damn things and he'll probably dot them all around the city in one go, if he hasn't already done it. From then on all he has to do is stay at home and watch it all on telly.'

'Bloody hell.' Denkhaus took the letter back and stared at it with disgust for a few seconds, then put it away. 'I know what you're saying, but you might be wrong there.'

'How so?'

'You got us here, didn't you? You were just not quick enough and you haven't got a clue why you brought us here. You're unmethodical, McLusky, that's your problem. Get yourself organized!'

They had arrived at the site of the explosion. Curious onlookers had formed a tight circle around the paramedics who were tending to a middle-aged man sitting on the grass, a woman and young boy kneeling by his side. Denkhaus waved his ID and bellowed at the civilians. 'Make your way to the nearest exit unless you're close relatives of the victim. Get going, this emergency isn't over. Walk, don't run, and for God's sake don't pick anything up, not even if you find the crown jewels.'

The man doesn't need a megaphone, McLusky thought. He squatted down by the victim, who drank shakily from a water bottle. 'How are you feeling, sir? What happened?'

'I nudged it. It was just back there.' He nodded his head at the hill behind him.

'What was?'

'It was a box of biscuits. I hadn't seen it before but I thought it might be ours. I had my hands full so I nudged it with the folding chair I was carrying. To see if it was full or empty. It knocked me back off my feet. Completely winded me. Thank God my wife and son had gone ahead.' The man's face and hands were peppered with angry red spots where debris from the device had hit him. 'I mean, I know we were told not to pick anything up but it was instinctive, you know?'

'Do you remember what kind of biscuits they were?'

'I don't know the brand. It had pictures of different sorts on it, what you call it, an assortment.'

McLusky left a sergeant in charge of getting personal details and securing the site and joined Denkhaus who was staring unhappily out across the park and the city beyond.

'We'll have to search the entire park again for devices. Possibly all the parks. How many are there, sir?'

'Too many. We might as well close the entire city. It can't be done without declaring martial law and imposing a curfew. People will just have to be extra vigilant. I'll arrange for another press conference but we can't have people panicking, that's what the bastard wants to happen.'

'I get the feeling he wants people to stay quietly at home.' So he can do what? McLusky had a mental image of a lone skateboarder moving through an empty town on an electric board, unimpeded by people or traffic. John Kerswill's dream.

'We don't have the resources to close and search every park, railway station, bus and public space.'

'I'm aware of it. We've had over five hundred false alarms so far, it seems we're doing little else but chasing up suspicious packages.' Each time a car backfired the phone lines got jammed with reports of bomb blasts. People saw bombs everywhere.

The sun disappeared and the first heavy drops of rain began to fall. McLusky cheered up. 'We did them all a favour closing down the festival, saves them getting soaked. All snug in their cars now.'

Denkhaus grunted and walked off quickly towards his own car. He hated getting wet. 'You're in charge. I'll call a press conference.'

McLusky stood on the knoll as the heavens opened. By the time Forensics turned up every officer in the park was soaked to the skin.

Chapter Fifteen

'I still can't get over how quickly you made up your mind. It would have taken me days of thinking about it. And you didn't even test drive it.'

'I've driven one before.'

Austin had given him a lift to the dealership. After spending half an hour looking at nothing but black cars he had turned around, pointed at an olive green Mazda 323 with excessive mileage and a thirsty engine and bought it.

'It's a kind of elimination process. If I look long enough at the wrong stuff then I suddenly find the right stuff.'

'Does that work with suspects?'

'Not so far.'

'Shame.' Austin rubbed a smoothing hand over the letter on the table to deflate the air bubbles in the evidence bag that protected the paper. He read out loud for the second time. *'Perhaps This will Shut you Up. I have Warned You. Now I will employ My Armies everywhere. Homes and Churches will be safe but Silence will settle on the Parks and Streets of this City.'*

'I know it by heart, Jane, there's nothing there, no hidden clues. Photocopy it and get it off to Forensics. Even they should know it's urgent by now though I expect them to find nothing.'

McLusky drove to Trinity Road, the central police station in St Phillips. At Technical Support he clicked the memory card from his mobile and handed it to a young suntanned technician. 'See if you can do something with this. I shot some video at the kite festival just as the bomb went off. It'll be crap quality – do you think you can sharpen it up somehow and stick it on a disk for us?'

'Yeah, no sweat, we do that all the time. I'll have a go at it now if you want to wait. Not got him yet, then?'

It was a rhetorical question and McLusky treated it as such. In turn he didn't ask any questions beginning with 'How on earth . . .' about imaging technology and video enhancing. To him it was pure witchcraft. How you could take a rubbish image and turn it into a clear one was beyond his comprehension. Surely if something wasn't there it wasn't there?

But apparently not; in less than twenty minutes the technician was back, handing him his card and a CD in a hard protective case. 'See how you get on with that. Hope you catch him soon.'

Back in his own office, still cramped with several TV monitors, he slipped the disk into his computer and settled down to watch with a mug of instant coffee and a custard Danish. There was only three minutes of footage. What Technical Support hadn't managed to fix was the jerkiness of the camera movement. Off screen a tin-voiced superintendent spoke of the kite festival's popularity. Then the sudden movement of the man falling backwards and the small plume of smoke blowing on the wind. People reacted by moving either away or towards the locus of the incident. Except . . .

Except one man. An elderly man carrying what looked like a canvas satchel on a strap across his chest and wheeling an electric bicycle. He looked up towards the victim, nodded – clearly nodded – and kept going. He was in shot for no more than four seconds but at least McLusky had been holding the mobile more or less still at the time. *Old boy on bicycle. Another* old boy on a bicycle. He remembered the man cycling away from the site of the burnt yacht *Eleni*. Had it also been an electric one? He couldn't remember. There had to be thousands of men over sixty riding bicycles in this city, electric or otherwise.

He dug about on his already cluttered desk and found the disks Technical Support had produced from the SD cards Austin had commandeered on Brandon Hill after the first explosion. Some contained video footage and pictures taken before the explosion as well as after the incident. It didn't take him long. There he was once more in a still photograph, obviously taken before the explosion. The camera was focused on the group in the centre, three middle-aged women posing in front of a bed of red and white flowers in the park. On the tarmac path behind he once more wheeled a bicycle, same man, same bicycle, same satchel. While zooming in on his target with clicks of the mouse he dialled the CID room number but before he got an answer there came a knock on his door. It was DC Dearlove with a sheaf of reports.

'Dearlove, where is DS Austin?'

'Ehm, haven't seen him.'

He hung up. 'Look at this man, Dearlove.' He swivelled the monitor for him. 'I think this might be our man.'

'The wrinkly with the bike?'

The phone rang. 'Hang on.' He snatched up the receiver. 'McLusky.'

'Inspector McLusky, it's Dr Thompson. At the Burns Unit, Southmead. We spoke in connection with a patient of mine, Ms Bendick.'

'Oh yes, how is Ms Bendick?'

'Recovering, though she will require extensive surgery. But that's not what I'm calling about.'

'Go on, then.'

'Well, it's a bit tricky for me. It would mean breaking patient confidentiality and puts me in an awkward position.'

'Look, doc, if you're calling me then you've already made up your mind to tell me so why don't you just go ahead and do it because I'm a bit busy right now.'

'Okay, sorry, I'll get to the point. I treated a patient in A&E the night before last. For burns to his right hand. These burns and the damage to his skin were quite severe in some places and will need aftercare but the point is he told me he had burned his hand at a barbecue. I've treated burns for eight years now and those injuries were not consistent with burning yourself on a barbecue. I have seen injuries like these before and they were invariably caused by fireworks going off in people's hands. Naturally I thought of all those devices going off. The man may just be an innocent victim, I want you to bear that in mind.'

'You were right to call me. You haven't still got him there, then?'

'Unfortunately not.'

'Do you have his name?'

'He didn't want to give his name. Then later he said his name was Dave. But one of the nurses recognized him from a previous injury he presented involving some barbed wire and she thought his surname was Daws.'

'Daws! Around twenty-eight years of age?'

'About that, yes.'

'Doctor, you did the right thing when you called me. I'll get back to you. In the meantime, if he shows his face for some more treatment you must call. Not just me, dial 999 and try and keep him there for as long as you can. I've gotta go now, thanks, doctor.'

For a few seconds he remained standing at his desk, staring at the image on the screen, then grabbed his jacket and keys. Old boy or Daws, what did it matter? He wasn't precious about his hunches. 'Dearlove, get this image printed out and distributed and put it up on the board in the incident room. I want that man found.'

'Okay. Where will you be, sir?'

'I'm going to check something out. Tell Austin to get in touch with me when you see him.' He walked down the corridor, then fell into a trot. Daws, Timothy Daws. They had never followed that up.

As he unlocked his car in his new reserved parking space he was hailed from the far end of the car park.

'DI McLusky, sir?'

He recognized the grey-haired officer from Traffic. 'What can I do for you, sergeant?'

'Not sure I should show my face here. I owe you an apology for leaving the mud sample in your lobby without telling anyone but I was in a hurry as usual. And I want to thank you for delivering the perpetrator as well. That was well beyond the call of duty, sir.'

'No problem, though I've had mud-jokes up to here.' He indicated a line below his chin. 'But while you're here, there's something that's been bugging me. Was it you who mentioned the kite festival to me?'

'Might have done. I think we were talking about the gridlock situation we had last year. The traffic from the kite festival was definitely a contributing factor.'

'Remind me what else went on.'

'A tourist bus broke down . . .'

'One of those Citytours things?'

'I don't remember what company. There was also a running fight between drunks and an abnormally wide load came in off the motorway from Wales.'

'What kind of abnormal load?'

'A boat, sir. It couldn't have come at a worse time. Big thing, they delivered it to the docks here. I didn't see it myself.'

'Why would a boat come by road rather than sea?'

'Not seaworthy?'

The *Eleni* had come overland from Cardiff, he was pretty sure that's what the owner had said. 'Bloody hell. Didn't you also say emergency services couldn't get through? Thanks, sergeant, I think we might be quits.'

Sitting in his car he dialled Austin's mobile. It was answered instantly. 'Jane, it's Liam. I'm in the car park about to pay Daws a visit.'

'You want me to come down?'

'No. I want you to check something urgently. Last year, I'm not sure of the date, you had virtual gridlock here one day.'

'Nothing virtual about it –'

'I want you to check the logs for all emergency calls for that day. Find any that had a long delay in being responded to. I think that's where our man's grievance might originate. Get back to me as soon as. I'm following up on Daws. Apparently he presented with a burnt paw at A&E.'

Timothy bloody Daws. Damn. Why hadn't he followed that up ages ago? Because he didn't fit the bill, that's why. A cheat and petty criminal of his age certainly had the potential to graduate to the big stuff, especially if he was sent to prison for any length of time, but a sustained campaign of terrorizing citizens with bombs surely was too long a jump?

Yet the boy he had living at his house had definitely been nervous about something, he thought, as he parked the Mazda out of sight of Daws' front door. He shouldn't be doing this by himself, really needed someone to cover the back of the house. Better check the back of the house first.

As soon as he rounded the corner McLusky began to feel uncomfortable, though he couldn't explain why. He hesitated at the entrance to the alley that ran along the rear of the fenced-off back gardens. Why should he suddenly feel spooked in the middle of the afternoon? Mentally shaking himself free of the strange feeling he nevertheless advanced cautiously to the locked back door of Daws' desolate little garden. He pulled himself up, peered across and dropped back instantly. Someone was in the kitchen, just behind the window, and it didn't look like the young kid. He walked back to the glass-strewn entrance of the alley. What was the rush? Better call for back-up.

As he reached inside his jacket for his phone he was grabbed by two men and slammed against the fence, face first. 'Police, don't move, don't speak!' Suddenly the place was busy. In the corner of his eye he saw uniformed officers in body armour troop past up the alley. Seconds later he heard the splintering of wood and the familiar shouts. 'Police! Show yourselves! Police, come out, keep your hands where we can see them!'

The two officers released their grip and swivelled McLusky around. Both were in their twenties, had shaved heads and weighed fifteen stone plus. 'Who are you, what are you doing here?'

'Detective Inspector McLusky.' He showed his ID.

'Ah. Sorry, sir. Bad timing. Drug squad raid. What were you doing here?'

'Is it Daws you're hoping to find in there?'

'That's who we should be finding there. And quite possibly a cannabis factory. Helicopter chased some kids around here a few days back, using infrared. Apart from the kids the infra showed up a huge heat signature for the roof of this house. Now unless he's converted his entire loft into a sauna that usually means it's full of heat lamps for growing pot.' A message over the radio soon confirmed it. 'Two in custody. Tropical gardens upstairs, wall to wall cannabis plants.'

McLusky nodded grimly. No wonder the kid had been nervous. 'Ask him if one of his prisoners answers to the name of Daws and if he has a bandaged hand.'

The answer came back instantly. 'Affirmative.'

'Gentlemen, I need to ask Daws a few questions and I need to ask them quickly.'

'Whatever he tells you he remains our prisoner.'

'First come first served, naturally.'

Daws was still in the kitchen cuffed by his left hand to a huge officer. Innis Cole, his young apprentice, sat bewildered and close to tears on a kitchen chair. The place was busy with officers. The front door had been knocked at the same time as the officers had entered the garden. McLusky showed his ID to Daws who tried to look bored, though fear had widened his eyes. 'Timothy Daws, I presume. That's entirely the wrong type of gardening you've been doing up there.'

Daws didn't meet his eyes but looked out through the window at the shed which was being searched. 'Just a few plants for private consumption.'

'I doubt the judge will see it like that. Even what's in that shed will be enough for a custodial sentence. But then I'm not really interested in your shed *or* your attic. *Or* your driving offences *or* your benefit fraud for that matter, though it all makes a tidy bundle for the CPS. I'm interested in this.' McLusky grabbed the prisoner's free arm and lifted his bandaged hand chest high. 'Where did you hurt yourself?'

Daws tried unsuccessfully to pull from the grasp. 'Burnt myself on the car engine.'

'I thought it was a barbecue. Try again, Mr Daws.' He turned to the officer in charge. 'Has he been arrested yet?'

'For drugs offences, intent to supply etc.'

'Marvellous.' He turned back to Daws. 'You got that injury when something unexpectedly blew up in or near your hand. I think you're involved with the spate of bombings in the city. I think we can safely add murder to the list.'

Daws met his eyes with an unbelieving stare. 'Nah, rubbish, that's got nothing to do with me.'

'Who has it to do with?'

'How the fuck would I know, I had nothing to do with that shit.'

'Who has, Daws?'

'I don't know his name, do I?'

'But you know where? Because you, Mr Daws, during your recent spree of burglaries, got a painful surprise somewhere.'

Daws clamped his mouth shut and stared out of the window.

'Daws, if you think it would incriminate you then I wouldn't worry about it. It'll be nothing compared to withholding evidence in a terrorism case. If one more person dies because you didn't tell us, we're going to add manslaughter to your charge sheet. I'll see to it personally.'

Daws appeared to be thinking it over but his shoulders had already sagged. 'Nelson Close, one of the old prefabs.'

'Which one?'

'At the end. The last one before the field. But it was an empty one, boarded up, no one lives there, so it wasn't even really breaking in or anything. Only I'd seen someone go in and out the back the day before so I thought I'd check it out. It had some kind of workshop in there. There was an MP3 player on the workbench. It blew up in my fucking hand. I got the hell out of there and down to A&E.'

'It didn't occur to you to let us know what you had stumbled upon there?'

Daws shrugged. 'It's not exactly my style, is it?'

The incident room was empty. DC Dearlove had enlarged the photograph of the old boy with the bicycle to A4 size and printed several copies, one of which he now pinned up on the board opposite the row of photos of the bomb victims, all thankfully taken before the explosions. The girl was the most upsetting, he thought, although the gym woman had been quite a looker too. It wasn't really fair, of course. The better looking you were the more sympathy you got. He had noticed that long ago. If you were ugly and covered in spots and had thin hair nobody really cared.

Where was everybody? Further down the corridor in the CID room he found only DC French listening to someone on the phone while demolishing a packet of Jaffa Cakes and ignoring him, both as per usual. Through the open door he spotted DS Sorbie in the corridor, moving past in a curious slow motion. When he called after him he only got a feeble wave in return. He drew level with him by the stairs. 'Are you okay, sir?' The DS certainly didn't look it.

His skin was glistening and he seemed to have shrunk into his suit.

'No, I'm not, thanks for asking. I've been throwing up merrily and worse and I feel shite. Drank too much river water the other day. I'm out of here.' Or it could have been the celebrations of course. Should have taken a couple of days off like Fairfield.

'It's only that DI McLusky asked me to disseminate this picture.' He held out a copy to him. 'He thinks this might be him. The bomber.'

'Oh yeah? About time. Hang on. I've seen him before, I'm sure of it.' And he hadn't been feeling too clever that day either. 'He's that grumpy bastard at Nelson Close, in those prefabs.' A new wave of nausea was gathering just above his navel. You'd have thought all that alcohol would have killed any bugs he might have swallowed with the river water but apparently not.

'You wouldn't have a name, would you?'

'For him? No. Last but one of the bungalows before the demolished brickworks.' He was feeling hot, sweat pricked his skin. 'Go get him, Deedee. Cover yourself in glory. Before I cover you in puke.'

Dearlove watched the DS turn away and shuffle back down the corridor towards the toilets like a very old man. 'Right. Okay.' Well, he would certainly have a look at him. One old dear he could deal with. And then if he found anything suspicious he would call it in, of course.

DS Austin was in the process of dialling the inspector's number when McLusky stuck his head into the incident room. 'Jane, what have you got?'

Austin consulted a sheet of notes. 'Well, there was a flood of calls as you'd expect on a day like that, most of them what you'd call nuisance calls, about being stuck in traffic and when the hell were they going to do something about it. But there were some serious calls. Two women in labour, for a start. They got attended by local midwives and a doctor legging it round there. But I just found this. The name is Cooke. The wife took an overdose and her husband found her and called for an ambulance. He called six times. When they eventually got her to the Royal Infirmary it was too late. She died later of liver failure.'

'And he lives in a prefab?'

'How did you know?'

'Because he's our man, Jane. Let's go, let's go.'

A thin, half-hearted rain began to fall as McLusky drove across town in his usual style, though he did refrain from using the pavements. Austin found he had to give fewer directions now; the inspector was getting to know the city.

'I think he always tried to watch, that was his mistake. He was certainly there when the bombs in the park went off. And I do think he was at the docks that morning looking at the aftermath of the firebomb on the *Eleni*. He enjoys the fruits of his work a bit too much.'

'It all makes hideous sense. He blames whatever caused the gridlock and takes his revenge.'

McLusky grunted with disgust and swerved to avoid a child struggling on a tiny bicycle into the middle of the road. 'Only it's gone far beyond that. He hates everyone, he hates the city. He wants us all to stay at home and be quiet. So he can grieve in peace.'

'If he was hoping to scare people into staying at home then he should have known better. Especially if he is the old boy in this picture.' Austin patted the photocopy on the dashboard. 'Even the blitz didn't make people stay at home.'

'I think it soon stopped being about getting a result and became all about doing it, hurting people. You hurt me – now I'll hurt you back.'

'We're nearly there. What kind of back-up have we got?'

McLusky checked the clock on the dashboard. 'Firearms unit will meet us in forty minutes. Just here actually.' He slowed down. They had arrived at the turn-off to the close.

A clump of trees, untidy shrubs and a substation obscured the view of the prefabs from the main road. 'It was the best place I could think of, not knowing the area too well. We'll send some of the boys across the other side through the demolished brickworks. But that's all academic until we know that the bastard's at home.'

'Do you think he'll be armed?'

'Hard to say. But we know he doesn't mind killing or maiming so he might not come quietly.' He turned the car down the narrow potholed road into Nelson Close and stopped by the first bungalow. 'This is number one, unsurprisingly, what number is he?'

'Last but one with the back to the service road, number thirty-five. Right at the back.'

Standing in the rain they surveyed the area. The bungalows were arranged in a rigid grid, with wide concrete paths between front and back gardens. Every two bungalows shared an area of perished concrete hard standing, most of which gave room to bins, rusting white goods, old paint tins and broken furniture. While all the bungalows looked identical – hunched, asbestos-grey shapes with moss-covered roofs – it was the gardens that had once given them their individuality. Waist-high weeds surrounded most of the boarded-up prefabs but some still showed signs of cultivation. There were only a few small cars visible in the close, parked in front of neatly kept houses. An old two-stroke disability vehicle rusted in front of a bungalow where the front garden had been concreted over.

Austin let out a long breath through puffed-up cheeks. 'Tumbleweed alert. The close that time forgot.'

As the sky darkened a light came on behind the small net-curtained window of number three.

'We'll try this one, have a chat, find out if anyone's seen him today.'

'I bet people round here know everything about everybody.'

'You'd have thought so. Yet obviously not everything.'

'Got a point there.' Austin pressed the tiny electric bell button in the centre of number three's front door.

A woman in her late fifties opened it as far as the chain allowed. McLusky showed his ID. 'I'm Detective Inspector McLusky from CID. With me is Detective Sergeant Austin. Could we have a word? Won't keep you long.'

'What is it now?' The door closed to allow for the removal of the chain, then opened wider.

'May we come in?'

'Make sure you wipe your feet. What is it you wanted?' The woman stood in the tiny carpeted hall, allowing them just enough space to come in out of the rain.

'Oh, it's nothing to worry about. May I ask your name?'

'I'm Mrs Woodley. Joan Woodley.'

'Mrs Woodley, we would like to ask you about Mr Cooke. He lives in number thirty-five, I believe. Do you know him at all?'

'Yes, poor Mr Cooke, well, of course we know *of* him.'

'He lost his wife.'

She shook her head at his ignorance. 'And his daughter. Both dead within two years. He lost everything really. His house, business, family.'

'His daughter too? I didn't know that. And his business? How . . .?'

'Yes, well, he used to have that electrical repair shop in the old town, I remember Frank getting our radio repaired there once, years and years ago now. But people don't have things repaired any more, do they? They just buy new things now, and then perhaps Mr Cooke didn't know how to repair all the new technology and that anyway. The business folded and then he lost the house too, they lived over the shop and he had remortgaged it to prop up the business.'

'His daughter, how did she die?'

'Jenny? She was run over. Well, squashed by a reversing lorry against a house. That's what sent Barbara, Mrs

289

Cooke, over the edge, I'm sure of it. They'd just lost the house and all and had moved here.'

The hall was so narrow Austin had to speak over McLusky's shoulder. 'Mrs Woodley, does Mr Cooke have an electric bicycle?'

'That's exactly what the other policeman asked. Yes, he does all his shopping on it. What's so important about it? Did he break the speed –'

McLusky interrupted. 'Other policeman, Mrs Woodley? When was that?'

'Today, earlier. Can't be more than an hour ago. Actually he looked too young to be a policeman, but you know what they say about policemen looking younger.'

McLusky fleshed out the picture for her. 'Thin hair, bad skin, terrible suit?'

She rewarded him with a broad smile. 'You describe him very well.'

Austin was already outside. McLusky thanked Mrs Woodley and urgently followed. 'Right, Jane, let's go check it out. That could only be Dearlove, what the hell does he think he's doing?' They walked fast towards the other end of the close. The further they came the more boarded-up prefabs they saw.

'Deedee's not the shiniest tool in the box.'

'He'll be the dullest bobby on the beat if he's spooked Cooke. Right.' He counted off the house numbers. 'There's his house, let's walk along the hedge out of sight.'

McLusky stalked along the fence among heaps of builder's rubble, some of which looked like dumped asbestos – he was glad it was still raining. Number thirty-five was entirely surrounded by uninhabited and partly derelict houses. It was a dark and desolate corner of the close, richly overgrown.

Austin nudged his boss. 'Look in there.'

McLusky followed the direction Austin indicated, into the wilderness of number thirty-four's garden. A car had been parked in here, then covered with bits of tarpaulin and partially surrounded with corrugated iron and chipboard.

'That's Deedee's little Ford.'

'You sure?'

Austin pulled more of the camouflage away and nodded. 'It's his.'

'Shit. Okay, we'll go in now.'

'Aren't we waiting for the firearms unit?'

'He didn't park it like that himself. If he's no longer in control of his car then he's in trouble. Sod the firearms unit, they're twenty minutes away.' He keyed his airwave radio. 'Alpha Nine to Control request immediate back-up my position Nelson Close number thirty-five one officer down ambulance required immediate officers McLusky and Austin attending over.' As soon as Control acknowledged he put the radio down and took his mobile out. 'Switch your mobile to vibrate.'

Austin did so, squinting into the thin drizzle. 'It's very quiet at this end away from the road.'

'Not for long. He's got net curtains on every window and the glass in the door. Probably the same at the back. He'll see us coming if he's in there. There's no time for subtlety. You take the back door, I'll take the front. Go, and move fast. If you hear me smashing through do the same at the back, otherwise wait.'

There was no possibility of approaching by stealth. They moved in quick strides past the front of the derelict house neighbouring Cooke's, then split up, Austin putting on a spurt to get to the back door. If Cooke was in there he must have noticed the movement. McLusky didn't hesitate: he turned the door handle, ready to break the half-glazed door down if it was locked. It wasn't. He opened it and moved quietly inside, listening. A narrow hall, identical in proportions to the first one they had visited. Cabbagey cooking smells mixed with the lemon scent of furniture polish. A half-open door to the left led into a small, sparsely furnished sitting room; two-seater sofa, half of it

291

taken up with piles of newsprint. A closed door to the right; he threw it open. A double bedroom, neatly made bed. Quickly on to the next closed door – a tiny bedroom, green carpet, empty apart from a silver electric bicycle leaning against the wall, connected to a charger on the floor. McLusky stepped through the final half-open door into the small kitchen. Behind the net-curtained half-glazed back door stood Austin, waiting patiently for a sign from his boss. McLusky stepped towards the door to open it for him, reaching out towards the handle. Below it a black round metal container, fixed to the door by an iron bracket, looked out of place. He withdrew his hand sharply and opened the tiny window above the sink instead. 'Step away from the door, Jane, it's booby-trapped. He's not in here.'

They met up by the front door. 'Was the booby trap meant for us?'

'Hard to say. Perhaps it's a burglar trap. No sign of Deedee or of a struggle. The door was unlocked and his electric bike is in there. He's in his workshop in one of these derelict houses.'

'Yes, but there's scores of them. Which one is it?'

McLusky pointed. 'It's that one.' Cooke had appeared from around the back of the last bungalow, whose garden backed on to the towpath. As he saw them he stopped in his tracks, then turned quickly back around the corner.

'Stop, police!' McLusky was running already. Austin sprinted around the front in case Cooke tried to escape that way. They met up by the back door, having seen nothing. Windows and door were boarded up and, to the casual observer, secure. Yet on closer inspection the chipboard over the back entrance was in fact a hinged door. A bolt lying on the ground beside it would secure the door from the outside. McLusky picked it up and flung it far into the long grass. There was no sign of Daws' break-in. It had either been repaired or he had come in a different way.

Carefully he pulled on the edge of the chipboard. It moved easily on its hinges and he folded it back completely until it rested against the side of the house, revealing the door underneath. It was ajar. Closer inspection showed that it had once been broken open, possibly with a crowbar. He shone his pen light into the gap around the door frame. Booby traps could take many forms, there might be one standing on the floor, waiting to be triggered as the door opened. McLusky doubted that there had been enough time but he pushed Austin aside. 'Get back.' Then he flattened himself against the wall and with one hand swung the door until it was half open. There was no resistance. 'Mr Cooke, it's the police! Come out, Mr Cooke, show yourself!'

It was dark inside with all the windows boarded up. What little light fell in through the door revealed a gutted kitchen and a filthy, half-perished floor. Something or somebody had been dragged through the dirt recently.

McLusky strained to listen through the drumming and splashing of the rain. A small noise, like something dropped on to the floor somewhere in the house, not in the kitchen. McLusky slipped into the gloom of the inside and moved to the door connecting the kitchen with the hall, with Austin close behind him. A thin cold light fell on to the mouldy hall carpet from a half-open door at the end of the hall, from what he guessed would have been the sitting room. He could now hear a hissing sound, too. It made him shiver.

He repeated his call. 'Police! Come out with your hands up, Mr Cooke!'

The answering voice was harsh and defiant, yet unmistakably that of an old man making an effort to sound strong and confident. 'Go away! I've got one of your lot in here. He's my hostage.'

McLusky moved slowly forward into the hall. 'Nonsense, Mr Cooke, it's over. You don't want a hostage. That's never worked before for anyone.'

'You're coming closer, I can hear you coming closer. Stay where you are or I'm going to hurt this officer.'

'You don't want to do that, Mr Cooke. How is the officer? He's very quiet.' As he moved closer to the door he thought he could detect the sound of laboured breathing. The hissing, he now realized, came from a hurricane lamp.

'He's not feeling too clever. I had to hit him on the head and I had to gag him. Don't come any closer now or he gets it.'

'I'm afraid I have to see him for myself, you could be lying.' Keep him talking, Cooke has no plan, don't give him time to make one.

'Lying? I don't lie, you are the liar, you are all liars, all that rubbish spouted about me.'

'Nevertheless, it's my duty to satisfy myself that my officer is alive. I'm going to come and look now.' He moved slowly sideways into the rectangle of hissing light and stood still.

The centre of the room was taken up by several small tables. Every inch appeared to be covered in tools, boxes, wires, a car battery, bottles, canisters and a vice. Under the dark windows stood shelves filled with more material; in the corners bin-liners were overflowing with the remains of carefully dismantled fireworks.

Dearlove sat rigidly on a kitchen chair. He had been tightly trussed up with cables and his limbs taped to the legs and backrest of the chair. There was drying blood on the side of his skull and face. Several lengths of silver gaffer tape had been used to gag him. Dearlove breathed with noisy effort through a nose and sinuses choked with his own vomit, some of which encrusted his nostrils. His eyes stared straight at McLusky with wide unblinking terror. Behind him stood Cooke, his deeply lined face thrown into sharp relief by the hurricane lamp hissing on a foldable workbench by his side. Standing quite still he looked like a figure made from leather. His right hand rested on a petrol can. It was uncapped and McLusky thought he could smell the contents.

'His name is David. I don't think David can breathe very well. There's no need for a gag any more, we're here now. Everyone knows we are here. Any chance of taking David's gag off?'

'Shut up about him, you're trying to distract me.'

'Distract you from what, Mr Cooke?' He took a casual step forward.

'Stay where you are. Distract me so you can rush me. But I warn you, I have lots of weapons at my disposal. And there's petrol in this. One false move and he'll burn.'

'Then we'd all burn. There's no use in that. It won't make any difference. It won't bring them back.' McLusky craned his neck left and right, leaning forward, looking about, moving forward a few inches. 'Is this what they would have wanted you to do? Your daughter? And your wife, Barbara?'

The name electrified Cooke. 'How dare you speak about them? How dare you mention her name?'

'Would Barbara approve of this? Would she have *liked* it?'

'Shut up. I warned you!' His hand jerked forward and petrol splashed over Dearlove's head and side. In response the DC let out a long insistent grunting noise of fear and pain as the noxious liquid bit into his head wound.

'How many bombs are there? Just out of interest.' McLusky spoke casually as though what had just happened was of no concern to him.

'That you will find out over time.'

'You've got none left, have you?' He looked about, displaying disappointment. 'All your arsenal deployed, all your little soldiers out there. It's all over then, isn't it.' A statement, not a question. 'Well, you outsmarted us then by the looks of it. So there's no longer any need for all this.' His hand gesture encompassed the room, indicating Dearlove. 'Well, that's it then. I'm going to go now, Mr Cooke.'

295

'You're going to go?' He looked puzzled.

'Are you going to tell me where you planted the remaining devices?'

A single flat syllable. 'No.'

'I didn't think so, and I can't make you, I know that too, so there's nothing I can do here.' McLusky spoke in a matter-of-fact voice. 'Obviously, I'll have to take him with me.' Three steps brought him into the middle of the room. Keeping his eyes entirely on Dearlove as though Cooke couldn't possibly have any more objections, he took hold of the back of the chair and dragged it around until Dearlove was facing the man with the petrol can. With one swift movement he ripped the gag off his mouth. Dearlove gasped, coughed, spat. McLusky tilted the chair back and began dragging the groaning constable through the door. As soon as there was room Austin took over and pulled him away. McLusky remained standing in the hall, facing Cooke. Several sirens could now be heard approaching. Cooke's head appeared to shake with tiny nods as he let the petrol flow from the can to the uneven vinyl floor where it pooled by his feet before creeping towards McLusky and the door.

'Why don't you come outside with me, Mr Cooke. It doesn't have to end in here. Not like that.' He searched the man's face for anything worth saving. Still holding the empty petrol can Cooke stood very still now, a leather statuette. He no longer appeared to be seeing him. One thin stream of petrol had reached the tip of his own shoes. McLusky nodded. 'But perhaps it's for the best. Goodbye, Mr Cooke.'

He stepped over the creeping stream of petrol and crossed the hall just as Constable Pym entered the kitchen. McLusky shouted at him: 'Get out!' The flash of igniting petrol reflected in Austin's eyes as it snatched the oxygen from the air. They tumbled out into the rain together. McLusky swung the outer chipboard door shut. It was a symbolic gesture rather than any attempt to deprive the fire of oxygen. Out here the close was busy with police and paramedics, many converging on the prefab. Just as he filled his lungs to shout a warning a window blew out in a vicious blast, making his warning superfluous. There had obviously been some gunpowder left.

An ambulance was leaving with DC Dearlove on board, its siren wailing as it neared the main road. McLusky found Austin standing by a defunct lamp-post. He lit a cigarette, offering one to the sergeant, who barely hesitated before accepting it. Both greedily inhaled while watching the black smoke and flames pouring from number thirty-five. 'Deedee all right, you think?'

Austin scratched the tip of his nose. 'I guess. He was cursing coherently.'

'Oh, good.'

'So we've no way of knowing how many devices are still out there?'

'No way at all. Could be one or two, could be dozens.'

'Isn't there some way we can stop people from picking the things up?'

McLusky shook his head and began walking towards his car. 'I shouldn't think so. Shouldn't think so for one minute.'

It was raining harder now. The remaining residents of Nelson Close saw the bungalow burn, though most stayed indoors to watch from their windows.